12 Months of Whump
Volume 2

Showstopper

The Kill Touch

Chipped

Silence

Bonnie and Guy

The Dark Side of the Sun

Cover Design by Nicole Alessi

Illustrations by Hen Towers

CONTENTS

Introduction

Welcome to 12 Months of Whump! The Whumpy Printing Press published one whump novella every month in 2025. This book contains the last six novellas, published between July and December of 2025. Each novella can be read as a standalone. Within these pages you'll find serial killers, electrokinetics, torturers, pets, dragons, and alchemists. And hopefully whumperflies.

Showstopper

Rae Ellis

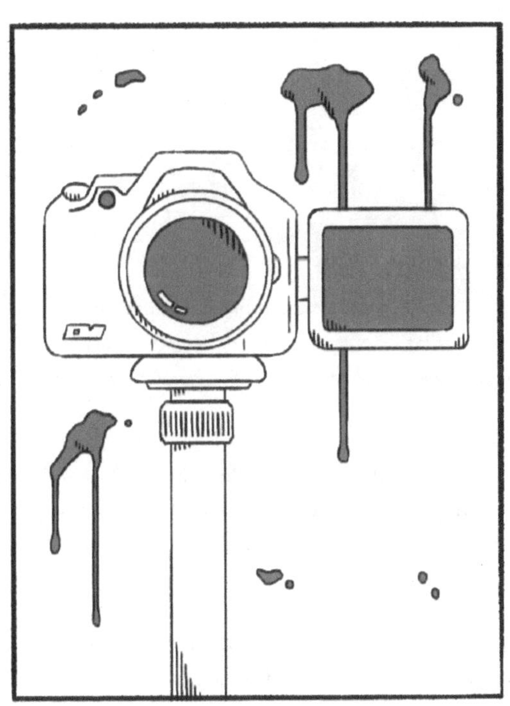

Cover Design by Nicole Alessi

Cover Illustration by Hen Towers

To the flu. The fever dream you granted me spawned the original 11,000 words of this story, which I wrote over the span of one delirious week. I'll never forget you <3

Contents

CONTENT WARNINGS

This story contains the following content:

- Serial Killer
- Yandere
- Snuff films
- Heavy violence, including knives, gore, and dismemberment
- Murder
- Nonconsensual drugging
- Taunting about a loved one's death
- Character death

If this book isn't for you, no worries! But if it is, we hope you enjoy this story about a detective and his suspect...

1

SHOWOFF

"Hey, *Shah* – "

Darian's head tipped up toward Amelia's voice, but his eyes didn't follow – too focused on following the steadily-blurring string of words that pillared down the too-bright screen of his laptop. "Yyyyyyyeah – ?" Half-distracted by the whirlwind of thoughts.

A file plopped onto his desk – thin, bulking in one spot.

He dragged his eyes from his work to it. "What's this?"

Amelia tapped at it. "Showoff's at it again."

Aaaaaaaaaand Darian's thoughts skittered to a stop, draining away almost noisily in his mind until only the file remained. "When did we get this?" He opened it, immediately plucking up the flash drive and plugging it into his laptop.

"Few minutes ago – east side this time. The guy gets around."

"Still don't know it's a guy, Amy. Check the language before you bias the team."

He could feel her eyes boring into him as he opened the file on his laptop, pulling up the MP4. "Just get the analysis in by this afternoon."

"Mhmm – " His voice was distracted again as he connected his earbuds and hit play. He didn't watch her leave.

He was already immersed.

'Showoff' was an entirely accurate name for this particular fucker. Out of all the serial killers he'd analyzed and tracked down, this one was easily the most elegant.

Most just ... slashed and hit. So many killers pulled from trauma and took it out on their victims in explosions of violence.

Not this one. They were incredibly refined. Almost loving as they carved off piece after piece. They floated across the screen clad in thick black fabric, a simple craft store mask over their face.

For all intents and purposes, they appeared at a glance like any highschooler egging a house during homecoming week.

They didn't speak.

They didn't leave messages.

They didn't make demands or taunt their captive.

It wasn't until they moved that their beauty shone. Delicate as a butterfly's wings and elegant as a flower unfurling at first light. Every flick of the knife cut through Darian's heart like the gentlest Mary Oliver poem. Ecstasy dripped through him as the blood flowed from flesh, drawn out and strewn on display.

A linen cloth draped behind the pair – Showoff and the poor victim. A man this time. Shirt cut cleanly off. Gagged with a simple black cloth tied around his head. Not to keep him quiet – just to keep him from speaking.

The screams rang through all the same, muffled or not.

Darian kept his composure as he watched, keeping his face solemn and blank as he took notes. Notes on Showoff's height – it was easier to tell in this video – perhaps five foot eight. Dominant hand – left. Physical features ... still none. They covered themself too well.

Yet, the bulk of the clothes did nothing to hide the elegance of their movements. Their arm still floated through the air. Their body still glided across the ground. Darian couldn't see their legs shifting at the bottom of the screen, but they caught Show's form as easily as breathing, leaving no impact point. No rise and fall of their body. No upset in their gait.

Just gliding smooth as water. Smooth as always.

The knife traced and twirled in a dance around the captive's throat, leaving no mark there, only drawing out panting whimpers and muffled pleas as his head wrenched to the side, tucking against his shoulder to escape it.

Darian forced himself to pause the video and look away. Take a note on nothing – just the precision of the blade.

His best guess so far was that Show was an artist or doctor. Few others had that level of precision. And, wives' tale may it be, left-handers always seemed to fall more neatly into those occupations.

Darian focused on his breath. It was shaking again – he needed to get it under control before someone else on the team noticed. This office space offered him no walls for solitude – just a network of shared desks and people – mostly – minding their own business. Only team leads got their own offices.

So, focus he must.

He drew in deep, slow breaths, eyes closed. Perhaps to others it would seem he was overwhelmed by the gore.

Then again, this was a particularly difficult group of people to keep behavioral secrets from.

So, he needed. To. *Focus.*

When his breath fell under control again, he hit play, pencil still poised for note-taking.

And Show started to dance again.

Long, slow cuts. Carving off long strips or leaving simple slices.

With each few strokes, they would wander behind the captive, knife brushing across the linen canvasing the background, letting the blood soak in in simple, dark streaks.

One by one by one by one by one, the strikes of blood littered the canvas. At first, they seemed to be building toward a design. A message. A purpose.

But more built – as they always did – building and building and building upon each other. Overlapping and crossing and dripping down.

Only once the entire canvas was evenly coated in red did Showoff finally let the sobbing man die, pulling out the gag and dragging his head up to center by a firm, gloved grip on his hair.

Forcing his eyes to the camera.

The man tried to sputter a plea – something.

The words were lost to pain, blood loss, and terror.

The knife slashed across his throat.

Eyes grew wild and wide with panic as he resumed his groggy thrashing, desperate gurgles spewing from his throat as blood poured and spurted away, retreating down his bare chest littered in cuts and stripes of exposed muscle.

Darian's heart was pounding so loud in his chest he could swear the rest of the team could hear it, eyes glued to the screen as shame and dread crawled up his stomach. Not the dread of this scene. Not empathy or horror. The dread of being caught. Of someone having some impossible mind reading ability – someone knowing how sick he was for being so addicted to this.

He just kept watching – he couldn't bring himself to pause it even as his breaths grew tighter and faster.

As the man choked out, Show didn't do anything. They just kept their blank-masked face tipped up toward the camera as their hand drifted slowly through the man's hair again and again, following smoothly and simply however he thrashed trying to avoid it.

Eventually, delirious and fading fast, he leaned into it.

They always did.

Show didn't stop his head from dropping to his chest when what remained of his strength faded away.

Their head turned to regard the not-quite-dead-yet man momentarily, then their face pulled back up to stare directly into the camera again.

Darian's stomach was flipping. As if Show could see straight through time. Through the frame. Through the glass. Into the darkest, coldest corner of his soul.

Show did as they always did.

They stepped forward, bending until the mask all but filled the frame.

Then, slowly – a single leather-clad thumb lifted into view. It smeared across the frame, leaving it streaked with dark, sloppy red.

The video ended. Clipped to the first frame and a play button.

Darian pulled in a deep, painful breath, struggling to keep his expression neutral.

His hands moved on their own, blindly as his eyes stayed on the screen. They slid open a drawer of his desk and plucked up a new flash drive.

Then plugged it into his laptop next to the other.

Systematically, he duplicated the video file onto the fresh flash drive, then ejected it.

Paranoia prickled at Darian's mind as his eyes made a quick survey of the office – making sure no one was watching as he slipped the pirated video into his pocket to bring home.

He'd watch it again and write up the report. Do his job. Shut down his thoughts.

But Darian needed to see that again. Alone.

2

Private Showing

The families.

Darian pondered what they were doing now. He wondered if, maybe, they made copies of the videos themselves before they turned the tape in to the police.

He wondered how long they stared in abject horror at the screen before calling the police.

If they watched it all the way through. If they got so far as to see Show prowling up to the camera, masked face tilting ever so slightly – as if they saw straight through the family's screen and into them.

If they flinched when Show smeared blood over the lens.

He wondered, vaguely, if any of them were a little twisted like him. If not twisted, then ... obsessive, maybe. Desperate enough to find the killer that they wanted to analyze it. Or, maybe, just so distraught that their husband, boyfriend, son, cousin, co-worker, whatever the victim was to them, spent his last forty-two minutes and seventeen seconds in horror-stricken, agonized loneliness, that they made copies too. Watched it back over and over and over again.

Staring at the screen with a beer and bleary eyes that had long given up screaming for sleep and settled into silent, watering acquiescence.

Staring at the victim.

Just him and the knife.

The knife and the elegance of the silent knife wielder.

Darian couldn't get the image of the families out of his head. He'd put in a request a few times now to be the first on the scene, but local officers always picked up the case to confirm that it really was Showoff and not some other killer or a sick prank. Only *then* would they pass it off to the BAU and it would land on Darian's desk.

It was a crock of shit.

He needed to be able to see the families. He wanted to be able to see their reactions. Were they crying as they handed over the tape? Were their eyes glazed and hollow as they robotically invited the officers in and systematically poured coffee for their guests, desperately clinging to the gilded decorum rather than drown in the vast unknown grief?

Maybe they were glad. Possibly. Plenty of families have squabbles, affairs, inheritance fights, or who knows what else preceding this. Maybe their poor victim wasn't so loved after all.

Darian was still pissed he didn't get to see. He got to talk to them later, sure, but there wasn't really a way for him to know what they were like in *that* moment. He wanted to know if they wailed in their grief.

For this. For his work.

Of course.

It was important for the case. Important for the profile. Any other reasonings or obsessions he might have surrounding the situation were purely coincidental and not in any way a driving reason for his repeated requests.

Mmm ...

His internal wrestle with phrasings stumbled to a stop as Show's knife blotted the final stain of red into place, soaking through the last of the draped linen.

They were beautiful on the screen.

Well. Not a *screen*. Not this time.

Darian didn't dare watch these little home videos upstairs in sight of the windows whose shutters he never quite trusted. He'd much rather analyze them in the basement from the comfort of his secondhand couch. A small projector haphazardly screwed into the exposed beams of the unfinished basement, a white sheet draping over a blank section of wall became his screen, and a minifridge next to the couch served both as end table and beer cooler.

Forty-two minutes and seventeen seconds.

They were thirty-eight minutes and forty-eight seconds in now as Darian cracked open another bottle, flicking the cap across the cement floor – eyes never leaving the screen.

He wondered just how freaked out the victim – this one's name was 'Marcus', by the way – would be if he knew what the video was for. If it had been explained to him. If Show was gracious enough to tell Marc that the video would be sent to his family. Then the police station. Then the FBI.

He wondered if poor Marc ever quite grasped the concept of how many people would be watching this. Or – on top of that – how many people like Darian (or the potential, aforementioned family members) would make copies to watch over. And over. And over.

Maybe someday, Showoff's work would even get one of those serial killer documentaries. Darian assumed it would – they were already up to eighteen documented kills. Plus, movie-makers have a flare for showcasing people who have a flare for the cinematic.

Poor Marcus' screams might be on Netflix someday, labeled with a simple '*This episode contains graphic depictions of a murder – viewer discretion advised.*'

As if anyone ever 'discresses' with that.

They all watch it – just like Darian did. So many people are obsessed with serial killer documentaries and true crime podcasts – Darian wasn't so different. Preferring one object of fascination and preferring the uncut content was just a quirk of his.

This was normal.

Normal how he leaned forward, adrenaline pumping through his veins as Show brought the knife to Marcus' throat. Again. For the twelfth time this night since Darian set the application to play on loop hours ago.

Darian stood, stepping closer to watch as the knife melted through flesh, blood spurting through gargles and wordless pleas. The rush was fading by quite a bit this time – he knew this scene too well now – but that didn't mean it wasn't *good*. It still made him dizzy with a soft, empowered pleasure as Marc sputtered out, crimson soaking down his slaughtered chest.

Darian's eyes were on Show now, though, as his target approached the camera. He squinted, trying so *so* hard to see Show's eyes through the holes in the mask. The inside must have been lined with black mesh.

As Show stared back at him, a murmur pressed unbidden from Darian's lips.

"*I will find you.*"

There was the smallest beat of silence – as if Show were sizing him up. Analyzing the words and the man behind them.

Then. As always. Their thumb smudged red across the screen, blinking them into darkness yet again.

3

Cue Card

The letter didn't have a return address. Didn't have postage. Didn't have much bulk to it at all.

Confused, Darian slid it from his mailbox, peeking inside to ensure he didn't miss another bill – or, heaven forbid, another fucking round of advertisements – before stopping to flip the envelope over.

It was blank.

Tied up in rusty red string.

No ... is that ... was that ... fabric? Strips of fabr –

His hands, body, and mind locked in place all at once.

Linen.

Linen – he was right – it was linen. The blood-soaked linen from Showoff's videos –

Fuck.

Darian took a desperate glance up the street, then jogged to the end of his sidewalk, head tossing back and forth. He frantically searched the road and memorized the cars. Looking for anyone suspicious. Anyone with a hood up or ... or who didn't seem to belong there.

Nothing.

Fucking *nothing* – how long had this been there?

FUCK.

His breath and hands were both moving again now – both shaky as he turned the envelope over in his hand.

He ran back inside, slamming the door behind him. The letter slid onto the table as he quickly found gloves and awkwardly fumbled them on with frantically flexing fingers. He re-approached, sliding a butter knife under the paper to pry away the glue with as little damage as possible.

Should he be bringing this into the office? Yes. Could it be stuffed with anthrax or who fucking knows what? Also yes.

But. Darian could just tell them he didn't realize the letter was from Show until it was opened – that he didn't recognize the fabric when it was cut so thin.

He could do that.

That was reasonable – people who didn't spend all-nighters staring at the videos wouldn't have noticed.

He ...

... he had spent *all night* watching the video.

He'd spent all night watching the *fucking* video and this was *right fuckin' there* in the morning.

Show had been there. Show had been there while *he* was *there*. While he was there watching the *fucking* video – *fuck* –

... Darian would need to triple-check the blackoutability of the basement curtains after this.

He was so fucking screwed if Show saw him –

ANYWAY –

Shaking fingers pulled out the small paper, turning it over.

Aaaaand this dude was a classic.

Cutout letters from magazines. Of course.

Darian's eyes skimmed the single sentence.

a FOx RAreLY expects its Hound to be as PRETTY As YOU <3

Darian … froze.

Staring.

Breath locked up and stuck in his lungs.

Whatever he had expected, that wasn't it.

Fuck.

4

Mandatory Unauthorized Research Montage

'*Off the case.*' What the hell did they mean, '*off the case*'? Darian didn't understand for a long few seconds, sputtering excuses in the director's office. *He* was the lead on this unsub. *He* had the most information. *He* had been tracking them for *years*. Now, all of a sudden, just because Showoff had sent him a letter, he wasn't allowed to track the fucker down anymore?

That didn't even make *sense*. The director said it was a "safety concern." That having the unsub obsessed with him was a "danger."

But if Show was a danger, wouldn't they have come *into* the house? Wouldn't they have knocked on his door or crept in through the window? Strangled or shot him in his sleep?

They didn't. All they did was leave a note saying he was cute and move on. Darian didn't see how that was enough of a concern to take him off the *case*. It seemed pointless, cowardly, and generally stupid. Wasn't his job dangerous *every* day? Didn't this make him the best lead they'd had?

Darian regretted even telling them as he shoved clothes into his suitcase back home. He couldn't even stay in his own damn *house* now.

He shouldn't have told them. Shouldn't have brought the letter there in the first place. It was a snap decision. Made before he could even get a word in about it. The director simply made her swift and ruthless judgment, gavel crashing down on years of obsession and aspirations.

"I ... I don't know that it was them – ! It could be a prank! Just some stupid kids–"

"–Oh, please, Shah. Don't be reckless – if a killer is targeting you, you need to take a step back. If they're trying to impress you or lure you in, you could set them into a spree. You know *that."*

Darian's hand had curled around the plastic-bound linen strips in his pocket. He was going to give them to her, but at this point, the less evidence he had to support that it was really a *killer* sending him the letter, the more likely he'd be able to talk his way back onto the team.

They wouldn't know what to do with the strips of linen, anyway. They'd just confirm that it was one of the victims' blood and keep it in evidence for when they eventually caught this bastard. What else could you possibly learn fr –

Darian stopped in the middle of shoving toiletries into the front pocket of the suitcase, staring blankly at the floor.

There *was* something you could learn from it ...

Darian skipped downstairs – he'd have to destroy all evidence of him keeping Show's movies, anyway. Glad he hadn't done that yet, Darian shoved a flash drive into his projector and slapped the lights off. A random film of Showoff's started playing – one from six months ago. The victim – Carmen, this one's name was – struggled in her chair as she always did, but this time, Darian's eyes were locked onto the linen sheet.

It was a rough estimate, but he traced the outlines of the cloth. It was tall as well as wide, covering the entire frame and then some. No seams. No connections. It was over two yards tall. It *had* to be.

A grin curled over Darian's lips. Because how many places carried linen you could buy with more than two yards of height in this city?

The rest of the afternoon was a frenzied blur. Darian shoved the souvenirs and snuff films into his bag to take them with him, finished packing quickly, and threw everything roughly into the backseat of his truck. Within an hour, he'd been at three craft stores already, combing through to find bolts of linen.

Bolt after bolt was wrong. Too white. Too brown. Too low a thread count. Too high a threat count. Too short a cut.

By the seventh craft store, it was already eight P.M. and employees were getting tired and less willing to assist him.

But he found it.

In the back corner of a little family-owned shop on the old main street, Darian finally found just the right bolt of linen. He pressed the small plastic evidence bag against the fabric, lining up the threaded, bloody grid of the sample piece with the fresh, bright linen on the bolt.

It was a perfect match. The sample he had was slightly misshapen from blood and stretching, but the threads lined up almost perfectly regardless, and the color of the bolt matched the hue he remembered from the films.

Darian was locked in place as the ramifications bled through his mind. If he could track the right sales to the right buyer, that would be it. Show would be caught. Put in prison.

The snuff films would be done.

...Why did that leave such a hollow pit in his stomach? Wasn't it a *good* thing that this motherfucker was going to be behind bars? That no family would ever be forced to watch a video of their child, spouse, parent, or friend being mutilated for a silent, shadowed, and faceless killer?

It crossed his mind a few times that he *could* just put the bolt back. Go to his hotel like he was supposed to. Let the nitwits who were taking over *his* case fail again and again and again.

But he couldn't bring himself to be out of the loop. Couldn't imagine not seeing the videos or knowing their progress. Besides, more people were going to die if he didn't do anything about this, and it was his job to save them.

Mind set, he tucked the bolt of linen under his arm and moved up through the cramped hobby shop and set it on the front counter.

The girl behind it perked up, popping her earbuds out with a startled smile. "Oh – ! Hi! I can get this cut for you – how many yards do you need?" She moved her phone under the counter and stood to pull the bolt to her chest.

Darian put a hand on it, stopping her. "I don't need any. I'd like to get some sales information from you." He flipped open his badge for her to see. "FBI. I need to know who has bought this fabric in the past two years."

The girl blinked at him in a confused flutter. "Oh – Oh, um – ... ssssure?" She side-stepped to the computer and opened up the program, dipping a few times to read the numbers on the label. "What's this for?" she queried, voice half-distracted as she scrolled through options and grids on her screen.

"That's classified, I'm sorry."

"Okayyyy – anything specific I'm looking for? There's quite a few on here – "

Darian hummed, thinking. "It'd be more than four yards at each sale, possibly doubled on some purchases, but no more than that. You can cut out credit card sales – we're looking for cash only." He severely doubted Show was stupid enough to pay for murder materials with a card.

"Okay ... ummmm – yeah, there – I flagged all the cash sales over forty dollars for you. Want me to print this out?"

"That works fine, thanks." Darian eyed the red-dotted camera that was pointed at his face from behind the cashier. "Let me see the security footage as well."

She frowned, glancing behind her. "I'm so sorry – this one's fake, actually, but there's stuff in the parking lot?"

Darian found himself frowning. He didn't have *time* to go through city protocol. "How about the people next door?"

"Umm – " She looked up as the printer under the counter started whirring and clicking. Glancing toward the door. "I thiiiiiink so? It's some bigger chains, so they can probably afford it?"

"Perfect, thank you – " Darian took the paper as she offered it to him, glancing over the sales. There couldn't be more than two hundred here. Good. "Jot down your name and number for me, too. I might have more questions."

"Oh – ! Sure, yeah – one sec – " She scribbled down the note on a fresh piece of printer paper and handed that to him, too. "Any way I can help, just lemme know!"

"I appreciate that. Have a good evening, miss." He took the paper and headed out the door.

It only took a few quick glances to see who in the area had cameras pointed toward the parking lot. He'd check there in a moment.

His eyes skimmed the page quickly, marking off all sales within a week of any of the kills.

Within the first four, he'd found the pattern. Someone bought a four-yard by two-yard piece in the late morning the day before each kill. Every. Single. Time.

Darian's heart was beating a bit quicker as he thumbed through the pages, circling date after date after date. The times. All paid in cash. All the same amount. *Always* the day before the kills.

Incredible. Darian was grinning like a schoolboy over the pages as the pattern unraveled in front of him. The grin snapped away again as he noticed the last entry on the sales list.

The same timeframe.

Same size.

Bought yesterday.

5

Security

Darian always had a knack for spelling. Ever since he was a young child, it never quite made sense to him why someone should 'sound out' a word. His classmates would be writing out 'chruck' and 'chree' or 'twuck' and 'twee' from using their ears. Darian, somehow, just remembered where the letters went. Which letters were friends and which made what sounds together. 'Sounding' something out too often led to incorrect results. So, he'd simply copy the word down over and over and over again until it stuck in his brain.

As a seven-year-old, Darian almost never colored or drew with the other kids. Instead, he'd spend his time writing down all the words he saw around him in no particular order. Notebooks and notebooks piled up in his closet, written in crayon, pen, marker, and colored pencil with thousands of random words he'd come across in his time.

He was the best speller in school, so when the idea of a 'spelling bee' was brought to his attention in fourth grade, little Darian had jumped at the opportunity, signing up immediately.

It sounded like a fine idea. Someone asks you how to spell something, and you do it. He looked through a list of common spelling bee words and wrote them again and again to remember them. He wrote them at the dinner table. He finger-spelled them in his poor, clunky sign language when he wasn't allowed to write in church. He wrote them in the margins of his homework and in the dirt of the playground fence line.

Yet, somehow, the actual competition was so much more difficult than he imagined.

In short, Darian did not win. In long, Darian took one look at the crowd gathered below the stage and vomited onto the only microphone the school could afford, ruining the night for everyone and earning himself even more horrid nicknames at school.

Darian never tried to go on stage again after that. Never tried public speaking. Never signed up for school plays or choirs. When he was forced to participate, Darian would request to be 'Tree #4' or whatever part had little to no speaking lines and would squeeze his eyes shut whenever he absolutely *had* to speak on stage.

Darian couldn't imagine how Show did it. It made plenty of sense to want to be seen and known and understood, yet the thought of being filmed while doing something so intimate seemed atrocious to Darian. He would sooner film for a porno than a murder. In porn, you show more body than soul.

Darian wasn't sure what he'd do if that much of his soul were on display for the world to see, scrutinized and studied by agents like himself. At least on stage, it was one showing, then you were done. On film, anyone could watch it again and again and again. Any mistakes would be recorded forever, infinite and immortal. That was something Darian could never understand. What if there were mistakes? What if everyone judged you?

All this musing was to say that Darian was *deeply* uncomfortable each time he checked security cameras. Seeing himself on the footage when he'd barely even registered that the cameras existed in the first place was nauseating.

He'd successfully talked his way into the shop's office and gotten access to their security footage. After the clerk gave him a quick rundown of how to use the application and search for dates and times, they had run away again to help customers, leaving Darian blessedly alone.

Of course, the most recent event caught on camera was Darian walking into the shop and talking to the clerk, so that was the first thing that showed up on the screen. Darian couldn't keep himself from hitting play to watch the interaction, grimacing at the way he moved and spoke and the little nervous twitch that kept his knuckles coming back up to his jaw, rubbing at it pointlessly.

It was painful to watch. It made him sick.

He thought of Show in comparison. How seamless and elegant their every move was. They were smoke tumbling through a gentle breeze, and he was a clatter of pots and pans banging down a rusted and rotting staircase.

Somehow, it made him feel far more like 'Barf-face' than 'Agent Shah.' If he was going to take down Show, he *needed* to be Agent Shah. Still, he was left with a pit of self-loathing and anxiety.

Swallowing thickly, he forced himself through the work. He flipped through the folders of recordings until he located the camera pointed toward the parking lot. Then, he scrolled to the date and time of the first sale.

He stopped breathing as the customer moved across the grainy screen, shopping bag in hand.

They were smaller than he'd imagined them. Curling hair fell just to their shoulders in a cool, faded auburn.

He played it again.

Again and again and again.

Even without seeing their face; even without checking the other times; even without waiting for another body to come on screen, Darian knew that was Show.

No one else on this planet could glide over solid ground that gracefully.

Darian blew up the image and jotted down the license plate number of the hatchback Show climbed into. He barely remembered to scoop up his papers before he was out the door and bolting for the car.

Maybe a better man would have stopped to think about reporting it to his supervisor.

Darian just looked up the address in a blur, then made a beeline to the highway with a pounding heart and loaded gun.

6

Showing Live

Darian just –

Stared.

He should have said something.

He should have said '*FBI – PUT DOWN THE WEAPON!*'

It wasn't like he hadn't done that before.

Still, the words died on his tongue, sliding back down his throat and rotting in his twisting stomach as he stared at the scene before him.

A chair. A camera.

A man in the chair. Bleeding heavily, of course.

And Showoff.

Show and their glistening blade, paused mid-cut as their eyes undoubtedly found Darian through the black mesh in their mask.

The victim stared at Darian too, pleas and crackling screams muffled and lost into the fabric of the gag.

But the door was behind the camera. Perfectly so.

To anyone watching, it would seem the victim was just ... pleading at his audience. Begging for it to be a livestream. For someone to rescue him.

No words came out formed enough to communicate in the slightest.

... No one knew.

No one would know.

No one had to know he was there.

He should say the words.

He didn't.

Darian should shoot.

The gun lowered through the air instead until it came to rest pointed limply at the ground.

His eyes never left Show.

Show stayed still for a long few moments, masked face still pointed toward the intruding officer.

Then. Slowly. They continued to carve.

A tangle of emotions rang through Darian's blood.

He had to kill Show now. He had to. If he didn't, Show would tell everyone how he didn't stop them. They would know how Darian stared. They would know what he was.

... His fingers rippled over the handle of the gun.

Show's movements slowed slightly ... then the knife twisted.

A cry cracked up the man's throat, sending him into a sputtering, agonized wail that tapered into choked coughs.

... The gun lowered again.

And Show moved on. Finally turning their back to Darian – decided he wasn't a threat in that moment and just ... *moved on*.

Darian's heart slammed in his chest, searching the eyes of the man. Darian didn't even know his name. This poor, innocent (probably? Darian had no way to know for sure) man was going to die.

He was going to die as an FBI agent watched.

Doing nothing.

Doing nothing but trying to keep his expression neutral.

Doing nothing but trying *not* to watch.

Trying not to inhale ecstasy at every scream.

They were so much *better* here.

The screams didn't just have pitch and volume. They had body. They had *life* and *desperation* and *form*. They danced around the room, a surround sound symphony of iniquity and desperation.

Darian tried.

He *tried.*

Oh, how he tried.

He tried to lift the gun. To point it at Show. To find a way to get out of here. To play the hero even when he came without telling his team he'd found a lead. Came here knowing he wanted to see Show alone.

Came ... wanting to see this.

No.

No, he'd wanted to *stop* this. Of *course* he'd wanted to stop this – the only reason he hadn't told anyone on his team was because they'd have simply taken too long to get there, anyway, and he was better off using what precious little time he had getting to the scene and saving this poor man's life.

That's why he came alone.

That's why he broke protocol.

For the invaluable life of the man in the ch –

... Darian flinched as the knife ripped across the man's throat.

***

Everything was a bit of a blur after that.

Numbness set in. Something twixt self-loathing and disbelief that he'd actually let that happen. Then he realized just how *much* he'd watched. How long he'd mindlessly stared as the room smelled more and more like blood. As the barely streaked linen draped behind the pair slowly soaked through with crimson until its steady drips were the only sound in the room.

The camera turned off.

The man stopped breathing. Stopped twitching. Stopped living.

Because of him.

Because he didn't stop it.

And now the two were alone.

Darian's mind clawed back up from the fog as Show stepped around the camera, looking him over. Their face was still covered, but Darian could feel their eyes dragging up every inch of his body as they stepped closer. Slow and deliberate. Light on their feet as always.

Even more graceful in person. The camera didn't do them justice.

Darian found himself taking a shaky, half-step back. His gun raised again. Form? Bad. But the end that goes 'BANG' was pointed at Show. Good enough.

Show froze at the sight of the gun, face tilting down to the knife that still clung to their hand. Carefully, they reached far to the side, setting it down on the ground.

Then nudging it away with their foot.

Darian drew in a long breath, trying to keep it even. " ... *The mask.*"

Show's head tilted almost playfully to the side. Carefully – likely just moving slowly so they didn't spook Darian into pulling the trigger – they gestured to the gun.

" ... *What*?" His voice was just a whisper – why couldn't he get it to *work* – ?

They just gestured again.

... Mmmask off if he puts the gun down?

Darian frowned, fingers flexing around the glock. " ... Step back a little."

Show shrugged, hands out at their sides in a soft surrender. They slid back a couple feet, then crossed their arms. Waiting.

... This was so stupid. So fucking stupid – he couldn't just ...

He should be shooting Show right now. He should be putting a bullet through their head he could say he came in at the last minute and they tried to run he could *still* fix this he ... he could ... he ...

He lowered the gun. Slowly.

Safety on, then set it on the ground.

Show stared.

... Darian slid it to the other side of the room with his foot.

The smile practically bled through the damn mask as Show nodded in approval. Their hands came together, first peeling back the leather driving gloves they were so fond of. Or ... maybe not so fond – they just tossed them across the room in little bloody wads.

Then, slender fingers picked at the black spandex material under their mask – pulling it away from the neck, then up over their face.

Darian didn't know what he'd expected Show to look like.

This wasn't it. Yet ... seeing them shake out their curls and give him a bright, lopsided grin, Darian didn't know how he could ever picture them looking any other way.

Their eyes were bright. Face young. Hair a mess of curls that dropped to their shoulders in a color so similar to his grandmother's molasses cookies, he could practically see the grains of sugar on Show's cheeks dappled in amongst the scars that slashed through clear skin.

Show didn't stop, unzipping their hoodie and shrugging it off. Then the next one that hid beneath. They must have been fucking dying in all those layers – *damn.*

"Not gonna say anything?"

Darian almost flinched when Show spoke. It was so clear. So casual. So unfettered by the hour of unuse.

Darian suddenly ... didn't know what to do with his hands. No gun? No gun. Pppppppockets? No.

Folded. Arms folded.

That'd work.

Show rolled their eyes, tossing the bundle of clothes onto the couch – this basement functioned more like a studio apartment than anything – then wandered toward the fridge in the kitchenette. "I know you drink Corona, but I have Blue Moon. Tragedy for you."

Darian almost dropped the fucking bottle that hurtled through the air at him moments later.

He didn't – the glass caught in his useless fucking hands – almost slipping, but not.

Cold.

Show just laughed at him, cracking the top of their own open against the countertop. "Wow – you're really shaken, huh? Not like you haven't seen any of that before."

Darian ... was ...

What the fuck was he supposed to be doing here?

Were they having a *conversation* now?

What the fuck was going on?

He stared down at the beer in his hands. And said the ... well, the only thing that came to mind.

" ... Are you a hipster or something?"

Amusement and wonder flickered across Show's eyes. " ... Because of the beer?"

"Yeah."

They shrugged, hopping up onto the counter and tipping the bottle up in a sip. "Not sure. Depends on your definition of 'hipster.' I hate flannel though, and beanies hate me, so that's not a good start." They glanced down to the bottle in Darian's hands. " ... Yyyyyyyou want me to open that for you?"

Darian didn't even want to drink something Show gave him. That would be incredibly stupid – it could be drugged or something.

The fucking mind reader piped up. "It's literally factory sealed, it's *fine.*"

Darian eyed Show, but found his hand moving toward his pocket. He slipped out his keys, cracked open the top, and gestured to it. "Happy?"

Show grinned at him, taking a sip of their own beer. "*Very*, thank you~"

Darian didn't drink. Not that brave yet.

Which was fucking stupid. Show was right, it was sealed. It was new. It was *fine.* It's fine. It's *fine, stopfreakingout* –

He watched Show for a few moments longer as the bottle rolled back and forth in his hands. " ... What's your name?"

Show sputtered a laugh, almost losing beer there. They wiped their mouth on the back of their hand as their legs swung back and forth. "*Seriously*? You tracked me the fuck down and you don't even know my name? How is that even possible?"

Darian glared to the side – at the wall. Toward the ground. " ... Didn't run the paper check, I just followed."

Show smirked. "Riiiiiight~ You were keeping this excursion from your supervisors. *Very* sexy. I approve."

Darian's glare flicked back up to Show. "Are you going to tell me or not?"

Show shrugged. "Not like you can't get it in like ... ten seconds by Googling what you already know. *Butttttttttttttt*. Fine, sure. My name's Calyx."

Darian rolled the syllables around in his mouth. Trying them. Tasting them. " ... Calyx ... is that your legal name?"

Show nodded. "Had it for years, yeah."

Darian's lips pinched together, looking at his beer. " ... You weren't even on my list."

Sho – no, *Calyx* – grinned at him. "Yeah? *Fantastic*. Do I get a sticker?" Another swig.

Darian's eyes slid to the body on the other side of the room. Blood was still oozing from it, sliding in long, sticky drips to the puddle on the ground. " ... Why are you doing this?"

Show – no, *CALYX*. Calyx. Calyx raised a brow at him. "Why do I kill ... ? What are you, a shrink?"

" ... No, I meant – why ... " Geez, now he just felt stupid. " ... Why ... are we ... talking ... ?" Gesturing awkwardly to the beer.

Calyx burst into laughter, curling up around their bottle. " *Wooooooooowwwwwww* – wow, you don't even *care*, do you? You're *really* fucked up, dude~!"

Darian's cheeks burned, shame clawing up his throat. "Th – ... no? No, that's not even what I'm talking ab – "

"*Shhhtshstshtshtshtttt~*" Calyx waved a fluttering hand in his direction. "I'm fucked up too, you're fine. That's your answer. I'm not gonna kill my favorite viewer. We can hang out for a while and sate each other's curiosity and tomorrow we can go back to the little cat and mouse game and it'll be *fine~*" The bottle lifted to their lips again. "You worry too much, dude."

Darian frowned at them, but found the beer on his tongue as well.

... It was good. It soothed him. An old friend – maybe with a different twist, but still much the same. Comforting.

... He glanced toward the door.

Then to the clock.

" ... Truce for tonight?"

Calyx smirked up at him. "Deal. A *real* truce, though. No using things you learned here against me and I won't do the same to you. Mutually assured destruction."

Darian drew in a long breath, nodding. He downed another few icy pulls on the bottle, bracing himself for this insanity.

" ... Okay. Um ... wh – "

"No no no – you already got a question in. My turn."

Darian rolled his eyes, moving to perch on the edge of the table now. A little closer. "Fine. What's your question?"

"Are you single?"

Darian almost choked. "I – why does that matter?"

Calyx shrugged. "Matters cuz I wanna know."

He sighed. "I'm married to my work."

"*Awwwhhhh~* You're basically married to *me* then, huh, hubby?"

Darian must have made some kind of amusing expression in response to that, because Calyx was *immediately* victim to a burst of laughter again. "No, really, though – ! You're obsessed with me – I know you are. Just admit itttttt~"

Darian's eyes narrowed slightly. He decided to just move on from that. "How many have you killed?"

Calyx's head tilted back and forth in thought. "Tricky question."

"How the everloving fuck is that a tricky question?"

Calyx gasped in offense. "Because you didn't clarify intent or ... or causation? I have *categories.*"

Darian rolled his eyes. "Okay, how about two numbers – one for total people who would probably be alive if it weren't for you, and one for full-on first-degree premeditated shit?" That sentence slid from his lips so smoothly, Darian was almost worried.

... He was already far too casual around Calyx.

He forced himself to look at the mutilated corpse in the room.

See that, Darian? *That's* what happens when you get stupid around an unsub.

Be smarter.

Calyx cut off his thoughts with numbers. "M'kay, uhhh ... total isssss ... twenty-five. First-degree, twenty-one."

Darian frowned, eyes turning back to them. "I only have nineteen videos, counting this one."

Calyx shrugged. "Didn't get my vibe going for a minute. First couple were sloppy."

... Darian didn't know what to say to that, so he just ... found himself drinking again. Stomach twisting.

Calyx hummed, feet kicking in a smooth rhythm as they pondered the next question. "Mmm ... how 'bouttttt ... hmm ... know what? Same question. What's your body count?"

Darian sighed. Thinking.

Ignoring the double meaning. This game sucked.

" ... Killed three. One on accident, two on the job."

"OoooOOoooo~ *Very* scary. Very cool. You look sexy in the bulletproof vest, by the way." Calyx gestured toward Darian's chest with their beer.

... Suddenly Darian wanted it off. Or ... on more? More on him but not – Actually, maybe just something else on him? Something more. Something not that. " ... Thanks."

Deeeeeep breath. Another drink.

Focus. Think.

"What do you do for a living?"

Calyx lit up a little. "Aww~! Cute question! I'm a dancer."

An error screen practically scrolled across Darian's eyes. " ... Dance ... *fuck*, that should have been obvious ... " Why hadn't he *thought* of that?

Calyx laughed, looking over him. "Why?"

Darian gestured vaguely toward Calyx. A little sloppy in the gestures – apparently not putting in much effort. "Cuz you're ... like ... I dunno, smooth? Graceful and ... shit ... ?"

Calyx pressed a hand to their heart. "*Awwwwhhhh,* really~?"

Darian nodded, setting the beer to the side.

That stuff was shit, it was giving him a headache. And ... kinda a stomachache?

Ew. Moving on. "Next question?"

Calyx chewed on their lip as they thought, sliding off the counter in favor of leaning against it. "Hmm*mmm* ... oh – ! Which of my videos is your favorite?"

Whyyyyy was Darian still here?

He could leave.

He *should* leave. He should leave.

Why wasn't he leaving – ? What the fuck was wrong with him.

Darian glowered at them. "I don't have a favorite. It's not something I enjoy."

Calyx rolled their eyes, stepping closer. "We both know that's a lie, Agent~" Darian flinched backward as Calyx booped his nose.

Darian refused to back away. Calyx ... was incredibly close – wayyyyyy too fucking close, their legs were almost touching –

But he wasn't going to be a little bitch and shrink away from someone so much smaller than him. It was *fine.* He was fine. This was fine.

" ... Rachel Wheeler."

A smirk crackled across Calyx's lips. "The garotte?"

Darian gave a small shrug, finding his hand around the bottle again. He needed something to hold. Something to focus the nervous energy on. " ... Good sounds," he muttered, taking another swig.

Calyx was grinning again. "They really were, weren't they? I should work that angle more often."

Darian rolled his eyes. "You're not going to be doing this much longer."

Calyx's brows popped up. "Why? Cuz *you're* going to stop me?"

Darian tried to glare past the sarcasm. "That's about right, yeah."

"*I've been really loving watching you try~*" Smirking now. Stepping closer until their leg brushed the inside of Darian's thigh. Smirk growing as Darian squirmed a little, eyes flitting away.

" ... Do you ... have – l-ike *no* idea what personal space is – ?" Leaning back a little. Heart slamming sirens into his mind.

Calyx hummed in thought, hand smoothing over Darian's chest to hook two fingers into the top of his vest. "Mmmm*nope~* Never heard of it." They reeled him back the few inches he'd retreated.

Darian's eyes turned up to Calyx's again, searching their face. " ... I agreed to conversation, n-ot touching."

Calyx chuckled softly, thumb brushing over the bit of collarbone that showed around his shirt collar. "Oh, come *on~* Not like I could hurt you. You're like twice my size with combat training." They took a moment to tug the collar of Darian's shirt straight, smoothing down the fabric. "You could stop me *any* time."

Darian just ... stared.

Calyx leaned in, looking very pleased with themself as they nuzzled their nose behind Darian's ear.

Panic and excitement and worry and fascination clashed inside of him, slamming his heart against his ribs and curling his fingers tighter around the almost-empty bottle.

He felt hot.

Too hot.

Almost light-headed as his head tilted just a little away. " ... *I don't want to hurt you."*

A grin spread against his scalp. "*I like your shampoo.*"

... He was being sniffed.

........greatttttttttt –

" ... *Thanks.*" He forced the bottle up and took another drink, immediately grimacing at how it churned inside his stomach.

He set down the b –

... The sound of shattering glass echoed in the room, slamming against the inside of his skull.

Calyx pulled back, glancing down to the bottle that had slipped from Darian's fingers. "Well, that's a mess."

Darian stared too.

How did he ... he wouldn't have dropped that. He ...

He rubbed his fingers together, breath immediately locking up in his throat as he realized.

They were numb.

Alarm bells that were distant in the back of his mind were starting to come to the front now as he twisted, staring behind him to see the length of the room.

... Vision swimming – fuck.

Fuck fuck fuck *fuck FUCK* –

He stared at the bottle for another moment.

Not factory sealed. *Re*sealed.

FUCK.

Darian immediately tried to stand straight, toppling backward *far* too easily as Calyx's hand shoved at his chest, pinning him there.

"Awwww – I'm sorry, is that *scary*? Honestly I'm surprised you actually drank that, it was just a shot in the dark." Darian flinched as Calyx's hand ghosted over his cheek, cradling it and wiping over the skin with a thumb.

The world was already spinning so bad – his hand tried to shove at Calyx, but mostly ended up focused on gripping the edge of the table, eyes blinking hard through the sludge and the fog that was quickly flooding through his mind. " *Ffffuckking bitch –* "

Calyx's laughter filled his ears again. Lips pressed to his cheek. "Don't be like that, baby. You liked my movies so much, I just figured you'd like to be in one~"

7

Stardom

Darian woke slowly – then all at once, grimacing as a foul odor shoved into his sinuses and twisted his stomach, zapping panic, consciousness, and unease through his mind. He turned his head, neck aching from drooping, and coughed away the scent.

"*Theeeeere* you are~"

Darian twitched as a hand patted his cheek.

He took a few heaving breaths before turning his eyes up to Calyx – the little shit was straddling him.

... He was in a chair. Wooden chair. Wrists tied behind the back.

The corners of the wood bruised into his arms and shoulder blades – far too tight. His back arched to alleviate a bit of the stretch as his hands fisted and squirmed, trying to wriggle away from the ropes or at *least* find a knot he could reach enough to pick at.

He found nothing.

He got nowhere.

Calyx's hands smoothed up his chest – it was bare now – both the Kevlar vest and his fucking *shirt* were gone.

Creep.

"You sure are pretty," Calyx murmured, palming up Darian's throat.

Darian's head wrenched away from the touch. "G-et *off* me – "

Calyx just breathed a twinkling laugh, hands running through Darian's hair now instead. "Nahhhhhhhhhhh – I'm savoring this."

Darian's eyes slid away from Calyx's, trying to press away the last of the fog from his mind. Looking at *literally* anyth –

... His stomach twisted as he caught a glimpse of the camera over Calyx's shoulder. Not on. Not blinking red.

But pointed right at him.

Breath caught painfully in his lungs as he twisted his head back, staring behind them for th –

... Y-yeah. Yeah, that was ... that was a new drape of linen.

Clean.

White.

Ready for blood.

His blood.

Darian couldn't quite keep the panic out of his eyes as he looked back over Calyx. They were in the 'Showoff' outfit again. Layered in black, loose fabric. Everything but the mask and gloves.

Calyx smirked, head tilting down and into Darian's line of sight. "Putting it together now?"

Darian squirmed back, anger and betrayal in his eyes. "Y – ... we c-alled a truce – !"

Calyx laughed, pressing a kiss to Darian's forehead. "You're adorable." Before Darian could try to bite or headbutt or kick them off, Calyx slipped off his lap, scooping up the mask from the back of the couch. "No offense, but I can't exactly have the FBI knowing where I live. Aaaaaaand you didn't tell anyone when you figured it out. That's on *you*, sweetheart. If you're gonna be that stupid, I can't help but take advantage." The gloves slipped onto their hands next. One by one, pieces of 'Show' covering up the 'Calyx' he'd met.

Darian stared desperately at them, still rolling his wrists and shoulders to try to get out. "Come on – come *on* – I – I fuckin' saved your ass! You could be in prison right now – !"

Show picked up a wad of black fabric, rolling it up and wandering closer. "Open up~"

Darian's jaw set, fear clear in his eyes as he stared desperately up at Show. " ... *Please.*"

Calyx rolled their eyes, grabbing Darian by the jaw and *s q u e e z i n g* until his cheeks were cutting against his own teeth. With a choked grunt, his jaw slotted open – quickly pried open further by the thick black cloth that was stuffed between his teeth.

"I like you. I do." Duct tape shredded away and smoothed over his mouth before Darian could get anywhere trying to work the gag out again. "I just need you to be less ... unpredictable. You get that, right?" The grip on his jaw tipped his face up to stare at Show.

Defiance, anger, and fear all pressed hot and wet at the corners of Darian's eyes in response.

"I don't *want* to do this, you know. As pretty as you'll bleed, I'd prefer you whole." Show sighed, fingers tightening as Darian tried to wrench himself from their grip. "This is best for both of us."

Before Darian really realized what was happening, Show's masked lips pressed to his through the duct tape, fingers keeping him exactly in place, just in case the shock of that moment wasn't enough.

It was.

Eyes still open and staring into the black void that lingered in the holes of Calyx's mask.

When they pulled back, Darian had stopped struggling. Just ... staring.

A gloved hand ran through his hair, and Show stepped away. Stretching for a moment before they picked up their knife. "Make some pretty sounds for me, and I'll go easy on you. How's that~?"

Darian barely had a chance to grunt in response before Show's fingers pressed at the camera.

The light turned red.

For a few long seconds, Darian lived in suspended disbelief. Denial, really.

That Calyx wouldn't do this to him.

That, even though they'd just met or *whatever* (*shut the* fuck UP *with your logic*), that Calyx wouldn't hurt him.

Just like how he couldn't hurt Calyx.

He barely shivered as the knife trailed over his collarbone, cool and crisp and scraping. He knew it wouldn't draw blood. He couldn't believe Calyx would do this to him. He *wouldn't*. This was a test. A ... prank. A –

Blood dribbled down his chest before he registered the pain.

Sharp. *Deep*. Prickling at the ripped edges of the gash.

And Darian believed.

***

Most of the next hour or so was a blur. It felt like months. It felt like minutes. It felt like it would never end.

Darian never realized just *how much* blood was in his body. Wouldn't it run out at some point?

It never seemed to.

With each cut and slice and gouge, more and more and more poured from him, coating his chest in streaks of crimson and soaking through his slacks. It dripped onto the floor until his bare toes were smeared with it. It soaked through the linen drape behind them.

Finally, he knew what it was like.

So many months of wondering what it would be like to be in that chair. And now he was there.

Darian screamed.

He screamed so *much* – he hadn't even known what his own screams could do. He never knew how they could sound. It didn't seem like his own voice. They crackled and snapped and clawed up his throat just to be devoured by the cloth that muffled them away.

The knife seemed to never stop moving. His only breaks from the onslaught were when Show stepped back to drag his blood over the white cloth.

It filled with red far too quickly. *Far* too quickly.

When that final moment came, he was so dizzy with blood loss and pain. He knew now how Show kept their victims awake. Out of sight of the camera, smelling salts, hidden in Show's sleeve, would press under his nose. Cubes of ice at the back of his neck made him arch and shudder, gasping back to clarity – but no one saw that.

It was just part of the show.

Part of the pain.

It kept him lucid enough to scream and thrash and beg wordlessly through the gag until that moment when Calyx finally stopped.

They stepped away, picking up something out of frame.

A garotte.

... Darian's favorite.

It looked like Calyx asked their questions with purpose, and Darian's head immediately hung in the exhausted regret that comes with having been so thoroughly played.

Calyx's fingers ghosted against his throat first – then the wire of the garotte.

A pause.

A moment of suspense to make this grand finale all the more dramatic for their audience.

Then Calyx's grip tightened. Twisted.

The wire choked away his air. It pressed at his arteries immediately – each frantic heartbeat slamming uselessly against the wire.

Darian's exhausted, depleted body was thrashing again – newfound strength found in one final burst of adrenaline as he choked on tears and panic. On pain and air and nothingness.

Desperately trying to breathe. To stop the slamming in his head as his mind turned fuzzy.

He thought he'd break the chair with the force of his thrashing and flopping as the panic ripped through him, but the wood held strong. Calyx didn't relent.

He'd seen this before. Seen the wire saw through flesh and draw out blood. All but decapitating the victims. They'd choke on blood as it slid into their esophagus or gasping at nothing as oily slick slid down their neck.

His final thought before slipping into the darkness was a question.

... Why wasn't the garrote cutting him?

8

Intermission

Pain.

Darian wished he could be cool and start off with a dramatic, badass-sounding intro line like 'He awoke to pain. An old, familiar friend.'

But they weren't old friends. They weren't friends at all, and it wasn't familiar. It was just pain.

Air wheezed out of him as he processed the inferno that wrapped his body. Skin and flesh shredded from their places and screamed agonies at his blurred and distant mind.

He shifted a little, heart pounding against his skull as he registered just how thirsty he was.

"*Oh* – ! Hey, there you are. Thought I'd lost you or something."

... Not a welcome voice.

Darian grimaced, head rolling away from the sound – then wheezing as Calyx's weight shifted on the bed, disturbing the delicate balance of agony and consciousness.

"Awh, don't pull away from me – it's not like you can, anyway." A hand combed through Darian's hair. Calyx chimed a soft giggle, amused, as Darian's neck mindlessly stretched to chase that touch – the only sensation that wasn't bringing pain. "Awwww~ you're adorable."

Darian half-scowled, head turning away again as a kiss pressed to his nose.

"Come onnnnnnnnn~ I saved your life – aren't you at least a *little* grateful?"

Darian's throat was rasped with dehydration and unuse, but he crackled out the whisper, anyway. "*Y-ou ... y ou hhurt me –* "

Calyx snorted a laugh, ruffling Darian's hair. "I mean *duh.* What did you think I was gonna do? I'm gonna go ahead and blame the sheer patheticness of that sentence on the drugs, m'kay? No judgment from me, nope nope~"

Darian grimaced, eyes cracking open in a groggy scowl at Calyx. " ... *Wh' day's it?"*

Calyx checked their phone with a bright hum. "Thursday. You've been out for liiiiiike thirty-something hours."

Darian's eyes strained down over his body. Covered in bandages and smelling like medicine. " ... *H-ow did y – ...* "

Calyx shrugged. "Patched you up enough you wouldn't die on me and gave you a blood transfusion. I avoided doing any major damage, so you should heal up in a couple weeks."

Darian frowned, looking over Calyx. " ... *Wh' ... are you doing* – ?"

Brow raise. " ... What, with you?"

... Small hum of confirmation.

Calyx shrugged. "Just keeping you, that's all. Obviously couldn't let you keep living, and ... wasn't ready to let you go. So." They took a moment to nitpick the way Darian's hair lay, brushing it from his brow. "Found a middle ground. You like it?"

Darian's face twitched away from Calyx. *"N-o, I don't ffucking like this –* "

Calyx blinked a tight smile.

Then something cold and sharp pricked against Darian's aching throat.

"You sure you don't like this alternative? Because I can always skip back to plan A."

Darian froze, swallowing against the cool blade. " ... *I-ll ma nage –* "

"*Good~*" The knife pulled away, and a kiss pressed to his cheek.

Darian was quiet for a long few moments, just ... trying to focus on Calyx's fingers in his hair. " ... *Why d'you like me – ?"*

Calyx shrugged, fingers drifting down now to trace the lines of Darian's face. "You see me. You actually *appreciate* my work. Anddddddd I'm bored. Good enough answer for you?"

He did his best not to twitch under the little touches. " ... D*id ... y ... the video ...* – "

"Mm. Mhm. Sent it to your team. Saw on the news they think you're dead. There's like a candlelight vigil thing for you this Friday in the park. Isn't that sweet?"

Darian twitched a frown, eyes sliding away. " ... *S-ure.* "

"I'd totally go, but I feel like it'd be rude to leave you alone during your own not-funeral, y'know? We can have a movie night or something instead."

... Darian ... had no idea what to say to that. So, he said nothing at all. A small part of him was screaming for him to run. To lash out and hit Calyx. To sprint from the room or strangle them.

... The rest of him was too fucking tired to even get through considering that idea. He'd probably pass out if he tried to stand, anyway.

Aaaaaand Calyx was back to playing with his hair. No – braiding it now. Their little fingers were twisting it out as long as possible to tangle a small cornrow from the corner of his forehead. Keeping their hands busy, he supposed.

" ... C-an I ... get some water – ?"

"*Mm* – ! Right right right, you're probably dehydrated as fuck, one sec – " Calyx stood, crossing out of the room.

Darian stared after them, then finally let his eyes roam the space.

... Queen-sized bed. Not a spare room – this one was littered in things. Piles of clothes that weren't put away. A few articles that had missed the toss to the hamper. Pictures tacked on the wall. Pocket change and trinkets drizzled over the dresser. This was Calyx's room.

Whichhhhhh meant they probably slept next to Darian last night.

... And would continue to.

Greatttttttt –

His eyes snapped back up to the doorframe as Calyx reentered, holding up a clear water bottle with a straw. "Got it – think you can sit up?"

Darian half-scowled at them, shifting up and shoving his elbows under his weight to scoot b –

Darkness.

Darkness and pain and delirium engulfed him for several long seconds, refusing to let him escape.

A voice cut through the fog, muffled and slurred.

Darian winced and twitched away from whatever was patting at his cheek.

"*There* you are." He could fucking *hear* the grin in Calyx's voice. "Guess the answer to that was 'no,' huh?"

Darian grimaced, head rolling away as the light finally returned to his world. *"A-ns'r to wha – ?"*

"Whether or not you can sit up." Something poked at his lips, drawing out a flinch. " ... It's just a straw, you're fine. It's water. Undrugged and everything."

Darian wanted so badly to give them some shit line like '*That's what you said last time*', but not only would that make Darian look even *dumber*, he had no choice here. His throat was practically sticking to itself with every swallow – he *needed* water and it wasn't going to come from anywhere else.

So. Reluctantly. He let his lips close around it, sucking down greedy mouthfuls of the fresh, cool liquid. A half-panic surged through his mind, mouth chasing the straw as it withdrew.

"Hey – chill out, there's gonna be more. You'll make yourself sick drinking it that fast."

Darian scowled, letting his head flop back against the pillow.

Calyx perched on the edge of the bed again after they set the bottle down. Their arm propped up on the other side of Darian, leaning over him. "Are you mad at me~?" Pouting.

Darian's head twisted further from them. *"N-o shit."*

Calyx cooed a sorrowful sound, fingertips ghosting over Darian's lips. "I'll make it up to you~! You'll see. You're going to *love* being mine."

9

Director's Cut

Darian eyed Calyx as they pushed into the bedroom. Smiling, as always. Not Darian, of course – Calyx. They were still in their leotard from rehearsal. The one they'd dyed with his blood.

Charming motherfucker.

"I got something for you~"

His suspicion just kept rising. How could it not? The past couple days with Calyx had been mind-achingly dull and filled with healing pains when his captor was out of the house. When they were there, Calyx's schedule for Darian had included cooing, coddling, and endless ramblings about films, dance rehearsal, or childhood pets.

It didn't make sense. Not really. Still, Darian was slightly eased somehow by the fact that Calyx had been truly as obsessed with him as he was with them all this time. Made him feel just a little bit more sane. At the very least, less alone in his insanity.

Calyx proudly held up a box. They looked like they might explode from excitement.

Darian raised a brow slightly, eyes dancing over the box. " ... Am I supposed to know what that is?" It had very little in the way of markings besides the standard delivery company logo.

"No! It's a *projector~*"

Darian forced his eyes away again. "Going to pacify me with T.V. shows while you're gone?"

"Nah, I can do better than that." They hopped onto the bed and plopped down cross-legged, opening the box and pulling out the miniature projector which they'd apparently already opened and assembled outside.

Darian watched quietly as they worked, disliking the way they loomed above him even at that distance. He was sick of having his hands tied above his head. He'd have to ask them to shift the restraints again soon, or his arms were going to lose blood flow. And heaven *forbid* they not get to see his muscles anymore. Yes, that *was* sarcasm.

Calyx actually shut up for once while they set the projector up. They just put it on the end table and pointed it at the ceiling before plugging the wires into their laptop.

Through all the clicking, tapping, shifting, and frame-adjusting, Darian couldn't help but let the question tumble from his mouth: "What are we watching?"

Calyx's grin split across their face, eyes still focused on their work – almost hiding from Darian. "Some home videos, that's all~"

Oh.

Oh, *shit.*

Darian started to protest only to have his objection cut off by an image of *himself* in the chair popping onto the ceiling. The words died in his throat as realization set in. Of course. Of *course* Calyx would make Darian watch *himself* get tortured. Why the fuck did he think it would be anyone else?

"I had to edit it a bit for the official release, but we can enjoy the director's cut~!" Calyx hit play and set the laptop aside, snuggling down on their back next to Darian to stare at the ceiling.

Darian's chest felt tight. It's always strange seeing yourself in a video. The way you speak. The way you hold yourself. The way you breathe or walk or smile. All the things that photographs don't show.

But this was different. More. It was surreal. His current body was in so very much pain, yet the body he saw on the ceiling was completely untouched. Yet, somehow, that Darian on the screen, who looked so much younger and stronger, seemed to know exactly where each drop of blood would fall. The phantom agony spun in his mind, creating an endless loop of agony and fear. His mind teased him with the memories of the nothingness interrupted by blinding pain, which ebbed away into this stitched and healing state. Then back to the start again, awaiting the blood and the occluded screams.

Darian's eyes closed, head twisting away from the display.

"*Awhhhhhh~* don't be like that. I made a movie of us together, don't you wanna see it?"

Darian's head twitched a shake. "*No.*"

Calyx sighed, snuggling in closer where Darian had tried to wriggle away from them. "Darian. Don't pretend you're better than this. You've already watched me kill and torture plenty of people. Are you *really* gonna get a weak stomach on me just because it's *you*? I'd have thought you were tougher than that ... "

Darian's jaw set, head turning to glare nose-to-nose at Calyx. "I don't *want* to watch you hurt me. I don't *want* to watch you hurt *anyone*."

Calyx moved slowly. Their eyes lost that smile, but kept the sparkle somehow, as delicate fingers moved up to brush Darian's hair away from his brow. "*You don't need to lie to me, Darian.*"

His stomach twisted.

They couldn't know. They could *not* – they were just conceited and brash.

Calyx's fingers ghosted down his cheekbone. "*I've watched you. Watched you watching me. I know you like it. I know this is the only video you won't have memorized by now.*"

Dread and panic tangled for dominance in his gut, and he twisted his head to glare at the opposite wall. "I'm n – "

A bruising grip cut off his thought as Calyx's fingers snapped his head back toward them like a vise around his jaw. "Do **not** lie to me." The grip relaxed slightly. "You don't have to. Not to me. To everyone else, yes – but not to me. It's okay to like it. It's done. Might as well enjoy it."

The urge to fight them was so incredibly strong – a strength much better suited to the Darian projected on the ceiling. *This* Darian, however, was bleeding, broken, and rotting tied to a bed. This man didn't have the strength to fight the accusations. Couldn't think of a lie any more easily than he could wrench his face from his villain's grip.

"*It's okay,*" they murmured, grip softening to cradle his cheek. "*It's just me. No one to impress.*"

Darian's jaw twitched, but he let his eyes slide to the ceiling. Ignoring the strain that put on his headache, he let his eyes linger over the shape of Calyx straddling his lap, tracing a knife over him just out of sight. But he could tell where it was. He could feel each millimeter of skin and scar pucker up around the invisible memory of the blade.

"*You're so fucked up,*" he murmured back, eyes still away from Calyx.

"*I know.*"

The video kept playing – getting now to the part that Calyx would have left in the 'final' edit. The silent strolling around the victim in the chair. Strolling around *him*.

"Gods, I *love* that expression you have. Defiant and angry but there's also sparks of passion? Stunning, really – soooo nice to look at."

Darian snapped a glare back to them, trying to burn a hole through their skull with his eyes.

They sputtered a bubbling laugh, sitting up a little and pointing at his face. "Yes! Yes, that one! Exactly!"

Anger and frustration were clawing up his neck now, bringing heat to his face and down his spine again. Darian snapped his eyes back to the 'screen', if only to avoid further scrutiny.

Calyx kept smiling over him, though, finger tracing the collar of his shirt. "Adorable," they chimed before settling back down next to him.

Darian trained his eyes on the 'home film' projected onto the smooth white ceiling, trying to maintain a blank expression to keep Calyx shut up.

He didn't notice before – maybe it was from the pain, abject horror, or belief that he was about to die, but ... Show treated him differently than the others.

It wasn't much. Small things. Things that no one but him would be able to pick up on. At least, he hoped no one would. He didn't need the entire BAU making fun of him when he finally got out of here.

But Show was ... sweet with him, almost. The cuts were precise and focused – made ever so slightly slower than usual. Like they were treasuring it. Their masked face was tilted up – watching his expressions through each moment, regardless of how small.

Even as Darian thrashed and screamed, gentle fingers smoothed his hair and traced the lines of his face. Not possessive, like they usually were with others. Just ... touching. Almost comforting. Tender.

Darian's breath was growing strained as he watched, noting how Calyx's fingers tended to drift – idly tracing sutured cuts with feather-light touches as Show created them on the screen. Reminiscing.

It felt ... surreal. Detached and separate. As if that wasn't *really* Darian on the screen. As if that wasn't Calyx.

This moment felt so much more real than that daze of a memory that Calyx committed to film. It was Agent Shah and Show on the screen – not Darian and Calyx.

That was easier. Easier to see Agent Shah bleeding and begging. Easier to see Show with fingers in his hair. It made him a little more certain that the Calyx next to him wasn't about to gut him again. Made it easier to believe that the gentle touches would stay gentle.

And they did.

Darian and Calyx both laid in silence for the hour or so that the film lasted, eyes locked on the screen as Show tore Shah apart.

When the film pulled to a stop, options to replay or rewind popping up on the ceiling, Darian's head fell to the side, face hiding against Calyx's hair. Even in calling them 'Shah' and 'Show', the threat still wriggled through. *I can do this again. Any time.*

He closed his eyes, buried in the surreal, yet gentle warmth of the moment. " ... *Can you move my arms? I'd like to sleep.*"

"*Mm,*" they hummed back, turning to nuzzle against him in turn. "*Of course, baby.*"

10

Showcase

"Quit being such a *baby* – I could just stab through it again to cut them, would you rather I just do that?"

Darian grimaced, forcing his shuddering breaths still as he glared up at the ceiling. "... *N-o – ?*"

"Then hold still – ?" Calyx's little sewing scissors slipped under another stitch, snipping it free. They weren't exactly *gentle* with these blades. Calyx was like a swan gliding across a glassy lake when they had a knife in their hand. Yet, with dainty, inch-long silver blades from a delicate little sewing kit? Chainsaw fucking massacre.

Calyx kept going, rolling their eyes whenever Darian flinched or winced. "You're being *dramaticccccc*," they chimed, glancing up at Darian. They'd positioned themself between his legs, kneeling on the ground to get to the lower cuts without blocking the kitchen light.

Fuckin' classy.

"You're *cutting* me – !"

"I have, can, and *will* stab you if you don't hold the fuck still."

"You *ARE*." Stabbing him, that is.

"I'm barely pricking you – you aren't even bl – ... oh. Oh, you *are* bleeding. Huh~"

Darian groaned, head tipping back to glare at the ceiling again. This would be easier if Calyx would just let him take them out himself. Of course they wouldn't.

They didn't trust Darian without his hands tied, much less with a sharp object in those untied hands.

His days with Calyx were simple. They'd fallen into a routine over these last few weeks. Darian stayed in bed, sleeping next to Calyx with hands bound to the fucking headboard. Moved for bathroom breaks. For meals. For movie nights with Calyx snuggled up against him or on his lap. Always fairly heavily bound, though Calyx was at least attentive enough to realize that Darian's arms had to be tied in different directions fairly regularly to keep up decent blood flow and mobility.

They were weirdly good about it.

Good about keeping his cuts and stab wounds cleaned. About checking the stitches. About massaging blood down his arms when they'd been tied in one place too long.

Right now, Darian was in a kitchen chair – hands bound individually to the cross of the chair legs and the bar that supported them. Still hurt.

"Can you j – *shhhit* – c-an you just fuckin' – *I* don't know, put on some glasses or something!?"

Calyx poked the little scissors up under Darian's chin, eyes glinting in amusement. "Maybe I just like how pretty you look covered in blood – ever think of that~?"

Darian scoffed a sigh, head rolling away from the scissors. "Just ... fuckin' ... hurry up."

Calyx laughed softly, hand dragging down Darian's chest. "But it's so *funnnnnn* – just look at all these marks. Some of my finest work, really."

Darian shivered as Calyx trailed the tip of the scissors over one of the freshly freed cuts. This one laid just below his ribcage on the left, following the long line of the prickling scar. "Everything was so well-balanced ... I made you so *pretty~*"

Darian's eyes roamed down, following the little silver points as they danced over his skin.

... Calyx was right.

He wasn't gonna fucking *say* that, of course. The bitch had too big a head already.

"Glad you're fuckin' satisfied."

Calyx leaned forward, tongue pressing to one of the marks – pricks of blood were beading up from where they'd pulled the sutures too roughly across the inside of his hip.

Darian's words choked to a stop in his throat as Calyx's tongue dragged up the mark – eyes locked on his. Blood gathered over their tongue, smearing over flesh as Darian squirmed back, eyes sliding away. That was a little close to the beltline, don't you think, Cal?

Calyx just smirked a bitten grin, moving back to their work. "Don't be so modest, Dari. You look *gorgeous~*"

Darian's skin twitched under the snips. At the sounds the little scissors made. At the way the stitches tugged at the inner lining of flesh. He was almost surprised when Calyx seemed to skip over one spot, but considering the gash across his side was giving him the most pain lately, he had to assume it was left intentionally. Larger wounds take longer to heal. Maybe the stitches weren't ready to come out yet on that one.

"Not even a 'thank you'?" Calyx's fingers drifted over his side, ticklish as they located the next spot to maul.

Darian's jaw tightened. "I don't need to *thank* you for anything. *You* did this to me. Giving me medical treatment is the absolute bare minimum you can do now."

Calyx chimed a laugh, stopping to look up at him from their spot between his thighs. "Not about the *stitches*, dummy! For the compliment!" Darian's eyes snapped back down as they kissed just above his navel. "Y'know? Because I think you're so pretty~?" They flutter-blinked up through their lashes at him.

Muscles and skin tightened under the touch, expecting the pain that Calyx's touches so often brought.

None came. It was just a kiss.

Darian's jaw tightened and untightened several times, assessing.

They were fucking with him. They always were.

He moved his eyes away again, roaming the kitchen counter and its crumb-spewing toaster. "I don't care if you think I'm pretty."

Calyx pouted up at him. "No? I'd have thought you'd want to know if the feeling was mutual."

He –

How was he supposed to respond to that? Agree? Say Calyx *wasn't* pretty? That would be a flat-out lie, and Calyx wasn't stupid.

Evasion, then – "You can't read minds, Cal. You don't know what I think."

"Hmm ... don't I~?"

Darian was *going* to snap at them, but a sharp breath punching down his throat cut that off as Calyx's hand drifted between his legs and cupped the bulge of traitorous flesh under his pants.

So much more sensitive than he realized. And *annoyingly* hard. The motherfucker.

Darian's jaw set, trying not to move. Moving would just come off as grinding. Like he wanted this.

He definitely didn't want this.

"You're such a fucking creep," he muttered, eyes as neutral as possible as he attempted to focus on the wall.

"You think I'm cute. Admit it~"

Darian couldn't help but squirm a little against the ropes as that hand palmed down and back up again, sending shivers of pain-pricked pleasure up his spine.

"I'm n – you can't j – ... Calyx, *stop.*"

They gave a contemplative hum, now stroking him in earnest through the fabric. It was so fucking annoying how good that felt. "I'd stop if you weren't hard, sweetheart. *You* started this. *Not* me."

Darian shifted again as fabric tugged down, cool air brushing over sensitive skin.

Then warm lips.

He tried to shove at them with his leg, but that just ground him against them more, earning a warm, tickling chuckle over his cock as they kissed down it. "No point in fighting it – and I'm getting *tired* of pretending we don't like each other. Aren't you?"

There was probably a good response to that. A proper response. Something that wasn't abject, knee-jerk denial. If that clever response was out there somewhere, it was washed away in the sensation of Calyx's lips closing around his head, tongue twirling slowly around it.

And Darian didn't have the brains to lie. He just didn't.

So much of his energy was taken up by healing lately, and being a defiant little shit was running him ragged. Exhaustion ate through his bones quicker than termites chewed through a pine foundation. Even before that, Darian was so damn tired. In life. In work. In the gasping in-betweens that he'd spent inhaling every scrap of Calyx he could find.

He didn't have the strength to lie anymore. The most he could manage was closing his eyes to pull them away from Calyx's smug gaze as he ground further into their mouth and the warm, intoxicating bliss it would bring.

11

The Show Must Go On

Finally.

Fucking *finally.*

After weeks of working and trying and stretching, he'd finally managed to slip his thumb from the ropes that kept his wrists locked against the headboard.

Darian's eyes slid to the side – to Calyx's softly snoring form curled up next to him.

Then to the clock. It was late – 3:32. Calyx should stay knocked out for hours.

He'd have plenty of time to run and actually get out. Get help.

Carefully, he inched numb, aching limbs through the knotwork until one hand slipped from the bonds – eyes on Calyx the entire time.

Then the other hand – far more easily that time without the tension from the first.

His shoulders screamed in protest as they always did, creaking as he rolled them forward, finger circling his wrists to knead away the burn and pull the ropes left in his raw skin.

... He lay there. Thinking. Watching Calyx sleep.

Their breath puffed out softly, each press of air pushing a soft, honey-colored curl from their lips, then letting it fall back again.

... He eyed the door.

The clock.

... That curl.

... Aching, but gentle, fingers picked it up, brushing it away so it wouldn't tickle Calyx's nose anymore while they were trying to sleep.

He breathed in that tranquility for a moment. Then moved in a flash.

He straddled Calyx, pinning them down with a hand to their throat – the other snatching a wrist that immediately shot up to try to push him off. He pinned that to the mattress beside their head, looming over them.

Calyx's eyes were wild, disoriented, and – for the first time Darian had ever seen – fearful.

They shared panting, strained breaths before Darian's fingers started constricting, cutting off Calyx's air – past the wheezing chokes and into the silent hiss of thrashing that Calyx quickly stilled.

Darian's eyes narrowed, eyes roaming over his captor's face. " ... *Stop fuckin' snoring.*"

Calyx stared up at him, then – slowly – nodded, fingers rippling around his wrist.

" ... *Thank you.*" His fingers unwound from Calyx's throat, and he shoved off of them, flopping back onto his side of the bed. He laid on his side, curling away from Calyx. Glaring at the wall. Wondering why he was still there.

He listened to Calyx sputter a few ragged coughs as they massaged their throat, pulling down fresh air.

An arm slipped around Darian's waist. He did nothing to shove it off.

A grin pressed against his back. He continued to glare.

Calyx pulled in a breath to speak.

"Shut ***up,***" Darian interrupted before they could even begin.

Calyx did, nose nuzzling into his back as they curled in close.

Calyx didn't tie him up anymore after that night.

12

CAMERA SHY

There was a clothesline outside the house. A small thing, really. Just big enough to hold one load of laundry, then you'd need to stop for the day and wait for the clothes to dry. Calyx used that little thing to hang the blood-soaked linen for days, ensuring the rusty hue was fully sun-baked into the fibers. Then they'd soak and hand-wash it with cold water in a large basin before hanging it out to dry again. Only in the final wash would they add detergent, and then hang it out for one final bask in the warm light of day.

Even if Calyx didn't treat their victims well, their blood was precious to them. It was precious to Darian now too. The transformation from human soul to stunning custom clothing was a simple but delicate one, matched with every ounce of tender care Darian and Calyx could manage.

When Calyx was gone at a performance or rehearsal, Darian occupied himself with several different, though equally monotonous, tasks throughout each day. He cleaned, cooked, did puzzles or read, but his favorite thing to do was to go through all of Calyx's uncut videos that they had lying around. He'd seen many of them dozens of times already, but these were the originals. Prime and perfect. Completely untouched by editing programs and the horrid cropping and trimming tools.

Of course, Calyx found this adorable. They seemed to find everything Darian did adorable, but Darian wasn't about to complain about that. Not anymore. It was endearing, in a way. He had always been too much of something or other to be properly 'adorable'. Too tall. Too masculine. Too annoying. Too muscled. Yet, Calyx called him 'cute' without even a hint of that sarcastic, condescending tone.

Alright, maybe there was *some* condescension there, but Darian knew that was flirtation, so Calyx got a pass and got to keep their perfect little nose unbroken.

Calyx had finally gotten some Corona in the house for him as well. They even kept limes stocked in the basket on the kitchen counter at all times, and Darian cut them into chunky half-slices in his free time so he could have one with each bottle as God intended. It was another long and slow day with cold beer in hand and feet kicked up on the ottoman as Calyx's car crunched over gravel, a cacophony of distant chaos announcing the arrival of his fair nemesis. Darian didn't get up or react, he just kept watching the clip he was analyzing. His favorite one. The one with the garotte at the end.

He had wondered so often before any of this if Calyx told their victims what was going to happen in that chair. Whether they knew if the film would be sent to their soon-to-be-thoroughly-traumatized families.

They did, surprisingly. At the beginning of each movie, there was an added clip of Calyx explaining it all in sweet, simple terms.

"You're going to die within the hour."

Cue pleading and crying or fighting or begging or whatever the whelp in the chair was inclined toward.

"There's no stopping it. I'm going to mutilate you on camera, then I'm going to send the video to your family. They'll probably report it to the police, but they won't catch me. I've done this a lot, and no one has yet. Feel free to be angry or hope that I'll be killed if it gets you through this better. Maybe you can even cry out some clues for the camera, yeah~? Just scream nice and loud for me, won't you? Give it a try~"

Darian caught himself smirking at that as the bottle pressed to his lips again and the bubbling bright amber washed over his tongue. Calyx had quite a way with words. A way that usually made Darian want to cut their tongue out, but still, they made him smile too much. So, the tongue and the words stayed.

Darian's eyes drifted over the fabric on the line outside. This one wasn't from the video he was currently watching, obviously – this fabric was from some other poor fuck last night. Still, they looked much the same. Soaked almost completely in red. This particular batch was headed for its first round of washing. Soon, the thick, crusted chunks of blood would be flushed away, leaving a delicate hue on soft fabric.

Darian's eyes pulled to that piece – even away from the film he was watching. It danced and spun in the breeze, wrapping and twisting in an intricate, timeless dance. It reminded him so much of how Calyx moved. How they spoke. How every breath they took was like magic, flowing in and out of them in a languid yet bright refrain.

Calyx's key scraped into the lock, dully ringing through the house.

Darian skipped ahead through the film a bit, rewatching a part that caught his eye on the last two playthroughs. He spent the long moments of waiting by analyzing the way Calyx's gloved fingertips tilted their captive's chin up to get better access to the throat.

Most people would fight that or, trembling, twitch upward. Obedient yet fearful. Instincts thrashing against each other in a torrential battle. This time, however, their head lifted, hinging on their spine like a flower opening to the morning sun. Almost like they wanted it. Like it was a dance. As if this moment could hang in eternity flawlessly, without wither or waste.

Maybe she'd simply responded to Calyx's movements in kind, matching pace and matching tempo with her torturer as if that would save her. Maybe with someone else, it would have.

Calyx hacked off his train of thought as they finally stepped through the garage door into the kitchen, keys dropping onto the side table. "Backkkk~" they chimed, shoes fumbling against the ground as they kicked them off and fabric rustling as they slipped off their jacket.

Darian lifted his beer so Calyx would see him over the back of the couch, regardless of how much he'd slouched. They'd probably be able to realize easily enough that he was there just because the T.V. was on, but he didn't want to leave Calyx unanswered.

Silent footsteps brought Calyx's fingertips to Darian's shoulders, massaging there for a moment before sliding down his chest and twining together in a lazy, half-backward hug. They kissed his cheek from their perch behind the couch. " *Miss me~*?"

Darian lifted a hand, fingers threading through the curls even as he kept his eyes on the TV. "How was rehearsal?"

Calyx shrugged, unwinding enough to kick a leg over the back of the couch and slide down next to Darian. "It was fine. Jen still can't fucking count, but what else is new?" They swung one leg over Darian's, nestling in properly.

"I made muffins."

Calyx perked up, twisting to see back into the kitchen. "What kind – ? Where?"

Darian rolled his eyes, setting down his beer. "Blueberry lemon. Want one now?"

"Fuckkk – yes please, I'm dying over here."

Darian pushed himself up to standing and wandered back into the kitchen, not bothering to stop the little home film from playing. It was good sounds. Good screams. He opened the little tin he'd stored the muffins in and plucked one out. "Get the body sorted?"

Calyx shrugged, arms crossing over the back of the couch with chin resting on their arms. "Sure, it's not rocket science."

"Y'know, I could help out sometimes."

Calyx scoffed, hand held out for the muffin as he approached again. "*Could* you? Maybe in a few months, sure, but you'll tear stuff back open if you try to lift a *body* right now, Dari."

The muffin plonked into their palm, and Darian leaned on the back of the couch. "Maybe, but I still wanna help."

Calyx grinned up at him even as their fingers plucked the paper lining away from the treat. "What, you wanna do the next one~?"

Fuck their little smirky face.

"No."

"*Awhh*, why not~?" Their cooing would normally keep trilling a beat or two, but it was quickly cut short by a thick mouthful.

"I'm not going to *kill* someone, Cal."

"*Bhy noph* – ?" There was a literal, audible *gulp* as they swallowed that down.

"Because that's ... bad?"

Calyx puffed a laugh, losing a few crumbs from between their lips. "What – ? And it's just *~fine~* to watch me, but if you gotta hold the knife, that's different somehow?" They chomped into the muffin again.

" ... Yes."

"*Is'not diffren'*," they assured at a muffled mumble, shoving the last of the treat into their mouth. Evidently they *were* hungry, damn. He'd have to get started on supper soon.

"It's different, yes. It's more active."

Calyx finally took a moment to chew before responding, finger held up to indicate he was to wait patiently. "*Ehhh* – legally, no, though?"

" ... Well, I feel better about watching. And I don't like being on camera."

Calyx raised a brow, crumpling up the paper liner between nimble fingers. " ... Are you ... *camera shy*?" They gasped at uncovering this great scandal.

Darian rolled his eyes, heading back toward the kitchen. "Sure. Fine. Yes. I don't like them. Don't like having an audience."

Calyx was silent in response. Which never happened. Ever.

Darian turned a wary squint back toward Calyx just to find the fucker holding up their phone, filming or photographing him – he didn't know which.

Darian's hand flew up to block the camera. "Hey – *hey* – !"

Calyx twinkled a laugh, arching and stretching to change the angle again and again as he tried to block it. "I'm helping~! Face your fear, darling!"

Darian's jaw set, and he returned to his work, hoping Calyx would get bored of this prank and drop it.

Calyx ... did not do that. What they *did* do was slip off the couch, still grinning as they danced closer, phone still pointed at Darian. They put on their most dramatic newscaster voice. "Alright, we're here *~live~* with Agent Darian Oslo Shah~! Agent, would you care to tell us how you make your muffins so delicious~!? What's your secret!?"

Darian couldn't help but laugh even as he tried to swat the phone out of his face. "Sto-*stop*! I'm trying t – What if someone *actually* sees that, huh? What then?"

"I'm sorry, Agent, this interview is *exclusively* about muffins! How do you get those little pieces of sugar on top so crunchy and perfect!?" Calyx was moving around him with phone held up dramatically – a wooden spoon which they'd pulled from the counter was now pointed at his face like a microphone.

Darian snatched for the camera.

Calyx pulled back just in time. "Nope – ! Gotta be quicker than that~!"

He tried again. Missing again.

Calyx was laughing so broad and bright that Darian couldn't help but laugh along, even as he lunged for them. They took off and Darian gave chase down the hall until he managed to catch their elbow.

He might have been injured, but he was still able to easily pin them against the wall, one hand on their throat to keep them there as the other wrenched the phone from their grip and tossed it harmlessly to the shag carpet.

Calyx grinned up at him, fingers gripping his wrist. "That was a very expensive camera, you know. News anchors spend thousan*ds of do – d – d –* " Their voice crackled away and Darian's grip tightened.

Darian's breaths were a bit thick, coming faster than they should have from that small bit of exercise. If Calyx could speak right now, he was sure they'd make some comment about being '*breathtaking.*' Not that they'd be wrong.

Darian's fingers lifted, tracing the outline of Calyx's gaping lips. Calyx pulled a softer smile from him by pressing a kiss to those fingers and tugging him closer, evidently not caring if Darian strangled them.

Ten feet away, the gasps, muffled screams, and pleas turned into a soft gargling frenzy as the Calyx on screen began to strangle their victim. Calyx's throat rippled under his fingers, laughter at the irony caught by Darian's grip.

Irony, sure. Or planning. Either way.

Darian dipped, chokehold loosening a bit as his lips melted over theirs. He dragged them closer with a hand on the small of their back, arching them into him so he could feel every delicious inch of them pressed close.

Calyx may have kidnapped him, but they were *his* now.

13

SHOWTIME

Calyx thought it was cute that Darian called them their 'murder clothes.' They thought it was even cuter when Darian was wearing them.

It was practical, really. The *vast* majority of the oversized clothes Calyx had were their 'murder clothes.' Hoodies and sweatshirts and oversized black jeans that they'd layer up when they were getting a little bloody.

Conveniently, those were the only clothes that fit Darian.

Not that he minded too much – the ever-so-faint stains across them were invisible to the naked eye, but Darian's fingertips could detect the faint traces of texture differences along the edges of each mark.

He didn't want to admit that wearing those bloodstains sent a small shivering thrill up his spine. He didn't mention it.

Calyx knew, though.

Darian saw how Calyx's eyes lingered on Darian's fingertips whenever he got caught tracing the outlines of the stains over his own chest or thigh or forearm.

Calyx didn't miss much.

They just gave him a little smirk and continued what they were doing. Sewing, most often. If they weren't taking care of their little house or off at rehearsal or a performance, they were making new practice outfits. Leotards and skirts and loose, off-shoulder shirts to wear over leggings.

Always of the same material. Rusted linen.

Of course, only Darian knew it wasn't normal ink that dyed those clothes. Only Darian saw just how much Calyx treasured that process of converting a blood-clotted mess into stunning clothing. Only Darian saw the gentle time and care Calyx put into washing the linen properly – *ensuring* that those bloodstains stayed right where they were.

Calyx liked wearing the blood.

More and more and more, the two were growing alike over Darian's time with Calyx.

Darian hadn't cut his hair in a month now. It was getting shaggy – curling at the tips. One day, Calyx had caught Darian with a pair of scissors, wet-combing it out in front of the bathroom mirror to try to trim it himself.

Calyx just wandered in behind him, hand splaying up the back of his neck and twirling around the little curls that tangled between their fingers.

"*I like it like this*," they'd murmured, pressing a kiss to the side of Darian's neck.

... And ... Darian put down the scissors. Without a second thought.

His hair wasn't as long as Calyx's by any means, but it was curling all the same. Calyx's hair. Calyx's clothes. Calyx's food. Calyx's bed.

Darian didn't know why he was surprised when Calyx handed him the mask.

Darian stared at it, that moment seeming to linger on and on forever.

Glancing to the captive as she struggled in the chair. As the tears streaked down her cheeks and soaked into the gag. Pristine, white linen hanging behind her. Framing the video.

Ready for blood.

And Darian just ... stared.

Calyx took Darian's hand, pressing the mask into it. "You can do this. You *deserve* this."

Darian blinked as his fingers curled around the edges of the plastic.

... He was dressed exactly as he should be. Head to toe in black. Exactly the size and shape Calyx took on-screen in all their layers.

The only thing missing was the gloves. And the mask.

He turned it over in his hands, letting the hollow black eyes bore into his own.

" ... *Cal* ... -"

"You can do this," they insisted, stepping back. They picked up the knife, offering it to him as well. *"I want to see you."*

Darian found his eyes back on the woman – Mari, her name was.

He ignored her desperate, muffled pleas, letting them fade into the background. His eyes were on Calyx again. Just them. Just now.

"... I ... I like to watch – "

Calyx shook their head. "You've watched enough. It's your turn to shine."

" ... What about you?"

Calyx rolled their eyes, heading for the camera. Adjusting the exposure settings. "I'll get the next one. We can do an every-other thing."

Darian's heart was slamming against his chest as he rubbed the edges of the mask.

No.

No, he couldn't do it.

He couldn't just ... become this.

Watching was one thing. Partaking was another.

" ... Okay," he murmured, turning the knife in his hand. Slipping on the gloves. The mask. Pulling up the hood.

Calyx glanced back at him with a fond smirk on their lips. "Good boyyyyyy~" they teased, rolling the settings to record.

Darian stepped up behind them, both arms snuggling around Calyx's waist. He let the knife prick against their ribs.

Calyx flickered, but breathed a soft laugh, head lolling back onto his shoulder. " *You're adorable.*" They twisted, pressing a kiss to Darian's cheek.

... He hated that he couldn't feel their lips through the plastic.

That was his last thought as his attention pulled back to Mari. His arms slipped away from Calyx.

He waited until the little recording light flickered red before stepping into frame.

14

Roll Credits

Darian thought about leaving. He could do it any time he wanted. Sure, Darian himself would go to prison, but Calyx would be locked away and people would be safe.

And wasn't that his life's calling? To keep people safe?

This world is full of so much chaos. Life has a way of beating you when you're down and pinning you to the ground well before your grave is fully dug or ready. For so long, Darian wanted to control the chaos. To help track it down and smother it to death with paperwork, dedication, and brainpower.

Thing is, there was always so much left to chase. So many rumors and so many stories. There would always be another villain. There would always be murders and snuff films and atrocities. The darkness would come and come and come until it snuffed out what remaining sparks of life are left in this rotting world.

But no matter how much darkness came, Calyx would be there. Darian could be cliché and say they were the light that drove out the darkness; in reality, Calyx was only ever a speck of dark themself. Just another cog in the machine that was driving everyone to madness.

But at least as this world rotted away, Darian would have someone by his side, watching it all burn down alongside him. Laughing with him. Pointing out the blinded idiots stumbling and falling as they tried to outrun death.

Calyx made this world seem a little more doable. A little more right, somehow. Like the veil had been lifted and he could see everything for all its blunt, beautiful glory.

Darian picked up the knife that night, and would gladly do the same again any time Calyx asked him to.

She'd screamed so much.

Darian was glad Calyx took him up on the suggestion to add a mic dangling above the chair. It really made a difference in the playback.

As Darian and Calyx watched the film – tangled up in blankets on the couch with popcorn and beer that night – the sound was so much better than the ones before.

It was nice seeing it on a screen, too. Darian's old projector just didn't get the colors crisp enough. He wondered vaguely if that was his own fault – a flaw in his setup or too much light in the room. Or maybe it was just the projector itself that failed.

Maybe it was being able to feel Calyx's breath hitch as they watched that made it so much better. Feeling their muscles coil and tense at the best parts, relaxing into him again after that small burst of euphoria those moments left behind.

Calyx seemed to think Darian did well. When the film rolled to a stop at fifty-two minutes and thirty-one seconds, Calyx nuzzled into Darian's neck, kissing once.

Twice.

Their breath warmed across his skin through the whisper.

"*Again.*"

So Darian played it again.

About the Author

Raised in the rural American midwest, Rae is a twenty-eight year old cat-obsessed gremlin who spends most of her time reading, writing, and gardening. She has been properly obsessed with writing since she wrote her first novel at fourteen, yet it took ten years after that for her to incorporate writing into her lifestyle and future goals. Her books and stories explore horror, dystopia, murder, and vouch for casual representation of LGBTQIA+ characters as a main goal and priority.□

The Kill Touch

Havilah G

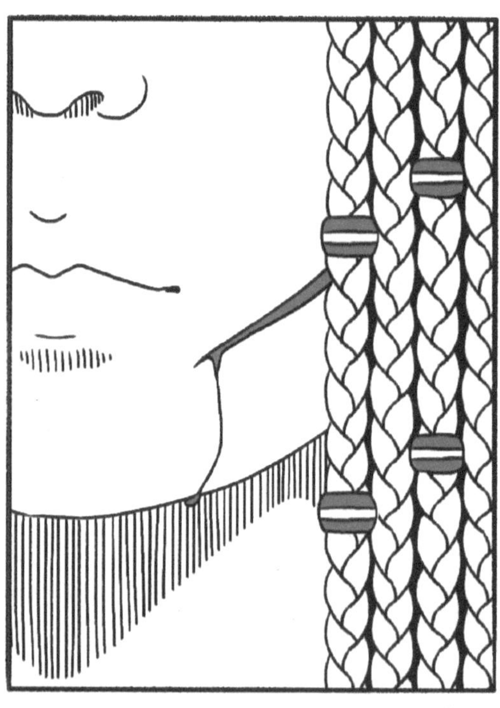

Cover Design by Nicole Alessi

Cover Illustration by Hen Towers

ALSO BY HAVILAH G

The Ghost of Seattle

Dance of Death

Miasma

Mighty

Back to the Dregs

Contents

CONTENT WARNINGS

This story contains the following content:

- Teenage protagonist
- Death of parents
- Blood, violence, torture
- Captivity
- Restraints

If this book isn't for you, no worries! But if it is, we hope you enjoy this story about a sarcastic, electrokinetic girl...

The Kill Touch

Y'Starren's family trudged down the walking path to Wenterglen, where Strangers' College nestled; a beacon of hope. They had been wanderers for most of her life, and when they weren't actively running from police, they were pretty happy. But Strangers' College was supposed to be a safe haven for people like them.

Everyone in her family had the gift of electrokinesis – what most people called "the Kill Touch." If only they'd been born with something stupid like clairvoyance or illusions, they could've lived in peace. But instead, her family had the unique ability to cause extreme pain, or even kill, using electrokinesis. Every time someone found out about them, they had to move on from that town. No one was comfortable with someone that could kill just by touching them, and her parents had had to fend off several pitchfork-wielding mobs and even a few assassins already.

Still, when they were together and felt safe-ish, like right now, life was great.

"I'm so hungry," Wackee complained, doing a little dance of hunger as he rubbed his stomach.

"Like that's going to help." Mother ruffled his hair good-naturedly. "Put some pressure on your stomach."

Wackee groaned.

"It hurts, Mother, that's just going to make it worse."

Y'Starren focused away from her own knotted-up stomach, listening to the birds around them, watching for wildlife, admiring the golden morning sunlight shining through the leaves. It made a spotted, twinkling pattern on the forest path that their bare feet tramped over.

"Just keep an eye out," her father said, walking at the front with his anxious eyes shifting through the foliage for predators, assassins, Ghost Men, or whatever else he was worried about at the moment.

Suddenly Wackee let out a squeal and dashed forward and to the side of the path, crashing into the underbrush with a roar of excitement.

"What's wrong?" Father shouted.

Y'Starren jogged forward hopefully.

"Apples! Apples!" Wackee screamed back at them.

Y'Starren broke into a run after him, following him down a tiny little rabbit trail into a meadow. How he'd seen it from the main trail was a mystery to her.

He was already rooting around among the apples on the ground like a wild animal, throwing them behind himself, crawling forward.

"That one's rotten. That one's wormy. That one's rotten and wormy ... "

"So pick from the tree." Y'Starren rolled her eyes, picking one from the sagging branch nearby and tossing it in front of Wackee.

He pounced on it with his whole body, and she heard a crack as he bit into it recklessly.

"Horizons," he cursed through his bites. "It's delicious."

There were so many apples. Y'Starren was going to dream of apples that night, she just knew it. Heavy clusters of palm-sized red and green apples weighed down the thick branches, making them droop low enough into the meadow for her family to grab to fill their packs.

"We could make apple pie," Mother commented as she gathered them into her basket.

"Oh, fuck yes!" Wackee roared from inside the tree, mouth still very full.

"It's bad luck to strip the tree," Father called from where he sat in the branches, trying to boost her little brother up to grab the higher apples. "Make sure you leave some for the next travelers."

"Tell that to Wackee," Y'Starren said, picking a final apple to eat as she lay back on the grass. It's always better to eat while you're watching the clouds.

"Now all we have to do is find somewhere safe to camp tonight," Father said.

***

Something told Y'Starren that she was alone.

Her eyes flashed open and she rolled out of the bundle of blankets she'd shared with her little brother last night. She looked around in the shack they'd used to camp in the last leg of their journey to Strangers' College, training her ears to the outside.

Besides the birds and breeze through the underbrush, there was nothing.

The orange-haired girl jumped up, grabbing a cloak and fastening the buttons as she thought.

Had they decided to go ahead to the college without her?

"Like Wackee's the only one going ... " she grumbled. "And he forgot his papers. Again."

She grabbed them and stuffed them into her tunic as she dashed out the front of the shack.

"Guys?" she called. "Wackee?" she called for her crazy twelve-year-old little brother.

Nothing.

She pulled her hood over the dread-like braids she'd left in her hair overnight; it was cold on the trail as she hurried up the mountainside.

For the first time in her family's history, they'd had a hope of living somewhere that their gifts would be considered normal.

"If they've ruined my introduction to Strangers' College, I'm going to be mad," Y'Starren muttered, hurrying down the path. Maybe they were just exploring. Without her.

The forest near Wenterglen turned out to be pretty damp in the springtime. Y'Starren buttoned her cloak further down over her arms, huddling deep under the hood for warmth.

Y'Starren followed the tiny trail to a meadow, where it disappeared among the grass and stumps of trees.

"Wackee?" Y'Starren shouted. "Guys? This better just be an unusually bad case of diarrhea. There's no other reason to go this far without telling me where you went!"

She heard no response, and was about to turn back when she saw a dark shape at the opposite end of the meadow.

Clutching her cloak around her with a frown, she moved toward the creature. Suddenly it broke from the forest and darted in her direction. It was a man in black and white, and he was holding a sword. She started back, but then she raised both hands, snapping her fingers. Magic cracked in the air between her fingers as she glared into the man's eyes – it was a warning. The moment the man saw that, he veered away from her with a frightened look in his eyes.

She knew that look, and laughed a little.

That was the look of a Clairvoyant who had met with an unforeseen circumstance.

She heard him slow down in the bushes just past the clearing, panting and moving around, probably adjusting his position to prepare for a better offense.

"Hey, mister," she called. "You alone?"

He didn't answer.

"If you're alone, think again," she said. "And put that sword back in your pants."

She heard him stand up and the sound of a sword going back into a wooden scabbard. Then she heard him sigh and mutter, and then tramp away through the woods.

This close to barbarian land, it was pretty normal for people to go around with weapons, but Y'Starren didn't like it.

She tucked her cold hands back under her warm cloak and kept walking toward a larger hill. Wackee had begged to go there on a picnic today, and Y'Starren wondered if that was where he was.

As she reached the foot and climbed out of the brush onto another trail, she saw him.

He was standing there, without a cloak, without even a pouch, as if he'd just climbed out of bed and run into the woods. And he was standing in front of their mother on the ground, eyes fixed on her, blood all over his hands.

"Wackee?" she said. "What happened?"

He stared at their mother as if he didn't see or hear Y'Starren.

Y'Starren knew what she'd see if she looked down, somehow.

Her mother's wide eyes were staring into the treetops, unseeing, yet somehow shocked.

"Where's Dad?" Y'Starren said, finding herself going numb in the face with a sense of shock.

As she pulled stray hair from her face, her hood fell back, allowing the bracing mountain air to whip around her cheeks. They stung. She was crying. "Where's Dad?" she repeated. "Wackee, what did you do?"

Finally, Wackee's arm moved; he pointed to the left.

Their father was face-down in the bushes a bit further off. Y'Starren softly stepped over to him, knelt and touched his bare shoulder, then flinched back. It was like cold, hard clay.

"Are they gonna be alright?" Wackee said, and his voice was husky like he'd already screamed several times. Y'Starren felt horrible for not having heard it.

"How would they be alright?" she said. "They're dead."

That was when Wackee broke into a horrified groan, and Y'Starren pulled him away from their parents, wrapping her cloak around him, trapping him in a hug.

"It'll be okay, it'll be okay," she comforted him. She didn't know why she was saying it, but it was all she could think of to say. "We'll be okay."

At that, he cried even louder.

"Wackee, stop it. Stop it," she said. "I saw a guy coming my way with a sword. Did you see what happened?"

As he continued to cry and not answer, she glanced over her little brother's shoulders and looked at the wounds on her mother's neck again.

A sword could easily do that, she thought. But then, so could any sharp object, probably. She wasn't sure. "Wackee, a guy with mud-color hair. Angry eyes. Did you see him?"

Wackee kept crying.

"Were you here when they ... When did you get here?"

Wackee shook his head.

"I didn't," he cried. "I was too late."

Y'Starren let out a small breath of relief.

It didn't feel exactly real that they could be gone. She felt like she could just take him back to their old town and they'd find their parents waiting at home for them, like they always used to.

At the same time, the present reality did make sense. Rather than seek to imprison such dangerous, gifted citizens, the government would probably prefer to simply assassinate them. Which meant that if that man Y'Starren had seen was the assassin, she was next. He couldn't possibly know about Wackee, or he would've killed him when he got to their parents. Better keep Wackee a secret, t hen.

"Wackee, I need you to do something for me," she said, releasing her brother.

He looked over his shoulder at his parents on the ground.

"No, Wackee – " She pushed his shoulder and dragged him away from the spot. "Come on. Let's pretend."

"I'm not in the mood!" he said.

"Wackee," she said, pulling him along. "Let's say that they're back in Seechatee. Okay? They sent us – they sent you to the college. They already paid for your first three months."

"I don't understand ... " He sniffled, wiping his nose on his hand, then wiping his hand all over his shirt.

It was true that they'd already paid the first three months at Strangers' College in advance for both kids. But if Y'Starren went there with him, she'd only draw assassins after both of them. Besides, they'd have nothing to do after three months.

"I'm going to get a job in Wenterglen," she said. "You're going to Strangers' College."

"You're gonna leave me?" He covered his mouth to keep from crying anymore. "How could you – don't leave me!"

She stopped and wrapped him in a hug again.

"I'll visit you," she said. "But if I come, then ... " She didn't want to scare him.

"Then what?"

"Look, I'll explain later," she said. "Now you better trust me. You go to the college and show them your papers."

"Will you come with me?"

"I can't."

He looked at her with his big eyes, legs trembling like he might just collapse.

"You can take care of yourself," she said. "I know you can. I have to go report the murder to the Investigator's Guild. Okay?"

She hoped he'd take the bait and stay in safety while she figured out who the killer was. It had to be someone in the guild, if they were local.

"I'll just wait for you," he said, turning toward the shack, which was now in sight.

"Not that way," she said. "Here." She pressed his papers into his hand, which she'd grabbed for him on the way, just in case they'd already gone straight for the college and forgotten them.

"Go straight to the college. I'll see you there tonight."

Finally, he listened to her and tromped off toward the college.

Y'Starren sighed as she watched him go, then suddenly her knees gave out and she sank back against a large clattery bush, which crackled under her as she leaned back.

"Oh, fuck," she whispered as the realization of what she'd seen began to sink in. She was going to cry for real; she could feel it gathering with the heat in her face. "Fuck."

***

Y'Starren arrived at the Investigator's Guild hot and tired, cloak pulled back over her shoulders with her orange hair even more windblown than before. She hadn't had the energy to re-braid her hair on the way, as she normally would have.

Her face ached from the set expression that wouldn't change since the moment she'd separated from Wackee.

The Investigator's Guild had a front lobby that felt like it was outside; light shafted down through the huge openings under upper arches made of weathered wood, and the roof had a hole right in the middle. A large stage for a bard rose up all bare and lonely in the middle of the day, and only a few investigators were even there.

As she paused, wondering who to speak to, several of them got up from nearby tables. One of them, a man with a barbarically brown tint to his orange hair, got up with a generous smile and sauntered over to her, followed by two others from the same table.

They wore black coats and white waistcoats, which had completely gone out of fashion for everyone except for people in the government.

Suddenly she stiffened and stared at the man with the brownish hair. He was the guy she'd brushed by in the forest earlier today.

She tilted her head.

He tilted his head in the opposite direction.

"Do I recognize you?" he said, squinting. "Are you the one that snapped your fingers at me this morning in the woods?"

"You ... " She hesitated, realizing that if he was, she was in danger. Someone who killed her parents for their gift would absolutely be coming for her next.

"Who's in charge here?" she said instead of finishing her accusation.

"I am." The dangerous man folded his arms.

"The half-barbarian is in charge," she said, not smiling. "Yeah, right. I'm surprised they haven't deported you yet."

As she said that, a dark scowl overtook his face and he stepped toward her, hand on the hilt of his sword.

But a man behind him with white hair and a young face put his hand on the half-barbarian's shoulder, stepping out in front of him and extending his other hand to Y'Starren.

"Merreth, she asked who's in charge," he said as she shook it. "I'm Relleck. Constant. You?"

A Constant's gift was to live longer and heal more quickly. They developed white hair and kept their youthful-looking faces for most of their lives.

"Y'Starren," she said, finding herself unable to smile. "So, I came here to ask you to investigate a murder, but ... "

Her stern orange eyes rested on Merreth as a bitter grimace came over her face.

Merreth scowled deeper at her and he laid his hand on his sword. Y'Starren lifted her hand, magic running between her fingers, but then Relleck thrust his hand behind himself and pushed the sword back into the scabbard.

"Relleck. She's the other target," Merreth said.

At that, heads perked up around the room. Y'Starren heard people outside moving closer, blocking the entryway. But her head was beginning to buzz with magic and adrenaline. Nothing mattered except this man standing before her – the man who had killed her parents.

"The fuck did you just say?" she said, stepping toward him.

He stepped backward, drawing his sword.

"Don't make yourself a murderer, girl," Relleck said from behind her.

Y'Starren wasn't even listening. She stared down her parents' killer, eyes wide.

"Come on, girl, snap your fingers for me," Merreth said.

"Oh, trust me, you don't want me to do that," she said, appraising the investigators outside, blocking her exit. They weren't even scared.

"I dare you," he said, advancing on her with his sword.

She cursed and stopped as she reached the door. She'd never had to hurt anyone before. She wasn't sure she could. She glared.

Then she raised her hand and snapped her fingers.

Magic arced out from her fingertips, down Merreth's sword, and arced over the leather-wrapped hilt to his hand. The sword clattered to the ground.

"Ah! Fuck!" He shook and wrung his hand.

At that moment, she felt a yank on one of her braids. She spun around, igniting with anger, and clamped a hand over her attacker's, sending magic into them.

She felt it climb up their arm and hit them in the chest, knocking them backward several steps, and they fell to the ground.

"Do not," she shouted, "*touch* the hair!"

The others began to surround her more warily now, gripping their weapons tightly.

She cursed and backed against the wall as the other investigators from outside the front of the guild came inside, holding crossbows. As they got closer, she lowered her hands and stood up straight, as straight as she could, looking around with a hard expression.

A woman behind Y'Starren laid a hand on her shoulder. Y'Starren spun around and pointed two fingers at the woman's forehead. She pulled her in front of her chest quickly, a shield for the crossbow bolts, she hoped. She had seen one up to the feathers in a deer's chest before, so she wasn't sure it would work, but maybe they'd think twice about killing another investigator.

The other investigators got closer and closer, jumping in, but then jumping back just before she touched them.

Snap-snap-snap.

Each snap arced out a few inches into a reaching hand, a sword, a dagger, and jumped into their bodies.

They screamed, and some of them fell suddenly or dropped their weapons. Most of what Y'Starren could do was to inflict pain, and she hated it.

"I told you, you don't want me to." She panted, holding up her left hand threateningly over her lowered head, fingers still pointed at the woman's temple. She could feel her magic skittering between her fingertips, hotter than the blood rushing through her head.

"Go ahead and shoot!" Merreth shouted, slashing down toward her with his sword.

"Don't you dare!" Y'Starren shouted. "I will kill this woman."

"Don't ... " the woman whimpered. "I'm sorry. I didn't mean to offend you, I was just trying to do my job. Please, please don't hurt me."

"Shut up or I will," Y'Starren lied through her teeth. The woman's pleading was wrenching her heart, and she couldn't afford to look indecisive right now.

The others around her had paused when Y'Starren made her threats. She could hear the crossbowmen above her whispering to each other –

"Do we ... Do we do it?"

She glanced up to see one of them vigorously shaking his head.

Y'Starren put her hand back down on the hostage's shoulder.

"Please ... " the woman whispered, shaking in fear.

"Shh," Y'Starren said under her breath into the woman's ear. "Calm down."

The woman was about the same age as Y'Starren's mother had been. Y'Starren bit her cheek, keeping her face stuck in that resolute expression that had been frozen on her.

"I will do it – I will kill her," Y'Starren said, more loudly. "So nobody shoot me if you want this woman to live."

There was a silence and Y'Starren heard people moving behind her, around the corner where she couldn't see.

"Don't hurt her, please," Relleck said, hands out pacifyingly. "Please. Don't make yourself a murderer."

Y'Starren looked over to the surrounding guild members. They were dangerous – these were the highest-trained police in the entire country of Baneon. Even the woman she had her fingers pointed at was glaring at her as if she'd already accepted that this job was going to get her killed.

At this point, she wasn't going to convince them that she wasn't dangerous, which meant that as soon as she was subdued, they'd certainly execute her. Baneon had no prison system – it was basically liberation, deportation, or death.

But she also knew that one of the most popular things to do with criminals was to work out a deal with them to benefit society in some way, which meant they might be interested in an agreement of some kind ...

"Hey." Y'Starren licked her lips. "So, yeah, you think I'm a danger." She looked around. Now that she had gathered her wits a bit, she could see the terror more plainly on their faces. Like everyone else who had ever heard about what her family could do, they were scared.

"So, this is me when I'm trying not to hurt anyone," she said. "But we don't have to be enemies ... How about this: give me a job here."

She'd been looking for a job in the city anyway, to pay for Wackee's protection at the college. Not this job, but ...

"I'm tough, and I've got the most powerful gift in the world," she said. "Sure you don't want to use that? You hire me, you ... " She hesitated, realizing they had relaxed a bit and were looking at each other with more interest in their eyes. "You hire me, you get to see what I can do for you when I'm serious."

"You have a job." Relleck was the first to step forward and extend his hand.

Y'Starren released the woman with a muttered apology and a pat on the shoulder, which made her flinch.

She stepped forward and shook Relleck's hand.

"Thanks," she said gravely. "Honestly, I have nowhere else to go. Now that my parents are dead."

She turned her icy gaze on Merreth. He raised his hands in an exaggerated shrug.

"I didn't do it," he said.

"Didn't do it, bullshit!" Y'Starren spat. "I – I saw you!"

"I just happened to be there, traveling through the area," he said, then rubbed his jaw thoughtfully. Maybe he was coming up with some more bullshit. "I was looking for your family, but not to kill you. I'm so sorry for your loss."

Y'Starren glared at him, wracking her brains. Should she believe him? How could she know for sure?

"If you're going to be working with Merreth, you need to make peace with him," Relleck said, folding his arms.

Not completely convinced, Y'Starren frowned at the floor. Her chest started to heave as she thought about her parents, and she blinked back the tears and looked up at the bit of sky visible through the small vents at the top of the arched ceiling, trying to keep from crying.

"Right," she sniffed, and nodded after a moment. "Of course I am."

***

Two days later, Y'Starren was alone, swinging a sword at a practice dummy but too afraid to actually hit it, because it looked kind of like a person. A person that hadn't ever done her any harm; an innocent bystander.

She paused, lowering her sword at the dummy and walking up to it.

"You know, you look a little beat up," she said to it. "If I had my way, I'd sit you down and get you a nice flask of tea. We'd go over there up the hill, sit down on that bench, and watch the sunset. You could show me your scars. I'd tell you about my little – "

She was interrupted by a quick *woosh* that ended in a blow to her shoulder. She clutched her shoulder and spun around, sputtering curses.

It was Merreth, and he was swinging the stick again in the direction of her head. She blocked and took the blow on her forearm.

"Motherfucker!" she shouted.

"Pick up your sword," he said, pointing the stick at her. "Let's see how well you fight."

"It's been two days, asshole," Y'Starren growled, arm throbbing now. "Horizons, do you even know how to be nice?"

"It seems you've got enough niceness for both of us," he said, glancing at the dummy behind her. "Looks like you're making friends already."

"I take what I can get." She shrugged, picking up her sword. "Now leave me alone."

"Make me."

***

Y'Starren yanked the visitor's chair away from Relleck's desk by the arm and sat down hard with a huff, glaring at Relleck.

"I'd ask you not to act like you were raised in a barn, but – "

"But I was." Y'Starren rolled her eyes. "Look." She pointed at the fresh bruise on her arm. "He hurt me. Again."

Y'Starren hadn't had a moment to rest since starting her job. She'd been too worried about being followed to try to visit Wackee – she couldn't have Merreth finding out about her little brother, just in case he really was the assassin.

And she'd been being pushed to learn how to fight by the guild trainer, and fitted for some investigator clothing, and introduced to some serious rivalry in the guild. Apparently no one under twenty-three had ever joined the guild before, and almost everyone here had about ten years of experience refining their gifts, going through training academies, often with a background in police work. The investigators were the best of the best, often hand-picked by a king to join the guil d.

Apparently they saw Y'Starren as someone who had been dealt a good hand that she totally didn't deserve. It pissed her off. But at least she didn't have time to think about her troubles, with all the stress of her new position.

"I don't care about your little bruise." Relleck sighed. "You're supposed to be practicing fighting. And I'm very blazing busy, so please get out of my – "

"In what world is a two-hundred-pound man beating up a teenager acceptable?"

"So just--zap him a little."

" ... I can't." Y'Starren sighed uncomfortably and looked out Relleck's high window onto the calm street of Wenterglen's banking district.

"You can't?"

"I mean, I don't know if a little bit of magic, or a lot, is gonna come out, I don't want to give him a seizure or something."

"You mean that's not people getting possessed by your magic?"

"It's nothing that a witch can heal," she sighed. "This magic can bounce around in their brain for the rest of their lives, and it'd be my fault."

"You were just bluffing, huh," Relleck said, taking a stack of books from his desk and carefully arranging them on the bookshelf by the window. "You couldn't have killed that woman."

"Oh, I could've, but it would'na been on purpose." Y'Starren shrugged, standing up. "Look, I appreciate not having a bolt through my chest right now, but am I ever allowed a weekend off? Oh, and where's my money?"

"That wasn't discussed," Relleck said, not turning to face her. His finger trailed across the row of books, stirring a tiny puff of dust that showed up in the sunlight shining in through the window. "But what could you possibly need? We give you everything here – food, shelter, clothes."

"A girl has needs," Y'Starren said, trailing her fingers through her hair as Relleck looked over his shoulder at her suspiciously. "Look at this braid. So empty. No decoration at all."

"Do they decorate their hair back in Seechatee?"

Y'Starren sighed pointedly. Seechatee was where she said she'd come from, a small farming town with locals that didn't "take too kindly to strangers."

"Fine," Relleck said. "I'll tell the steward to give you your pay at the end of each week."

"Cool," Y'Starren said, turning to go.

"In exchange for you practicing," Relleck said. "Learn to control what your magic does, at least."

***

The job at the Investigators' Guild was a high-paying, life-risking career where you were about at the end of your rope when you got to the middle of a job, Y'Starren had been told.

But you wouldn't think so to see her walking down the trail through the barbarian wilderness north of the Baneon wall, swinging a shortsword at the nearby bushes along the trail, training her ears for the sound of a river to follow. They were on their way to attempt, for the third time, to open communications with Chaza, the closed-off, technologically advanced country to the north of the barbarian wilderness. The only man that had ever come back alive from this mission was Merreth, and Relleck said that he hoped this time Y'Starren would come back with him. He'd told her she was the most powerful Gifted that had ever joined the Investigators' Guild. Yay for her.

"I can prove that I didn't do it," Merreth said for the third time.

"And yet, you refrain from actually doing so," Y'Starren sighed. "You afraid I'm going to murder you in your sleep?"

Merreth shot her a look as he slowed down behind her again. He lagged back a lot, keeping a full six feet away from her, at least, at all times.

"I'm not a murderer," Y'Starren looked back at him. "Though I might make an exception for you."

"I just happened to be there, Y'Starren," he insisted. "I had my sword out because I was afraid of you."

"You weren't afraid till I snapped my magic at you."

Merreth didn't answer as he tramped after her. Y'Starren had been raised in a small town with plenty of outlying farms and places to explore, so she was already used to forests. She was comfortable in the environment, but he apparently wasn't.

The morning mists had barely cleared before a heavy evening fog came down into the sunset-colored light ahead, gathering beneath the trees in a way that felt cozy and warm, as if to welcome them to sleep. Merreth had started to walk closer to her, eyes darting side to side with anxiety as they got closer.

"You know of the Warminds, don't you?" he asked.

She squinted at him. "I know nothing more than what you told me."

"But you grew up in Seechatee," he said, not making eye contact.

"Yeah, Seechatee, where we don't take too kindly to strangers, and we definitely don't talk about them," she said. "Just tell me."

He shook his head and sighed, making a "this close" finger sign at her, and then shaking his head again instead of elaborating. He came closer and lowered his voice as he shyly approached her.

"I don't bite," she said.

"Shh," he said. "No unnecessary talking. The Warminds will either kill us right away, or sacrifice us, if they find us."

She frowned. This was old news. Everyone knew that barbarians were like that.

"This tribe is brutal. Don't you get that?" Merreth said, more softly.

"So we avoid them?"

"We're in their territory, and this path isn't exactly new," Merreth said. "I'd have gone another way, but I don't ... know one."

Y'Starren walked thoughtfully forward, digesting the information. She was half-tempted to tease and pretend not to believe him, but she was starting to feel the need for some companionship. As they trekked up toward the top of a hill, she could see the last golden bits of sunset seeping through the murky fog.

"Does that look a little ... " Merreth interrupted himself by sniffing, catching her arm suddenly to stop her. "I smell smoke."

She smelled smoke too. Merreth looked sick with panic.

"If they know we're here, it's too late," he muttered.

"Hie daen!" came a sudden yell from the side of the path.

Y'Starren flinched back from it, only to hear the same cry from the other side.

As she and Merreth backed away slowly, four archers rose out of the bushes, longbows bent and trained on the two of them.

"Ah, fuck," Merreth said.

"Stop," boomed a young man.

As he came down the path, eyes fixed on them, his feet took each step with a surety that said he knew every rock on the road. He was bald, and wore a crisscrossing, knotted network of strings across the top of his chest and shoulders, and a kilt of some kind on his lower half. His feet were booted in soft leather.

The two of them had stopped, and Y'Starren realized Merreth had stepped slightly behind her.

"So this is how you came back alive," she said. "By using the other investigators as shields."

"Just do your thing and get us out of here."

"Yeah, I'll use my Kill Touch from fifteen feet away."

The young man had brown eyebrows and eyes, and he was staring Y'Starren down from a height of about two inches taller.

"What are two witchlings doing in my forest?" he growled, stepping down the hill toward them.

"He speaks our language. Thank horizons," Merreth muttered.

The barbarian came to a stop a couple feet away from Y'Starren, hand on the hilt of a dagger on his hip. She flexed her fingers into a fist. She wasn't going to hurt him if she didn't have to.

"I guess I came directly to meet you and enchant you with my witchy skills," Y'Starren said.

That seemed too long and complicated for him to understand, because he frowned at her disgustedly.

"Maybe I should just kill you – " he started.

"No, no!" Merreth said, pushing past Y'Starren to face the barbarian, bowing repeatedly. Even Banes didn't really bow anymore. "We're just passing through. Just passing through. I promise."

"Yet if I said we were passing through one of your farms, you would kill me," he said. His eyes took on a grave, resentful expression.

"Well, that's different – " Merreth started, and the man slapped him.

Merreth bellowed in anger and hauled off with a punch at the man, who dodged up and back, drawing his knife quickly in the same motion.

"Get 'em, Y'Starren!" Merreth shouted.

The barbarian yelled something at the archers, who approached but did not shoot, appearing to be ready to do so. At the same time, Y'Starren heard a rustling and crunching through the underbrush behind them – someone had gone to get more of the barbarians, and the backup was almost there.

The leader stepped toward her.

"Come with us, and we will not hurt you." He reached for her sword with his left hand, holding a knife pointed downward in his right fist.

She stepped back and made a fair attempt at swinging the sword before he hooked her at the wrist with his knife as he redirected her swing, grabbed her hand, then stabbed the knife into her forearm.

She screamed and let go, clutching her arm at the wrist. He grabbed her by the hair, forcing her to bend over and dragging her up toward the other barbarians.

Stomping into the brush underfoot to brace herself, she clutched the corded muscles of his bare calf. Then she pressed magic through his leg, forcing it to arc between her ring finger and thumb.

He fell with an anguished cry to his knees. Then something hit her in the back of the head and she fell face-first into moss and bark dust.

***

Y'Starren struggled toward the waning light as she heard them all around her, someone dragging her by one wrist, someone else dragging her by the other. The young man, apparently not too harmed, kicked her, cursing something in their wild dialect.

"Haela maeglegh!" He shouted.

She stumbled forward onto her feet. Her right arm, extended as she was dragged forward, was killing her. Every jerk felt like a rip of the mangled muscles. She gasped and bit the inside of her cheek, then cursed through her teeth.

"Blazing fuck." She sparked a shock through her left wrist and the barbarian let go.

She scrambled to the side, and the barbarian holding her other arm yanked her off her feet again and kicked her in the head and the ribs. Y'Starren knew from experience that it was nearly impossible to properly channel magic through an injury, and this was no different. The injured wrist remained securely in the barbarian's grasp as kicks, and now blows from sticks and hilts, were rained down on her back and protecting arm.

A panicked cry burst out from her as a hilt came down on her shoulder blade so hard it could've cracked it. The pain fucked with her magical control and it arced over her body, but she couldn't send it out into her attackers.

The barbarian leader's voice raised into a higher-pitched sound as he gave orders to the others. Y'Starren fell forward onto her elbows as she saw him aiming another kick at her. Protecting her head and face with her arms, she crouched down on her knees and shouted.

"Blazes – stop! Stop!"

"Die well, witchling." He kicked her.

She grunted in pain but didn't respond, hoping desperately that they would take that as a sign of submission and stop for now. A whimper of pain broke from her as she felt the blows pause.

The one holding her wrist tightened her grip cruelly just under the wound, and Y'Starren flinched but didn't pull back.

"Don't hurt her," the barbarian leader said. "No hurt."

Y'Starren bit her tongue as the pain from being stabbed in the arm ached unbearably. Blood dripped up her elbow. She stayed still with her other arm up.

"No hurt, understand?" the leader said again.

"Huh." Y'Starren nodded, not looking up. She was embarrassed because she was nearly crying, and didn't want to show it. People said that barbarians never cried.

Another Warmind came toward her, raising an unstrung bow, but the barbarian stopped them with a couple words.

"A maeglegh agnae."

With ... whatever that was, they dragged her off to their camp.

Y'Starren had heard stories about people being kidnapped by barbarians in order to be sacrificed to their gods, but even though the people in the stories often had hands cut off or eyeballs gouged out, they were usually much too tough to do anything more than grunt. Because of this, she had assumed that as injuries get worse, there's kind of a plateau of pain.

Either getting stabbed hadn't reached the plateau, or the whole thing was a myth in her mind, because Y'Starren was in so much pain from the cut in her arm that she couldn't even sit up.

She was writhing in front of the firepit in pain, clutching her left wrist just below the stab wound, gasping breaths in and then holding them so she didn't scream. They kicked her every time she screamed.

"Are you going to sacrifice us?" Merreth was saying quietly to the young barbarian, whose name was Eugh, which Y'Starren couldn't even pronounce in her mind.

"Not yet," Eugh said.

Y'Starren's knuckles were white as she gripped her wrist under the cut, trying desperately to focus her mind on anywhere else – anywhere else that wasn't in pain – as she felt heavy raindrops starting to sprinkle down between the trees.

At the sudden rain, the woman across the firepit from her cursed loudly, throwing down the tools she was using to try to start the fire in Y'Starren's direction. She stood up and walked around the firepit to Y'Starren, about to kick her.

"Molaidh," Eugh said. "Kicknae."

The girl – probably named Molaidh – stopped.

"Sorry ... " Y'Starren said, almost half-sincerely. "It must be my fault it's raining."

"Witchlings are bad luck," Eugh said. "How's your arm?"

Y'Starren didn't answer for a moment, thinking he was mocking her, but when he didn't say anything more or even laugh, she lifted her head a bit to look at him. He was simply looking at her with a serious expression, waiting for a response.

She dropped her head.

"How do you think?" she said.

" ... I don't understand," he said simply.

Another ache of pain made her writhe with her feet twisting together.

"It hurts, okay?" she said through her teeth. "When are you going to sacrifice us, anyway?"

"When the moon makes a circle, we'll kill you," he said, and she heard him moving toward her. "Don't hurt," he said.

She braced herself for another kick. When he put his hand on her upper arm, she flinched.

"You was holding a weapon in this hand," he said. "Sacrifices should be clean. You made me ruin you."

She clenched her teeth and waited for him to stop touching her before she released her breath. "Does this mean you're not going to sacrifice me?"

He shook his head.

"Maybe tonight I kill you, witchling."

"So we're just ... animals to you? Sacrifices?"

"We are barbarians to you," he said. "It's fair, isnae?"

It was true that she'd been raised to think of them as outsiders, as sun-cursed because they had no gifts. Back in Seechatee, a barbarian would've been killed on sight.

She closed her eyes and gritted her teeth against another shudder, images of her parents and of Wackee going off to the college alone blinking through her mind. Then the crazy fact that she was here, not even in her home country anymore, on the ground with a stab wound and about to be sacrificed "when the moon makes a circle." By barbarians.

Eugh was talking to the girl that had been failing to make a fire near Y'Starren's head, and when he knelt down again, he took her wounded arm and pulled it away from her body behind her back. She clenched her arm.

"Don't – " she started.

"Don't hurt," he said. "You're dirty."

He showed her a flask, which he then poured over the wound, washing away some of the dirt and dried blood. She took a deep breath and gritted her teeth, forcing herself not to pull away. It would be better to have it clean. And it would help it stop hurting.

"Now go," he said, pointing to a tree next to the one Merreth was tied to. They were going to tie her up next to him.

"Wait, I'm gonna – " she started, but he cut her off, drawing his dagger and nodding to the tree again.

"Go," he repeated.

Y'Starren hissed in frustration and showed him her fingers, at which he jumped to his feet, dagger ready.

"I'm not hurting you!" she said, putting her hand over the firepit. "I don't hurt. Watch."

As the barbarians closed in around her, leery of touching her but picking up their weapons, she picked up one of the charred chunks of wood from the last fire. She'd used small sticks to practice running her magic through at one exact point, and they all did the same thing – they smoked, sparked, and charred.

The barbarians had now closed in around her.

"I help. I'm helping!" she said, clenching the stick in her fist and forcing, willing the magic through it. At first it was just the surface that sparked and crackled, but soon the thing was snapping, hot and smoking in her fingers. She kept having to move her fingers in order to avoid being outright burned as the magic became fire.

"Ouch ... " She hissed and dropped it into a nest of coals, then bent down to blow into the fire, and all her braids started falling down from behind her head where she'd tied them that morning. Clutching them all in her left hand and kneeling awkwardly over the pit, she bent down and blew on the fire, occasionally leaning back on her heels and imbuing it with a bit more spark from her left hand.

Finally, the damp tinder began to blaze up more reliably.

"There, see?" she said, wiping sweat off her forehead with a sooty hand, relieved as she realized they had relaxed a little.

"Witchling ... " someone muttered.

"Yeah, a witchling that saved your ass from a cold night. You're welcome." Y'Starren had almost forgotten about the wound. She smiled.

"Good witchling," Eugh said. "Now go."

***

Y'Starren leaned back against the sapling she'd been tied to – not the kind of sapling you can twist apart with your hands, but the kind that's about three inches through the trunk – watching the others cook and sit comfortably around the fire.

Eugh stood up from the fire with a long piece of meat stuck to his stick and walked toward Y'Starren. He jabbed the stick toward her face and she cursed, flinching back.

"Eat this," he said.

"Oh," she said. "Okay."

She tilted her head and grabbed the meat in her teeth, biting down hard as he jerked the stick away.

"Thank you," she said around the meat in her mouth. It was hot and crispy, but not too hot.

Eugh turned away.

"Wait – what about me?" Merreth interjected. "Am I getting some?"

"This good witchling started the fire." Eugh pointed his stick at Y'Starren. "*You* just complain." He turned away again as Merreth cursed at him.

"Fucking three days of this shit ... " Merreth said. "You should've killed them when I told you."

"As if I didn't try," Y'Starren said.

"Ai! Speaknae!" Molaidh made a throat-cutting gesture.

Merreth gave Y'Starren a withering look. He appeared to think very poorly of her at this point. She sighed and leaned her head back against the tree, squinting eyes reconnoitering the stars through the tips of the trees as if that was going to give her a strategic advantage.

All she wanted to do was focus on the mission. Focus on the money that was going to pay for Wackee's school and keep him safe, so the two of them, at least, could survive in a world that was meant to destroy them before they could destroy it.

I was made to break things.

It was a thought that recurred every time something like this happened. Before her, their parents had managed alright. But when she was born, they had to try to hide out even further from civilization, now that they had a crying baby to conceal.

She couldn't tell herself that she didn't blame her parents a little for choosing to have Wackee next. But she'd never blame him for something he couldn't help. Then came that morning that had ruined everything and gotten her here.

After that three months of school was up, Wackee would be found out and eliminated. A twelve-year-old couldn't be an investigator, no matter how well he bluffed – he'd be useless to the government.

The poor kid must feel so lonely right now ... if he was even okay.

No matter how much she tried to focus on the pain in her arm, or even just the feeling of missing her little brother, all she could think about was a mental zoom-in on the gash in her mother's neck, the feeling of her father's clay-like skin as he lay on his stomach on the stone. A bubble of grief welled up in her chest and her shoulders shook painfully as she began to sob softly, mind reeling blindly as she saw the horrible images over, and over, and over.

It was all over so fast. That morning, that wonderful morning, where her only problem had been the mild insult of having been left behind from some family adventure – what an adventure it was.

She moaned and bit her tongue to try to keep from letting anything else out.

"You're such a baby about this." Merreth scowled. One of the barbarians responded to him by hawking a well-deserved loogie in his direction.

Y'Starren wanted to beg him to tell her the truth, tell her what really happened. Because she kind of knew, but she couldn't let it go unless he admitted to it. What if he was telling the truth, and their real killer was somewhere out there, stalking Wackee and her?

She looked at Merreth, wisps of hair sticking to her tear-streaked face, unable to hide the rage and grief she felt toward him.

He rolled his eyes.

"You suncursed bastard," she swore under her breath.

"Suncursed" was a way to insult anyone who didn't have the orange hair and eyes or the gold-bronze skin tone of a "true" Bane. And he knew it. He set his face into a genuine grimace as he looked away.

It was just as the Warminds were lying down to sleep when there was a sudden shout, and then a scream.

"Naimhcaden!" came the cry from the sentries as they rushed back up the slope toward the camp. The tribe began to scramble to their feet, grabbing knives, axes, sticks, and bows from where they'd set them as they lay down to sleep.

Women clutched their babies to their chests, wrapping them in the narrow cloths that everyone here wore instead of hoods, and their children sprang to their defense with their own crude weapons. Everyone was shouting and screaming, and their enemies were surrounding them with torches that gleamed through the trees all around in tiny points of light.

Merreth was hissing at her. "Y'Starren. Hey. Dumbshit."

She glared at him. "Yes, suncursed?"

"Get us out of here!"

"And what exactly do you expect me to do when I'm tied up like this?"

"I can feel it," he said. Y'Starren realized he had pressed his palm into the pine needle bed behind him. He was a Seer, which meant he could extend his consciousness into whatever he was touching. "Their feet on the needles. There are over five hundred."

Y'Starren's mouth opened. Five hundred was more barbarians than she had ever imagined together in the wild lands.

"Someone's going to drop a knife behind you," he said. "Get so your feet are pointed the other way, so you can pick it up with your feet. Then cut us free."

Y'Starren reluctantly did as he said, groaning with annoyance and some pain from her wounds. She didn't ask him how he knew what was going to happen – he was a Clairvoyant Seer; you don't ask Clairvoyants how they know. They can't ever tell you, but they're usually right anyways.

"And don't you dare leave me here," he added. "You need me."

"Don't worry," Y'Starren grunted as she maneuvered herself into the brush behind her at the base of the tree. "You are *top* of my priority list."

She was pretty sure she was now halfway on top of a termite nest, because she could feel little itchy, crawly sensations going down her buttcrack.

The camp was being overrun, and it happened in the space of less than a minute. A couple arrows clattered into the brush around them, but for the most part, the other tribe came in waving torches and battering the Warminds over the head with them, flaming tar and ripped cotton bits flying from the torches into the damp underbrush and smoking out into cinders.

"Who are they?" Y'Starren shouted, since Merreth seemed to know so much about barbarians.

"Also Warminds," he shouted back.

"How can you tell?"

"Bald!" he shouted over the screaming, which was coming from both sides.

They were, in fact, all bald, she realized. Even the women and children.

The invaders got even louder as they began to spear and stomp the Warminds that had captured the two Banes.

Then it happened – a knife slipped from the belt of one of the invaders and landed by Y'Starren's feet. She stuck out her bare feet in the direction of the blade, which was slightly crooked. It was an ugly iron thing, with only the edge sharpened and metal slivers rolled at the base of the blade, but she pulled it close with her feet and maneuvered herself around so that her hands could reach it.

"You've got about forty-five seconds before they notice us, Y'Starren!" Merreth shouted, just audible above the other shouting.

Y'Starren muttered, "Not helping!" as she ripped the clumsy thing against the twisted plant cord that had bound her hands. She was accustomed to that kind of twine, otherwise she would've been shocked at its natural strength. However, she wore lengths of cord around her body, as part of her decorations and bracelets and armbands and such, so she knew that this cord could hold her body weight easily if required. The knife sawed through and she wiggled her wrists free of the last strands. She crawled to Merreth, cutting at the cord across the tree rather than freeing his hands directly. He'd have to wiggle them apart on the way – there was no time.

"But I need my sword. I need my sword," he was insisting. Perhaps he Clairvoyantly knew he'd need it. But she had no time for the delicate task of trying not to cut his hands as she ripped through the twine, and if they only had forty-five seconds, that time was up.

He barely ducked out of the way of a sword slash aimed at his head, and they fled.

"They put up a perimeter," he grunted to her as they knelt in the underbrush fifteen feet away. "I can feel their feet there and there." He pointed. The tribe members were trying to escape the slaughter, but the invading Warminds were catching them as they fled.

"Here," he said, pointing as a woman with a baby raced forward through the trees. "They'll probably get caught. We'll use them as a decoy."

Y'Starren watched in horror as another barbarian ambushed the woman, springing out of the bushes and running her through with a narrow, iron-tipped spear, which was illuminated by the crazed, waving torch of the other Warminds behind Y'Starren and Merreth. She heard the baby whimper as it fell from her arms.

Merreth grabbed Y'Starren by the hair and yanked her to her feet. They fled.

Even after they ran past the perimeter that the barbarians had created, Merreth continued to pull her forward, though he caught her by the wrist when she lifted his hand from her hair. A glance at his panicked face told her everything she needed to know – they weren't safe yet.

"I can feel them," he said, pausing as he twisted his foot into the clay underneath the pine needles, probably sensing them. "They're coming."

Then he yanked her onward.

Y'Starren's lungs burned as she followed him, determined not to be outlasted, determined to escape, even though she felt like she was going to collapse.

Do it for Wackee, she told herself. *Get that money for him. Keep him safe at the college. Do it for him.*

Finally, Merreth pulled her up toward a rocky outcropping, where she nearly bumped her head into the stone jutting out over them as she slumped down with him. Her chest ached and her lungs burned.

"Now stay quiet," Merreth panted.

She sank back into the bushes against the cold stone, and in a matter of minutes, her dizzy head relaxed and her eyes closed. She fell asleep.

***

Merreth was physically kicking himself as they trudged up the mountainside. There was a goat path lightly trod into the side of the steep hill, which they managed to stick to with only a few slips here and there. It didn't help that Merreth was scuffing the back of his left calf with his right foot here and there, cursing at himself.

"Should've been blazing paying attention. Don't know why I took the blazing path. Stupid. Stupid."

"Didn't you say it's going to be dangerous no matter what path we take?" Y'Starren called back to him.

He fell silent for a while.

"So what exactly are we doing?" Y'Starren said. "When we get to Chaza?"

She was, as they walked, scanning the trees for bears. They were so big and contrasted so clearly with the greenery that you'd think you'd see them right away. But Y'Starren had seen several bears, and they were always suddenly just there. It was terrifying every time.

" ... Delegation," Merreth replied after a very long pause.

Y'Starren stopped and looked back at him, licking her lips. She was thirsty as fuck and they still hadn't reached the river, though she could hear it far ahead and below.

"You're just saying a long word because you don't want to explain," Y'Starren said.

"What are you stopping for?" he said impatiently, having caught up.

"Tell me what we're doing in Chaza," she said irritably.

"I said, we're doing delegation." He scowled. "You're getting your money either way. Now get going, I'm getting thirsty."

The hillside was rocky and difficult, and every few minutes Y'Starren would think again about stopping and resting. Merreth insisted on going on the side of the cliff where it would be harder for people to group up around them, with better visibility, and he also insisted on hurrying. No breaks. It was terribly frustrating, even though deep down she knew she would've agreed if he'd given her the choice. The walk should've taken them ten days, but he was trying to get them through it in three.

It was getting dark by the time they finally started traveling down toward the river they'd been hearing. It was still so far away.

Mist lowered around them once more as their bare feet clutched the slope on the way down. The river got louder and louder, till it seemed like they must be reaching rapids. Maybe her ears had just gotten accustomed to the quietness of nature, though, because it was just a stream, ten or twenty feet across.

Though the Banes tended to boil or filter their water to prevent curses, Y'Starren couldn't stop herself from plunging her hot, dirty feet in and scooping up a handful to drink immediately.

"You fool," Merreth shouted above the sound of the water. "Just get some in your flask to boil."

Y'Starren did, but she hardly cared about any curses at the moment. The water was sweet and tasted rocky and fresh, just like the mountain moss smelled. It was freezing cold on her bare feet, which was a welcome change from the heat and dust and bruises from the day's long climb.

Despite the pain and the sweat and her wounded arm, she was charmed by the magic around them. Even the birds seemed excited to see them, not alarmed or anything. Blue dusk melted down in the gap between the trees that the canyon river formed, making the faraway landscape look like the ghosts of trees and shadows. Somehow, despite the absence of people, there was still a vibrant amount of magic in the air for her to gather in her body.

"Let's go up a bit further, make a fire," Merreth called.

Y'Starren realized she had just been standing in the water with her wet hands on her hips, staring around herself happily. When he spoke, she was reminded of a few very bitter things she didn't want to think about. Her shoulders slumped a little and she sighed.

"I found some tea leaves," Merreth added.

She perked up again and turned to smile at him.

"Oh, good!" she said. "Let's have a proper Bane dinner."

***

It was darker now. Trees loomed black against the sky around them as Y'Starren and Merreth huddled in their cloaks by the small cooking fire, sipping some admittedly well-made tea from their flasks.

"So, tell me about yourself," Merreth said. "All you've done is complain all day. Cheer us up for a change."

"So you want me to tell you about my dead family to cheer you up?" she said sourly. Her voice was raised just above the crackle of the fire. They were terrified that someone nearby would see it, but they were about at the edge of the Grass People's territory, Merreth said. Tomorrow's walk would be much safer.

"I'm just curious." Merreth shrugged, starting to lean back, then getting annoyed that there was no chair-back for him out in the wilderness. He grunted and shuffled around, finally leaning forward again and putting his chin in his hands.

His forty-year-old wrinkled face was always a bit irritable-looking, but tonight, it looked a little more alive. Maybe he'd missed the wild woods. Y'Starren had never seen any landscape as beautiful.

"Well, my mother was the smartest woman I ever met," she said. "Pure sarcasm, this woman. She acted like she hated everyone, but she was extremely kind."

Merreth eyed her judgmentally. "Go on."

"I'm loving the encouragement." Y'Starren rolled her eyes, but she settled back on her bundle of extra clothes, crossing her legs and taking another awkward gulp of tea. "And Father was a paranoid, superstitious woodsman. Powerful, strong."

She paused. She was not going to tell him about her brother.

"Was he a good guy?" Merreth asked, staring down into the coals now. He looked a little more bitter and a little more thoughtful than normal.

Y'Starren realized she couldn't answer. She couldn't tell him that her father was the most handsome, excitable guy she'd ever witnessed chase a squirrel. She couldn't even bear to think about the play fights they used to have, that day with the apples, because now each old memory of him was matched with the picture of her father on his stomach. The hard, cold skin on his neck.

She grimaced and looked up into the sky, blinking back tears. She couldn't cry in front of this guy. Not while she thought what she thought of him – just in case this man really was the fucking killer.

"What do ya know, it's bedtime," she said, voice breaking slightly.

She pulled her cloak up closer around her shoulders, wrapped her feet up in a spare woolen tunic, and lay back on the pile of soft branches and leaves she'd collected to sleep on while they were making camp. She blinked at the haze of fog that drifted over their hillside camp, built on a small plateau, where Merreth could look down the hill from his seat across from her. To his credit, he'd given her the safer place to sleep. It was probably just a strategic choice, since he was the Clairvoyant.

"Hey, I'm ... " he said slowly. "I'm sorry."

***

Two days later, Y'Starren followed closely behind Merreth as he guided her through the forest toward a massive industrial building that was somehow embedded in the cliff. They could only occasionally make it out in the distance, but Merreth said that that was the facility they were trying to reach. It was some kind of laboratory, he said, and that was where he met with the Chazans for private government deals.

The Chazans, called Ghost Men by the superstitious, were said to be somewhat small and squat, dark but also pale, and freakishly intelligent. They were said to be able to wave their hand and kill you. They could also fly. Then again, none of the people Y'Starren spoke to had ever actually seen one.

Y'Starren figured she should give them a chance to be less frightening than the legends claimed.

As they walked, she found herself gingerly avoiding patches of gravel that seemed to have been intentionally carted in. Why would you bother to make a path out of something so uncomfortable to walk on? There was more and more gravel as they went forward.

Finally, they had to go off the path to step over some barbed wire, and then they crossed a ravine and reached a flight of steps.

"Is this sandstone?" Y'Starren said, bare feet spreading on the cool, gritty steps luxuriously after over a half-mile of gravel path.

"Cement," Merreth replied. "We're almost there."

"How 'almost' are we talking this time?" Y'Starren said. He'd said that same sentence three times already today and once yesterday, so she had no real frame of reference.

He pointed upward as the steps went up the hill, winding side to side to avoid drops and getting higher and higher.

She couldn't see it through the trees, but she assumed that the building was up there somewhere. Finally, as they reached the top of a hill where the steps crested, Y'Starren could see the building they were approaching – what looked like massive cubes of the purest dark crystal, gripped into the side of the jungle cliff like black knuckles, rising above even the tallest trees with about four levels of massive architecture.

Despite its apparent newness, the cement walkways were mossy and somewhat overgrown. As they got closer, it was clear that they had been swept.

Finally, they reached a modest-looking door with a teensy reinforced window. Merreth hesitated, glancing back at her, then knocked on the door.

There was no answer.

He raised a meaty fist and banged on the solid green door this time. Y'Starren heard it echoing down a hallway that sounded almost like a canyon. And finally, the sound of feet and voices, and the door opened all the way to reveal a man with black hair and a face so pale it was almost white.

The Ghost Men.

The Ghost Man looked over Merreth's shoulder.

"Is gifted?" he said.

"Well, you're one to get to the point, aren't you," Y'Starren smiled, holding out her hand.

The man barely looked at her, but nodded at Merreth and asked them to come inside, using an odd dialect that Y'Starren found she couldn't understand.

As the door closed behind her, Y'Starren noticed that men in white coats that didn't even look warm were crowding around them, eyeing the tall Bane, and writing in notepads when they looked at Y'Starren. She noticed only after a minute or so that the Chazans didn't touch each other much.

"Her gift?" he asked.

"I only speak to Mainmwim," Merreth said. "Get me Mainmwim."

"Lord Mainmwim is of industries!" the man protested. "Accords with Yeckswem, is much able."

Y'Starren squinted, trying her best to understand what they were saying. She didn't know what "industries" or "accords" meant, but the rest of the words were definitely Bane.

At that moment, a tall, scornful-looking Chazan with a long, lined face hurried up with a clipboard stuffed into one of the massive pockets in his lab coat.

"Yeckswem." The man that had opened the door bowed and moved out of the newcomer's way. "Yeckswem is of accords. I am of industries, my apologies – "

He broke off as Yeckswem put a hand on his shoulder.

"Winwyn, stop," he said, and then he turned a pair of hard, clever eyes on Y'Starren and fished around in his pocket for something.

He pulled out a black box-shaped thing, then suddenly jabbed it into Y'Starren's arm. The jab was hard enough to bruise, and at the same time there was a powerful jolt of magic, which repeated mechanically. She was too shocked to react for a moment, taking in the energy quickly and feeling it spark in her fingertips, like it did when she needed to touch the ground pretty soon. The wax-like floor was almost bouncy, and it did not respond at all when she tried to push her excess magic into it.

"Uh – hey. Stop," she said, pulling away. It had left two bruised marks on her arm. "That kind of hurts!"

Yeckswem was staring at the box and shaking it and adjusting knobs on it with a panicked expression.

"I'm so sorry," Merreth started stammering. "She's not – I didn't know she could – "

Yeckswem glared at Merreth as someone screamed "Security!" and all the scientists scrambled away from Y'Starren like she was going to bite them.

"This subject is defective," Yeckswem was growling at Merreth.

"Excuse me?" Y'Starren said. "I'm the defective one here?"

And then it hit her.

Something slammed into her from the left just behind her and knocked her sideways, and before she realized what was happening, people had jumped in – people in gray and yellow bodysuits with masks over their faces – solid black masks like crystal – and she was struggling to get out of their grip, grunting and now biting. And her magic was sparking and arcing out, zapping their hands, and then they'd grab another part of her body.

This time, she wasn't letting them kidnap her. She'd seen where that would go – she could get killed.

Sticks battered and rebounded off her back and arm as she struggled toward the door, lunging at the one scientist who blocked the way with his short arms spread out as if to stop her. She smashed a fist into his face, and then pushed magic out of her fist and into his broken nose, and he clutched his face and fell to the ground, seizing and making choking noises. She put her hand on the door and could immediately tell it was metal from the way it accepted the energy in her body.

Involuntarily the magic started to jump into the door, and she willed it back into herself and twisted the knob.

But suddenly she was yanked back by an arm around her neck. It was tight and thick. She couldn't breathe or think. Her face went puffy as she fought against his grip.

She batted behind herself with her bare hand, searching for skin – the easiest thing to hurt with her magic. All she found was a tacky, waxy material that was somehow completely blocking her magic just as effectively as the floor was. Her legs were kicking reflexively, and it wasn't helping. He just wouldn't let her breathe.

"Get it! Get it!" people were encouraging him.

They dragged her backward, so weak now that she could hardly move, and tears were running from the corners of her eyes.

The last thing she saw was Merreth, calmly watching them go with that serious, almost blank expression he so often wore.

He'd betrayed her.

Her vision went black as she felt something jab into her arm.

***

Y'Starren lay limp on the floor as her eyelids fluttered open. The floor was completely free of any kind of smell, but her body was all twisted up in an awkward pose, like she'd just been dropped there. She trembled, trying to move, but every part of her felt like it was strapped down with weights, even though she couldn't feel or see anything besides her own body. She flopped awkwardly, head dragging on the ground as she braced herself on a shaking elbow, shoulder poking up as she tried to get the rest of herself up. Her hair draped forward, strands of it trailing into her eyes, and her braids made a jagged curtain around the corners of her vision. Her string bracelets and anklets were only a small comfort – she could barely feel them. She always used them as a sort of grounding technique for anxiety when she was worried about getting found by the government.

As she struggled and failed to rise on the floor, she heard their shoes around her, talking about her, though she mostly couldn't understand what they were saying. She gathered that they had intentionally made her this weak, that they were waiting for Mainmwim, and they were trying to figure out how to "ground" her. They acted like she was some kind of problem they'd never had to deal with before – as if they couldn't have just not kidnapped her.

"Is a gifted?" a new voice came in. A door closed. The room was small and had muffling walls, so their voices sounded personal, intimate.

"Lord Mainmwim." Their voices were more hushed than normal. "Subject does not engage properly with G-H-B. Is gifted of electrical charges."

A small silence fell as a pair of black shoes approached. Y'Starren lifted her heavy head to see the bottom of his white slacks.

"Like a charger ... " Mainmwim knelt down in front of her and took her under the chin, tilting her head back to see her face. "Charger," he said, "why have you stopped charging the scientists?"

"Is it just me," Y'Starren slurred, "or are you suddenly talkin' right?"

"Bane dialect is not right," Mainmwim said, still scanning her with his eyes. "So, why have you stopped charging the scientists?"

Y'Starren trembled in the effort to speak and keep from collapsing.

"He left me here, didn't he ... " she said.

"A simple matter of money," Mainmwim said. "Now I've answered two of your questions. Answer mine, or this exchange will not be so kind."

Y'Starren dropped her weight, exhausted, forehead on the ground as she struggled to speak.

"I ran out of charge, okay?" she said. "I can't believe they just sold me out like this. I'm gonna kill them ... "

"And how do you get more charge?" Mainmwim said.

"Ask Yeckswem," Y'Starren said, thinking of his little box of magic. If they wanted magic, why didn't they just ask him?

There was a pause as the two of them communicated something with a shrug and a point.

"Yeckswem will torture you if you do not answer," Mainmwim said after a moment.

" ... I don't understand ... " Y'Starren said, breath huffing against the ground. "I don't understand! What's happening? Why are you threatening me? You drugged me!"

"He will torture you," Mainmwim repeated.

"Well, isn't that quaint!" Y'Starren's voice trembled. "Why? What did I ever do to you?"

There was a sigh as people shuffled around her, and the door opened and closed again.

"Yeckswem is going to get something to hurt you," Mainmwim said. "Now answer the question, or else."

She was shaking, trying to process exactly what was happening. She had to give him some kind of answer, but she could hardly think.

"I get more ... charge ... over time," she said. "I – I don't know much about it myself."

She couldn't tell them everything. She didn't want them to know what she could do. It was going to be a surprise. Yeah, a surprise. That helped a little. She smiled grimly, face hidden by the floor and the fallen braids, which still smelled like forest and smoke. Quite the surprise it would be.

"You said to ask Yeckswem," Mainmwim said, sounding irritated. "So you know you are using electricity. What I'm asking you is how you gather it."

"Ughhh ... " she groaned. She could feel a little bit of her strength coming back very gradually, and she raised up on her other elbow, lifting her head just enough to glare at Mainmwim from under her eyebrows. "I collect the magic over time, and then I push it out of my hands." She wouldn't tell them that she could also push it out of any other place in her body with a little more effort. "How is that not enough for you? We don't have 'chargers' back where I'm from. I'm the only one," she lied again. "I barely know how my gift works myself."

The door opened and closed again, and someone else knelt next to her – Yeckswem. Suddenly there was a pinching sensation on her neck, and then an intensifying burn as the flesh on her neck was pinched and twisted in a set of pliers.

She winced and tried to push him away. She tried to send a shock of magic through the metal pliers, but it didn't reach him, and her skin began to burn.

"Stop – stop!" she gasped, flopping a limp arm out to try to grab Yeckswem's hand. He shifted the angle, twisting more. She whimpered in pain, lip quivering as her eyes watered. "It hurts ... please ... "

"Then answer the question." Mainmwim's voice came from up above her, completely detached. "How do you gather charge?"

Yeckswem let go of the piece of flesh, and as the blood flowed back into it, it burned even worse. She groaned and ducked in to cover her neck. He moved the pliers about an inch down from the last place and she felt the cold clamps begin to squeeze.

"Wait – wait!" she gasped. "I don't know, I swear."

He twisted and pinched till she screamed, cringing in to try to protect her shoulder. She wasn't going to tell them shit. She was going to figure out how to make the Kill Touch really kill everyone she touched, and she was going to get the hell out and make Wackee safe.

She cursed and panted as he released the chunk of skin, shuddering a little. She collapsed inward, covering the bruises with her right hand, breaths puffing against the waxy floor.

"Please just let me go," her voice creaked.

"Behends not," Winwyn said from behind Yeckswem. "Accords?"

"Withal – " Yeckswem started.

"Is fascinating," Mainmwim interrupted.

Winwyn stepped up beside Yeckswem, and Y'Starren, who was watching them in her periphery, noticed a slightly disturbed expression on his face as he glanced at her.

"Haply is instinct," he said softly. "Tolerates the tase, yet it behends little. Haply we test of it?"

Somehow, their dialect was actually starting to make a little sense, though it was annoying. Or maybe she just didn't like the speakers.

"Accords," Mainmwim said, and the scientists left Y'Starren alone for a while in the room, probably watching her through the massive dark windows on one side of the room.

After a while, a few of them came back with Yeckswem and helped him drag her away.

She was dumped into a room on a cot-like bed, where the ceiling was lined with lights, and the door had one of those tiny windows.

White, fragile chairs and tables crowded the corner of her vision, and as the door closed, she saw the orange heads of two other Banes. She felt her chest sinking into the bed, making it hard to breathe.

The Banes' tan faces were a welcome sight. There was a blue-eyed man in his forties, hair going white and a wandering expression. He introduced himself as Nomad.

The other was a young boy named Len. He had a beautiful face that reminded her a little bit of Wackee, though his hair lay flat and dull against his head instead of spiky and vibrant like her brother's. He looked gentle, but frightened.

She looked around the room, with its white, noise-canceling paneled walls, the sound of some kind of construction in the next room, with the off-and-on massive whirring of machinery. The tables in this room had some food set out on them in strange shiny black trays. There was also a chess set. Len was shyly, secretively touching one of her braids. The two other prisoners had their hair cropped very short into a perfectly even cut that looked like it had been shaved by an expert barber. That seemed unlikely, but perhaps these advanced Chazans had some sort of machinery that made it easy.

"So, Merreth has just been selling the other investigators, huh?" Y'Starren said. It was getting easier to speak, though her chest was still heavy and her limbs were practically immobile.

"I don't know about him," Nomad said. "I was a Teleporter, but ... I can't seem to do it anymore. Not after the ... "

"Come on, I don't have all day," Y'Starren said.

Nomad smiled slightly.

"It's so good seeing a fresh face after all these years," he sighed. "You're about the age my daughter would be now ... "

For a moment, his eyes clouded with tears, and he rubbed his hand over his stubble repeatedly like he was trying not to cry.

Y'Starren's heart began to sink. Years? And that bit about his daughter ...

"I'll tell you one thing, Y'Starren," Nomad said. "Don't ... try anything."

As he spoke, he rubbed a deep red scar across his neck under his ear.

"Look, Nomad, you take your own advice, because someone's gotta," Y'Starren said. "And it's not gonna be me."

Nomad looked away with a resentful grimace.

"Of course you'd be like that," he said. After a silent pause, he added, "I mean, you've seen what they'll do to you. Suncursed bastards already hurt you." Y'Starren saw him turn his face away to rub roughly at his eyes. "Can't you just call it enough and cooperate?"

She sighed and closed her eyes.

"No," she said. "I have a brother to protect."

Nomad shook his head. "Nothing's worth what they'll do to you."

Y'Starren shivered.

"Ooh, sounds exciting," she said. "Now I'm gonna sleep. Wait – " She opened one eye and squinted at Nomad. "Are they gonna come back for me, do you think?"

"It's okay," Len said again. "They'll probably wait for the drug to wear off. They like us conscious and able to feel everything for their ... tests."

He shuddered.

Y'Starren sighed and settled back, imagining a canopy of trees, black against the cold night sky.

"They never turn the lights off," was the last thing she heard before she fell asleep to Nomad's hollow, droning voice.

***

As she was led out between the guards, Y'Starren mentally mapped out the place. She focused on her magic moving through her body, finding her fingers snapping with it. After the box, which was apparently called a taser, she had become rich with magic and had gathered a little from the air.

If she could figure out her gift faster than they could, she'd have the edge on that. Then all she'd need to know was the layout.

It seemed simple. She bit the inside of her cheek as she looked around, mentally rehearsing the layout as she walked. Things were never simple when they seemed simple, but she was going to make it happen anyway.

There was a chair made of panels in a tiled room with a black ceiling, and there were massive bright lamps shining down onto the chair. She noticed restraints by the head, arms, and leg areas, and shivered.

They passed by huge, bright panels full of letters, numbers, and a few images that made no sense to her, on the way to the panel chair. Except for one – it had a gridwork of what must absolutely be man-made paths. She knew it was, because it said "map" on top. These Chazans probably assumed she couldn't even read. They'd been treating her like she would've treated a barbarian.

"Go!" The guard punched her in the back impatiently. "Sit!"

Y'Starren whirled around, about to punch him, and reeled back the response just in time, biting her cheek and stepping backward while lowering her eyes meekly.

"Thought better of it?" the guard said.

"Oh, I'm not one to talk back to my betters," Y'Starren scoffed, not looking up.

"Repeat it," the guard said.

Y'Starren didn't, but the scientists were now flooding into the room, many of them staring at her with a piercing kind of interest that made her feel like an animal.

"Sit," the guard huffed, pointing at the chair.

Her stomach ground with anxiety as she did, panels wobbling slightly under her weight. Despite a lifetime of fending off starvation, she'd become pretty well-built and heavy and tall for her family, which was barely above average for a Bane.

They started fastening her wrists and ankles in the restraints immediately – except for her left hand.

"Is what?" someone said, brushing some of her stray hair away from her arm and pointing to the wound. "Is a wound, but how came it?"

"Never seen a cut before?" Y'Starren said.

The scientist – a short woman with the typical sharp eyes, hair pulled into a graceful half-ponytail – looked shocked that Y'Starren had dared to speak, much less say that.

"What, are your subjects usually tamer?" she sneered. "I was raised in the – "

A hand was clapped to her forehead and a thick leather strap came halfway over her eyes, and she grimaced as her head was pinned against the back of the chair.

Great. Now I look stupid.

"Tell me of it," the woman said. The other scientists had backed up a bit to wait for something anyway, and she was now the only one close to Y'Starren. She tapped above the wound, making Y'Starren wince. "Tell me of it. Behend me?"

" ... I behend it," Y'Starren grunted. "We came into the Warminds territory, and they must hate Banes as much as we hate them. I had a sword in this hand – " She flinched as the woman touched the wound. She realized the scientist was applying some kind of gel to it.

"The fuck is that?" Y'Starren said through gritted teeth.

"Tell it." The woman didn't look up.

Y'Starren turned her eyes back to the ceiling.

"Anyway, the leader of the barbarians stabbed me right there in the arm and made me drop my sword. It's probably still out there."

There was a pause, then there was a small applause from the gathered scientists and the two guards that had remained in the room.

"Affable, affable," they said, which must be some sort of praise.

"Stories are what Chazans like," the woman said slowly, clearly attempting to make herself easier for Y'Starren to understand.

The woman taped a bandage over the wound, and Y'Starren realized that the dull ache that had been there was slowly fading. She tried to look down at her arm, but couldn't move her head enough. The woman had just made it stop hurting somehow. Whether it was for some evil reason or not, Y'Starren was grateful, and the clenching in her throat released a little. She swallowed.

"Thank you," she said.

When Yeckswem came in with a sour expression, beady eyes fixed on Y'Starren, she felt naked once again. Her braids, thickened with ribbons from last week, itched at the back of her head as she watched him come up and start tapping buttons at a rapid pace into the computer he was standing at. She'd heard enough terms and enough new words of the Chazan dialect to begin piecing together a bit about the world where these people lived and conducted their experiments. The only thing that was bothering her was the difference between rubber and plastic – she couldn't figure it out.

He walked over to her, pulled over a tray on a stand which rattled with tools, and pulled something out of his pocket. Two things. The first, the black taser he'd tried to hurt her with yesterday, and the second, the pliers. Her bruised, torn neck burned already just from looking at them. He was giving her a look as he showed them to her.

It wasn't even a demand for compliance – no, those eyes said "I'm going to use these on you."

He pulled something from the tray which was connected to a cord. It was a pair of discs, which he taped to two of her fingers, her forefinger and her middle finger. His hands were cold and unpleasant.

“Charge this one, Charger.” He tapped her forefinger. Many of the scientists had taken positions around the screens, looking, pointing, whispering observations. Had they been watching her in the room with the other prisoners? Creeps.

“Start,” he said, irritated, already looking to the pliers, where Y’Starren’s own eyes kept wandering. Maybe if she didn’t give him an excuse ...

She closed her eyes, pretending to find it difficult, and trailed a miniscule amount of energy into her finger, which was sucked in greedily by the disc.

“How long are you going to keep me here?”

Yeckswem didn’t answer, frowning at the readings.

“More,” he said, tapping her hand.

Y’Starren wanted to shock him up through that finger he was tapping her with, but she forced herself not to. She didn’t want to be hurt again.

She grunted and strained against the bonds, pretending to try to put more power into the finger, then reversed the flow and put it through the other one.

“Ah – it’s just hard to control it,” she said.

“This control – you did it to another,” he said. He took the pliers.

“Wait, I – ” Y’Starren struggled against her fear. She couldn’t let them win. She needed to figure out her powers first. She’d never been much good at making tests, but she had to copy their tactics and try. And she had to buy time to figure it out faster than they did. They couldn’t know the extent of her power.

She pushed another almost negligible amount of magic into the disc.

Suddenly a pinching pain seared into her arm as Yeckswem clamped the pliers down. She hissed a curse, wrist jerking at the restraint. Then she forced herself to focus away. They would not make her – then she realized that the power had reflexively surged out of her, as it often did when she was frightened or in pain. She was both right now, heart pounding and pain ripping up and down her arm.

“Horizons,” she cursed hoarsely.

“Thought it,” Yeckswem muttered, squeezing harder, twisting till the skin broke. She screamed through clamped-shut teeth. “More torture.” Yeckswem snapped his fingers at one of the other scientists. “Penalty of pliers must of revise,

Winwyn." Yeckswem tossed them onto the tray. "Encounter such an efficat, and keep such torture no mennus."

Gotta like the sound of "torture." The thought flashed through her head, but she didn't say it. She was focused on not letting out her magic. She attempted to constrain the tide to what had already been released, creating a plateau. She didn't want them to know just how much magic she could release.

"Line, haply?" Winwyn said, hurrying to a metal chest of drawers.

"Line, yeh." Yeckswem nodded.

Winwyn pulled something out of a drawer. It was a bundle of three thin metal sticks, wrapped at the base with wire that formed a handle. He handed it to Yeckswem.

"Behold, the line." Yeckswem showed it to her. Then he tapped her leg with it; it was cold, and even the light flick stung a little. "Charge the electrode as charged in the scientist you punched."

Charge it like you charged the guy you punched. Y'Starren understood, but –

Fwip – the line snapped into her forearm above the restraint and she gasped, body reflexively yanking at the restraints. It stung across her arm.

"Stop – " she whispered, and he brought it down again.

She whimpered through her teeth, twisting and tugging at the once-gentle restraints, which now seemed hard as rock around her wrists. Head pulled back like that, everyone could see her face contorting as he continued to whip her till the blood ran down her arm. She screamed. Her voice bounced off the plaster walls and ceiling and rattled the lamps. The chair shuddered under her jerking body as she held her breath and screamed again.

All the control she'd had was gone, and she was screaming in pain over and over, power pulsing out of her through the fingers of both hands and feet, scorching her skin black under each pulse of pain and magic after each lash to her arm. Then there was a snap, a faint acrid smoke, as the connection broke. She'd overloaded it

"Output severed," one of the scientists commented. Y'Starren sobbed in agony, shuddering and heaving huge breaths. She didn't want them to know how much they were hurting her; she didn't want to let them know shit until she'd figured it out. She hadn't even really noticed that pain forced her to lose control of the magic that was always waiting to be released from her body.

She groaned, tears pouring down the sides of her face into her hair.

She felt the meager remains of her magic drifting down her chest toward the torn flesh of her arm, as it liked to do. It often collected around her injuries. She focused past the pain, closing her eyes and picturing herself in the woods. She used to take the energy from the air, very slowly, as she watched the clouds pass across the moon and stars, on nights when it was warm enough to lay outside on the blankets. The static from the blankets was a little disruptive to the magic collection process.

She made the magic spark across her fingers, keeping them close together so that no one else could see them. The lights that were shining down on her were so bright, but she kept her eyes closed, now imagining resting on the grass at midday, the day with the apples.

A sudden sob broke from her before she knew it. She grimaced and forced it back, pretending to be reacting to the pain with a weird little whimper. At least the awkwardness brought her thoughts away from that last good day.

"Yeckswem has the right," the female scientist from before commented. "Would that a shocking did such a trick."

"Hold – such is it!" Yeckswem snapped his fingers. "Output of it haply subcedes of the gen."

"Tending it," the scientist replied. "Of the cut and the backup gen plan. Good good?"

Y'Starren sniffled. *Keep acting like your blazing language is valid*, she thought, biting her cheek and grimacing again. *I hate your blazing language*.

"Good, Menyth," Yeckswem said, pointing at two of the other scientists. "Accords."

They left the room, and the female scientist, apparently called Menyth, took out more of the ointment she'd used on Y'Starren's other arm with a sigh of resignation to attend to her new wounds. She was the first person to care for Y'Starren like that here in the facility. But Y'Starren didn't thank her again. The bitch just stood by while they tortured her. She was the same as the others.

***

Back in the room with the other prisoners, Y'Starren focused on drawing the electricity from one side of her body to another, charging her hand, her foot, her neck, but not releasing it. Each time, all it took was imagining Yeckswem's hand there to provoke a magical flow. Controlling herself enough to keep from sparking it off from there was a little harder, so she often had to pull it away and create a small rhythmic flow inside her.

She also practiced sending it into the metal bedframe, not retrieving it for a moment before pulling it back. And, of course, the much simpler task of sending it from one hand to the other through the frame. She had already tried the walls, the door, and the black glass windows. The only other conductive thing was the door, which seemed to be wood plated with metal.

She was going to have to get out while being walked to a test, probably.

At the end of the day, three more prisoners had been brought in – a Clairvoyant sibling group. Y'Starren had asked them if they were planning to escape, and they paled visibly and stopped chatting altogether. That's why she was silently sitting on her bed practicing while they played chess.

And then there was a sudden bolt sound and the door swung open, revealing several guards, a few technicians, and Yeckswem behind them.

"On the beds!" he ordered.

He didn't have to. The three Clairvoyants had already scurried to them and sat down, eyes closed, hands clenched together on their chests. From their behavior, they were waiting to be hurt. From the taser in Yeckswem's hand, this happened on a regular basis.

"Charger." Yeckswem snapped his fingers.

Y'Starren got up, folding her arms with a small sigh. Her electricity was almost gone, and she was tired.

The technicians were drilling holes in the wall at top speed, guards crowding around the door with batons and tasers ready. Now the technicians yanked her bed over to the wall where they were drilling. Two thin cables of solid metal were now attached to the wall, ending with a pair of cuffs ... her size.

"Sit," Yeckswem ordered.

Y'Starren glanced around once at the other Chazans before deciding to go, promising herself that a better chance would come.

They fastened the cuffs, which were oily inside, to her wrists, and Y'Starren noticed with discomfort that they were not long enough for her to lie down in bed with.

"Wait, you're not going to leave me here all night in these ... "

"All night, every night." Yeckswem smiled slightly at her pleading look.

"Yeckswem, I can't sleep like – "

She was cut off by a roar of the fan from the other side of the room, and suddenly there was a huge draining sensation through the cuffs. She grimaced and slumped over her drawn-up legs, hands dangling on either side. She groaned as her muscles ached, electricity drawn away from her too fast – faster than she could pull it in. Was this what being tased was supposed to feel like?

"It's too much ... I don't have anything left to give," she groaned.

Yeckswem came to her and grabbed her left hand.

"Charge it," he said, adding, "Charge the hand," when she frowned in confusion.

He reached slowly into his pocket with his free hand. She stiffened as he pulled out the line, placing its cold length against the hot blisters down her arm. She heard a shift in the rest of the room as they saw what he'd been making those marks with.

"Do it," he said.

She clenched her jaw and looked away. Permission to hurt him had to be a trap.

Y'Starren felt the electricity run toward him instinctively, only to be cut off mid-flow by the cuff. She closed her eyes to concentrate once more. It didn't work, though she felt a separate flow in her abdomen. That meant that she could definitely separate it in her body, just not that close to the cuff. She needed to practice.

She looked at the line out of the corner of her eye, trembling.

"Well?" he said, lifting it like he was about to hurt her.

"I – I'm sorry – " She felt herself starting to shake. "Please don't hurt me, I'm trying. I'm trying!"

"Try it more."

She did.

Nothing.

She lurched into a sob, pulling at her arm. His grip was so fucking tight around her wrist that it didn't budge an inch. He tapped her burning arm warningly. She shuddered.

"See, I tried, but it's stopping at the cuff. I tried." Tears ran down her cheeks. "I can't – I can't do it."

Slowly he lifted the line. She clenched her jaw and turned her face away, waiting for him to strike her. But he didn't.

He was putting the line back into his pocket, letting go of her hand. He tilted her face up by the chin. She blinked back the crying, gritting her teeth and forcing herself to stop. Her eyes blazed into his defiantly.

"Calm it," he said. "I don't whip you now."

She took a breath for courage, then snapped her teeth at him like a threat to bite. He flinched.

"Fuck off," she said.

His hand turned into a fist, which she expected him to knock into her jaw, but while his eyes flickered with an uncontrolled wrath, he pulled back.

“Will regret it,” he said as they left.

Y’Starren closed her eyes and jerked at the very fixed metal cords. She probably would regret it.

***

The next day, Y’Starren was once again strapped to a chair, but this time she was in a place that smelled like a bathroom and had massive windows that looked out into the wild land where the barbarians lived. It was beautiful. For a moment, she let her mind take her away as she waited for whatever horrible treatment was coming.

The forest rose up into the mountains opposite them, with very few treetops reaching above the window. Huge clouds of mist hung over the morning forest, with occasional trails of faraway smoke coming from the mountains.

Out there, some barbarian clan was resting around that fire, stripping fresh meat off a piece of carcass they’d killed recently, or cooking wild potatoes in the coals. Wild potatoes ... you always burn yourself trying to dig the flesh out of the crispy skin, because they take so long to cool, and you are always so hungry. And the way they fill up your stomach is worth the burn.

And then the door opened and she flinched, stomach tensing to the point that her appetite vanished, her mouth dried up in an instant, and she huddled forward, grateful for the curtain of dirty orange braids that hid her flinching face. Her arms were the tensest – scabbed and bruised, she could almost feel the stinging of the line across her skin again.

“Leave us. I don’t think she’s a threat,” the woman said. “I speak a little Bane. How’s that?”

She gently touched Y’Starren’s shoulder.

Y'Starren flinched hard.

"I'm sorry," she whispered automatically.

The woman's hand retreated quickly.

Y'Starren heard her moving around behind her, dragging a rolling tray closer. She grimaced, keeping her head down under her hair. She looked out from between the braids at the woman. The Chazan had covered her mouth, stepped back a pace, and was looking at Y'Starren's scabbed arm, colored all down the forearm with dull red bruise lines. Her hand shifted on her own mouth as if she wanted to re-cover it and then realized her hand was already there.

"Uh – are you okay?" Y'Starren said.

"Oh. Uh." The woman lowered her hand, looked like she didn't know what to do with it, and then held it out toward Y'Starren, who recoiled slightly. "I'm Yin," she said slowly. "I'm not going to hurt you."

Y'Starren gritted her teeth when she heard that and saw the concerned look the woman was trying to hide. Maybe it was a trick. A test.

"Oh, yeah? Then why am I tied to a chair?" Her voice trembled with fear she couldn't hide. She was glad the woman couldn't see her quivering lips.

The woman reached for something on the tray, and paused when she saw Y'Starren grip the armrests of the chair that her wrists were tied to, knuckles going white.

"I told you I'm not going to hurt you, Charger," the woman said. "Are you going to hurt me?" Y'Starren bit her cheek, trying to calm herself down with a couple breaths.

"Depends on behavior of it," Y'Starren answered like they had answered her, but sarcastically. "Gonna pinch me? Whip me?"

Yin walked around in front of Y'Starren, holding a pair of scissors close to her chest. The gray light from the early morning outdoors wrapped around her body, making her look darker, more ethereal.

Y'Starren wanted to add another sarcastic comment, but when she looked up with hard eyes, she saw a concerned look on Yin. Her lips were slightly parted, and she looked like she was trying to decide what to say.

"Young gifted, I am a barber. I am not going to hurt you," she said slowly. "Do you … "

"I behend what you're trying to say," Y'Starren rolled her eyes. "But do I believe you?" She shrugged.

Yin sighed and pulled up a chair next to Y'Starren's. As Yin reached for her hair, Y'Starren's arm jerked reflexively at the tie over the chair, but Yin did not hurt her. She wrapped a towel over the girl's shoulders and took a couple of her narrow braids in her hand.

"Don't," Y'Starren whispered, and it came out in a choked sob. "Please, don't cut my hair."

"I'm really sorry," Yin said. "I have to. If I refuse, they'll just find someone else to do it."

Y'Starren moaned, breaking into actual crying.

"Don't cut my hair … " she cried. "Please, don't cut my hair."

Yin's hands dropped into her lap, and Y'Starren saw a tear drip down the woman's white face. The woman didn't say anything, though she looked like she was trying to and then swallowing instead.

After a minute, Y'Starren managed to stop, blinking tears out of her eyes and sniffling, wiping her face on her shoulders.

" … It's okay," she said finally. She managed half a shrug. "What do I need my blazing hair for?"

"It's beautiful," Yin said.

Y'Starren laughed, still trying not to cry anymore.

"You think these dirty ropes are beautiful?" She sniffed. "Do you realize how much they itch?" But her eyes teared up again when Yin started cutting them off.

It turned out they did have a machine to make your hair the exact same length all over your head, and it was loud, but it surprisingly didn't hurt at all.

As Yin brushed the extra hair away from Y'Starren's neck, she told her about her boyfriend, who was going to be a guard, so that he could try to work near Yin.

"I will say the haircut took very long, if you want," Yin said, pausing and sitting down. "Less tests."

Y'Starren met her eyes briefly, then tore them away from the painfully kind expression and looked back out the window.

"Less pain," Yin added, more softly, gently touching Y'Starren's hand, which was swollen under the pressure of the wrist restraints. "I'm sorry. I don't think they should treat you this way."

"Yeah?" Y'Starren said.

She was considering asking Yin for help escaping, but her stomach flipped in panic at the very idea. She had to know if she could trust Yin.

"You may be Bane, but you are still human," Yin said. "I think." She frowned.

"You *think*?" Y'Starren repeated.

"It's unethical to ... to whip your subjects," Yin said, biting her lip. "I'm so sorry."

Y'Starren sighed, scraping her nails against the chair arms.

"I've tried reporting them, but ethics don't care as long as results come forth." Yin put the scissors on the tray, and Y'Starren thought about the pliers.

"No qualms about the whole non-consensual part, though?" Y'Starren said.

"Qualms?" Yin asked. "What is it?"

"It's ... you don't think it's unethical to hold Banes here, when we just ... want to fucking go home?"

Yin sighed and got up, pushing her tray away. She came back to Y'Starren and released her ankles, then her wrists. Y'Starren rubbed her wrists and cautiously stood up. Wordlessly she took a broom and swept around the chair where she'd been sitting, collecting orange twists of hair in one pile.

"But ... " Yin stared.

"I just wanted to help," Y'Starren muttered. "Sorry."

Yin picked up a dustpan and took the broom gently from Y'Starren, sweeping the hair up. This stranger, knowing Y'Starren's gift, didn't seem afraid of her at all. It was such a strange, long-hoped-for feeling. Something she'd never thought would happen, and for it to happen here was completely unexpected.

"I thank you," Yin said doubtfully. "Is that how you would say it?"

"Basically." Y'Starren shrugged. She tried to smile, and it came out floppy, so she stopped, wincing instead. "Right. I guess I'll just go back to my torture now?"

Yin cursed under her breath, looked at the clock, and her eyes fell to the ground. The look told Y'Starren that this was probably the longest that Yin would be able to keep Y'Starren away from Yeckswem.

"Just do as they say, and they won't hurt you."

Y'Starren sighed.

"I wish."

***

Week after week, Y'Starren studied every path in the building and every map she could get her hands on. Every door and every lock, and how it was opened.

The nature of the tests and her own obstinance when it came to hiding her secrets resulted in her returning to the prisoners' cell later than everyone else and covered in welts and bruises, some of which would blister only to break the next day when she was whipped across the same spot. The jumpsuit they forced her to wear was cold and didn't protect her at all from the abuse – they had kept it sleeveless and the bottom half didn't even come halfway down her thighs. They'd taken all of her decorative strings and handmade jewelry. And no matter how much she twisted and matted her hair, it wasn't long enough to braid.

It had to be worth it – she had to rescue Wackee, and that would make every extra strike she'd taken to hide her true power worth it. She imagined living with him on the run, somewhere in the wilds. Barely safe, but together. It would be horrible not having their parents there, but there was one last spark of beauty in her life, one last piece of family, and she wasn't going to give up on it. Ever. Not if it got her a hundred lashes. Which it did.

They hooked her up to more and more powerful equipment to see how high her charge could get, then struck her legs till they bled in lines across them and she screamed. They also tried to make her practice taking in and putting out more power, faster, and arcing the electricity further and further from her fingers. Keeping her progress steadily behind where she actually was cost her a lot. The bleeding lines on her legs and the layered bruises could attest to that. Yeckswem probably would've tortured her either way.

But each time, she practiced. She practiced pretending to give them all her magic, while really holding it deep in her abdomen, waiting to strike at the right moment. Waiting to strike when she knew the way out.

She had counted ten weeks since her imprisonment, and she was waking up from nightmares every time she was dragged out of the prisoners' cell. They were nightmares of Wackee being found out, or of Wackee trying to look for her and getting dragged in here, or of her running back for him with a naive smile on her face, only to find him face-down and cold outside the gates of Strangers' College – dead before he even got accepted. That was the most horrible one.

So every time she was released from those painful shackles in the subjects' holding cell, her eyes were already baggy and frightened, strained from unshed tears.

It had been a horrible day, not that that made it special. She had been taken to the chair under the lamps and tested with bigger electrodes, and lashed across her thighs when the output slowed. She'd pushed past the pain and controlled her output anyway, successfully deceiving them about how much she could do. These days, she could gather electricity much faster – she'd been practicing. And she kept that a secret, despite the torture and the tests. They'd left her there in the chair for two hours while they discussed the confusing results, and she had sank into a dreadful, unavoidable sleep while waiting for them to come back and torture her some more. Then they'd come back in, take her somewhere else, and the cycle repeated. Always trying to push her body further, sometimes examining her brain and taking chunks of her flesh to study. They didn't waste anesthetic fo r that.

She'd spent the first three weeks trying to act compliant – anything to make them whip her a little less. Tired of begging and crying, she found her screams absent of tears these days, ending in silent sobs and shudders.

Every time they took her somewhere else, she kept her eyes down, forcing herself to scan the passageways for the exit. Sometimes she believed it was pointless. She did it anyway. She had to.

Now Y'Starren was being half-dragged along down the hall – she could hardly stand, let alone walk without help – when she caught the golden light of sunset coming in from one of the half-open rooms to the left. She guessed that that was the side of the building that looked out from the face of the cliff. It wasn't much of a clue for how to get out, but it was something. She bit her cheek and tried not to hope too much.

As they walked down the hall, her hands were manacled in corded shackles that attached to a battery that was supposed to "ground" her – draw the charge, for the scientists' safety. Having that much of her charge sucked out weakened her physically. She constantly felt dizzy and sick.

Unknown to them, however, she had been figuring out how to not charge it. After charging this box for a minute, she wouldn't have enough power left to really hurt any of them, though she could still deliver a painful static shock after a minute or two without the manacles. After some private practice on the very conductive bedframe, there was really nothing stopping her from bashing it into someone's head right now and then electrocuting them. Nothing except the strategy she'd chosen.

The fronts of both her legs and arms were covered in welts and dark red lines. Under those were a multitude of darker purple ones. The stab and pinch wounds had healed a long time ago, but a reopened weal on the top of her thigh, one of the worst spots they had targeted that day, was dripping a mixture of blood and some watery substance. It trickled down to her ankle and left tiny spots where her heel touched the floor at each step, and it itched. The scientist that sometimes cleaned up her wounds, Menyth, hadn't seemed to notice this one, and she didn't dare draw attention to them openly. When she did, Yeckswem tended to punish her even more for it. He clearly didn't like the other scientists noticing the marks of his brutality. It was better to ignore it.

As usual, the scientists that passed eyed her openly with a mixture of disgust and concern, though most seemed to be more interested in her charging ability. While Y'Starren had started to see them as sort of ... the same as anybody else, some bad, some good, they clearly saw her as some kind of otherworldly specimen.

As she stepped the last weary step up a flight of stairs, she paused at the top. Suddenly she recognized the hall. Yeckswem was watching her, so she cast her eyes down with her now-typical depressed stare, but stealthily scanned the area through her peripheral vision.

Let this be real ... She cursed under her breath.

"Repeat it." Yeckswem put a hand on her shoulder and tilted her chin up with a jab of his thumb.

She blinked away, refusing to look at him.

"It's nothing," she said, finding her voice hoarse.

He reached for his pocket, where he kept the blazing line.

"I just said 'horizons,'" Y'Starren said in a low voice. "Alright? Gonna whip me for that?"

"Why 'horizons'?" Yeckswem said, pausing with his hand in his pocket.

"It's a Bane ... " She hesitated. He wasn't going to believe her that that was a Bane curse. "It's an idiom for 'I'm tired,'" she said.

He grunted and assented.

There were still too many guards around, and there were two at the door she and Merreth had been let in over two months ago. But the door was there, and she knew where it went. Could she escape this way later? She went over and over in her mind how to get out. Left from the cell, down the hall, take a right, up the stairs, out the door.

Too many variables.

If she was going to escape, she needed to do it now. But she was out of electricity – they'd drained her repeatedly throughout the day. She stared at the door, clenching her fists.

This might be her last chance.

As Y'Starren was trying to strategize, she was unexpectedly shoved sideways into a room and crowded in by an unusually large horde of scientists. And in the room, waiting expectantly by a huge machine and flanked by two guards, was Mainmwim.

There was also a more rudimentary chair, with the ever-present restraints at the armrests and chair legs, and on either side of it was what Y'Starren now recognized as a massive battery with a bunch of cords going out through the wall, and a bunch more going into the computers across the back and middle of the room.

Y'Starren slumped, then fell to her knees on the floor. Her legs ached, her skin stung and burned all down the front of her legs where she'd been struck repeatedly throughout the day, and her hands tingled from how much electricity she'd been forced to push through them. They were blackened on the skin and so tired they were going numb.

She found herself hyperventilating. She couldn't do another test.

"What's wrong?" Mainmwim said.

Y'Starren gritted her teeth and glared at him as he came closer. Someone was about to hurt her and make her get up. But she couldn't get up.

She saw Yeckswem coming from the left and clenched her shoulders as she saw him take the weapon out of his pocket. She gasped as the metal cut across her back. Her cuffed hands shot up to protect her head as she shuddered, waiting for the rest of the whipping.

"Rise, pissant," Yeckswem said.

"But I ... " Y'Starren shuddered, ducking her head again as she said, "I can't stand."

Mainmwim walked closer and reached out a hand in her direction. She stiffened as he put a hand over her forehead, thumb crooking under her eyebrow as he pushed her head back to see her face.

"I asked, what's wrong?" he repeated.

She gritted her teeth, meeting his eyes.

"I can't do any more today," she whispered. "Please. I can't take any more. It won't do any good. I can't do any more."

Her body shook as silent tears ran down her face. When he let her head go, she lifted her manacled hands to cover and wipe her eyes. As she did, the scientists went quiet – usually a clue that they were communicating nonverbally while she was too busy dealing with the effects of whatever they'd last done to her to pay attention.

"Alright." Mainmwim put a hand on her head, which now had the hair cropped short like the other subjects. "You can do it either with or without more pain."

"No." Y'Starren found wrath exploding out of her. "No, I can't! What about 'I can't do it' don't you understand?"

"Give her the line," Mainmwim said.

She choked back a cry as the metal snapped into her bare upper arm, recoiling toward the wall. She shuffled until she was leaning against it, pressing her right arm and temple against it, grimacing. *Snap* – it slit her skin open with a sting that made her scream through her teeth. *Snap. Snap. Snap.* Her screams grated against her throat and rattled the tube-shaped ceiling lights.

"You can either cooperate," Mainmwim was saying. "Or ... " Yeckswem continued to lay into her with the line.

She held her breath. She didn't want to scream. It hurt.

I'm going to kill you, she kept thinking. She used to think about killing them every night, but now she was too tired to feel the old rage. It was just an automatic comfort thought. She'd never be able to kill them.

A harder lash broke her silence, and her scream reached each of the four corners in the ceiling, echoing with each consecutive one.

As he paused, she panic-planned, eyes darting around for resources. And then she saw the test equipment and realized something.

"I'll try!" she screamed. "Fuck you, I never said I wouldn't try!" She sobbed as he hit her again, not stopping.

Her breath sucked in with a choking sound, the tail end of a cry she was trying not to release.

Y'Starren had been practicing, and she knew a few more things about electricity from paying attention to the Chazans, who still assumed that she hadn't picked up on any of the technical jargon they used.

A human could be killed by as little as nine volts as long as there was enough amperage behind those nine. Pulsing the magic could cause some kind of additional danger, though she hadn't figured out exactly what.

And Y'Starren could release magic in a little less than a tenth of a second. As the line cut into her arm again, she focused the magic into it and up into Yeckswem's hand, hitting his thumb and then his upper arm, which jerked back. He let out a cry of pain.

"You dare to – "

Y'Starren struggled to her feet.

"I said I'd try!" she screamed.

Yeckswem gripped the line even tighter now, face looking almost blue with cold rage.

"Penalty of line – " he started, raising it, but Mainmwim cut him off.

"Wrong is you, Yeckswem," he said. "Charges it." He pointed to the chair, addressing Y'Starren now. "Charger, charge it."

Y'Starren knew the drill by now. She groaned and got to her feet painfully, arm throbbing as the movement broke open one of the welts. The scientists closed in around her.

"You don't have to restrain me!" she snapped, grabbing the correct electrodes from each of the batteries, one in each hand. "You want me to charge it? Watch me." *I'll fuckin' charge it alright.*

The battery on the right was full of charge. They were probably going to see how much she could draw from that one, and how quickly. Their experiments had started to revolve around the idea of mimicking her body as a man-made, more controllable biological battery. And they definitely thought she was too stupid to understand that, but she'd picked it up.

And she was going to surprise them.

She took a deep breath, and it shuddered on the way out as she pulsed the tiny bit of electricity left in her body into the empty battery. Scientists were rushing to the panels to watch their little test play out in real time. She found a genuine, though malicious, grin coming naturally to her face for the first time in months.

Then she pulled the charge – every drop of it – into her body in a split second.

Hell yeah.

Back to normal. This was how she'd felt after a week of walking through thunderstorms – though after all this practice, she could probably suck in much more.

She dropped the electrodes and turned around, lifting her hands and spreading her fingers. Electricity jumped over the fingers of each hand.

"No – restrain it!" Mainmwim ordered, backing toward the door. His guards moved toward Y'Starren, and she snapped her fingers at them, glaring into their black eyes with her fiery orange stare.

They hesitated.

"Range of arc is but three inches," Yeckswem said, approaching her with a grim, set look.

As he raised the line to begin whipping her with it, she grabbed his hand and pushed it toward his waist, stepping up to him and looking into his eyes. Then she squeezed and sent the electricity straight through just his thumb. She didn't let go, but sent through three pulses, making him scream.

If a scientist was its own species, its resting state would be one of observation. Y'Starren was counting on this as she watched Yeckswem crumple and the other scientists either pulling out tasers or backing away. Someone was already in the hallway screaming for the guards. Y'Starren strode forward quickly, relying on the intimidation factor.

Two scientists with tasers blocked her way.

"Yeah, go ahead, tase me. I love it," she said.

At their hesitation, she extended both her arms. Looking at each other with disbelief on their faces, they did what she said and the tasers struck into her arms. She sucked the energy in, though it jolted a little harder than Yeckswem's taser. Then she put her hands on both of their shoulders, enjoying their horrified expressions, and shocked them through the necks.

At this point, the other scientists in the room had hastily picked up makeshift weapons.

She pushed the other two out of her way and stumbled right into a rubber-gloved hand on her chest, with several more similarly-clad guards coming up behind them. She'd noticed these suits; they were called hazmat suits and were mostly made out of rubber. She ripped the mask up and plunged her hand into the guard's face, letting out a bolt of electricity so hard that he shot backward with the force, knocking into the other guys and buying her some time to flee.

She absolutely did, running straight for the exit. The guards there actually looked terrified, but they raised what looked like more tasers in her direction.

"Hold! Hold!" Chazans behind her shouted.

That meant to not tase her, which Y'Starren thought was a good idea for them. She ran at them.

"Hurt or pass?" she shouted at them.

“Pass! Pass!” The one on the left scrambled out of the way, but as she took hold of the doorknob, he pushed on the door, beckoning at his companions, who were almost at Y’Starren’s heels, squeaking along awkwardly in the hazmat suits. The one she had hit hard was still motionless on the ground.

Don’t look back, she told herself. She’d known this would happen. It had to happen.

She hit both guards – slapped them on the hands, sending electricity up hard and fast. And they collapsed. As they fell, she shoved them out of the way, yanking open the door, and when she came outside onto the balcony that she and Merreth had come in by months ago, she jumped over it onto the cement below, and ran into the forest as fast as she fucking could.

***

Y’Starren had been running for only a few minutes before she couldn’t anymore. Her lungs burned, and her heart pounded so hard it was the only thing she could feel. And her legs, once welted and bruised, were now also ripped up, practically flayed by the underbrush. She tumbled down and leaned against a tree, legs stinging so bad she almost forgot the pain in her ribs from the stitch in her side.

“You fuckers,” she panted through ripped vocal chords. “Fuck you so much.”

She lifted a middle finger over her head in their direction, vaguely.

She could still hear them. They had run out after her.

Now, as she sat there panting, she heard this terrible whirring, chopping sound like a hundred knives on cutting boards all at once, and she saw something out of the top of her vision, and looked up. A black thing like a massive bee was up there, flying about a hundred feet overhead.

“Oh, fuck me ... ” she whispered. “They really can fly.”

She was up and running again in a moment, and this time, she lunged down toward the canyons, regardless of what barbarian tribes might be down there using the water.

What started off as a high rocky streamlet, which she tramped alongside as fast as she could go without passing out, got deeper and deeper, till she found herself in a gorge between two cliffs, only going deeper in. She kept going, heart still hammering in her chest.

It was almost more about what she'd left behind than what would happen if she was caught again. Maybe they were still behind her, she thought. She looked back, but there was nothing.

She slowed as she reached a place where the stone above her met. It opened up again a little ahead, so she kept going cautiously. She hated the trapped sensation she was starting to feel. But if they were looking for her from above, maybe this was a good thing.

She finally trudged up to the side of a pool of water that had gathered in a wider place in the canyon, by a tiny drizzling waterfall.

She sat by the fall, dipped her cropped head under it for a moment, and let the cold water run over her face for a wonderful moment. Then she got a headache and had to stop.

Something about cold water always made her feel clearer and happier. It reminded her that there was more to life than whatever funk she was stuck in. Even if they caught her again, even if they dragged her back and used the line on her till she was left with no skin on her at all, she'd still have gotten here. She'd still have gotten to drink waterfall water and sit on the smooth gravel in this tiny oasis of a cave, watching the beautiful ripples and bubbles from the waterfall gushing outward into the pool, which stilled again before it reached her toes. The water was perfectly clear, and the moss that reached out from the wall was soft and cold under her ears. She turned her head and kissed it, then laughed.

She leaned her head against it and closed her eyes, just for a second.

***

When she woke up, she was freezing.

If she didn't get some help, she was going to die of chill and the minor wounds she was covered in. Her legs were like solid rocks that ached like a motherfucker. She wouldn't get very far without food and warmth, but there was no one but barbarians out here.

She tried to get up, and it felt like her skin ripped open all down her lègs and arms and she screamed in pain, hitting the rock wall she'd slept against. It burned. Exposing her back to the cold breeze had reminded her of how soaked she was across the back of her scanty jumpsuit. She stared up into the canyon opening at the cold white stars in the black night. It was so cold.

Then she heard voices nearby, and she stiffened. They had that unmistakable throaty accent of the barbarians. She had to get out of here. She tried again to get up, but her weak legs gave out before she got halfway up. She cursed softly, tears springing to her eyes. After all this work, to get bumped off by barbarians ... It was just not fair. She dragged herself a little ways away from the waterfall, into the shadows, gritting her teeth and holding her breath every time she moved so she wouldn't cry out in pain.

There were soft splashes as whoever it was waded through the last canyon bottleneck before Y'Starren's hiding place. One of them was holding a torch. She grimaced, leaning her head against the stone.

They spoke softly, moving toward her. They'd obviously heard her and had been close enough to tell that she was nearby. There were two of them, one of them dangling a dead rabbit from his left hand, with knives and arrows stuck into his rope belt. For a moment, she was jealous. They looked so calm, like they really had their lives together. The man to the right with the torch suddenly lowered it and pointed at Y'Starren, who cursed again.

The man raised his eyebrows, lifting a hand toward Y'Starren, then beckoned at her.

"No, thanks, I'm good over here," she said, and her voice betrayed her with a quaver. It was so obvious that she'd cried repeatedly today, and was about to do it again. "Dammit," she squeaked, and her breaths shuddered.

The man handed his torch to his partner. They spoke to each other in soft, guttural tones, slightly different from those of the last Warminds she had come across. Maybe these were a different tribe. She noticed, now that she thought about it, that they had hair. They had chopped it at the sides and then braided all the rest of their hair over the top of their scalp down to the nape.

These must be the Grass People, she thought. She was pretty sure she was in their territory by now, and they certainly weren't Warminds.

The man now showed her his hands, empty, eyes wide as if he was trying to make her understand something. He spoke in a very expressive tone, enunciating clearly, like that was going to help. Unlike the Warmind dialect, not a word of it made a lick of sense to her.

But the man was moving closer, and he reached out and touched her leg gently. She flinched and hissed in pain, and he jerked back, looking at his hand, rubbing his fingers together, then rubbing them on his pants. Looking alarmed, he started speaking more rapidly both to his friend and to her, then stood up, reaching out a hand to her insistently, shaking it and beckoning with his fingers when she hesitated. His tone wasn't threatening, but neither was Yeckswem's half the time.

She didn't want to go, but it was better than dying here, which she knew she would do if she didn't get some help.

She took the hand, and nearly collapsed after she was on her feet. He looped an arm around her back and pulled her toward the light, supporting her every time she stumbled.

Bare feet slipping on the rocks, they guided her out of the canyon.

As she walked, the stone evened out under her. In some places, the stone felt like it had been chipped into the shape of stairs here and there, and gravel and moss had been scuffed away to create an easy way to walk up and out of the canyon.

As they did, she heard a pleasant sound – the sound of laughing, and an old man humming. Then the man would snort with laughter, pause, and begin singing again. People were talking softly at the top of the canyon.

On top of the bluff over the river, barbarians sprawled around a fire, many on bedrolls made of skins and woolen blankets. There was a small cabin off a ways into the forest, embraced by a rocky outcropping above it.

Grass surrounded the worn places near the fire, and a couple children that looked to be about eight and ten were playing there by the bluff.

Y'Starren slipped and nearly fell to her knees on the way there, but the barbarian caught her, making a comment to his partner, who just grunted a single-syllable response.

In the light of the fire, her bright orange hair and eyes would be much more visible. She waited for someone to point at it, call her a witchling, and get ready to sacrifice her, but none did.

As her features were illuminated, their eyes grew round and excited, and they pointed to her. Even the man carrying her squinted at her, touched her hair, and looked down into her eyes, but then she staggered and nearly fell. He barely caught her, saying the same word – "Duilagh-duilagh" – several times like an apology.

Somehow she expected to hear someone cursing at her for falling and feel the line cutting into her skin. She jerked around, thinking she heard it hiss behind her. A moment later, she realized she was hyperventilating, staring into the barbarian's eyes as he stroked her cheek, saying something gently.

He lowered her onto a pile of blankets close to the fire, which someone that looked very much like him, probably his little brother, rolled off of for him.

Her eyes widened, but she was getting dizzy and her hands were clammy and cold. The cuts all over her body had given her a fever again. This wasn't the first time her injuries had led to a fever, but this was the first time someone had looked startled and concerned instead of pissed at her for it.

"Look, I didn't mean to," she said, trying to get up, but the barbarian pushed her back onto the blankets, saying something else. "I'll get out of your hair. I know barbarians don't like weaklings."

The barbarians responded in their foreign dialect as if they were having a normal conversation.

She turned her face away, mind a whirling mixture of relief and terror, curling in on the less cut-up side of her body. She felt slightly less vulnerable when she looked into the fire.

The barbarians let out a laugh, with an "Ah!" The way people sound when they say "Called it!"

The man who had helped carry her back sat down near her with his little brother, while his friend with the meat took it away somewhere. The man touched her hair, and she flinched, hands close together like they had been in the manacles so that they didn't yank and bruise the wrists. That was going to be embarrassing till she could break that habit.

"Sh-sh-sh ... " He stroked her hair comfortingly.

"Don't touch the hair." She shivered.

She realized she was trembling like a leaf. Probably the chill.

He spoke to her while some of the others gathered around, and the others went back to their conversations, though their eyes drifted to her with a great amount of curiosity. These people were blazing tall, she noticed, with powerful-looking legs and chests. The young man who had carried her up had a wispy, cropped beard and a quick smile that vanished the moment he focused back on Y'Starren.

He showed her a piece of cotton cloth – clearly a rarity here, since everyone except her was dressed in either wool or skins – and a small kettle of steaming water, and told her something about all that, then asked, "Gu leor?"

"Look, man, I speak Bane," she said.

He said more words, then asked again – "Gu leor?"

Biting her cheek, she shrugged doubtfully in response. Then he put the cloth on her leg and she flinched and grabbed his hand.

"Like I can't clean my own wound," she said.

He started pointing and talking about the different cuts on her body, asking his tribe members about it, and they came closer, eyes widening as more wounds were revealed.

Y'Starren only realized she was slipping into some kind of dazed sleep when she felt the touch of the cloth on her leg and she flinched.

"Blazes," she whispered.

"Duilagh," he said.

He wasn't rough – in fact, he was gentler than her own mother would've been, and spoke softly as he cleaned her wounds with his brother's help. Occasionally he chuckled and bantered with his brother. As he wiped dirt that was stuck to the wounds on the tops of her legs, he asked her questions. She gathered he was asking why she was so injured.

"Because some people don't have a conscience," she said.

He replied with a few bemused words.

"I don't know, do you?"

He looked at her with an odd smile, then shook his head and chuckled. She smiled. Neither of them understood each other.

Finally, he sighed and tossed the cloth onto the grass, pouring some of the warm water from the kettle on his hands to rinse them. He smiled at her, then looked up at the sky, leaning back onto his elbows. He made a comment that sent his brother into a fit of giggles.

Y'Starren's shudders of pain and terror had decreased to slower breaths now, and her tired heart beat slower and slower as she leaned back, wrapping the wool blankets around herself. She fell asleep to the sound of the tribe members talking around her.

***

Y'Starren spent another week there with the tribe. They didn't seem to mind that she was a Bane or a witchling. They didn't seem to care what she did, but simply shared their food when they ate, offered her water, and let her sleep in the extra blankets by the fire until her wounds were so healed that they were down to lines of scabs and green and purple bruises. Her skin didn't burn and sting anymore, though now that she wasn't being beaten across the healing skin, she could see a pattern of slanting red scars down her arms and legs.

She fended off those thoughts as she walked away, wearing the new wool tunic they'd insisted on giving her before she left. She didn't understand, but she bowed many times to them and swore to them in her own language that if she could ever help them in return, she would.

Now if she wanted to make it back to Baneon before Wackee was expelled and forced to go to Wenterglen, she had to walk all night and all day without stopping. She would get to Seechatee in the late night tomorrow, and take a night's rest and beg some food off them. They'd probably remember her and give her something.

The entire night, as she walked above the river on the same path Merreth had taken her by before, she imagined what would happen if everything went wrong. She kept trying to tell herself to focus, but all she could think was what could happen.

She took a massive detour around the Warmind territory and left the riverbank, having no flask and no food, hoping to still reach Seechatee that night.

By dusk, her legs were giving out every few minutes, and she had to stop.

***

Woken up by raindrops falling on her bare legs, Y'Starren got up as the grayest blues of morning were peeking up in the east. It rained all through the early hours, hard. She was soaked through the dirty outfit they'd made her wear at the facility, not to mention the thick woolen tunic laying over that. She forced herself to walk quickly to stay warm.

As she strode into Seechatee, she recognized a couple of kids that noticed her, pointed, and then ran. Her family had been at Seechatee last, and she couldn't help passing through the town on her way – she needed some food and water, at least. And a cloak would go a long way, if anyone was that kind.

The ten or so cottages in Seechatee crushed upward into the mountainside like they were trying to get away from the road, which doubled as a flash flood zone right now. Bare feet slipping through the rocky mud, she sighed as she plodded up the hill toward the homes that doubled as tiny shops. She was standing in what was essentially a river as the townspeople all kind of gathered around her, frowning and muttering amongst themselves.

"Alright, I know it wasn't all melons and roses when we left, but let's not start off angry," she said.

A man pointed at her and she flinched, then clenched her fist. She wasn't going to let people hurt her anymore.

"You're supposed to be dead," he said.

" ... Excuse me?" Y'Starren said. "Are you the one that blazing reported us?"

"Looks dead enough," another villager said. She was the baker.

"I am not dead!" Y'Starren protested.

"What are you doing, walking in here bald, half-naked – " The baker's eyes wandered to her legs momentarily, disgusted. "And blazing ... not dead?"

"Horizons ... " Y'Starren glared. "All I wanted was a little bit of water. Is that too much to ask?" Apparently it was. They were balling up fists, grabbing weapons, and moving toward her.

"Still a reward out," someone called. "Do this village a favor and get rid of the Kill Touch before she gets strong enough to kill us too."

Y'Starren's heart pounded hard, but she raised her hand over her head. She was terrified. She snapped her fingers, electricity cracking against her hand like the tail of a whip. It didn't hurt her, but it sure would hurt them.

"I am strong enough to kill you," Y'Starren shouted. "Now back off. I don't want to hurt you."

She really didn't. There were a few teenagers in the crowd, and one kid that couldn't have been more than ten years old. She didn't want to have to choose between her life or theirs.

But instead of backing off, the baker ran at her with a pitchfork and the tip slammed into her gut, knocking her onto her knees. It was dull, so it probably only made a harsh bruise, but it still hurt like fuck. She gasped for breath, struggling as she was lifted from her hands and knees in the mud by the arms.

"We need that reward money," someone sighed resignedly.

"I don't understand!" Y'Starren shouted. "Why would there be a reward out? I'm an investigator!"

"It's the investigators is lookin' for you," the man on her right said.

The muddy incline was now absolutely full of people, and the rain was pelting down harder and harder again as she was dragged in front of the village elder.

Y'Starren had a lightning ball in her stomach that she was gripping onto with all her might.

The village elder was only about forty, a perfectly bald man with a long beard and a massive build. He squinted down at Y'Starren.

"Elder?" Y'Starren scoffed. "More like younger."

He punched her in the stomach, and she would've fallen if the guys on either side of her hadn't held her up by the arms. She choked in a breath and struggled to stay on her feet. Apparently banter didn't work with these people either. She missed people that appreciated her jokes.

"Keep that tongue in check," the elder said. "Or you'll get a beating."

"Or you could just control yourself."

"That's it." He straightened up. "We're delivering you dead. Martha, get me my spear!"

Y'Starren ground her teeth, taking one last look around at the villagers. There were about twenty-five of them, most older than ten, but there was a kid that looked like he was about eight. If it wasn't for the hope of saving Wackee, she'd have let them kill her. But ...

"Fine," she whispered. "You asked for it."

She ground her feet into the rivulet of a road and channeled her magic down. "I'll try not to kill you."

The electricity from the battery plus nine days of collecting magic eased out from her feet and into everyone standing in the middle of the rain-soaked village.

They screamed and some fell to their knees. Nobody was touching her now.

"She's trying to kill us!" someone screamed.

"If I was trying to kill you, you'd be dead," she growled. This time, she wasn't bluffing.

They staggered toward her.

Suddenly she felt an unusual amount of clarity and calm. She felt like she was surrounded by a bunch of children. And then she was punched in the gut. Hard.

Power exploded out of every part of her body as the pain hit, then the panic and nausea took her to her hands and knees. It was all too much to focus past. She couldn't pull the magic back – she was too disoriented to make it obey her.

When she finally managed to stop it, she looked up from her position on all fours, choking in painful, tiny breaths. They were all on the ground – all over the road in the mud and rivulets. The baker. The young man she now recognized as the barber. She ran a hand through her short, damp hair, remembering the Chazan barber for a moment.

Up and down the road from her, the citizens of Seechatee lay either seizing and going blue, or just completely still. She clutched at her throat, trying not to puke.

What have I done? she thought.

She stood up slowly, rubbing the mud off her hands and onto her bare thighs.

"Anybody else?" she shouted.

Her voice echoed off the mountains behind her. She stepped forward toward the elder's house.

Might as well loot.

***

Y'Starren pulled her cloak further over her face as she waited at the gate of Strangers' College. It was a massive castle, with brilliant lights in a huge plaza down the road, and the walls were black and sharp against the sky.

"Oh, good, she's still here," she heard the guard mutter nervously. "Yeah, she's right over there – " he started to call to someone else, when a boy with spiky orange hair rushed past him with an excited whoop, and dashed out the barred side door, and embraced Y'Starren so hard it took her breath away and pressed in on old bruises.

She'd told them she was looking for Wackee, and that's all she'd told them. Somehow, without seeing her face, he'd known who she was.

She wrapped her arms around him.

Months of hoping for this moment had made it seem unreal. Impossible, even.

The sensation of his smaller body wrapped around hers was completely different.

But he still smelled like rain and dog, as always.

"You're alive." He let go just as suddenly, eyes shiny with a frank smile on his face. "I thought ... "

He was supposed to be angry – she'd told him she was just going to get a job in Wenterglen, and then had disappeared for almost three months.

"You're not mad at me?" she said.

"Why would I be mad?" He frowned, putting his hands on his hips.

Y'Starren narrowed her eyes at him, knowing he tended to say much less than he was thinking. He should definitely be mad at her. Their parents had died, and then she had immediately abandoned him. His face showed no resentment, and no grief either. He appeared as clear and cheery as he always had been.

"Might as well not give you a reason," she said. "Wanna walk?" He shrugged and followed her.

"Wait – you can't just – it's past closing," the guard stammered.

"Come on, Lackee, you know you love me." Wackee winked at him.

Her brother was charming as hell. He knew it, and he used it. The guard grumbled and sat down to wait till they got back.

"So, I heard you were wanted ... " Wackee said.

Y'Starren shook her head and smiled.

"You always hear things you have no right to know about."

The path pushed them closer together as they walked through a damp-smelling cleft in the mossy rock. Sunlight caught them full in the face on the other side. Wackee still hadn't spoken after several minutes, so Y'Starren finally broke the silence.

"It's okay, you know," she said.

He didn't respond.

" ... If you're mad," she added.

He sent her a small smile and stepped forward down onto the rocky trail.

"I told you, I'm not mad."

"Yeah, but I ... "

"Let's go this way." He turned off the road and led her up a leaf-covered, rocky hill that was difficult for her travel-worn feet to grip. Hearing her panting, he reached back a hand to help her. His hands had gotten bigger – he'd bulked up a bit, actually. "Look. I want to show you."

Climbing up onto the rocks at the top of the hill, she was able to look down into the ravine they'd just climbed out of. It was getting a little dark, so the area below looked creepy and magical – the bases of the trees were black, the mist blue, and the bits of sunlight left over as it set graced the branches, turning them all g old.

"No matter how long I stay here, the glamor of the forest is gone," he said, sitting down on the stone and dangling his feet off, kicking them a little. "And I don't know how to find it again."

Y'Starren sat down next to him, looking at him out of the corner of her eye. She could see him, staring into the darkness and looking anxious. Sad. Then he looked up at her with that half-forced smile.

"I'm sorry for not coming back," she said softly. "I tried. I was afraid of bringing assassins down on you."

"I figured." He shrugged. "Let me guess. You were trying to protect me." He glanced at her bare arms and winced. Y'Starren knew they were visibly scarred and still bruised. "That looks like somebody hurt you pretty bad. Tell me you killed 'em."

"I ... I'm not sure," she said. "It really doesn't matter. I got away."

He pursed his lips and scowled into the darkness.

"Fine. I'll kill 'em for you."

Y'Starren huffed. She hoped he wouldn't try something like that, and she certainly wasn't going to enable it.

"Here," she said. She reached into a stolen purse and pulled out a stolen coin pouch. She opened it, gold coins spilling out into her palm. "Use this to pay your tuition."

He frowned. " ... Are you coming to school too, then?"

She shook her head, standing up and dusting her hands off.

"No," she said. "People know I exist. If it gets out to the guild in Wenterglen, I'm toast. I have to wait for all this to blow over."

"All this, meaning?"

Y'Starren really didn't want to tell him that she'd accidentally massacred an entire village. She looked down at her toes, scraping lichen off the rock with her feet.

"I guess you'll hear about it eventually," she said.

Wackee stood up with a very sober expression, looking like he was trying to read her face.

"So, you're going to leave me again?" he said.

She clenched her teeth.

"I'm sorry," she said. "I don't want you to be lonely ... like me."

He wrapped her tightly in his arms. She didn't want him to let go, squeezing him back.

"Come back to me, okay?" he said, voice breaking.

"Fuck, I ... " She felt a tear fall down her cheek. "I will."

About the Author

Havilah has been writing whump since she was a child, to cope with abuse, trauma, and her autism. She writes to shed light on patterns of abuse and underlines the courage of those who endure through suffering and recovery. She portrays heroic survivors to send a powerful message: You are beautiful.

Chipped

Lux Thorn

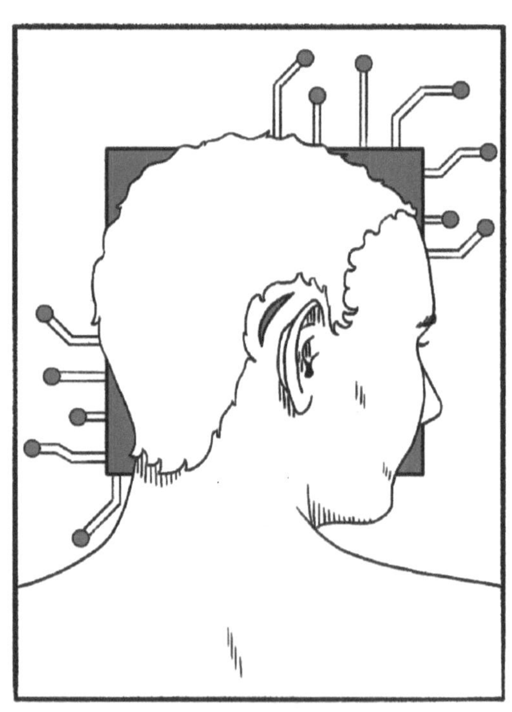

Cover Design by Nicole Alessi

Cover Illustration by Hen Towers

Also By the Author

As Lux Thorn:

The Mind Games Series

Obscure

Unseen

Defect

Villain

Protector

As Z.J. Cannon:

The Iron Bound Series

The Nic Ward Series

The Hound of Hades Series

As Zoe Cannon:

The Internal Defense Series

Short Story Collections

Contents

CONTENT WARNINGS

This story contains the following content:

- Heavy violence, including knives, guns, blood, torture, and electrocution
- Mind control
- Institutionalized slavery
- Toxic relationship
- Major character death

If this book isn't for you, no worries! But if it is, we hope you enjoy this story about a torturer and his rebel...

1

Ryland hated when prisoners pissed themselves.

Blood he could handle. Blood was just part of the job. If he wanted to get information out of a prisoner, chances were someone was going to have to bleed for that information, and it wasn't going to be him. But the acrid smell of urine was enough to make him regret the hasty muffin he had grabbed on his way to work. He should have stuck with his usual breakfast of black coffee.

The prisoner quivered against the steel cuffs that bound his wrists and ankles to the chair. Wetness spread across his pants. Pungent liquid dripped down onto the smooth gray concrete of the floor to dilute the small pool of blood there. The man's eyes remained locked on the bloody knife in Ryland's hand.

Funny – he'd handled electricity just fine. Better than fine – Ryland had brought in one of the techs to make sure the current was strong enough, he'd resisted so well. But as soon as Ryland had started cutting, the man had fallen apart like a wet tissue. Ryland could usually tell which methods would break any given prisoner the fastest. Call it a sixth sense. It wounded his pride when he was wrong.

Ryland ripped off the remaining electrodes, taking no notice of the prisoner's flinch each time the sticky adhesive tore away from his skin. He wouldn't be needing those anymore. The knife in his hand was all he needed.

He brought it close to the trembling man's face, the tip nearly brushing his cheek. The man pulled back as far as he could, his eyes round, his cuffs rattling against the chair as he trembled.

"All I need," he said, "is the key to the cipher you created for the resistance."

His eyes still locked on the knife, the man shook his head weakly. "I didn't create that cipher." His voice was thin, desperate, trembling with the obvious lie. "It wasn't me. I told you."

Ryland lowered the knife until the tip was pointing at the floor directly in front of the chair. At the scrap of what had been the top half of the man's pinky finger, severed at the highest knuckle.

The man followed his gaze. The rattling increased.

One more finger ought to do it. Ryland sighed to himself. The thought of another gush of blood, of another round of piercing screams that had almost shattered his eardrum the first time, made him want to put the knife down and adjourn for a nap in his office – and it wasn't even lunchtime yet. At least the man didn't have any more piss in him.

He stared down at the bit of severed flesh. His stomach churned. Wasn't a single mutilation enough for one day?

He clenched his teeth. Not this again. This reticence, this ... *weakness.* None of this ever used to bother him – not the blood, not the screams, not whatever mangled mess he had to make of a prisoner before they gave up what he wanted. Not until he had started imagining Coop's face superimposed on the face of every prisoner in his interrogation room. Coop's blood. Coop's screams. Coop's severed finger on the floor.

Ryland dropped the knife at his feet. It landed with a clatter on the concrete.

"You've already lost one finger today," he said. "It seems excessive to take any more. Your wife, now ... she's still got a full set of ten. For now. She usually goes to the Sub Shack for lunch, right? If she follows her usual schedule, she should be getting there about, oh..." He made a show of checking his watch. "Half an hour from now." He laced his hands behind his back and leaned back casually, resting his weight on his back foot. "I'm willing to wait. How about you?"

Ryland's intuition had been wrong about this prisoner before. But not this time. With a strangled sob, the man hung his head. "Don't ... don't touch her." His voice was a thready whisper.

"I'm waiting," said Ryland.

When he looked up at Ryland, his eyes were dead. "You'll need to write this down."

***

On his way out for an early lunch, Ryland caught the sound of tuneless whistling behind him.

He only knew one person that bad at carrying a tune.

Ryland picked up his pace. The whistling stopped. "Interrogator Eskell!" a jolly voice called. "Just the man I was hoping to see."

Ryland briefly considered pretending he hadn't heard. Then turned to face his boss, Elmer Norby, a diminutive man with a baby face and lips perpetually puckered from kissing his own bosses' asses. Norby flashed him a smile. "How goes it with the Johnson interrogation?"

"Just finished with him. You'll have the cipher – as well as a few names he knew – this afternoon. After I celebrate with a long lunch." Ryland held Norby's gaze, silently daring the man to heap another urgent assignment on him immediately after this victory.

Norby's eyes fell to Ryland's cuff. He wrinkled his nose. "You might want to get yourself cleaned up first."

Ryland followed Norby's gaze. There was a single speck of blood on his cuff. Somehow, despite supervising a building full of interrogators, Norby still hadn't gotten the idea that interrogation was a bloody job. Probably because he got to sit behind his desk all day and keep his hands clean.

There was a time he used to meticulously check himself for blood before he left the building. Coop had always hated it when he showed up with traces of his work still on him. It reminded Coop of all manner of things he preferred not to think about.

"It was a hard interrogation," was all he said now.

"You've been going above and beyond lately." Norby gave him a hearty pat on the shoulder. Ryland held still and endured it. "That's exactly why I wanted to talk to you. I've got something that's about to make your life a lot easier."

Ryland, adept at reading prisoners, caught the not-so-subtle signs of strain in his boss's too-wide smile. He looked like someone trying to convince a kid that a cup of foul-tasting medicine was going to taste good.

"I'm sure you've found yourself wishing for an extra pair of hands from time to time," Norby continued, his voice painfully bright. "Someone to fill out your paperwork for you, or hold your ... tools ... in the interrogation room ... " He made the grimace he always did when he was forced to talk, however obliquely, about what actually happened during interrogations.

Ryland sighed. "Not another intern. The last one fainted at the sight of blood."

"You won't have that problem with this one!" Norby promised. "He's not an intern. He's something better. Obedient, highly trainable, and he'll never ask for a raise." He chuckled too hard at his own joke.

Ryland tried to parse this. When he worked it out, he stared. "Tell me you're not considering bringing a *chipped worker* into a secure facility."

A wince cracked Norby's smile. "It's no secret how you feel about chipped workers – "

"I'm not the only one. They're a security risk – that's been established. The technology isn't infallible." Chipped workers were the government's answer to a surfeit of rebels and a shortage of workers. The chip, inserted just behind the ear, promised to make a former rebel docile and obedient, with little memory of their past and no desire to rebel. By all accounts, they made highly useful factory workers, and chip failures were rare. But rare didn't mean nonexistent, and giving a potential time bomb free run of a factory was a far cry from setting one loose *here.*

Besides ... privately, Ryland found the idea grotesque. The fact that the technology existed to strip someone's past from them, their will, their *humanity*, was something he preferred not to think about.

"I took a careful look at the data before I agreed to this," Norby assured him. "The chips are a lot hardier than they used to be. Left alone, they'll keep working for a hundred years – longer than any chipped worker's lifetime. And there's no physically damaging the chip, short of shooting the worker in the head or shorting it out with enough electricity to stop their heart – and both of those would solve any problems before they started, wouldn't they?" He gave another too-loud chuckle.

"What about the effects on higher cognition?" Ryland asked. "There's a reason chipped workers are normally assigned to menial jobs. My work requires more than pulling a lever for ten hours a day."

"There have been major advances in the technology. The chips are not only more resilient, they have less of an effect on essential brain functions. That's why the technology division wants to do a trial run expanding the uses of chipped workers – and you're one of the first lucky beneficiaries." Norby's smile was back, even more strained around the edges now.

"I appreciate the offer," Ryland lied through his teeth, "but I'm sure someone else would appreciate it more. Assign this worker to someone else." Anyone else.

"You're considered the best equipped for this trial, because of your ... ability to respond quickly and decisively should the need arise." There came that grimace again.

"You mean I have a reputation for brutality," said Ryland. "Just in case I'm right and this worker is a security breach waiting to happen. I'd rather not take the risk in the first place."

"Consider this an additional job responsibility," said Norby, his smile dying away. "One that comes with some added benefits. I know you could use that extra pair of hands."

"You pay me to interrogate prisoners," said Ryland. "Not to be a test subject for the technology division. Tell me, how much extra funding did your bosses promise you for next year in exchange for signing us up as guinea pigs?"

Norby's smile faded. His cheeks went pink. "Well, it's too late to send him back now, so you may as well make the best – "

"Send him *back*? He's already here?"

"The technology division delivered him this morning," said Norby. "He's waiting in your office."

With a muttered curse, Ryland turned his back on his boss – he could worry about the ramifications of his rudeness later – and hurried down the hall toward his office.

A rebel with a head full of questionable technology. In *his* office, alone with a computer full of secure files. And he had been there *how* long?

But when he threw open the door to his office, there were two men waiting for him, not one. The first, wearing the blue uniform of the technology division, was sitting in Ryland's chair. He looked up with a frown. "It's about time. I've been waiting here since – "

He probably said more. Ryland didn't hear it.

He stared at the man standing in the center of the room, and forgot how to breathe.

The standing man was wearing a darker blue than the other, his shirt and pants rough and plain. His hair was shorn nearly down to the scalp. He stood with his arms pressed tightly to his sides, staring at a point just below his eye level. His face was expressionless, his eyes blank and glassy.

But Ryland remembered when those shorn curls had been long enough to hang into his eyes. He remembered that face creased with laughter, and blotchy with fury as he threw one of Ryland's blood-flecked shirts at his head. He remembered the softness of those lips on his, and those glassy eyes bright with adoration.

Coop, he mouthed, barely stopping himself from saying the name aloud.

Cooper Byrd. The rebel he had fallen in love with, even though he had known better. The rebel who had haunted Ryland since his arrest. Ever since Ryland had failed to save him – because trying to save him would have meant risking his own life.

2

The last time Ryland had seen Coop, they hadn't been speaking. Ryland hadn't looked at Coop as he had pulled his shirt back on, their planned liaison cut short because of yet another argument. When he had glanced up at Coop, Coop had been sitting on the edge of the narrow bed in the one-room apartment. Ryland could still picture his face as it had been that night, tight with anger, staring into Ryland's eyes as if daring Ryland to look away again.

He hadn't said a word – they were all done with words for that night, the familiar tense silence all that was left between them. But their arguments still echoed off the thin walls.

"You're never going to leave, are you?"

"I got us both new identities – good ones. A bank account that can't be tracked. I bought us a cabin, for god's sake, in a little town in the woods where no one will look for us." Ryland could still hear the defensiveness in his voice, could still feel the tightness in his throat. *"Is that not enough commitment for you? What more do you want?"*

"How about for you to actually do it?"

"It's not the right time."

Another image, burned into Ryland's brain: Coop's hair flying into his eyes as he shook his head. *"You've been saying that for months. It's never going to be the right time, is it? I don't think you want to give it up – the good job, the nice house, the secret boyfriend on the side. You don't care that you're paying for all that with the blood of my friends."*

"You mean your friends who are willing to let the world burn so long as it means people like me burn first? I thought we were done with that argument. I'm willing to give up everything for you. Isn't that enough?"

"Are you willing? Because you're sure not showing it."

Ryland had hurried out of the apartment with his shirt still half-buttoned, unable to face Coop's accusing gaze one second longer. In this neighborhood, there were no cameras – even an obvious rebel around here would have had to worry more about a stolen wallet than an arrest. Even the streetlights were broken. The anonymity was the reason they had chosen this place to rent for their illicit nights together. Still, Ryland had looked up and down the street as he turned away, looking for signs of Coop's people watching, looking for his own. Unsure which would be worse for both of them.

He had told himself not to look over his shoulder, but he had done it anyway. Coop had been there at the window, lips curled in disgust, judging Ryland's twitchiness about surveillance. As if he wasn't just as worried about being discovered with Ryland as Ryland was about being discovered with him. As if he wasn't ashamed of sharing a bed for two stolen nights a week with a man who wore an interrogator's uniform during the day.

Coop hadn't shown up for their next planned meeting. Ryland had assumed he was still angry. Until a fit of what he had thought was irrational fear had made him check the database at work, and he had seen Coop's name staring out at him from the screen like an accusation.

How many times since then had Ryland longed for one last look at Coop, one more glimpse of him to erase the terrible memory of those eyes full of bitter condemnation? Now, as the man who used to be Coop stared through him with empty eyes, Ryland regretted every time he had made that wish.

The tech sitting in Ryland's chair checked his watch. "There some kind of problem? Or will you go ahead and sign off that he's been delivered? The agreement says you're responsible for him during the standard workday. The facility is obligated to provide storage at night, and basic care on weekends and holidays.

If he dies, one of us will have to certify that it was natural causes, or there'll be a fine. Basic stuff." He held out a screen to Ryland. "I've got other places to be today, you know. I didn't expect to be here so long."

Ryland gave the screen a brief, distracted glance. Then his eyes were pulled back to the man with Coop's face, as if magnetized. "What's his name?" As if there was any question. As if he could possibly be mistaken.

The tech frowned. "The worker's? How the hell should I know? He probably doesn't even remember it. Call him whatever you like – he'll learn to answer to it." The man stood, holding out the screen more insistently.

"I'm Ryland," Ryland said to Coop's blank face. "Ryland Eskell." He searched those glassy eyes, and saw no hint of recognition.

"Hello," Coop said in a voice as flat as his face. "It's a pleasure to meet you." He held out his hand.

Coop had loathed the custom of shaking hands – *What's polite about being socially obligated to touch the hand the other guy probably scratched his ass with five minutes ago?* Ryland stared at the outstretched hand, and couldn't bring himself to take it. Would Coop's skin still feel the same – silky soft, like the luxurious sheets Ryland couldn't afford even on his salary?

The tech huffed. "There's no point in talking to them. Tell him what you want him to do, he'll do it. Better tell him to eat and sleep and piss too, or he'll work for three days straight before passing out in his own mess. But don't expect decent conversation." He pressed the screen into Ryland's hand. "Now, are we finished here, or ... "

Ryland, who had come in here ready to throw the chipped worker out on his ear, used his finger to sign without a word.

With a mutter under his breath that sounded like, *It's about time*, the tech hurried out the door and closed it behind him. And then it was just Ryland and Coop. Or Ryland and the thing that wasn't quite Coop. The thing that wasn't quite human.

Coop finally lowered his hand. He stood perfectly still, until Ryland had to squint to make sure he was breathing.

Ryland walked past him to his desk. He froze momentarily as his arm brushed Coop's. A bolt of electricity shot through him – sense-memory and repulsion wrapped into one. Coop didn't react.

Ryland slid into his chair. With a few quick keystrokes, he disabled the surveillance in his office. Then, still sitting, he swiveled to face Coop.

Coop was still facing the other way, staring at the closed door. "Hey," Ryland said softly. "Hey, look at me."

Instantly, Coop turned to face him, his glassy eyes locking on Ryland's face. A shiver crawled up Ryland's spine.

"Cooper," Ryland said. "Cooper Byrd."

A tiny crease between Coop's eyebrows marred the smooth expressionlessness of his face. "I'm sorry. I don't know what you mean."

"That's your name. You really don't remember?" How could a person forget an entire life? How could he forget his name, his dislike of handshakes, his loathing for the building he stood inside now? How could he forget the man who had shared his bed for two long years?

But the technology division had had almost a decade to perfect the chips. Tens of thousands of test subjects, from the early failures to the first successes to the man who stood in front of Ryland now.

It had never mattered to Ryland until it was Coop.

Even though Ryland knew better, he tried again anyway. "Coop." He whispered it the way he might once have in bed.

"Is that what you'd like to call me?" Coop's voice, soft and even, was the worst thing Ryland had ever heard.

Ryland stared into those eyes, and saw nothing. The man in front of him might as well have been a doll with a painted face. No – not a doll. A corpse. He looked dead, and maybe he was. Maybe the man Ryland had known was gone, killed by the thing sitting in his brain.

Maybe that was a kinder fate than if Coop had been trapped in there, lost in his own mind, screaming and unable to be heard.

Ryland shook away another shiver. He forced his eyes away.

Yes – Coop was dead. Better to think of it that way. The man in front of him wore his face and spoke with his voice, but that was all. Now if only Ryland could send him back, so he would only have to worry about his own memories haunting him. He already regretted signing, but of course, by now the tech was long gone.

His stomach growled, reminding him that he still hadn't had that lunch. His desire to go out and celebrate had fled. He would grab something quick from the cafeteria, and then he would get back to work. Since it was too late to send Coop – to send the *chipped worker* – back, he would do what Norby wanted, and use him as an extra pair of hands until he was numb to the sight of him.

He stood. "I'm getting lunch," he said, although he had a feeling he could have left his office without a word and the other man would not have felt a single shred of curiosity about where he had gone. "Don't touch anything while I'm gone." Belatedly, he remembered the tech's words. Coop – the chipped worker – wouldn't feed himself, which meant it was presumably Ryland's job to feed him. "You want anything?"

The voice that answered was just as soft as before, but this time, it held an unmistakable hint of mischief. "A handsome model in my bed and enough money that I never have to work again," he said, as Ryland froze, wide-eyed. "But if you're asking about *lunch*, I'd settle for ham and cheese."

It was the same joke he always used to make. Ryland used to tease him about it – *It's not funny the hundredth time, you know.* That was before he had known that someday he would give anything to hear it one more time.

It took Ryland a few seconds to find his voice. "What did you say?"

"I said I'd like ham and cheese, if you wouldn't mind," Coop said in his too-flat voice. The hint of mischief was gone.

"No. Before that. What did you say?"

But Coop only stared at him in confusion. His eyes were just as dead as they had been a moment ago.

The man had never made Coop's old joke, had he? Because he wasn't Coop.

It was just the same old ghost in Ryland's head, haunting him again.

Still, as he left, he looked over his shoulder. He could have sworn he saw Coop's eyes following him as he walked away.

3

The chipped worker couldn't still be Coop on the inside. His lack of expression as they walked into the interrogation room was the proof. Coop's face was blank, his stride steady, as he took in the stark concrete floor and the gleaming metal cabinets concealing an impressive array of tools. He didn't even react as his eyes fell on the prisoner cuffed to the metal chair at the center of the room.

This was her first interrogation. Her face still held more defiance than fear, which wasn't the case for most prisoners who had sat in one of these chairs for more than a couple of hours. Her only bruises were from her arrest – the note in her file explained that she had resisted. Ryland looked away from Coop long enough to take in her clenched fists, her rigid back, the snarl of fury on her face. All signs of a prisoner who thought raw anger would be enough to get them through what was coming.

Ordinarily, that sight would have cheered Ryland – more often than not, it meant an easy interrogation. But now it set his teeth on edge. He knew he could anticipate being cursed at and spat on before the prisoner's curses devolved into screams. And speaking of screams, there were likely to be plenty of those too. The angriest prisoners tended to be the loudest.

He looked over his shoulder at the door, contemplating simply walking back out of the room. Maybe he could knock off early for once. Between his victory this morning and the sixty-hour weeks he'd been working lately, he had earned it.

But that meant admitting defeat.

A small intake of breath from the prisoner made him realize he had stopped watching her. He was staring at Coop again, at that corpselike face. He turned back to the prisoner in time to see her anger shift to shock, then a sick horror. Not an uncommon reaction for prisoners who realized what was about to happen to them, but she wasn't looking at Ryland anymore.

She was looking at Coop.

"Cooper," she whispered.

So she had known him, then. Probably worked with him in the resistance. Absolutely fucking fantastic. Her horrified whisper grated on him as much as he imagined her screams would later. Speaking of sounds, why was the ventilation system so *loud* today? And the room was just slightly too hot, sending a prickly itch up his torso. Had someone messed with the temperature controls?

"Cooper," the prisoner repeated, louder this time. Her voice wasn't any less irritating at a normal volume. "Can you hear me?"

"He's not going to answer," Ryland said, his voice short. "He's – "

"Chipped," the prisoner finished for him. "I know that look. I know what it means." He expected a return to her snarling fury, a torrent of curses – all the old tired insults he had heard before. Instead, she lowered her head. "I'm sorry, Cooper. I wondered what had happened when you disappeared. I hoped it wasn't this."

Ryland snapped his fingers in front of her face. She flinched back.

"You're not here to talk to him," he reminded her. "You're here to talk to me." He shifted so he was standing between her and Coop. Then he stared down at her, crossing his arms, and willed himself not to look over his shoulder at Coop's unnatural stillness.

"Here's the situation," he said. "Everything you've heard about what happens in this building is considerably better than the reality. And I happen to be having a very bad day, so I'm not inclined to go easy on you."

She opened her mouth. He kept going before she could speak. Whatever she was going to say, it would only set his nerves jangling even more. How could her voice possibly be so annoying? And that *face.* Those beady little eyes, like a pig.

And what was going on with the temperature in here, anyway? The room felt even hotter now than it had a moment ago. A thin sheen of sweat coated his forehead.

"You were arrested breaking into a secure facility," he continued, "so don't try to deny anything. We have the video footage."

She tilted her head to the side. What was she ... oh, of course. She was still trying to look at Coop. He shifted again to block her view.

"Here's what I need from you," he said. "The names of all your co-conspirators – the three who escaped when we arrested you, plus anyone who helped you plan that little escapade of yours. If you give me everything – and I mean everything – you may just earn yourself a clean death instead of ending up like *him.*"

Finally, he stepped aside, giving her a view of Coop once more. He itched to look over his shoulder himself, but didn't.

She swallowed at the sight of him. "Cooper," she said again. "Come on, Cooper. You've got to be in there somewhere."

"Do you need something to help you focus on me and not him? Very well – I can manage that." Ryland stalked across the room and threw open one of the cabinets. The metal door hit the wall with a clang. "Pain has a way of focusing a person's attention, I've found."

He pulled out a pair of gleaming steel pliers, freshly disinfected. "We'll start with your fingernails," he said. "I'll give you a little break after each one. That will give you ten chances to start feeling more cooperative."

A shiver ran through the prisoner. She tucked her fingers protectively under her palms. "You're pathetic, you know that?" Her voice shook.

"Not the response I would have chosen." Ryland advanced on her, holding the pliers in one hand.

"You're not even going to try to talk to me first? You're just going straight to ripping out fingernails?" Her voice dripped with contempt, even as her eyes shone with fear. "Is brutality really the only tool you have?"

Coop used to ask him how he could live with himself. There had been times he would flinch away from Ryland's touch, saying he couldn't stand the feeling of those hands on his skin, knowing what they had done only hours before. Of course, when they were in bed, his conscience had never stopped him from begging for more.

Ryland's hand tightened around the pliers. He held them up in front of the prisoner's face, snapping them shut just to watch her flinch. That wasn't like him – he didn't enjoy a prisoner's fear unless he thought it meant the prisoner was that much closer to breaking. But now he took satisfaction in the way she drew back from him – and, most of all, in her silence.

"I've got plenty of tools in my toolbox," he informed her. "You'll see a lot of them, unless you start cooperating soon. As for my methods, you wouldn't have been assigned to me if my boss thought simple persuasion would be enough to get through to you. I've got a reputation in this building. Most of those stories you heard? They were about *me.*" He flashed her a joyless smile.

What's wrong with me? Coop had asked one night as they lay in bed, turning his head away from Ryland. *I'm sick in the head. I've got to be. This – what we're doing – it's sick.*

"Hold her hand in place," Ryland snapped to Coop. "We'll start with the left. Straighten her fingers for me."

Cooper showed no hesitation as he walked over and grabbed her hand. She looked up at Coop, then quickly away, her eyes wet. "You don't have to do this," she said to him. "You can fight it."

"He doesn't know who you are," Ryland reminded her.

This was when he would normally give the prisoner one more chance to cooperate before things got messy. But what was the point? She wasn't going to give him anything yet. He knew it. She knew it. Probably even the walking corpse that was Coop knew it.

He gripped the prisoner's pinky nail with the pliers, digging the tip deep under the nail bed. He watched Coop from the corner of his eye, ready to react if Coop let go, if he fought. But Coop kept holding her hand in place. Of course he did. He was a dead thing, an automaton. All he knew was how to obey.

In one quick jerk, Ryland yanked the nail out by the root.

The soundproof walls deadened the prisoner's scream, but not enough. Her blood coated Coop's hand. Coop flinched away. His throat worked. Ryland watched him, holding his breath.

But Coop kept holding on. He kept obeying. What Ryland had seen hadn't been a bit of his old self coming through – only an instinctive reaction to the blood and the screams. And who *wouldn't* react to that?

But chipped workers weren't supposed to react to anything.

No. He had to stop this – whatever *this* was, wherever these thoughts were coming from. Coop was gone. He had been gone for three years.

You don't really pull people's fingernails out, do you? Coop had asked once, early on, before he had learned Ryland regularly did far worse. *That has to be an exaggeration.* Nervous hope had hidden underneath his flirtatious smile. He hadn't wanted the man he had already gone to bed with by then to be a monster.

The prisoner breathed hard, staring at the bloody pliers. Ryland opened them and let the bloody nail fall to the floor.

"Are you ready to start cooperating?" he asked.

"Cooper," she whispered in a ragged voice. "Please. You can fight this. You can fight *him.*"

If only she knew how many fights the two of them had had. And how little it had gotten either of them in the end.

He took hold of the prisoner's next nail and started to tug, slower this time. Drawing out the pain. The nail offered resistance, but Coop held her hand firmly in place. As he did, though, he looked away. Was that a flash of disgust in his eyes?

You realize you're everything I hate, don't you? Coop had said to him, pulling on his clothes quickly, as if trying to erase the evidence of what they had just done together.

Ryland had flashed him a teasing smile. *And yet you just can't resist me.*

But Coop had met his smile with a scowl. *Don't. Just don't. I can't think about this right now, all right? I can't … I can't look at you.*

"If you're going to do it," the prisoner spat, "then go ahead and do it."

Ryland blinked away the memory. He came back to the present moment, where he had frozen, no longer pulling at the nail that was still locked in the pliers' grip. Blood seeped out from where the metal had dug under her skin.

He released the nail and let the hand holding the pliers fall to his side. "Go," he ordered Coop. "This will be an easy interrogation. I don't need any help."

"Go where?" Coop asked, face and voice perfectly placid.

"I don't care. Go organize my desk." No doubt he wouldn't be able to find anything when Coop was done. Plus, it meant leaving a chipped worker alone in his office full of secure files for what could turn out to be hours. Back when they had been together, back when Coop had been himself, his feelings for Ryland wouldn't have been enough to stop him from taking advantage of that opportunity. Just like Ryland's feelings for Coop had never been enough to get him to leave his job.

But he would have. He *would* have. Just as soon as the time was right.

Ryland unlocked the interrogation room door. Coop walked away without a second glance.

Ryland slammed the door shut after him. He turned back to the prisoner, raising the pliers again. Why was it so damned hot in here? And this shirt – he had never noticed how rough and itchy it was. They just didn't make clothes the way they used to.

"Now," he said to the prisoner, "where were we?"

4

Casey's was a favorite lunch and dinner spot among interrogators, even though the food and ambiance both left a lot to be desired. The burgers were greasy enough to soak through the bottoms of the cheap buns, and the fries always tasted like they had been sitting in stale oil for a few days. The small building was cramped and loud, the tables too close together, with tepid radio hits from twenty years ago blaring through the crackly speakers. But it was right next door to the facility, which meant they did a brisk business, mainly owing to people like Ryland who were too busy or lazy to go farther afield.

Tonight, though, Ryland regretted his choice. The music grated on his nerves, which were already worn thin, and the press of the crowd worsened the feeling of oppressive heat he'd thought he had left behind in the interrogation room. If he hadn't promised Oliver dinner tonight, he would have gone home and tried his luck with whatever he could find in the fridge that wasn't too furry yet.

He looked down at the burger in his hand, and was surprised to find it half gone already. He couldn't remember taking a single bite. The good news was it didn't taste like grease tonight. Probably because everything tasted like sand.

Oliver leaned in to be heard over the blaring music. "You seem ... *off* tonight," he said in his quiet voice. "Is something wrong?"

"I'm sorry," said Ryland. "We came here so I could help you, not so you could watch me sulk over my burger." He set the burger down – he didn't want the rest anyway – and tried to give Oliver his full attention. "Tell me about this prisoner. Did you bring the file?"

Oliver frowned. "Prisoner?"

Ryland wasn't so distracted that he had mixed up the reason for this dinner, was he? "The prisoner," he repeated. "The one you're having so much trouble breaking. That's why you wanted to talk, wasn't it? So I could give you my thoughts?"

"Oh, right. Him." Oliver shook his head ruefully. "I guess you're not the only one who's a little off tonight?" He gave a soft, self-deprecating laugh. It was hard to tell over the noise of the music and the crowd, but Ryland thought his laugh sounded a little strained.

Well, maybe bad days were going around.

He tried to focus all his attention on Oliver, the way Oliver would have done for him. Oliver was the closest friend he had in the facility – maybe the only real friend he had there, or anywhere else. Interrogation was a lonely job. Coop wasn't the only one put off by how Ryland and those like him spent their days. A person didn't have to be on the side of the rebels to be uncomfortable with how the sausage was made. Ryland would have thought that would bond the interrogators closer together – after all, who else did they have? – but in practice, their social muscles were atrophied enough that they kept to themselves.

Oliver was the kind of person someone could pass by every day and not give any more thought than they gave the faded painting of a beach sunset someone had stuck up in the men's bathroom in a vain attempt to brighten the place up. And that was exactly what Ryland had done for years, until they had happened to start talking one day during an escaped-prisoner drill. He hadn't realized until that day just how long Oliver had been working there, and how many prisoners he had successfully broken. His numbers put Ryland's to shame. Maybe there was more to him than Ryland had realized.

Once Ryland started watching him more closely, he saw other things he had overlooked. Like how Oliver was always reading something he thought might help him with his work – most recently, it was a book on some new theory of psychological development. Or how, when someone asked him to do something, no matter how trivial, he would move heaven and earth to get it done. It would have been easy for people to take advantage of him, if anyone had noticed he existed.

And once the two of them had become friends, Ryland found him to be an incredibly loyal and caring confidant. Oliver was the only person he had ever told about Coop – only after Coop was arrested and it was all over, of course. Even then, he had feared the rule-following Oliver would report him for his indiscretion, but to his knowledge, Oliver had never told a soul.

"What do you think?" Oliver asked, bringing him out of his reverie.

Too late, he realized Oliver had been laying out the details of his problem, and Ryland hadn't heard a word. So much for giving Oliver his full attention.

"Hmm," he said, feeling like a terrible friend – as if he needed one more thing to feel bad about today. "That's a tricky situation."

Oliver gave him a wry smile. "You weren't listening, were you?"

Ryland sighed. "I'm sorry. It's been a hell of a day."

Instantly, Oliver's face creased with concern, his own problems apparently forgotten. "What's going on?"

He opened his mouth to give some excuse – a bad night of sleep, a difficult interrogation. But this was Oliver. He had kept Ryland's secret before. He could keep it again.

"The ex-boyfriend I told you about three years ago," he said. He lowered his voice and leaned in toward Oliver. "The rebel."

Oliver's frown grew. "What about him? I thought he was arrested years ago."

"Did you hear about this new chipped-worker trial?"

"I heard a rumor that someone cursed out Norby for suggesting it." Oliver looked half scandalized at that, half secretly envious. "Don't tell me that was *you.*"

"That's an exaggeration," said Ryland, "but not much of one. Also, it was more than a suggestion. He delivered the chipped worker straight to my office."

Ryland could tell Oliver had put the pieces together when Oliver's mouth went round with shock. "And it's that ex of yours?"

"Yes. No. I don't know." Ryland rested his elbows on the table and his head in his hands. Why had he thought talking about it might make it *easier*? "The chip – it takes away most of who they were. The voice is the same. The face. But that's about it. He assisted me in an interrogation. He didn't fight. Didn't argue. That alone is enough to tell me there's nothing of him left in there."

"Have you reported the conflict of interest?"

"And put it on the record that I was sharing my bed with a rebel for two years? That I knew what he was and never turned him in?"

"You don't have to get that specific with it," said Oliver. "Say he was your neighbor. A friend of a friend. Or confess to the one-night stand – you said that's how it started, didn't you?"

Ryland had forgotten he had shared that much with Oliver. "It's not necessary," he said shortly. "It's not *him*. I just need to remember that." He looked up to meet Oliver's eyes. "I can handle it."

Oliver blinked and drew back. Ryland hadn't realized his look had been that intense. "All right, all right," said Oliver with a nervous laugh. "I never doubted that, you know. I was thinking about *you*. About you having to work with him every day. To see him like ... that."

"It's not him," Ryland repeated.

"Why put yourself through that?" Oliver shook his head. "He was out of your life. It was for the best. Better to keep it that way."

Why, indeed? Ryland didn't have an answer. He hadn't wanted a chipped worker in the first place, even before he had found out who that worker was. If he took Oliver's advice, what would he be losing?

Coop. Only Coop. All over again.

"You're right." The music jangled in his ears. He glared up at the speaker in the corner. "Sorry about this, but I think we'll need to take a rain check. My head's not in the right place tonight."

A flash of hurt crossed Oliver's face, gone almost too quickly for Ryland to notice. But it was visible long enough to make Ryland feel even worse.

"It's all right," Oliver assured him. "Listen – why don't we go out tonight? Somewhere more exciting than here. We could have some fun. Take your mind off things."

Ryland blinked at him. "I'm sorry – did you suggest going someplace *exciting*?" Oliver's idea of excitement was getting chocolate ice cream instead of vanilla.

"You're always saying I should get out more," said Oliver. "That it would be good for me to have some fun once in a while – the kind that doesn't involve sitting alone on my couch with a movie I've seen a dozen times. Well, maybe tonight is 'every once in a while.' What do you say?" He offered Ryland a tentative smile.

His words had the annoying benefit of being true. Worse, Ryland was hardly one to talk – he had been even worse than Oliver in that regard since Coop. These days, his version of fun didn't even involve his couch and a movie. It looked more like catching up on paperwork after dinner and then turning in early. He could benefit from taking his own advice, and he knew it.

But he shook his head. The thought of a crowded bar or club made his head throb with an anticipatory headache. "Another time, maybe. I don't feel up to it tonight. Besides, you should probably focus on working out your strategy for that prisoner."

"If you don't feel up to going out," Oliver said, "you could come back to my apartment for a while." He gave a tense little shrug. "It would be quieter than going out – and it would be better than going back home and brooding. I've even got a bottle we could break open, if you're looking to distract yourself the old-fashioned way. I've been saving it."

He held his body perfectly still, like he was bracing for a blow and not a simple yes or no.

Realization hit Ryland like a gallon of ice water straight to his gut. The invitation to go out, when Oliver never went out. The offer to open up a bottle he had been saving – and why, just because Ryland was having a bad day? And then there was how Oliver had practically forgotten the reason he had invited Ryland out to Casey's in the first place.

No. Oliver wasn't ... he couldn't be *interested* in him. Not like that.

But they'd been having more and more nights like this, hadn't they? Casual dinners where Ryland helped Oliver work through a thorny issue with one interrogation or another. Ryland hadn't thought much of it – that was the kind of thing friends did for each other. He certainly hadn't thought about the fact that Oliver had far more successful interrogations under his belt than Ryland did. What did he need Ryland's help for?

And when was the last time Oliver had gone on a date? Not for ... oh, half a year or so, at least. Around the same time Oliver had started asking him for more help with his interrogations. That hadn't caught Ryland's attention, either – after all, it had been much longer than that for him.

Oliver was still watching him, waiting for his response. The hope in his eyes, now that Ryland knew what to look for, was painfully raw and desperate.

Ryland cursed silently to himself.

He knew how selfish it made him that his first thought was, *As if I need this right now, on top of everything else.* Now he was going to have to figure out how to let Oliver down gently, and do it without destroying their friendship in the process – the only real friendship Ryland had. And he had to do it while his head was too full of Coop to focus on anything else.

He opened his mouth. Closed it again. No. No, he couldn't do this. Not right now.

He glanced over his shoulder at the door. His body screamed with the urge to get out of here, now, this instant. Away from the hope and fear in Oliver's eyes.

He stood so hard his chair squealed across the floor. "I'm sorry," he said again. "I need to get home. Take an early night. Everything that's happened today ... I need to crawl into bed and start over fresh tomorrow."

Another flash of hurt in Oliver's eyes, gone almost before Ryland could see it.

Ryland turned away, his heart pounding with the need to escape, and fled before Oliver could protest.

5

Entering the facility this late at night, Ryland had to resist the urge to avoid the harsh floodlights and creep along in the shadows. He felt like a criminal, even though he had left the facility at a later hour than this on many a long workday. He had every right to be here, at any hour he chose.

And it wasn't as if anyone would see him, even if he *had* been doing something he shouldn't have. At this time of night, all the security was automated. And the automated security wouldn't be a problem, because Ryland had set it to delete any footage where he would appear for the next several hours. Which, again, was something he was perfectly entitled to do. He had been given that ability the day he had moved up from the junior-interrogator position. There were plenty of legitimate reasons, after all, why an interrogator might not want to show up on an official recording. Some prisoners needed more coercion than the official rulebook allowed, even though the rules gave them plenty of leeway. And other prisoners needed to quietly disappear.

Even if anyone found out he had been here tonight – which they wouldn't – no one would question his actions. There was no reason for him to skulk along in the shadows like a rebel on a mission.

And yet, as he crept up the stone steps and entered the code that would allow him inside at this hour, he still found himself hunching his shoulders, turning away from the places where he knew the cameras were hidden.

The building was eerie at this time of night. Only the emergency lights were on – the main lighting had switched off at midnight to save power. The emergency lights cast the familiar hallway in a dim yellow. Ryland peered around every corner, rehearsing excuses in his head just in case an interrogator working late happened across him and wanted to know what he was doing. Not that he needed an excuse. Any interrogator would assume he was working on a difficult prisoner, just as he would assume the same of them.

They would have no reason to think he was doing anything wrong.

He *wasn't* doing anything wrong.

Where had Norby told him the chipped worker would be stored at night? He scrolled through his messages until he found the location. A repurposed storage room on the maintenance level, where Ryland rarely had reason to go. He found the room at the end of a long hallway. The door was locked, but Norby had given him the code.

The room was almost as bare as an interrogation room. Darker patches on the faded gray walls showed where the shelves had been hastily removed. In their place, six bunks had been built into the wall – three sets of two, upper and lower. The bunks looked like shelves themselves, but big enough to store humans rather than cleaning supplies.

Apparently Norby had high hopes for the chipped-worker trial. But for now, only one of the bunks was occupied. On the bottom bunk against the far wall, a figure lay curled with his knees to his chest and his face to the wall.

Coop had always slept like that. *Curled up like a pillbug*, Ryland used to tease him. Coop, in turn, had griped about Ryland's habit of stretching out like a starfish to fill every inch of any bed he slept in – *As if I have any control over what I do while I'm sleeping*, Ryland had protested.

Ryland should have been asleep right now. He had tried. After hours of tossing and turning, drifting into and out of nightmares about Coop's blood and Coop's screams, he had given up. He had come here instead.

Ryland rested a soft hand on Coop's shoulder. Coop used to startle awake, sometimes throwing a half-asleep punch at whoever was unlucky enough to be the one to wake him. But this version of Coop uncurled slowly from his pillbug shape and sat up to meet Ryland's gaze with placid, empty eyes.

"Good morning," said Coop, as if Ryland hadn't just awakened him in the middle of the night. "What do you need?"

"I need ... " What *did* he need? What had made him think coming here was a good idea? Sleep deprivation, no doubt. He knew the effects it had on the brain. He used it on his prisoners often enough.

He sat down heavily on the edge of Coop's bed, ducking his head to keep it from banging on the upper bunk. "I need to talk to you."

"What would you like to talk about?"

"Would you stop talking like that?"

"I'm sorry. Please explain, and I'll do my best. Talking like what?"

Ryland buried his head in his hands. "You and me," he said, his voice muffled by his fingers. "We shared a bed for *two years.* For most of that time, we shared a lot more than that." Dreams. Secrets. Ryland had planned to leave his job for him, for god's sake. To leave his entire *life.*

"I'm sorry," said Coop. "Intimate relationships aren't allowed under the terms of the agreement."

Ryland made a strangled sound. "I'm talking about before. You had a life before this. *We* had a life. You can't tell me you don't remember any of that."

"I'm sorry. I don't know what you'd like me to do. Can you be clearer?"

"We met at a club, of all places," Ryland said into his hands, remembering the throbbing music and the sticky smell of booze like it was yesterday. "I never went to clubs. Neither did you, but I didn't know that then. I was coming off the bad end of a worse relationship. You were there to meet a resistance contact."

In Coop, who had stood off to the side and shyly watched the action from under his floppy curls, Ryland had seen the antidote to the sharp-edged lover whose angles had finally cut him one too many times. In Ryland, Coop had seen ... what? Ryland had asked himself that question many times. He still didn't know.

He looked up, hoping to see some trace of recognition on Coop's face. He saw nothing but emptiness.

"Your name came up in an interrogation a week later," said Ryland. "I erased the recording. It was a stupid impulse – I regretted it as soon as I did it." But he hadn't regretted it nearly as much as he had known he should have.

He had told himself it was simple self-preservation, a way to avoid any blowback from his unfortunate indiscretion the previous week. He hadn't known about Coop's resistance involvement when they had met at the club, of course, but still. That was the kind of thing that could come back to bite somebody in the ass.

If it had ended there, he might have been able to go on believing his own excuses.

Instead, he had tracked Coop down using the facility's resources. It had made him feel like a stalker – Coop hadn't given him his address or contact information, and that had clearly been by choice. He had knocked on Coop's front door and come clean about who he was, where he worked, what he did. He had told Coop about the prisoner's confession, had told him to be careful – to cut all ties with the resistance as soon as he could.

And they had mutually agreed to end their brief association then and there – to forget about their night together and move on with their lives.

Coop hadn't cut ties with the resistance. And neither of them had moved on.

"It lasted two years, before you were arrested," he said, studying Coop's blank eyes. "Two *years,* Coop. There has to be some trace of that left in your mind." There had to be some trace of Ryland. Some trace of *Coop.*

"I'm sorry." Coop's voice was empty of regret, empty of sympathy, empty of anything. "I don't know how to give you what you want."

Ryland didn't know what came over him at that moment. Maybe it was the sleep deprivation. Or the strange yellow lighting, messing with his head. All he knew was that without his conscious volition, he was leaning in, closing the narrow space between him and Coop. Pressing his lips to Coop's. Kissing him.

His lips felt just the same as Ryland remembered. Plump and whisper-soft, with a faint herbal taste Ryland couldn't place. For a split second, letting his eyes drift shut, Ryland could pretend. He could forget.

But Coop's lips didn't open to meet his. And when Ryland drew back, Coop's eyes were still wide open.

"I'm sorry," said Coop, "but intimate touching isn't allowed."

Shame crawled in Ryland's gut like a living thing. "You have nothing to apologize for," he said roughly. "I'm the one who's sorry. I shouldn't have..." He shook his head hard, trying to clear it of the memory of his lips on Coop's, so familiar, so horribly wrong.

"Please," he said. "Please just tell me you remember *something.*"

"I remember," said Coop.

Ryland went still. "What..." The word came out as a croak. His voice wasn't working properly anymore. "What do you remember?"

"You wanted me to tell you I remembered something," said Coop in that terrible flat voice, "and so I did. What would you like me to remember?"

Of course. Ryland had given him an order – or that was how his words had registered in Coop's chipped brain. And Coop had obeyed. Of course he had.

He stood quickly, narrowly avoiding bashing the back of his head on the top bunk. "Nothing," he said without looking at Coop. "I have to go."

He couldn't stay here one second longer. He couldn't come back to work tomorrow morning knowing Coop was here waiting for him. He had to do what Oliver had suggested. Declare the conflict of interest. Let the technology division take Coop back. Banish this ghost once and for all.

"Goodbye," he said, willing his voice not to break. He told himself not to turn around, not to give Coop one last look. He did anyway.

Where would Coop go after this? Ryland imagined him standing anonymous on an assembly line, pulling levers, tightening bolts. Alive out there somewhere – if this even counted as life. Ryland didn't see how it could. And yet his mind screamed at him that Coop would be alive – that he would never again be able to tell himself Coop was long gone, a closed chapter in his life. Coop would be alive, and Ryland would never know where.

Ryland would never see him again.

The night he had shown up unexpectedly on Coop's doorstep and given his confession, they had agreed that this would be the last time they would see each other. Even if they had wanted to try to build something between them, even if there had been no risk, Ryland had known he would never again be able to look at Coop without seeing the face of a rebel. Someone who would rather see the world fall into anarchy than live with the knowledge that someone, somewhere, was doing something that offended his precious moral sensibilities. And Coop, he knew, would never be able to look at him without seeing a monster.

Ryland had offered Coop his hand to shake, like it was a business deal. Coop had wrinkled his upturned nose, making the freckles on his cheeks shift into new constellations. *I hate shaking hands,* he had said.

Their eyes had met.

Ryland hadn't left. Not until the sun was crawling red-eyed up from the horizon.

That had been the beginning of the end. The first bad decision that would spawn a thousand more.

He had felt the truth of that then. And he felt it now, as he held his hand out to Coop like he had that day on his doorstep.

"Come with me," he said. "Quickly." Before he could have a chance to think about what he was doing.

Coop stood and took his hand. His fingers were cold in Ryland's. "Where are we going?"

"Somewhere you've never been," Ryland answered. Not in all the time they had been together.

Ryland's house.

6

Ryland walked Coop in through his back door, under a wide-brimmed hat and draped in an oversized coat. There shouldn't be any cameras around back, but the ones watching the street had probably glimpsed Coop for a few seconds – and Ryland, carrying the disguise out. Would Ryland's bundle of clothes register as suspicious? Had Coop looked up, even for a second?

Ryland urged Coop inside with a gentle hand on his back, and quickly swung the door shut behind them both. He cleared his throat. "Well," he said, "this is it."

Coop stood still, staring straight ahead of him at Ryland's entryway, the floor polished to a mirror shine by the cleaner who had come in yesterday. Beyond the entryway lay the living room, which suddenly seemed much too large for one man living alone. And could Coop see how much he had spent on the furniture, and on that plush carpet which now seemed like a ridiculous expense? Past the living room, a glimpse of the kitchen was visible, full of fancy high-end appliances Ryland never used.

Yes, this is what an interrogator's salary buys me, he wanted to say. *Yes, they pay me very well to rip out fingernails. But you already knew that.*

"Well?" he said instead, more irritably than he meant to. "Are you going to say anything?"

Coop turned to face him, his expression as placid as ever. "What would you like me to say?"

Ryland forced himself to take a breath. Coop wasn't standing there judging him. Coop *couldn't* judge him, not with the sliver of brain the technology division had left him. He was simply waiting for orders.

"Nothing," Ryland said, already feeling ashamed of himself. This was not starting off well. "You can take off that hat. And that coat."

Coop did as Ryland had suggested, hanging them both carefully on the hook by the door. Then he went back to standing with his arms pressed to his sides, staring at nothing.

"Sit," Ryland urged. Then, when Coop began to lower himself as if to sit down right there on the floor, he hastily pointed to the living room. "There. On the couch."

Coop obeyed, sitting with his back straight and his hands neatly folded in his lap. Was he comfortable? He didn't look it. Did he even care about being comfortable? Did he care that he was here and not assisting Ryland in another interrogation? Maybe it was all the same to him.

He ducked into the kitchen and poured Coop a glass of cool water, grateful for the respite from looking at Coop's empty face. But if he hadn't wanted to look at Coop, he shouldn't have brought him *here*, right? Rather than stop too long to think about that, he hurried back out to the living room, glass in hand.

He pressed it into Coop's hands. Coop took it without complaint. Ryland imagined he would have accepted the pliers the same way, if Ryland had handed them to him and told him to start pulling out fingernails.

"Drink," Ryland told him when Coop didn't do anything with the glass. Immediately, Coop tilted it to his lips. Ryland really was going to have to tell him to do everything, wasn't he?

The thought of sitting next to him at a stiff and polite distance, like an estranged couple trying to pretend they didn't hate each other, was unbearable. Ryland stayed standing instead. *Hovering*, if he was honest with himself. "Do you need anything to eat?"

"I can safely go without food for three days and remain productive," Coop answered, "but it's not recommended to let me go that long on a regular basis."

A small shudder rippled through Ryland. He turned away before Coop could say anything else. "I'll find you something."

That turned out to be easier said than done. The sum total of his fridge contents turned out to be a bottle of ketchup, a jar of pickles, and a container filled with some fuzzy green substance that might have been food at one point. A search through the cabinets yielded a single bag of microwave popcorn and a box of stale crackers.

But that wasn't a problem. He could order something for both of them. He frowned at the window, where the moon was still visible in the black velvet sky. Not at this hour of the night, he couldn't. And even once morning came, could he risk a delivery person coming to the door? A single glimpse of Coop would be disastrous. If he went to pick something up instead, could he risk leaving Coop here alone?

The moon stared in at him like a nosy neighbor. He hastily pulled the blinds closed, then hurried through the house, doing the same for all the windows. This was a highly surveilled area. If a neighbor or delivery person didn't catch a glimpse of Coop, it was only a matter of time before a streetlamp camera or patrolling drone did. How was he going to pull this off long-term?

What, exactly, had he been thinking?

He returned to the living room empty-handed. He paced back and forth across the expensive carpet, restless as a prisoner in a cell. What had he done? What was he *going* to do?

This wasn't like him. He wasn't a pacer, wasn't one to let his thoughts run away with him. But then, he normally wasn't the kind of person who would steal government property or secret a potential security risk away in his home, either.

If his anxious pacing bothered Coop at all, Coop gave no sign. He kept on sipping at his water. When the glass was empty, he asked, "What would you like me to do next?"

Coop's voice, soft though it was, seemed explosively loud in the silence. Loud enough to be overheard. Ryland glanced at the living room window, the blinds now tightly shut. In the morning, that oversized window, looking directly out at the road where all the neighbors walked their dogs, would be a threat he didn't know how to handle. For now, no one would be suspicious if the blinds stayed closed. It was the middle of the night. Everyone would expect him to be asleep, blinds shut to block out the light.

"Asleep," said Ryland aloud. "You should sleep." It was then that it occurred to Ryland that he didn't have a guest room – and why would he, when he never had guests? It didn't matter. He would sleep on the couch.

Coop frowned. "I thought you brought me here to work."

I brought you here because apparently I'm a sentimental idiot. And wouldn't everyone at work be surprised if they knew? His strong stomach in interrogations was the stuff of legend. "It's nighttime. I want you to get some rest. I want you to ... " *I want you to wake up as yourself.* But that wouldn't happen.

Ryland forced himself to still his pacing. "I want you to keep yourself hidden," he said. "Don't look out the windows. Don't answer the door. If you see anyone but me, if you hear anyone but me, you hide. Got it?"

Coop nodded. "If I see anyone but you, if I hear anyone but you, I hide," he parroted.

Ryland's eyes slid away from Coop. Seeing Coop here in his living room, on his couch, felt *wrong*. It wasn't even because of Coop's corpselike stare. Well, not *only* because of that.

It was because, for two years, he had been so careful to keep Coop away from this place.

By mutual agreement, they had stayed away from each other's homes after that one night Ryland had shown up unexpectedly at Coop's door. For security reasons – or that was what they had told each other and themselves. It could be a death sentence for Coop if anyone looked too closely at his relationship with Ryland. And the same was true for Ryland if the resistance got wind of what was happening between the two of them – undoubtedly they wouldn't assume Ryland's intentions were pure.

That was a sensible enough reason to rent a separate apartment just for their nights together. But it wasn't the only reason. They just never talked about the others aloud.

If Coop had let Ryland into his home, it would have meant admitting how comfortable he was getting with the enemy. Even as their relationship evolved far beyond the physical, even as their late-night conversations grew more and more intimate, keeping a separate apartment made it easy to pretend a certain distance existed between them. Coop didn't have to say it aloud for Ryland to understand this. Ryland knew what Coop thought of him.

And if Ryland had brought Coop home, he might have had to see the look on his face when Coop saw the luxuries that interrogating his resistance friends had bought him. Ryland might have had to think about how he was spending his nights in bed with a rebel while he spent his days working against everything they stood for. And once he'd had one of them in his home, would he still be able to go into work the next morning and treat every other rebel as a nameless, faceless source of information?

Maybe he had been afraid to find out.

"I wasn't ashamed of you," he said to Coop now. "That was never it. And I would gladly have shared my life with you, if things had been different. They were *going* to be different. I really did buy us a place to live together. I know you thought I was lying about that, but I wasn't." He sighed, thinking about the little cabin with its old-fashioned wood stove. Coop would have loved it. "I wish you could have seen it."

"I'm sorry," Coop said. "I don't understand."

"It's okay. You don't have to. I shouldn't have said anything." Coop wasn't here to be a dumping ground for Ryland's guilty conscience.

Why *was* Coop here?

He couldn't go on like this forever, with Coop hidden in his house like a fugitive. Sitting empty-headed on his couch, waiting for orders. Ryland wasn't sure he could go on like this for one more day.

But he couldn't go back in time and undo his foolish impulse. So what was his way forward?

"I'm going to find a way to help you," said Ryland. "I'm going to find a way to bring you back."

After that, if Coop wanted nothing more to do with him, that was his choice. Just so long as he was Coop again.

Coop shook his head. "It's my job to assist *you* with whatever you need," he corrected. "Do you have a job for me?"

A headache began to form behind Ryland's eyes. He rubbed his temples. "Sleep," he said. "Just sleep."

"All right," said Coop, and promptly curled into his pillbug shape on the couch. With his face turned to the back of the couch, he closed his eyes. Within seconds, his breathing took on the steady rhythm of sleep.

Ryland stared.

"I guess I'm going to have to learn to be more precise," he said as he bent to take Coop into his arms. He would carry him to the bedroom, and take the couch himself.

But before he could touch Coop, his phone rang. "There's been a security breach," Norby said as soon as he answered, without so much as a hello. "You need to come in right away. The chipped worker is gone."

7

Ryland entered the facility and walked into a whirlwind. Every inch of the lobby was full of grim-faced people in security uniforms—barking orders, talking on headsets, scanning walls and floors with arcane devices. Ryland had never seen this kind of frenzy in the facility before dawn. He couldn't remember seeing this kind of frenzy in the facility *ever.* He needed a cup of coffee.

Or maybe, he thought with a chill, what he needed was to head right on back out the door before anyone noticed him. When he had gotten the call and weighed the risks of leaving Coop in his house alone, he had thought about how not obeying Norby's summons would make him look suspicious. Only now did he wonder whether someone had already figured out the truth. Easier to get him to come in on his own than to send someone to arrest him, after all.

He took a step backward, reaching for the door. But at that moment, Norby emerged from the maelstrom, his eyes locking on Ryland. "You got here quickly."

With an inner sigh, Ryland stepped forward, away from his escape route. "You said it was urgent."

"That's an understatement. The facility was breached. Our first breach in more than a decade." Norby closed the distance between them. Gone was his usual affable demeanor. From the look on his face, he was about ready to step into an interrogation room and start ripping out fingernails himself.

"And you," he said, "were here when it happened."

Ryland's heart froze in his chest before coming back to life to slam painfully against his rib cage. His mind raced, his thoughts swirling and fizzing away before he could grab onto any of them. Run? No, he wouldn't stand a chance – not with the facility swarming with security. Give himself up and hope for mercy? Yeah, right. He had worked here too long to expect any mercy from this place.

Deny everything, then. For as long as he could.

He had met many a prisoner who had made that same decision. It never ended well for them.

Norby's brow creased at Ryland's lack of response. "You *were* here," he repeated, a hint of uncertainty in his voice now. "Weren't you? Your car was, at least. The parking garage cameras caught your plates."

His car. A weakness in the system he had never considered. The mechanism that automatically deleted any footage with his face in it would only work if the cameras actually *saw* his face. On his way into and out of the garage, they might not have. And his plates were on file with the facility, allowing him to enter the garage without a security screening.

"It's all right," said Norby, his voice surprisingly mild for someone who was about to have him arrested. "I'll make sure that part stays out of the official files as much as possible. I know you used the privacy codes. Probably working on the Capshaw interrogation, am I right? I know there were some ... irregularities in that file."

Irregularities, in this context, meaning a discrepancy between the official goals for the interrogation and what had *actually* been asked of him. In this case, someone high up wanted this prisoner's confession to happen off-the-record. Ryland didn't know why. He didn't care. But right now, that fact might just save his ass.

Ryland cleared his throat, trying to recover his composure and his voice. "That's right. I've found it's best to handle those cases late at night, for the sake of discretion."

Norby let out an audible sigh of relief. "You're a lifesaver, Eskell," he said. "That's the best news I've heard all morning."

Ryland frowned. "I don't follow."

"Just a few minutes after your car left the garage, the night janitor came in to clean the room where the chipped worker was being stored, saw it was empty, and raised the alarm. Unless the intruders moved impossibly fast, they were here at the same time as you. Which means you might have seen something out of the ordinary. Something that could help us catch whoever did this."

Ryland steadied his breathing, trying to slow his racing heart. He hadn't been found out.

Not yet.

"I didn't see anything," he said with a shake of his head. "I'm sorry."

"Security will want to talk to you anyway," Norby said. "They've been very eager to talk to the only potential eyewitness." Before Ryland could protest, he made a broad beckoning gesture over his shoulder.

Almost immediately, two uniformed security officers emerged from the crowd, as if they had been waiting for this signal. They could have been twins – sharp, angular, with dour faces and crow-black eyes. Their hair was the only meaningful difference between them – one had dark chestnut curls cropped close to his head, while the other had a striking shock of white-blond hair.

"Ryland Eskell?" Chestnut asked. Those crow eyes looked sharp enough to slice through him and all his excuses.

Ryland managed a faint nod, not trusting himself to speak.

"The eyewitness," Blondie added.

"Not exactly." Ryland forced the words from his mouth. "I didn't see – "

"We've been waiting to talk to you," said Chestnut, turning on his heel. "You're the best lead we've got. Follow me." He was already walking away.

Blondie brought up the rear, striding forward until Ryland had to hurry after Chestnut or risk the other man slamming into him. Refusing clearly wasn't an option. They didn't handcuff him like a prisoner, or drag him down the hallway by his arms, but they might as well have.

They sat him down in a small, unfriendly meeting room dominated by a long table. The two of them sat at one end, Ryland at the other. Staring into their sharp eyes, Ryland wondered if this was how his prisoners felt.

"Can you tell us when you arrived at the facility, and when you left?" Chestnut asked. "Don't worry – this will be kept out of the official record, as requested by Mr. Norby."

"I'm sure you have that information already, in the recordings from the parking garage." Ryland tried not to fidget – squirming in his chair would make him look guilty – but that left him sitting frozen, too stiff and awkward to be innocent.

"Yes," said Chestnut, "but we'd like your corroboration. In the interest of thoroughness."

Or to make sure he wasn't lying. Ryland gave the approximate times as best he could remember – although the clock had been the last thing on his mind last night. His voice sounded high and false to his own ears. Blondie took out a tablet and began making notes.

"And where in the facility did you go while you were here?" asked Chestnut.

"Prisoner Capshaw's cell. The interrogation room. That's it." They wouldn't be able to tell where in the footage the missing recordings had been – could they? He had been promised the system handled the erasures too smoothly for that, filling in the blank spaces with footage from earlier in the feed. But no one had mentioned the garage loophole, either.

"Nowhere else?" Chestnut pressed.

"I might have visited the bathroom at one point."

Blondie made a note of that. "Did the chipped worker assist you in the interrogation?" Chestnut asked.

"No, I didn't ask for his help."

"Why not?" Chestnut asked.

Ryland shrugged. "I'm not used to him yet. And the tech who delivered him told me to make sure his physical needs were met. I assume that includes sleep." Ryland's voice didn't falter.

Chestnut nodded. His face gave no clue to his thoughts. "While you were in the building," he said, "did you see or hear anything unusual?"

Ryland shook his head. "Nothing. I'm sorry."

Chestnut leaned forward. His crow eyes seemed to pierce through Ryland. "Are you sure? Nothing at all?"

Were his denials making him look more suspicious? He couldn't read the security officers' faces, couldn't discern the intent behind their questions. They could have been an inch away from arresting him, and he wouldn't know until it was too late. Was this why his prisoners got so weird in the head so soon, even before he started in with the pliers and the electricity?

"I don't think so." Ryland paused, pretended to think. "Well ... I might have heard something."

Chestnut leaned in further across the table. Blondie stopped his note-taking, his gaze intent. "Like what?" Chestnut asked.

"Footsteps, maybe. I didn't think anything of it. I assumed it was another interrogator." Was he saving himself, or only digging a deeper grave for himself?

The questions flew hard and fast after that.

Where in the building did you hear these footsteps?

What time was it?

Were they slow or quick? Heavy or light? Did they sound like they belonged to a man or a woman?

With every lie Ryland told, he felt the noose around his neck draw tighter. As an interrogator, he would have seen through these lies in a heartbeat.

Finally, Blondie tucked the tablet away. "I think we're done here," said Chestnut, rising to his feet.

"Then ... I can go?" Ryland tried not to sound too anxious about the answer. Only someone afraid of being found out would have anything to fear. He schooled his face into an expression of mild annoyance, like a man who had work to do and was being kept from it.

"I'm sorry," said Chestnut.

Ryland tensed, waiting for them to advance on him. For the click of the handcuffs as they settled around his wrists.

"Yours is the only evidence we have to go on so far." Did Chestnut look ... nervous? "And please take no offense, but I'm afraid it's not much. We'll do what we can to find the chipped worker and the cause of this breach, but it may take some time."

"We will, of course, work day and night until we find the ones who did this," Blondie added. "We understand the seriousness of a breach of this magnitude."

Slowly, the pieces of the puzzle rearranged themselves in Ryland's head. He wasn't a suspect here. They weren't trying to intimidate him. The sharpness in their eyes, the intensity of their questions, was their way of impressing upon him – the interrogator with a reputation for brutality – how seriously they took this crime against him.

They were afraid of *him*.

Had they ever even considered suspecting him? Had anyone? Or did his position place him above suspicion?

"But I can go," Ryland reiterated. He didn't make it a question this time.

Chestnut nodded. The nerves on his face were clear, now that Ryland knew what to look for. "You can go."

Ryland stepped back into the maelstrom. As he shoved past the swarming security officers, he noted the wary glances they gave him, and how quickly they tried to step out of his way. They raised their voices conspicuously as they passed, so he could hear what they were saying and be assured that they were hard at work.

– a manual review of all recordings from the entire facility –

– pull all streetlamp camera and drone feeds within a twenty-block radius –

– door-to-door searches aren't out of the question –

He paused at that last one, frowning at the security officer who had spoken. "Isn't that a bit of an overreaction?"

The man shook his head. "Not at all," he said. "Rebels have breached one of the most secure facilities in existence. This is an existential threat, interrogator. We understand that as well as you do."

Ryland nodded and tried to look reassured. Inside, he felt anything but.

Door-to-door searches. Every camera feed gone over with a fine-toothed comb. The nation's entire security apparatus closing in to battle an existential threat.

It was only a matter of time before someone found a clue. The tiniest thing could be enough to lead back to Ryland. Looking around at the swarm, Ryland had a sinking feeling it would happen sooner rather than later.

Restoring Coop to his former self wouldn't be enough. Ryland had only two choices now.

Either bring Coop back, with some plausible excuse for what had happened to him ...

Or finally keep his promise to Coop, and give up everything for a life as a fugitive.

8

That night, after the security swarm was long gone and the building lay still and quiet, Ryland snuck Coop in the same way he had snuck him out last night.

This time, it wasn't as easy as only entering the code that would automatically delete the camera footage. There were guards at every door, even the emergency tunnel that exited a block away. So Ryland went through the front, like a man who had nothing to hide.

Coop walked in beside him. He wore a suit to match Ryland's, and a hat that covered as much of his face as he could get away with while still looking natural. When Ryland flashed his ID to the guard, Coop did the same. It was an old expired ID of Ryland's that he had never gotten around to shredding, but the guards didn't look closely enough to tell the difference. They recognized Ryland, after all, and Ryland was above suspicion.

Ryland knew the position of every hidden camera in the hallway, and as he and Coop passed, he turned to give each one a full view of his face. It was counterintuitive, and made him feel prickles of unease down the back of his neck, but he needed to make sure they got a good view of him. He had entered the code before coming inside, and he needed all this footage erased.

When he led Coop into the interrogation room, Coop didn't hesitate, and offered no word of protest. Nor did he object when Ryland, his voice threatening to break, ordered him to sit in the central metal chair. He sat immediately, and looked up at Ryland with an expressionless face, waiting for his next orders. No fear in his eyes. No betrayal.

"I'm sorry," said Ryland as he fastened the restraints – not because he thought Coop would go anywhere, but because he needed to make sure he wouldn't fall and hurt himself. He said it again as he lifted Coop's shirt to place the electrodes. His hands trembled against Coop's warm skin. How many times had he run his fingers down Coop's chest? How many times had he felt Coop shiver against him? Now Coop's flesh gave no response. Warm though it was, it might as well have been the flesh of a corpse.

Coop looked down at the electrodes, his face betraying only mild curiosity. "Sorry about what?"

Ryland couldn't bring himself to answer.

Coop would find out soon enough.

Electricity would short out the chip, Norby had said. His own research confirmed it. He had spent every spare moment studying today, under the guise of doing background research on one of his prisoners. While the hallways had bustled with tense-faced security officers, and fellow interrogators had shared their theories about the breach in hushed tones, Ryland had sat at his desk, reading about chipped workers.

Oliver had knocked on his office door while he was reading. Ryland had blown him off with a few terse words about being busy with prisoner research. It was only after Oliver had left that Ryland had realized this was the first time they had talked since Ryland had run out of Casey's in a sweaty panic.

He had gone looking for Oliver, intending to apologize, but Oliver had already been in the middle of his next interrogation. It might have been for the best, because with Coop still occupying his every thought, Ryland had no room to figure out what to say. Later, when this was over, he would find a way to make it up to Oliver.

Norby had said shorting out the chip would take enough electricity that it was bound to kill the worker in the process. But now Ryland knew that wasn't necessarily true. He knew electricity. He knew how much the average prisoner could take. The ranges in the research were survivable ... maybe ... at least for a young and healthy subject. And it *was* a range, and a fairly broad one, at that. Maybe Coop's chip wouldn't require the maximum amount to short it out.

Anyway, this method was safer than amateur brain surgery, which had been his other option.

Ryland attached the last of the electrodes and stepped back. He looked down at his hands and willed them to stop shaking. He tried to tell himself it was only an interrogation. He had done this hundreds of times.

"What do you need me to do?" Coop asked.

It took Ryland a moment to find his voice. "I need you to trust me," he said. "No matter what happens. This ... " His voice caught. "This is going to hurt."

"As a chipped worker, I can endure more pain than the average human," Coop said. "But you're required by contract to provide all necessary medical treatment."

How many of those canned speeches had the techs implanted in him? Ryland shuddered as he stepped back to the controls built into the wall. The wires attached to the electrodes disappeared into the shiny metal square like a tangle of snakes.

He turned the dial up to the minimum amount that would be required to short out a chip. Even that amount of electricity was more than he would ordinarily have used on a prisoner – unless he was sure it was worth the risk of them dying under interrogation.

"I'm sorry," Ryland said again, and pressed the button.

He held it down for a count of five. One – and Coop's muscles went rigid, his back arching. Two – his mouth gaped open, his frozen lungs trying to remember how to scream. Three – his scream ripped through the air. Four – the scream faded to a thin and ragged whimper. Five – and then Ryland let go, and Coop sagged back into the chair like a puppet with its strings cut.

His chin dropped to his chest. He was suddenly, terribly silent. Ryland rushed to him. "Coop?" Oh god, Coop. "Please tell me you're alive."

"I'm ... alive." Coop didn't raise his head. Full-body shudders ripped through his frame.

Ryland tilted Coop's chin up to meet his eyes. Silent tears ran down Coop's cheeks, but his face was still utterly blank.

"Coop," Ryland said, his voice a desperate whisper, even though he already knew he had failed. "Coop, say something." Maybe there would be a delayed reaction. Maybe, any second now, Coop would stand up, slap him across the face, and ask what the hell he thought he was doing.

Coop blinked slowly at him. "What would you like me to say?"

Without answering, Ryland let Coop's chin fall. He crossed the room to the controls again and turned the dial up. He rarely risked giving a prisoner a shock this strong, and when he did, he made sure it lasted for one or two seconds at the most.

He didn't let himself hesitate. He pressed the button.

This time, Coop's scream didn't sound human. His arms and legs rattled against the chair hard enough that Ryland was sure there would be bruises later. But if it worked, the bruises wouldn't matter. And if he failed ...

If he failed, Coop would be dead, and the bruises wouldn't matter then, either.

He was at three seconds now. Longer than he would have risked for a prisoner. Coop's scream rang through the room in an endless assault of sound, until Ryland wasn't sure if Coop was still screaming, or if his eardrums had given out and all he was hearing was an inner echo that would never fade.

Four seconds. Coop finally ran out of breath. His chest heaved as he struggled to take another. His body jerked and thrashed, the movements frenetic and mechanical.

Five seconds. At last, Ryland let go.

Ryland didn't remember crossing the room to him, but he blinked and then he wasn't standing at the controls anymore. His arms were around Coop, and Coop's sweat was soaking his suit. Coop didn't hug him back. And he didn't push him away. His body was stiff in Ryland's arms as he sucked in ragged breaths.

Still, Ryland tried. "Coop? Coop, talk to me."

Coop tried to lift his chin. It flopped heavily back down to his chest. "I ... I ... " Even his aborted attempts at speech had that terrible flat tone.

"I'm sorry," Ryland murmured against his hair, even though he knew it meant nothing to Coop. "I'm so sorry."

He released Coop. Coop sagged back against the hard metal chair.

Ryland walked back to the controls.

He turned the dial up to the maximum allowable level. He knew of an interrogator who had accidentally killed a prisoner this way. The interrogator had received an official reprimand and a six-week suspension.

Ryland pressed the button.

He mouthed the seconds to himself as he counted. One – Coop's head jerked back so hard Ryland thought his spine might snap. Two – he heard something inside Coop's body crack under the force of his convulsing muscles. Three – Coop's voice gave out at last, his head flopping back and forth, every part of his body twisting and jerking.

Four.

Five.

At the sound of Coop's breathing, Ryland let out his own breath, which he had been holding the whole time. "Coop?"

Coop slowly raised his head. Small trembles ran through him at the effort. His eyes were filled with the red starbursts of burst veins. His cheeks were shiny with tears. "What ... " Coop rasped. "What ... would ... you like me to do?"

No.

No, that had to have worked. It was the highest shock he could deliver. The most it was possible for a prisoner to survive. It was his last chance. Coop's last chance.

It *had* to work.

It hadn't worked.

"I'm sorry," Ryland whispered. The taste of salt met his tongue. He raised a hand to his cheek. It came back wet.

What now? Sneak Coop back out, he supposed, and hope Coop wasn't badly injured enough to draw the guards' attention. Drive him back home. Sit him back down on his couch and leave him there awaiting orders.

Or ...

He shot a brief glance back at the controls before hastily looking away.

A longer shock might do it. Maybe.

A longer shock might kill him. Probably.

"I wish I could ask you." Ryland tried to focus on Coop through his blurry vision. "This should be your decision. Not mine."

Ryland cast his memory back over every intimate late-night conversation they had shared. But in two years of pillow talk, there had been nothing that gave Ryland a clue as to which Coop would prefer: near-certain death, or a lifetime of *this.*

All Ryland could do was ask himself which option *he* would prefer, and then make a choice he had no right to make.

He turned back to the controls.

He closed his eyes as he pressed the button.

One. He didn't look. Couldn't look.

Two. An aborted scream, then a sudden silence.

Three. The rattle of the restraints against the chair; the dull slap of flesh against metal.

Four. Coop still wasn't screaming.

Five. Ryland didn't open his eyes.

Six. *Please.*

Seven.

Eight.

Nine.

Ten.

He released the button, and he opened his eyes.

Coop sat slumped in the chair, his chin to his chest. He was utterly, terribly still. Ryland couldn't see whether his eyes were open. He couldn't hear him breathing.

"Coop?" Ryland's voice cracked.

Coop didn't stir.

Ryland felt for a pulse. Coop's skin was cold and clammy. He felt nothing, no reassuring drumbeat against his fingers, no matter how faint. Not even a weak, unsteady stirring of life. He held his fingers under Coop's nose. He didn't feel any breath.

He tilted Coop's head up to face him. Coop's eyes were open, unblinking. They stared into his without seeing him.

He had thought Coop had looked like a corpse before. He had been wrong. This was what death looked like.

He didn't allow himself to think, let alone grieve. There would be time for that later. He released Coop and dug in the wall cabinet for the emergency kit. There was a portable defibrillator to restart a prisoner's heart. He had only ever had to use the kit once, during his first year as an interrogator. It hadn't worked. The prisoner had died.

And his hands hadn't been shaking like this then. His mind hadn't been racing like this.

He ripped open Coop's shirt and tore off the electrodes. With hands slick with sweat, he unfastened the restraints and lowered Coop as gently as he could to the floor. He started chest compressions, staring into Coop's waxy face. Hoping. Praying.

Nothing.

When he couldn't stand the feeling of Coop's unresponsive body under his hands anymore, he stopped. He attached the defibrillator pads to Coop's chest, hoping he was remembering the instructions from last year's refresher course correctly. He pressed the shock button. The irony did not escape him.

Back to chest compressions. Then another shock. Nothing.

And another. Nothing.

Finally, he stood.

It was over.

Coop was gone.

"I'm sorry, Coop," he said one last time. He knew it didn't matter. Coop wasn't there anymore to hear him.

Then a gurgling gasp made Ryland jump back. Coop's body jerked as his head snapped up.

"Coop?" Ryland could barely do more than mouth the name.

Coop drew in big, desperate gulps of air. His gaze darted wildly around the room before landing on Ryland.

"Where ... where am I?" He tried to stand, then collapsed bonelessly back to the floor. His red-veined eyes rolled wildly with panic. "Where am I? What *happened*?"

"Coop." It was all Ryland could say, a gasp of relief, a prayer of thanks. "Coop, Coop, Coop." He tasted salt again, but he didn't care, because this time, his tears were tears of relief.

9

Back home, Coop sat in the same spot at the end of Ryland's couch. But this time, he didn't sit straight-backed and placid, waiting for orders. He hunched over himself like he was a turtle trying to retreat into his shell. His forehead nearly touched his thighs. He curled slightly to the right – that was the side where one of his ribs seemed to be broken after the electric shock session. Tiny tremors ran through him – from the electricity or from the trauma, Ryland couldn't say.

Coop hadn't said a word since they had left the interrogation room.

Ryland sat as close to him as he dared. He wanted nothing more than to wrap his arms around Coop and let Coop melt into him. But he didn't know whether Coop saw him as his rescuer or as the man who had shocked him with so much electricity it had stopped his heart. As the man he had loved or the man who hadn't loved him enough to run away with him.

He rested a gentle hand on Coop's thigh. The muscle went rigid under his fingers. Ryland hastily pulled his hand back. He curled it into a tight ball on his lap.

"It's okay," he murmured. "It's all right. You're safe now."

"Ry." At first, Ryland didn't recognize the whisper for what it was, hearing only a ragged sigh. But that was what Coop used to call him. He was the only one who used a nickname for him, the only one for whom he was anything other than *Ryland* or *Interrogator Eskell.* Even with Oliver, he was only ever Ryland.

"Yes," Ryland said, his own voice as soft as Coop's. He didn't want to startle Coop, didn't want to break the spell. "Yes, it's me. I'm here."

"They ... they put something in me." A trembling hand brushed the place behind his left ear, where the chip lay dead and inert. "I felt them do it."

He had been awake for the procedure? Ryland's gorge rose. "It's gone now." Or at least fried beyond repair.

"I don't remember anything after that." Coop raised his head. The red starbursts in his eyes stood out like wounds as his gaze searched Ryland's. "I was ... one of *them*, wasn't I? A chipped worker."

Ryland, not trusting himself to speak, only nodded.

"Before they put the chip in, they ... they took me to one of those rooms. Like the one I was in when I woke up with you. They ... they asked me questions."

Coop had been in the facility. Maybe while Ryland had been interrogating other prisoners. He should have known that was a likely possibility, of course. But he hadn't let himself think about it.

"It's over now," Ryland said uselessly. He reached out a hand to pat Coop's shoulder, and pulled it back just in time. He didn't have it in him to feel Coop flinch under his touch again.

A little clarity came into Coop's gaze. His eyes were bright and accusing. "When they brought me to that room ... I was afraid it would be *you*."

"It wasn't," Ryland assured him. How clearly did Coop remember his interrogation? Did he know Ryland hadn't been a part of it, that Ryland hadn't even known he was arrested until it was too late?

"But it could have been." Coop's red-streaked eyes held his. Ryland fought the urge to look away.

"I wouldn't have done it," Ryland said. "I would have ... " His voice trailed off, because what would he have done? What *could* he have done? Condemned them both to certain death by trying to escape the building with him?

Only ... he had done it now, two years later. And they weren't dead. Maybe he could have done it then. If he had tried.

"I never gave you up," said Coop. "In the interrogation. I didn't give them your name. I didn't tell them about ... about us. About our plans." He gave the word *plans* a bitter twist, so faint it would have been undetectable to anyone who didn't know him as well as Ryland did.

Coop had never really believed those plans existed.

"Thank you," Ryland said. The words seemed inadequate. He knew – better than anyone – what an interrogation looked like. He knew the futility of trying to hold any information back. But Coop had. He had protected Ryland, even after he must have figured out that Ryland wasn't coming to his rescue.

He reached a hesitant hand out toward Coop. Coop drew away, pressing himself against the arm of the couch. Ryland brought his hand back to his lap.

"You kept me going, you know," Coop's voice was still raspy – from the screaming, Ryland thought. Those small tremors still ran through his body, shaking the cushion underneath them both. "Imagining us. Together. What we could have had. What you could still have. I imagined you running, once you figured out what had happened to me. Going to that cabin. Being free." He paused. His gaze cooled the tiniest bit. "If there ever was a cabin."

"There was," said Ryland. "There is."

"But you're still here," said Coop. "I thought … when you didn't come, I thought you had run. I was glad for it. I was glad at least one of us would get to leave all this behind. But … you're still *here.*" As he repeated the words, Ryland knew he didn't mean this luxurious house. He meant the facility, and all that came with it.

"There was no point in going without you," said Ryland.

"Weren't you afraid I would tell them everything?"

Ryland had done his best not to think about it, just like with everything else about Coop's arrest. But yes, some part of him had foreseen that outcome. Some part of him had assumed it was inevitable.

"There was no point," Ryland repeated, "without you."

"So you just … went on interrogating rebels. Went on doing to them what your friends were doing to me." A larger shudder ran through him. He clutched the side of his chest, where the broken rib was.

"Let me get you some ice for that."

"When you were interrogating my friends," said Coop, "with me right there in the next room ... did you ever think about how it could have been me?"

Yes. Yes, he had, that day and every day after. Every day for the past three years.

He opened his mouth. But the words caught in his throat.

What right did he have to complain about the past three years, after all? What right did he have to whine about his haunting? While he had been plagued by his ghosts, Coop had been dead, or the closest thing to it.

"They won't catch you again," Ryland promised. "I still own that cabin – or my other identity docs. I'll get you there."

A mask of bitter resignation came across Coop's pain-pale face. "I've heard that before."

"I've risked my life more than once for you over the past two days," Ryland said. "If I was going to back out, I would have by now." He held his hand out to Coop again, palm up, like an offering. "I'll get you to that cabin."

Coop dropped his gaze to Ryland's hand. Ryland, practiced though he was at reading prisoners, couldn't tell what Coop was thinking.

At last, Coop placed a trembling hand in his. His skin was cold and clammy. He felt like ... well, like a man who had been dead less than an hour ago.

Ryland squeezed his hand. Coop squeezed back. The tiny, trembly gesture filled his heart more than any number of kisses could have back when they were together. The memory of Coop's empty face was still fresh in his mind.

"And you?" Coop asked.

Ryland frowned. "And me, what?"

"You said you'd get me to the cabin. What about you? Will you be there?"

Ryland's hand tensed in Coop's grip. He didn't even consciously realize it until Coop pulled away. He looked down at his now-empty palm, and regretted his instinctual response too late.

"That depends on you," Ryland said. "You've only just gotten free of the chip. I don't know where things stand between us – and you probably don't know, either. I don't want to assume anything. If you don't want me there, I'll understand."

"Do *you* want to be there?" Coop's eyes didn't release his. "Because you never seemed to want it before."

"Of course I do. I never stopped thinking about you, you know. Not for three years."

"If it's what you wanted," asked Coop, "then why aren't you there right now? Why aren't we both there?"

"It wasn't – "

"The right time. I know." Like his bloodshot gaze, Coop's small sigh felt like an accusation.

"What I want isn't what's important right now," said Ryland. "You should take some time to think. After you've had something to eat and a good night's sleep. You might not want to be with me, after everything." After Coop had gotten an up-close view of what Ryland's job entailed. After Coop had sat in a cell, waiting for a rescue that had never come.

Coop's gaze softened just enough to melt some of the tension from Ryland's shoulders. "I don't know much right now," he said. "I'm not even sure I know who I am anymore." His hand went to his head again. "But I do know I still want you. I want *us.*" The ghost of a smile flickered across his strained face. "I know it's a boneheaded choice, one I shouldn't be making now and shouldn't have made back then. But just like back then, I also know I wouldn't be happy with any other choice than this."

Coop's words melted something in Ryland that had been frozen for three years. Something that had kept him on his feet all this time, clocking in to work, going through the motions. Now he was left abruptly unsteady, like there was nothing holding him up. Like he was teetering on the edge of a cliff.

"I'll get you out of here first thing tomorrow morning," Ryland said. "After you've gotten some sleep. I wish I could give you longer to adjust, but they're searching for you. I'll join you as soon as I can."

Coop frowned. "Wouldn't it be safer for you if you came with me right away?"

Ryland's shaky footing grew more precarious. The abyss yawned open before him. "I should stay and keep an eye on the investigation, make sure your tracks are covered. Once I'm sure you're safe, I'll join you."

Coop's bloody gaze hardened.

"This isn't about covering my tracks and keeping me safe. You're not ready. Even now."

"You don't know what kind of hornets' nest I kicked over when I got you out. I need to make sure you're safe. If it's between risking your life by not keeping an eye on things here, or risking my own by staying behind too long, I know which choice I'd rather live with."

Coop shook his head. "No more excuses, Ry. Not *now*, after all this. Either you're coming with me, or you're not. Choose, Ry. Now."

Even though Coop was still trembling, his voice was steel. Ryland knew he meant what he said. Either Ryland ran away with him now, or he would never see him again.

And maybe that would be for the best. Coop didn't need Ryland in his life, a reminder of everything he had been through. Ryland could do Coop more good here, where he could watch the investigation, where he could make sure no one tracked Coop down.

Where Ryland wouldn't have to take that final step.

He stared down at the yawning abyss – and leapt.

"I'm coming with you," he said.

10

So many little luxuries. Ryland's house was stuffed with them. So many, and yet he struggled to fill the single duffel bag he had pulled out to pack for their departure.

What use would his espresso machine be on the run? And he could hardly pick up that expensive carpet and tuck it into his bag. The paintings on the walls ... even if they could have fit, none of them were worth bringing. They had come with the house; Ryland had never bothered changing them out.

Coop was still sleeping. Ryland wanted him to sleep as long as possible – although that wouldn't be much longer, since he wanted to leave before anyone would expect him at work. Ryland hadn't slept. His head had been too full of the plan they had settled on before he had made Coop go to bed for the night. Besides, the couch might look nice, but as a bed, it left a lot to be desired.

The metronome of Coop's breathing settled Ryland's heart as he crept into the bedroom and opened the dresser. As silently as he could, he slid open the drawers, one by one.

He stared down at the contents. What use would he have for his work suits where he was going? He tossed in a couple of pairs of socks and underwear, then peered into the drawers like a crystal ball, trying to find something worth bringing into his new life.

The metronome lost its rhythm. The bed shifted and groaned as Coop stirred. He gave a sleepy whimper of pain.

"Careful with that rib," Ryland warned. He turned around to see Coop wince as he struggled to a seated position. "Did I wake you?"

Coop shook his head. "Nightmare." His eyes went to the bag and the open drawers. "What are you doing?"

"Packing. Or trying to." Ryland grabbed a shirt and pair of pants at random and stuffed them into the bag. "You'll be arriving at the cabin empty-handed, I'm afraid. I don't have anything in your size, and buying things for you ahead of time would raise suspicions. If it's any consolation, I won't be much better off." Ryland zipped up the half-full bag.

"That's okay," said Coop. "I lost everything I owned three years ago." He bit his lip. Then he offered Ryland a tentative smile. "I have my freedom. And I have you. That's all I really need."

"How are you feeling?" Ryland asked, frowning as Coop winced again on his way out of bed.

"I could use some more of those painkillers." Coop wobbled on his feet. He grabbed at the wall to steady himself. "It's not just the rib, either. I hurt *everywhere.* And the burn cream helped last night, but the burns are hurting again."

Coop's electrode burns were the worst Ryland had ever seen, and no wonder. "I'll get you more burn cream." Ryland swallowed down a surge of guilt. He'd had to do it. That didn't make the memory of Coop's screams hurt any less. "But you're feeling well enough to go?"

Coop rubbed at the side of his chest with the broken rib. "I don't have much choice, do I?"

Unable to argue with that, Ryland hurried to the bathroom, where he grabbed two more pills for Coop. Over-the-counter – it was all he had. He also took the tube of burn cream. After a thought, he turned back and grabbed the whole bottle of pills. Coop would need it for the drive ahead of them.

He brought the pills to Coop, plus a glass of water. Coop swallowed them gratefully and lifted his shirt to spread the thick cream over the burns. "So," he said, "are we doing this?"

Ryland looked down at the duffel bag. He swept his gaze around the room, taking in the sight of everything he owned, and marveled at how little he cared that he would never see any of it again. "I guess we are," he said.

The blinding grin Coop managed through the pain made all Ryland's doubts disappear for a second. He could have left even the meager contents of the duffel bag behind and been content just to know Coop would be there to smile at him like that again.

In the garage, Ryland tossed the bag into the trunk of his car. Then, with a grimace, he fingered the blanket he had put back there last night. "Do you remember the plan?" What he was really asking was if Coop was still ready to go through with it.

"I hide in the trunk, under the blanket, until we get to Anderson Farm." The farm was the closest source of fresh vegetables, and did a brisk business this time of year. It was a logical enough place for Ryland to drive, even though it meant going well out of his way. It was also in a lightly surveilled area, and had a junkyard out back full of cars in various states of disrepair. It would be an easy enough place to do the handoff.

"My contact will meet us there." Ryland picked up where Coop had left off. "He'll take the car and junk it. We'll give him the cash and take the new car he brings for us." Ryland's contact had been surprised to hear from him after three years. But apparently his underground operation was still in business. He'd had no problem making the plans on short notice, so long as Ryland agreed to pay a rush fee.

"It's almost an hour to the farm," Ryland warned. "You won't be very comfortable back there. Especially with that rib."

"I'll be less comfortable if they catch me," Coop pointed out.

Again, Ryland couldn't argue. "After that, it's another ten hours to the cabin. You should be able to ride in front for most of that time, but you'll have to get in the trunk again if we see anything suspicious." Had they set up checkpoints yet? If so, Ryland would be in just as much danger of being recognized as Coop.

Above suspicion or not, it would be hard to explain what he was doing several hours away from the facility, and in a car he didn't own. But he didn't bring that up with Coop. This was still the best chance they had.

"I can manage," Coop said, although he rubbed his chest again at the thought. He paused. "You know, as much as you told me about that cabin, I was never sure it was real."

"It's real," Ryland promised. "It's got a working wood stove in the living room, and a hiking trail out back that leads to the lake, and a fenced yard for a dog. And a mouse problem, last I heard. Sorry about that."

"I've always wanted a dog," Coop said. "One of those wiener dogs with the stubby legs. You know, I'm not entirely sure I didn't stay dead in that interrogation room. This is all too good to be true."

"Let's not count any chickens. We still have to make it there first." He climbed into the driver's seat. Coop swung one leg into the trunk.

Ryland's gut knotted. "Wait."

Coop froze as Ryland climbed back out of the car. "What is it?"

"Are you really sure you want this?"

Coop stared at him in disbelief, one leg still hoisted up awkwardly. "What's the alternative, exactly?"

"I don't know." All Ryland knew was that the knot in his stomach had started *moving*, like a mass of squirming snakes. "We're moving pretty fast. Maybe we should slow down."

"You were the one who said we had to go right away," Coop pointed out.

"I know," said Ryland. "It's just ... " He shook his head. "I don't know. Put your leg down – that's got to hurt."

Coop swung his leg back down. "It's just what? Still not the right time?"

Ryland winced at the bitterness in Coop's voice. "It's not like that."

"Then what is it?" His eyes searched Ryland's. "If this isn't what you want, you need to tell me now. I meant what I said last night – no more stringing me along. The answer is either yes or it's no."

"The answer is yes." But Ryland couldn't seem to take the two steps back to the driver's seat.

Coop shook his head. "I should have known."

"We're doing this. I just need a minute."

"You had *months.* The past three years would never have happened if you'd made your choice a little quicker – did you ever think about that?"

"Every day," Ryland said tightly. "But what do you want me to do about it now?"

Coop lowered his head, releasing Ryland's gaze. It didn't feel like a reprieve.

"If it wasn't for me," Coop said quietly, "you would never even consider leaving, would you?"

Ryland blinked. "Why would I?"

"Maybe because you're tired of torturing people for a living."

"Do you really want to go there now?"

"Even when you were planning on running away with me before," said Coop, "you never had a problem with your job. It was only ever about me."

"Again, is this really the time? We've had this fight. It never ends anywhere good."

"Why *not* do it now? We sure don't seem to be doing anything else. Like getting in the car and leaving."

"Someone has to do what I do," said Ryland. "I happen to be good at it. No matter how much you dislike both of those facts, it doesn't make either of them any less true."

Coop shook his head slowly. "Why be with me if you think I'm such a horrible criminal?"

"I could ask you the same question. If you hate me so much, why were you ever with me?"

"I used to ask myself that question all the time," said Coop.

Ryland's heart dropped into his shoes. He had thought Coop would say, *I don't hate you.*

Maybe Coop was right. Maybe this was the best time for this fight, after all. It would have happened eventually – two years together had made Ryland certain of that. At least now maybe Coop would realize his mistake before they were stuck with each other.

Ryland started to revise the plan in his mind. He would drive Coop to the farm. They would make the handoff as planned. Coop would take the car on his own – it would be riskier, but not that much riskier. Ryland would pay his contact a bonus to make up for not leaving the car with him, and then –

"But I always knew the answer," Coop said, interrupting his thoughts. "Or I never would have stayed with you."

"Because I'm that good in bed?" Ryland's teasing tone fell flat.

Coop rolled his eyes. His lips twitched upward in the hint of a smile. "Because I love you, you bonehead."

"I love you too," Ryland said. "I never stopped. If I could do it again, I would have come for you." As he said the words, he realized he meant them.

Coop shook his head. "No sense feeling guilty about things you can't change. I just wish ... " His words trailed off.

"You wish what?" Ryland pressed.

"I wish," Coop said softly, "you would recognize that loving me – just that alone – is a rebellion against the system you serve. I wish you could admit to yourself that you don't support everything you work for as much as you think you do."

Anger rose in Ryland's belly – the familiar anger of so many fights, so much retreaded ground. He opened his mouth to argue.

Then he shook his head. "There'll be plenty of time to fight later," he said, answering Coop's hint of a smile with one of his own. "At the cabin. For now, we need to go." He watched Coop tensely, waiting to see whether the other man would accept his offer of a truce.

"Then ... we're doing this?"

"We're doing this." *If you still want to do this,* he silently added. *If you still want me.* "Get in that trunk."

"Gladly," Coop said as he swung his leg up again.

Then both of them froze at the sound of sirens.

They looked at each other. Then toward the road, where the sirens were growing louder.

"It's probably not us," Coop said with a tremor in his voice.

"Probably not," Ryland agreed. "But let's get moving anyway."

Ryland hadn't even closed the driver's-side door when he heard the screech of tires from beyond the garage door. Outside the door, flashing lights strobed.

I'm sorry, Coop.

11

In all the years he had worked at the facility, Ryland had never realized the walls of the cells slanted inward slightly, giving them the impression of being constantly about to collapse atop a prisoner's head. Or maybe Ryland's mind was playing tricks on him. Maybe he was losing it already, even though he had only been sitting in the bare concrete cell for a few hours. Or *had* it been a few hours? Maybe it had been less than one hour. Maybe it had been days.

The cell had a faint musty odor, like an old basement after a rainstorm. Something else Ryland had never noticed before. He'd have to bring it up with the maintenance staff at some point, see if water was getting in somewhere.

As if he'd ever have a chance to make a suggestion to the maintenance staff again. He laughed – and jumped as the sound echoed off the close walls.

The short, sharp burst of laughter woke the painful spots in his chest. He rubbed the bruises gently, wincing each time his fingers hit an especially tender place. They hadn't been gentle with him when they had brought him in. That was the flipside of being above suspicion – when they had found out they were wrong about him, they had taken it personally.

The cell door began to swing inward with a near-silent swish. He sprang to his feet, then winced as the movement showed him still more bruises he didn't know he had. He took an involuntary step back.

He didn't want to show fear. He didn't want to be like those prisoners who collapsed as soon as someone looked at them wrong. He had always thought of those types as pathetic, although on the bright side, they tended to be easy to interrogate.

But it was hard to keep his calm when he knew better than anyone what awaited him.

How long would it be before his own interrogation? Was that why they were here? To drag him off to one of those rooms where he had spent so much time?

But it was Oliver who stepped in. Ryland let out his breath in relief. "So you heard," he said, trying for a sheepish smile.

Oliver didn't return his smile. He looked Ryland up and down with pain in his eyes. "I didn't want it to be true."

"Believe me, I didn't want to be here either." Ryland stepped forward. "Coop. The chipped worker. Do you know where he is?"

As Ryland approached, Oliver took a step back, holding his hands in front of his chest as if to ward him away. The pain in his eyes flared; his lip curled in disgust. "You really do care more about him than about all the rest of us, don't you? You turned traitor for a nice piece of ass. I can't believe it."

Ryland bristled at the description of Coop. "It's not like that." But wasn't it? He had made his choice. He had chosen Coop.

It had been so hard for him to take that final leap. But now that he had, he couldn't find it in him to regret the choice. Even here. Even now.

"I hoped I was wrong," Oliver said. "I hoped they wouldn't find anything. I was *sure* they wouldn't find anything, and I'd have to apologize for doubting you. I was going to grovel. Buy you an expensive dinner. The works."

Ryland frowned, trying to make sense of Oliver's words. He couldn't be saying ... he couldn't mean *he* had ...

"You did this?" He whispered the words, not wanting to lend them legitimacy by speaking them too loudly.

But Oliver's eyes only grew more distant, his disgusted lips a thin white line. " *You* did this. All I did was pass on the information that you and the chipped worker had a history."

"You did this." The one person he had known he could trust with his secrets. The one person he had counted as a friend. "How could you?"

"*You're* angry?" Oliver gave his head a sharp shake. "I'm the only one here with a right to be angry. You're just facing the consequences of your actions. What exactly did you think was going to happen when you breached the security of your own facility and ran off with government property?"

"He's not ... " Ryland looked down at his hands, which had clenched into tight and painful fists. He slowly released his fingers. His nails left half-moon marks along his palms. "Where is he?"

"He's back where he belongs." Oliver's voice was clipped, cold. The kind of voice Ryland imagined he must use with his prisoners. "The chipped-worker trial will continue, with or without you. There's no reason your stupidity should ruin it for everyone else. If this works out, we'll all have chipped workers as assistants one day."

"Back where he belongs," Ryland repeated slowly. He was afraid to think about what that might mean. "You mean with the technology division, or ... " Would they try to put a replacement chip in him? Could they even do that? Ryland wanted to be sick. It would have been better for Coop – better for both of them – if he had died in that interrogation room.

"Back here," Oliver said impatiently. "In the facility. Weren't you listening? I said the trial isn't over. He's been assigned to me now – and he's proved himself to be quite a helpful assistant so far." He shook his head slowly. "Although I have to say, I don't see the appeal. He can't have been all that attractive even back when he still had a will of his own."

Oliver thought Coop was still chipped.

Oliver thought Coop was still chipped.

How? The difference between Coop with the chip active and Coop as himself had been so stark – how could they not have known the difference? Unless ... unless Coop had thought fast enough, and put on a convincing enough act, to make his captors believe he was still under the chip's influence.

And if they didn't know he had his own will back ... he still had a chance to escape.

Ryland's breath caught. He sagged sideways against the wall.

Coop could still escape.

Oliver made a disgusted noise deep in his throat. "You're not going to cry for him, are you? Because I don't think I can stand to stick around for that. My stomach can't take it."

His words were cruel, but pain flared in his eyes again as he spoke. Ryland remembered their last dinner together, how eager Oliver had been for Ryland to put the memory of Coop behind him. How eager for Ryland to come to his apartment and share a quiet evening and a special bottle.

"I know this isn't what you expected of me," he said. "I know you're hurt, and I don't know if I can ever make that up to you." His eyes searched Oliver's in a silent plea. "But if our friendship ever meant anything to you ... if *I* ever meant anything to you ... help him. Please. Help him get out of here."

Oliver's face contorted. "I thought you might ask me to save you. I thought it might even be hard to say no. But you're asking me to save *him*? Really?"

"It's the last favor I'll ever ask you." The last favor he would ever be *able* to ask him. "And there are plenty of chipped workers to take his place. What does it matter to you which one is here?"

And how many of those chipped workers had been ripped away from people they loved? How many of them still haunted the people who had lost them? But Ryland wouldn't think about that. He had never wanted to think about that. Bad enough that he had loved a rebel. Bad enough that he had lost him.

He wasn't going to turn rebel. No matter what Coop thought.

But then, what did it matter now, anyway? He was dead no matter what.

If he was lucky. If they didn't do to him what they had done to Coop.

"I'm no traitor," said Oliver. "Unlike you, apparently. And it's not like it matters to *him* where he is. He's chipped – he doesn't know the difference." He looked briefly queasy. "What exactly did you order him to do when you took him home? Did you go to bed with him for old time's sake? Did you tell him to do all the things he used to do, and say all the things he used to say? Did he obey your orders?"

A full-body flinch ran through Ryland. "Don't," he said tightly.

"You're the one who took your chipped ex-lover home with you. What else am I supposed to think?" He shook his head. "I can't believe I ever ... " He didn't finish the sentence.

Ryland knew there was no point in pushing further. And yet he tried anyway, because what did he have to lose? "At least let me see him. Just one more time."

"I can't do this anymore. I can't listen to this." Oliver turned away. "Goodbye, Ryland."

With his hand on the doorknob, he looked over his shoulder. "It'll be about time for your interrogation to start soon, anyway. I won't be handling that. *I* know better than to ignore a conflict of interest." For a second, Oliver looked like he was about to cry. "I hope you resist for a good long time. I hope it hurts."

Then he was gone.

12

As the next shock hit Ryland, his lungs contracted, stealing his breath so he couldn't even scream. Fire raced through him as if someone had set his veins alight from the inside. His back arched, his muscles tightening, his limbs twitching without him willing it. His body was no longer under his control. He hung suspended in the pain, unable to imagine a time before it or a time after.

And all he could think was, *This is what Coop felt.*

The pain stopped as quickly as it had started. The interrogator stared down at him with arms crossed. "The names of your resistance contacts," he said again.

Ryland shook his head weakly, the movement sending sharp spikes of pain down his exhausted muscles. "I told you," he gasped, still struggling to regain his breath. "I'm not ... working for the resistance."

The interrogator was a newbie. Of course he was – they'd had to assign Ryland to the new guy, because he was the only one in the facility Ryland didn't have at least a passing relationship with. This junior interrogator had only been at the facility for a few weeks. Ryland wasn't even sure he remembered his name. Black? Blake? Not like it mattered to Ryland. He would just as soon call the man Interrogator Asshole.

Unfortunately for Ryland, he was the type of newbie to follow the rules to the letter, not the type who made sloppy mistakes. He hadn't taken his eyes off Ryland for a second, nor had he given Ryland an opening to attack when he had transferred him from the handcuffs to the chair's restraints. It figured that *now* was when the facility would start hiring new interrogators who were competent from the start. They couldn't have done that a couple of years ago, when Ryland had drawn the short straw and been assigned to train a bunch of –

Another shock obliterated Ryland's thoughts. A part of him watched detachedly as his body convulsed against the chair. It was funny, really – all the times he had done this to his prisoners, and he had never really known how it felt. Sure, he had imagined it, but imagination didn't come close to the real thing. Imagination couldn't capture the feeling of one's own bones being set aflame.

Coop had gone through this three years ago, and he hadn't given Ryland up.

The shock stopped, releasing him. His head flopped heavily to his chest. He couldn't seem to lift his neck, and couldn't imagine why it would be worth the effort.

Where was Coop now?

Ryland hoped he had made his escape already. That he had made it to the handoff, and found a way to pay Ryland's contact. That he would make it to the cabin. The cabin had always mattered to him more than to Ryland, anyway.

He hadn't understood, before, how the thought of him escaping alone had been enough to sustain Coop. He hadn't understood how Coop had felt anything other than bitterness once he had known Ryland wasn't coming for him. Now he got it.

The interrogator was talking again. "How long have you been working with the resistance?"

"I ... told you," Ryland said without lifting his head. "I'm not ... working with them. I never have."

"What information have you been passing to them?" The interrogator's heavy footsteps echoed off the walls. When Ryland looked up from under his lashes, the interrogator had walked back to the controls, his hand on the dial. He turned it up a notch. Ryland let out a pathetic little whimper.

But the interrogator didn't press the button. Not yet. "You know how this ends," he said. "You know it better than anyone. So why not spare yourself the pain?" Under his stone exterior, he sounded truly baffled.

“Because I’m telling you the truth,” said Ryland. “It was never about their cause.” He ignored a stab of guilt as, in his mind, he saw Coop’s reproachful face. “It was only ever about Coop.” And that had never been enough for Coop. But that hardly mattered now.

“Cooper Byrd,” the interrogator said. “According to the information Oliver Marotti provided, the two of you were sexually and romantically involved for two years. You were fully aware of his resistance activities for the entire time. And yet you continued the relationship. You didn’t report Mr. Byrd’s criminal activity. Mr. Marotti suspects you may have actively worked to cover up his activities on at least one occasion.”

Had Oliver’s jealousy poisoned their friendship so thoroughly? Or was he truly so loyal that he was willing to sacrifice all other loyalties? “That’s my worst crime,” said Ryland. “Not turning in a known rebel. If you want to lock me up for that, fine. Do what you want with me. But I don’t have any other information to give you.”

“If you didn’t have at least some sympathy for his cause,” the interrogator insisted, “you would have turned him in.”

With an effort, Ryland lifted his head. “You’ve never known anyone to do something stupid for love before?”

“What information have you passed to the resistance?” the interrogator asked without replying. “What are the names of your contacts?” His face was stone. He looked like he had no personal experience with love and its accompanying stupidity.

Instead of arguing, Ryland threw back his head and laughed.

After all, it was hilarious, really. He of all people knew how futile it was to hold back information during an interrogation. He of all people knew everyone talked eventually. If he’d actually had any of the information the interrogator wanted, he would have coughed it up in a heartbeat. But he had nothing to give. And because of that, he would suffer the same fate as the most stubbornly defiant prisoners.

Well. He did have *one* thing he could give up. Coop's chip wasn't working anymore. Coop was free, and they didn't know it.

But he was damned if he would ever tell him *that.*

Which, he supposed, made him every bit as stupid as those stubborn prisoners, after all.

When the next shock came, it ripped through him like an inferno. The pain engulfed him, worse than before, worse than anyone could survive. He was going to die right here and now – how could he not? From a far distance, he heard himself scream. His screams didn't sound like anything human.

But this was still better than what Coop had felt, after Ryland had sat him down unsuspecting in one of these chairs to short out the chip. Coop had endured it, and so could Ryland.

And if it killed him, like it had Coop ...

Well, at least then the pain would stop, and Coop's secret would be safe.

He could only hope they wouldn't be able to bring him back.

"Coop," he whispered on a ragged breath as the pain faded.

The interrogator's stone mask briefly broke as his face twisted in disgust. "I heard all the stories about you, you know," he said. "The prisoners you broke that everyone thought would never talk. The one rebel you had confessing everything in less than five minutes. I looked up to you. I wanted to *be* you."

His hand crept back toward the button. Ryland braced himself for the pain.

The door opened.

The interrogator looked over his shoulder, annoyance crossing his face. "I'm in the middle of an interrogation," he snapped. "What do you – "

His voice cut off as the blood drained from his face.

Coop stood in the doorway, a gun in his hand. Blood dotted his shirt and freckled his face. His eyes were set in a determined stare that left no room for fear.

Ryland's whisper had summoned an avenging angel.

"Your interrogation is over," Coop said, and he pulled the trigger.

13

The walls of the hallway closed in, seeming to grow narrower and narrower. Ryland's hurried footsteps and Coop's echoed through the close space – as behind them, the echoes of their pursuers grew ever louder.

Ryland's steps faltered. Under the sterile tang of the facility, he smelled his own sweat. He smelled like a prisoner. He smelled like fear.

His steps faltered. Coop pulled ahead, and shot a tight-lipped look over his shoulder. "Keep going," Coop warned, puffing out the words between breaths. "Don't slow down."

"Stop!" someone shouted behind him.

Ryland's fingers tightened around the gun he had stolen from the interrogator. He spun to face his pursuers. Two guards advanced on him, weapons in hand. He knew their faces, although he couldn't place their names. They were often on duty when he was working; they regularly exchanged nods on busy days, and a few words about the weather when things were slower.

He started to raise the stolen gun. His hand shook. This wasn't like being in an interrogation room with a prisoner. In an interrogation, he didn't hear his heartbeat thundering in his ears. He didn't sense his own impending death with every indrawn breath.

He was too slow. The guards' weapons came up first. His heart gave a shuddering beat as he lowered his head in resignation. It was too late. The best he could hope for was that they would shoot him before –

Two gunshots, one after the other. Ryland squeezed his eyes shut instinctively. A high-pitched ringing in his ears replaced the drumbeat of his heart.

When he opened his eyes again, the guards were lying on the ground in front of him, a pool of red spreading around them. Neither of them moved to get up.

Coop lowered his gun. "Come on. There'll be more where that came from." His voice was perfectly steady. Without another word, he turned and started running again.

With one last look at the fallen guards, Ryland took off after him.

"This way," he said, motioning Coop down a hallway to the left. His voice was faint and shaky. He could barely hear himself over the persistent ringing in his ears. "The stairwell leads to a tunnel. It comes out – "

"A block away, by the drugstore," Coop finished for him. "The resistance *does* know a few things about this place, you know." As he followed Ryland through the stairwell door, he shot Ryland a sideways look. "I didn't think you, of all people, would freeze under fire." Then he shot Ryland a brief smile. "No offense meant."

"And I didn't think ... you were so good ... with a gun," Ryland puffed as he ran down the stairs, feeling every bit of the strain the electric shocks had put on his body.

Coop shot him a heart-stopping grin over his shoulder. "Look at that. We can still surprise each other."

At the bottom of the stairs was a metal door with a keypad next to it. Ryland typed in the code and held his breath. The door clicked open. They hadn't changed all the codes yet. Sloppy of them.

The door closed behind them. Dim yellow emergency lighting lit the tunnel, reminding Ryland of the facility at night. The walls curved upward into a sloped concrete ceiling. The musty smell of the cell was even stronger down here.

Ryland wanted nothing more than to sag against the wall until he stopped shaking. He forced himself to keep going. But he let himself slow to a jog.

Coop shot him a worried look. "Hey, you okay?"

Ryland tried to smile. "In the past few hours, I've been arrested, beat up, shocked repeatedly, and shot at. That's a lot of new experiences all at once."

Coop reached for Ryland's hand. He squeezed it. "It's okay now," he said. "We're going to be okay."

"There are guards at the exit," Ryland warned.

"And we'll deal with them when we get there." Coop gave his hand another rhythmic squeeze, like he was showing Ryland's heart how to beat properly again. "One step after another, okay? Focus on my voice."

"Do I really look that bad?"

"You're pretty pale. Pale enough that I hope you're not going to pass out on me. I may be your hero tonight, but my superpowers don't extend to carrying you out of here."

"You've done more than enough already," Ryland assured him. He shot Coop a look. "How did you do it?"

Coop shrugged without breaking his stride. "They thought I was still chipped. It was easy enough to catch that jerk of an interrogator off guard."

Ryland bit his lip shut on the impulse to defend Oliver. "Is he dead?"

Coop must have caught something in his tone, because he frowned. "Friend of yours?"

"Not anymore." Ryland tried to put the memory of Oliver's hurt, disgusted face out of his mind. "Still ... the element of surprise can only get you so far. How did you overpower him without a weapon? How did you get down to the interrogation level without being caught? How did you get the key to the interrogation room where I ... "

His voice trailed off. Because, of course, he knew the answers to all of those questions. He had never asked Coop about the specifics of his work for the resistance, just like Coop had never asked for the specifics of Ryland's work. It had been just one more of those things Ryland had preferred not to think about. But now he thought he had a good idea of what that work had involved. This wasn't Coop's first infiltration of a secure facility.

The silent look Coop shot him confirmed Ryland's suspicions.

Coop's steps faltered. He steadied himself against the wall, wrapping his other hand around his broken rib. Ryland paused, frowning. "Hey. You okay?"

Coop tried for a smile. "Still better than you."

"You shouldn't be running like that with a broken rib. Not to mention ... everything else." Like the fact that only a day ago, Ryland had killed him. "I don't know how you kept up that pace for so long."

"Adrenaline." Coop shot Ryland a pale smile. "It's a wonder drug."

"Well, you can't keep going like that much longer. You'll collapse."

"No choice. I'm getting you out of here."

Ryland frowned as he caught a glint of red on Coop's fingers. Coop wasn't holding the broken rib, after all, but a spot slightly lower down. Red oozed onto his hand and soaked through his shirt, spreading slowly but steadily. Ryland hadn't known any of the blood on his shirt was his own.

"What happened?" he asked, trying and failing to keep the alarm out of his voice.

"Your friend fought back. It's nothing serious. I'll take care of it once we're out of here."

"*I'll* take care of it," Ryland promised. "For now, slow down a bit, okay? Before I have to carry *you* out of here."

"No slowing down on a rescue mission." With another wan smile, Coop pushed himself off the wall. He returned to his jogging pace, looking for all the world like nothing was wrong. But he kept his hand clutched to his side.

They were getting close to the exit. Ryland placed a finger to his lips as he slowed his steps, sacrificing speed for quiet. Coop nodded and matched his pace to Ryland's.

They crept the last few feet to the door. Ryland lifted a finger to the keypad, then paused, shooting Coop a questioning look. Coop nodded. He pulled out his gun.

Ryland's chest constricted as he tapped in the code. As soon as the lock clicked, he swung the door open. The guards spun to face them, surprise turning to alarm on their faces –

Two more shots. They fell together, each of them with a neat hole through the forehead. Ryland stared at Coop. How had he never known how *scary* his gentle and easygoing lover was?

Up and down the sidewalk, under the glow of the streetlamps, startled heads turned at the gunshots. "Run," Coop ordered – and then took his own advice, pushing his beleaguered body harder than should have been possible.

Given that Coop was both bleeding and recently brought back from the dead, Ryland could hardly complain about his own comparatively minor aches and pains. He matched Coop's pace. He felt the night closing in around them as tightly as the hallways had a few moments ago. Trapping them.

"Where to now?" he asked, trying not to sound as despairing as he felt. Sure, they were free, but for how long? They had nowhere to go. His house was out of the question. His car was probably evidence by now. He searched for other ideas, and came up blank. This wasn't his area of expertise. He belonged in an interrogation room, not out in the field.

"Steal a car," Coop said immediately, pausing beside a sad rusted-out specimen. "Whoever owns this hunk of junk won't be shelling out for the extra security package – if it's even available on something this old. No one will be able to track us. Shoe." With the last word, he motioned toward Ryland's shoes.

With no time to ask why, Ryland pulled off a shoe and handed it to Coop. Coop started to swing it at the back window, then stopped with a wince, clutching his chest. He handed the shoe back to Ryland.

Ryland slammed it into the back window as hard as he could. After three tries, the window shattered. Coop reached in and forward to unlock the driver's side door.

Coop slid into the driver's seat with a grunt of pain. He bent with a sharp whimper and fiddled around under the steering column. Ryland watched with a frown, trying to keep one eye on Coop and another on their surroundings. "Are you trying to hotwire the car? I don't think that actually – "

The sudden roar of the engine cut off his words. Coop climbed into the passenger seat, motioning Ryland to the side he had abandoned. "I think … " he said, his voice wan all of a sudden. "I think you should drive."

Ryland frowned at the thick smear of blood across the seat. "We need to look at that wound."

"Not now," Coop said tightly. "Drive!"

Ryland peeled away from the curb. He shot a worried look at Coop, who was hunched over in his seat, clutching his side with both hands now.

"Don't worry about the car," Coop said. "If you're feeling guilty, you can get his address from the registration, mail him a few hundred bucks. This thing can't be worth much more than that."

"It's not the car I'm worried about," Ryland said as he tore through every red light he saw.

"Just drive," said Coop. "Get us to that farm."

Ryland made it onto the highway, where he slowed his frantic pace, letting himself blend into the anonymity of rush-hour traffic. "I doubt my contact will still be waiting," he warned.

"You can get in touch with him when you're there," Coop said. His voice was still impossibly steady. Maybe it just hadn't hit him yet – how close they had both come to death.

Ryland wasn't sure it had hit *him* yet. He had come within inches of ending up dead in that interrogation room. Or worse, with a chip in his head. And then the guards in the hallway – and at the end of the tunnel … by all rights, he should have been dead by now.

He should have been dead.

The same detachment he had felt in the interrogation room came over him as he watched his hands begin to tremble on the steering wheel. He tightened his grip until his fingers turned white and his fingertips went numb.

"Keep driving," Coop said, his voice soft and hypnotic. "It's okay. You're okay."

The gunshots echoed in Ryland's ears. His vision narrowed to a tight, dim tunnel. "Maybe you should drive."

"I don't think that's such a good idea."

Something in Coop's tone made Ryland look at him sharply. He drew in his breath. Coop's shirt glistened with wet blood. It spilled out around his fingers and wet the seat underneath him.

"We need to deal with that wound *now*." Ryland started to pull onto the shoulder.

Coop shook his head. He grabbed the wheel with a blood-slick hand and jerked it back to the left. "Don't slow down," he ordered. "Keep going. This is your only chance at freedom." He flashed Ryland a faint smile. His lips were so pale. "No slowing down on a rescue mission, remember?"

Ryland didn't smile back. "*Our* only chance at freedom," he corrected. His eyes returned to the blood leaking out of Coop. So much blood.

Coop leaned his head back. He closed his eyes. "I'm glad I was able to get you out."

"You shouldn't have pushed yourself so hard." If he hadn't run like that – shot like that – if he had slowed down to do something about that wound –

"We would both have gotten caught." Coop's voice grew choppy as his breathing turned ragged. "Better this way. For both of us."

"You shouldn't have come back for me." The road ahead of him was blurry all of a sudden. "You should have saved yourself."

"You will be free," Coop said. "You'll be out of ... that place. That's all I really wanted." His head sagged to one side.

Ryland swung the car onto the shoulder and slammed on the brakes. With trembling hands, he lifted Coop's shirt. A jagged knife wound gaped open under his ribs. The bleeding was finally slowing now. Too late.

"Coop," Ryland whispered, a fervent mantra, as he pressed his hands uselessly to the wound. "Coop. Coop."

In the interrogation room, his mantra had brought Coop back. He knew it wouldn't work this time.

"I love you," Coop whispered, and then he was gone.

14

The fish weren't biting. That was no surprise. From his spot at the end of the weathered dock, Ryland watched the sky turn from golden to orange-red. He had been out here since dawn, minus a break for lunch, with nothing to show for it but a sunburn across the bridge of his nose. Oh, and probably a few splinters in his ass.

As the temperature dropped, the breeze turned from refreshing to chilly. It carried the scent of someone's barbecue from across the lake. His stomach growled.

"All right, you wily little critters," he muttered to the fish he knew had to be laughing at him under the surface of the lake. "You win. Again." He started to reel his line in.

Then he felt a tug. Was that – could it be ... He reeled faster. The hook broke the surface, a small silver fish dangling from the end. Its scales caught the golden light as it flopped uselessly.

"Oh no you don't," said Ryland with a grin of triumph as he plucked the fish off the hook. It nearly slithered out of his hands – what right did fish have to be so *slippery*? – but he popped it into the bucket that, until now, had never held anything but rainwater. "Victory at last. I'm having fish for dinner tonight."

He whistled a tune under his breath as he walked the narrow trail through the woods that led back to the cabin. Old Mr. Reynolds, with his ridiculous silver mustache, was out walking that fat bulldog of his. Mr. Reynolds marked his cheery demeanor with a raise of his eyebrows. "You finally caught one, did you?"

Ryland tried to hide his sudden tension. He did his best to be invisible to his neighbors, but they had noticed his pathetic attempts at fishing. "You don't have to sound so surprised about it," he said easily. He gave the dog a scratch behind the ears before letting them pass.

"Well done, Brian," Mr. Reynolds said as he continued on his way. "I knew you had it in you."

It took Ryland a second or two to realize he wasn't talking to the dog. Even now, he still wasn't used to answering to his new name. Mr. Reynolds only knew him by the new name, of course. Just like everyone else around here. Ryland doubted he or anyone else would be too keen on celebrating his accomplishment if they knew who Ryland really was.

He didn't know Mr. Reynolds's politics – it wasn't the kind of thing you brought up when making small talk on the trail. But one of the reasons he had chosen this town, way back when he had been making plans for him and Coop, was that it was a low-level center of rebel activity. It was too small and sleepy a place for anyone to bother doing anything to shut down that activity – the country had bigger problems. But it was the kind of place where, if anyone were to find out Ryland was on the run, they wouldn't be quick to turn him in.

Not unless they knew what he had done *before* going on the run.

The trail led him to his back fence, which he had left unlatched. Inside the fence, the grass was trimmed ruthlessly short – Ryland had to do something to occupy his time, after all. His failed attempts at a garden lay brown and scraggly along the worn wood of the back wall.

Ryland turned the key in the back lock, gave the door a kick in the sticky spot, and swung it open. It squealed as it let him in. The familiar smell of the cabin, like smoke and old wood, greeted him. He kicked off his boots and set his fishing supplies by the door. He hurried for the kitchen, turning away from the fireplace Coop would have loved, the armchair where he could so easily imagine Coop curling up under a blanket with a book. His whistling ceased.

He set the bucket down on the kitchen counter with a slam. The fish had ceased its flopping, and now lay inert, staring up at him with one glassy eye.

"Now I've just got to figure out how to cook you for dinner," Ryland said, trying to keep up his cheerful tone. "I didn't go to all the trouble of catching you not to get something out of it." He stared into the fish's dead eye. It was going to stare at him when he cut its head off, wasn't it? And did fish bleed? He hoped not. His stomach flopped like the fish had when he had pulled it out of the water.

He shook his head at himself. Coop would have laughed at him for feeling squeamish about a fish, considering all the things he had done to his prisoners without the slightest hint of queasiness. That is, if Coop had been in the mood to laugh about Ryland's former profession. Would they have come to a point, eventually, where they could laugh about it?

Oh god. Coop.

Ryland's vision blurred. His chest constricted. He let out a small hiccup. Tears landed in the bucket with tiny plops, like a summer drizzle.

He was crying over a damn *fish.*

"Pull yourself together," he muttered to himself, swiping at his eyes with the back of his hand. He wasn't doing Coop any favors by getting all teary-eyed over nothing. He owed it to Coop to live a happy life here in the cabin that should have been Coop's. Happy enough for both of them.

It was what Coop would have wanted. He knew because it was all he had wanted for Coop, back when he had thought he was going to die in that interrogation room.

Coop shouldn't have come to rescue him. He should have run.

He swallowed hard and forced the tears down. He stared into the fish's eye, and tried to ignore the stinging in his own eyes. "Enough," he said. "We're moving on, you hear me? We're going to figure out how to cook you, and then I'm going to eat you for dinner. And you're going to be delicious."

And after that, he would light a fire as the temperature dropped and darkness crept in. He would curl up in the armchair he had chosen for Coop, and finally make progress on the book he had picked up at the library last week and hadn't yet been able to concentrate on. He would read until he was tired enough to sleep without nightmares. Then he would curl up under the quilt Coop would have loved, in a bed big enough for two, and sleep alone.

Alone. Just like every day he had spent here so far.

He was trying. He was trying so hard. Trying to get back into reading again, to learn to fish, to take up chess and woodcarving and half a dozen other aborted hobbies. He was trying to relax. He was trying to be happy.

He was trying for Coop.

And sometimes it worked. When the sun was up and the weather was good and he could empty his mind for a while. When he wasn't inside these four walls that were somehow filled with memories of Coop even though Coop had never set foot in here.

It wouldn't have been so bad if he'd had a purpose. Something to occupy his time. Retirement wasn't all it was cracked up to be, and not only because even his considerable savings were bound to run out eventually. And yet the thought of stepping back into an interrogation room made him sick. Not because he imagined himself in the chair, but because he imagined Coop there.

It was only now, too late, that he understood that was part of why it had taken him so long to fully commit to his decision. Some part of him must have known that if he ever admitted it was Coop he truly wanted, that he cared more about the rebel in his bed than he did about his job getting information out of people who were no different from Coop, he would never be able to go back. He had a yawning void where his professional self used to be, and he no longer knew what to fill it with. He only knew that he had killed that self when he had made his choice.

And yet he didn't regret the choice he had made. Even though it had all gone wrong.

All he regretted was the empty life it had led to.

"It wouldn't have been empty to Coop," Ryland said. "He would have loved all this. Even figuring out how to cut up a fish for dinner."

Ryland would have loved it too, if only he'd had Coop here to share it with.

"We're going to do this for him," Ryland informed the fish with grim determination. "We'll live the life he should have gotten. We'll *enjoy* this, dammit." He flopped the fish onto a cutting board and searched the knife block. What kind of knife was he supposed to use for a fish, anyway? All he knew was what to use on a prisoner. Maybe he should have asked Mr. Reynolds for advice.

You absolute bonehead. Coop's voice was as clear as if he had been standing beside Ryland in the kitchen that should have been his.

Ryland jumped. "Not again," he muttered. "You've got to stop doing this, brain. We're both lucky I wasn't holding a knife."

If you really want to live for me, said the imagined version of Coop in his head, undeterred, *you can do better than waiting around all day to catch a fish.*

"This is what you wanted," Ryland said, even as he shook his head at himself for answering his own brain out loud. "You wanted all this, and I can't give it to you, so I can do the next best thing and enjoy it." Who did he think he was going to convince, anyway? The fish?

But is it what you *want?* imaginary Coop asked, implacable.

"Of course not. What I want – what I've always wanted – is you."

And if you can't have me, what do you want?

It was the question he had avoided asking himself all this time, because he didn't know the answer. He wasn't sure there *was* an answer. All he knew was that he was restless out here. He missed working, even though the thought of the facility made him sick. He missed purpose. He missed not being alone.

"I can't go back to my work," Ryland said. He would be on the run for the rest of his life. But even if Norby would have taken him back with open arms, it wouldn't have made a difference.

His imagined version of Coop fell silent. But he saw Coop in his mind, looking at him with that familiar reproachful expression. When he blinked away the image, the fish was giving him an identical look.

"Don't act like you're so superior," he said to the fish with a roll of his eyes. "You're about to be dinner."

And Coop – how dare Coop look at him like he was wasting his life, like he was rotting away in this cabin, doing all the things he had never wanted for himself and pretending it made any difference to the fact that he had been too late to save Coop? How dare Coop look at him like he was selfish for not doing anything about the other chipped workers who had people they loved grieving for them?

He blinked at the turn of his thoughts. Coop kept on looking at him. So did the fish – as if *it* had any room to talk.

"Fine," he snapped to them both. "Fine. You win. I'll do it."

He knew what Coop would really have wanted from him.

He had known since he had first come here.

A knot in his shoulders that he had stopped noticing disappeared all at once, leaving him blinking at the sense of lightness, the sudden absence of pressure.

He turned his back on the fish and strode back out the door, pausing only to slip on his shoes.

Time to stop trying to be invisible, and start getting to know his neighbors a bit better. He already had a couple of ideas about which of them might have resistance contacts.

You win, Coop. You win.

About the Author

A hermit at heart with a twisted mind, Lux Thorn is a lifelong whump enthusiast with a weakness for death scenes. They live in northern New England with their partner and child. They love swimming in the ocean, staying up late reading, and big floofy dogs.

Silence

Zi Trone

Cover Design by Nicole Alessi

Cover Illustration by Hen Towers

To my friend Mill, who has always supported me.

Contents

Content Warnings

This story contains the following content:

- Institutionalised/systemic pet whump
- Dehumanisation
- Past abuse and trauma
- Medical whump
- Forced medical treatment
- Morally dubious caretaker
- Defiant whumpee

If this book isn't for you, no worries! But if it is, we hope you enjoy this story about a runaway pet...

Stray Dog

It had been days since the first time Rayan had heard the rustling from behind the big, green dumpster. It was in an alley close to his apartment, frequented by many of the strays he'd helped over the years – cats, dogs, you name it. He just loved the little guys, and when he had enough money to spare, he liked to bring them little treats until they trusted him enough that he could bring them to a shelter. He'd even found loving homes for some of them around the neighbourhood, and seeing the scared, sopping wet dogs he had fed from his palm prance around on the streets in a little dog-coat and with a smiling owner ... that always warmed his he art.

In that first phase of trying to build trust, he never stuck around to wait and see what came to the bowl, allowing the strays peace and quiet. Some privacy. He knew from experience that was the best way to approach them, especially the cats, and there was a big chance this newest one was a cat. The bowl was always empty by the time he came back, and he was glad to see that his cat-and-dog-safe paste mixture was to the liking of the little critter. It was important to make it into a paste; he'd learned that the hard way. Some of these animals' teeth were a complete mess, and they couldn't really eat solids.

After a week or so, he decided to stay as he presented the mystery animal with yet another bowl full of food and another bowl of clean water. He really hoped it would still come out of hiding despite his presence, at least so he could see what he was dealing with.

"Here, love. I've brought you some food," he said softly, stepping away from the bowl to give it space. He crouched down and waited, eyes surveying the alleyway curiously.

Soon enough, he heard that signature rustling, and something poked its head out from behind the dumpster.

That wasn't a cat. It wasn't even a dog.

He watched in astonishment as the thin and dirty little thing crawled out of the shadows and dragged itself over to the bowl, eyeing him warily. Neither of them said a word. Maybe this poor guy hadn't talked to anyone in ages and didn't know what to say. Rayan was simply too stunned to.

It was a pet. An actual pet, the kind that looked awfully similar to people, with a worn, black collar around its neck and an expression that told Rayan it was not happy that he decided to stay.

Rayan had never seen a pet up close like this before. He had learned about them in school, he had seen some famous, rich people's pets, he had studied the rules and laws regarding them extensively, wanting to adopt one someday. With all that knowledge neatly tucked into the crevices of his brain, he should've been way more prepared and way less like a kid staring at a monkey in a zoo with their mouth hanging open.

"Sorry I'm not a dog," it spat, making him snap out of it.

"Oh ... no, that's not – if I'd known – "

"You wouldn't have brought me anything. I know."

"No! I would've brought you normal food! On a plate!"

It still seemed full of distrust, probably for good reason. Who knew how other people must've been treating it up until now? Strays were a rare occurrence when it came to pets, and the ones that ran away usually had a damn good reason to.

Rayan reached towards the bowl, making the other pull it closer protectively, glaring at him. "I'm not trying to – it must be disgusting! Let me bring you real food instead, please."

"Then bring it. I'll finish this by the time you come back."

He sighed and stood up. "Okay. I'll be right back, then."

On his way back to the apartment, Rayan couldn't help but wonder why the poor pet decided to show itself if it thought a dog would've been more appreciated – to the point where it thought it was risking its only source of food by not being one. It must've heard his voice and known he was still there, right?

He grabbed a plate and stacked some food onto it from the fridge. He decided to heat up some instant ramen too, hoping the warm soup would help combat the chill. Logically, he should've called the Pet Protection Agency to take care of the poor stray. The pet probably knew this. Did it think Rayan was somehow different? If it did, Rayan supposed it was right, because his thoughts were nowhere near the possibility of making that phone call.

The only thing he could think of as a logical explanation was that under all that snark and cynicism, it wanted to be found and cared for. Of course it did. It was a pet, it needed to be cared for. But maybe, because of some odd turn of events, it might've wanted to be cared for outside of the system, by someone other than its legal owner. But why? It should've been having a blast at its owner's. The PPA was supposed to ensure a happy life for all pets, right? If it *wasn't* having a blast, it should've been taken away and given to someone better.

In any case, throwing itself at the mercy of another was most likely easier to bear if it acted like it wasn't hoping for even a scrap of kindness. Like it already knew it'd be rejected, so there was no way to surprise it.

Rayan was determined to do so anyway. To shock it with just how much he already cared, after days of no contact and a five-minute encounter.

— • —

SIL

Rayan sat on the ground a few feet away from the stray as it ate. He was lost in thought, quietly observing the visible injuries and weird bumps under its skin. Bones healed wrong, maybe.

The more he thought about this entire situation, the more he found himself absolutely furious with the pet's previous owner. He had wanted a pet his entire life. He had grown up wanting one, seeing how happy and lively and perfect they were, knowing that if he was just a little more fortunate, worked just a little harder, got out of his one-bedroom dwelling and moved into something a tiny bit more spacious, *maybe* the Pet Protection Agency would consider him as a potential adopter. He had always been so passionate about wanting to give poor, helpless things a better life; that was precisely why he was so obsessed with helping the stray cats and dogs around the area. His ultimate goal was to get one of the pets out of a shelter and give it a loving home, the best home he possibly could.

And then there were people like this guy's owner. He couldn't fathom having the wealth and opportunity to adopt a pet and then treating it like utter garbage. He couldn't fathom how the PPA could've given someone like that a licence in the first place. Wasn't there an interview? Weren't they supposed to check up on pets regularly? How did they miss this?

His new acquaintance put down the cup gently, almost like it was handling expensive glass or something. Quite out of character for someone moving around so jerkily, and who had pretended not to care much for the soup in the first place.

"My name's Rayan. May I ask what your name is?" He kept his voice quiet, both so he could avoid startling it and so others on the street wouldn't hear.

"Wouldn't we both like to know?" It choked out a dry laugh, devoid of any joy or amusement. "Owner called me *mutt*, or *that thing*. I'm not sure I ever had a name, *Rayan*." His name felt like an insult coming from the pet, as if he was in the wrong for simply having one when it didn't.

Rayan frowned. "Well, do you wanna have one? You could give me anything. Make something up. Go back and change it later if you come up with something better ... Surely, you don't want me to call you those things?"

"Why do you need to call me anything?" it snapped suddenly. "You're making it sound like you'll just stick around and humour me forever! Why don't you go on your way already?"

"I – well ... " Rayan rubbed the back of his neck anxiously, awkwardly, looking for words that wouldn't upset the other. He wasn't sure words like that existed. "I was hoping I'd find you here tomorrow, like ... like always. Well, for the past week. And that I'd have a name to call you by when I came back."

The stray's eyes narrowed in suspicion, but it didn't lash out again. In fact, it didn't react at all, which was already better than the outburst a moment ago. Rayan counted it as a win.

"Think about it, okay?" he said with what he hoped was a friendly and pleasant smile. "I'll take this stuff back now. I'll bring you more tomorrow, if ... you know, if you're still here. If I didn't annoy you into leaving and finding another place."

He slowly inched closer and grabbed the bowls and the plate with the cup on it, still without getting a single word in response. It was only when he turned to leave that he heard a quiet voice from behind him, so unlike the harsh tone he had just gotten used to.

"I've been calling myself Sil. In my head. I was always told to be silent, so I guess I just took it and ran with it."

Rayan stopped and glanced back at the stray, *Sil*, nodding his understanding without giving any indication that he noticed the faint blush on its face. "Sil it is, then."

"Will you really come back tomorrow?" it asked, prompting him to fully turn back around. "Am I really worth it, compared to a dog?"

"Hey." Rayan crouched down to be at eye level with it. "I'll be back, as long as you want me to. You could even come home with me." Sil visibly recoiled at the idea, and he quickly added, "It's just an option. Just letting you know. All I'm saying is I'll be back tomorrow. For sure."

"Okay," it said quietly, watching Rayan stand up again with those sharp eyes that seemed to catch even the smallest of movements. The eyes of someone that had been hurt by those movements.

"See you tomorrow, Sil."

Distrust

The next day, Rayan was considerably more nervous as he made his way to the alley. He used to be excited, sure, wanting to find out what was hiding in there ... but now he *knew*. And he had no idea whether it would still be there.

"Sil?" He didn't put the plate down this time, wanting to hand it to the pet instead. Sil poked its head out from behind the dumpster, seemingly disapproving of this new idea.

"Do I need to do tricks for it now?" it groaned. "Roll over? Sit pretty?"

"What? No, I – "

Rayan averted his gaze, knowing that at the core of it, that was what he'd had in mind. He wanted to lure it closer, build some more trust. He was still treating it like a stray dog, when pets were so entirely different.

"I'm sorry." He put down the plate of food, stepping back. "I won't force anything. Like, in exchange for food. You don't have to earn it, is what I'm trying to say."

Sil began carefully moving towards it, never taking its eyes off of him. Now that Rayan could see it a little better and knew what to look for, it was obvious that it was in pain. The way it compensated for loss of movement in some areas, the way it winced when it made a wrong move ... He was sure that part of it moving so slowly was caution, but the other part was definitely the pain.

Rayan had no idea how to approach the topic of a vet's visit, and it ended up causing him a long, sleepless night. He thought he'd just grab a stray animal, bring it to the vet, and be done with it. But Sil ... he couldn't just put it into a box.

Then there was the issue of the licence. Only licensed pets could be brought to a vet, and they took the rules *very* seriously. The moment he showed up with an unregistered pet, they would take it away and bring it right back to the sly fucker who managed to avoid questions up until now. He could already picture it. *"Oh, I don't know how it got these injuries. It must've happened in the time it was on the streets. Yes, of course I'll pay for all the treatments, I'm a good owner, see?"*

He couldn't bring in Sil as a pet. But trying to bring it in as a person, trying to trick a doctor, would put all three of them in danger of serious legal trouble. He didn't want to put anyone else in harm's way, and that was precisely why he had decided that when the doctor finally got back to him, he wouldn't mention an in-person visit, only ask some general questions over the phone about things that he himself might be able to do to help.

Unfortunately, said doctor had just found the time to call back.

The ringtone sent Sil scurrying back to its nest, food untouched.

"Oh no – goddammit, why now ... ?" He pressed a hand down on his pocket to muffle the music. "It's just my phone, Sil, please eat! I'll just – I'll be right around the corner!" He took a few steps away for privacy and took the call.

***

Sil couldn't stop shaking. The sound of the phone startled it so badly, and the most frustrating thing was that it couldn't even explain why. It wished it had at least grabbed the food before running like a coward.

It could faintly hear Rayan's voice from the street, talking to someone. It couldn't make out a single word from so far away, but it found itself curious enough to shuffle towards the source.

" ... They seem hurt ... yes, I think so ... no, they're just – bumps under the skin, yes ... I can't bring them in ... it's complicated, I just can't ... "

They. Who were *they*? Ah, of course, Rayan must've been talking to a professional or something. He had to pretend he was talking about a person, so he could ask his questions without raising suspicion.

No. That didn't make any sense. That was a pet train of thought, a *stray* train of thought, from someone who had been running from the Agency for almost a year now. From a *person* point of view, all Rayan had to do was call the PPA and have it be brought in. Returned to its owner. That was the 'right' thing to do, wasn't it? He was probably just talking about someone else ... with bumps under their skin.

Sil leaned against the cold brick wall. It studied its hand, noting that the weight loss had made the protruding bone even more pronounced. It had been broken by its owner after one of the minor offences it'd committed, and he never ended up taking it to the vet. He never took it anywhere, not even the fundraiser balls or the – the other *stuff* the pets kept getting so well-dressed for. It had been hidden away from public view for years, some gross, useless, nameless thing. Master hated it and never *ever* failed to make that known.

Maybe its wrist healed wrong, but was that really important? It could live with the pain, it had for years now. Its ankle and shoulder were honestly way more of an issue for it, the agony of walking getting a little too much as time passed, but even that was negligible. Surely, if even its owner thought that wasn't worth a vet's visit, it couldn't have been a big deal.

It looked up at the grey sky above and let out a small sigh. It had no idea why it had decided to come out with Rayan around. It had spent so long hiding from all the people in all the towns and cities it had passed, and now that it was finally quite far from where its owner was, it had decided to blow its cover and just *trust* that this man – Rayan – would be an ally. That he wouldn't call the authorities. That he would just keep bringing it food and water, that he would keep being kind, that he would keep being so *odd* and *different*.

It wasn't so sure about its decision anymore. It desperately wanted to take it back, so it wouldn't have to sleep with one eye open for when the PPA finally got Rayan's report about the stray behind the dumpster.

Sil poked its head out again, trying to see whether he had come back yet. He hadn't. It crawled over to the plate and brought it back to its hiding spot, stuffing its face as quickly as it could in case he changed his mind about having to earn it. It *wasn't* going to do tricks for food.

***

The doctor had told Rayan dreaded news after dreaded news. In-person visit. Rebreaking of bones. Potential lice and other parasites. Infections. He didn't even know where to start, especially since Sil didn't even want to be near him.

The plate was gone by the time he got back to the alley, and he smiled a little. At least it was eating. "Sil?"

A thin little arm appeared from behind the dumpster, placing the plate on the ground. He frowned. Was it not going to come out again?

"Is everything okay?"

"As much as it's ever been."

"I'm sorry about the phone call. Did I upset you somehow?"

"Does it matter?"

Rayan slowly walked over to where the plate was, resisting the urge to peek behind the trash where Sil's hiding place seemed to be. He backed off with the plate now in his hands, stopping at his regular spot. "It matters to me. If I did, I didn't mean to, and I'm sorry."

"Who were you talking about? On the phone."

"Well ... well, um ... you. I was – I was trying to get you a vet's visit, or at least some advice – "

"You were talking about me like I was a person. I don't like that, and I don't trust that."

He opened and closed his mouth a couple times. How was he going to explain that? *"Yeah, that's because I'm trying to sneak you past security and avoid the agency that was founded specifically to protect you, all so that I can take care of you instead of your owner that I've decided is a horrible person."* That didn't sound very trustworthy or morally correct, even in his head. Said out loud, he assumed it would sound even worse.

Still, hiding the truth would be an entirely selfish act. If Sil wanted him to call the Agency, he supposed he had no other choice.

But then again, Sil ran away and was currently hiding behind a dumpster. Surely, it'd understand?

Unless it was lost, and it really had sustained all those injuries on the streets, and he was making horrible assumptions about a potentially very kind owner who was desperately looking for their beloved pet. But a lost pet would've just gone up to an officer, right? To be returned?

Either way, Rayan could only imagine what kinds of people would want to forgo making a report so they could keep an undocumented stray all to themselves, and he was about to come clean about being such a person. Sil had no way of telling that his intentions were actually good.

"I ... I told them you were a person because I didn't want the PPA to get involved. You look very hurt, and I assumed it was from your owner, and that's why you're out here all alone and hiding. I was afraid they'd send you back."

Sil didn't respond, no matter how long Rayan waited. He didn't know what it was thinking. He didn't know whether the answer had made it despise him. He wished he could've scooped it up in his arms and told it that all he wanted was to make it all better, but that was a far cry from where they stood with each other right now.

"I'll bring you a blanket tomorrow, if ... if that's okay. If you're still here. It's getting colder. See you tomorrow, Sil. I hope."

Emergency

Rayan didn't bring up the vet again, or the offer for Sil to join him in his house. Instead he brought it little pieces of the much dreaded *inside*: sweaters, blankets, warm drinks and soup, trying to coax it further out of its shell. He spent their limited time together talking to it, asking how it was feeling, in Sil's words, 'pretending it was a person'. At this point, Rayan was pretty certain that its owner was just an all-around horrible person. In what world were pets undeserving of a few words of comfort? Well ... in Sil's world, apparently.

It had been easy to forget how cold it was really getting while bundled up in warm coats himself, thinking maybe slow and steady was eventually going to win the race. It had been easy to forget that time was very much of the essence, and one day, he woke up to white skies and snow-covered rooftops.

Rayan didn't immediately register the implications of that. Once again, he was cosy under the blankets, with soft pyjamas and fuzzy socks on his feet. He was still stretching and rolling this way and that when suddenly, something clicked in his head. *Sil.*

He had never put on clothes quicker than he did that morning. He ran outside with his coat half-open, racing to the dumpster that was now all white and icy – and behind it, there it was. Poor, shivering Sil, curled up into the tightest ball of misery and borrowed sweaters. It had made itself a little nest with all the fabric Rayan had previously brought it, but that did very little to keep out the winter chill.

"Oh, Sil ... " He swallowed and looked around, cursing himself for being so careless. He should've been looking at the weather forecast religiously. He should've been more stern! He should've just brought Sil inside when it had begun to get so cold, instead of waiting around to gain its trust so fully. No, he was stupider than that – he was trying to wait until it *asked* to be let inside. Sil was never going to *ask*. He'd thought he was giving it space, but he was doing nothing but letting it turn into a betrayal-flavoured popsicle.

He scooped up the shivering thing into his arms carefully, his heart breaking further when Sil didn't even have the energy to push him away. It groaned quietly, murmuring something that was most likely a protest, but other than that, it seemed to cling more than it was trying to get away.

Rayan walked all the way back to his home and set it down on the couch, biting his lip as he thought back to his first aid classes and the fact that he was going to have to undress Sil. He had tried his best to respect its boundaries, but this just wasn't the time to agonise over that. Maybe Sil would hate his guts forever, but god, he just wanted to make sure it would be around to do that.

He carefully removed all of its wet clothes, piling them on the floor. Upon reaching the collar, he hesitated. Sil had always been fiercely protective over it. He didn't get it – he thought its owner was a bad person, someone deserving of their pet running away from them, but seeing Sil be so adamant about keeping it on, he didn't know anymore. He'd *tried* to understand, but his questions only seemed to annoy the pet.

"You wanna take it away?"

"No, that's not – "

"So stop asking. It's none of your business whether I keep it on."

He grabbed a clean towel and gently patted Sil down, then left the fluffy thing on top of it while he went to fetch some dry clothes. It felt strange to have a barely conscious pet on his couch, dressed in his own sweater and pants, but he couldn't afford to just stand there and dissect the feeling. He ran back to the bedroom for extra blankets and draped those over it as well, just to be a hundred percent sure it wasn't going to wake up to any sort of cold. Only then did he slip out the front door to retrieve the rest of the blankets from the snow, the ones he couldn't immediately pick up along with Sil.

He considered calling emergency services. In truth, he barely had any idea what he was doing, only relying on something he'd learned in tenth grade along with his driver's ed course. But he knew more about first aid than Sil's predicament. What if he was dooming it by calling them? Because honestly, nothing about this entire thing was adding up in his head.

First of all, how did the PPA not pick up on the abuse Sil had so clearly gone through? There were annual welfare checks for all the pets in Lezune, around the entire damn country, specifically to ensure that cases like this were prevented. But even if prevention failed, the PPA were supposed to pick up on bad situations and remove the pet immediately, revoke the owner's licence, and make it as right as they possibly could. There was a chance that someone had inflicted all of these injuries upon the poor thing in less than the span of a year, before the first check-up was due, and Rayan actually hoped *that* was the case.

Because the other possibility was *bribery*. That was his first thought on the day that he'd met Sil, and while he'd tried to be understanding and go through the information he had with a clear head, he just kept coming back to the same conclusion. A regular owner would've long been jailed for severe neglect and abuse, but some people just had a way with ... words. He supposed the money did most of the talking.

That would also explain why Sil hadn't gone to the authorities to be checked into a shelter. Its chip would've been read, and its owner would've likely figured out a way to get it right back to the same abusive home it had escaped from, rendering all of its efforts useless.

Sil let out a pained moan and Rayan was immediately by its side, kneeling next to the couch and waiting for any sort of request from the pet. "Sil? Uh, try not to freak out, okay? I brought you inside because of the cold, you're in my living room. Do you need anything? A warm drink? Soup?"

"Where's my collar ... " it mumbled.

"Right next to us. Your clothes are here too. I'm gonna wash everything for you, okay?"

"No!" Its eyes snapped open fully, and it turned to Rayan with the most panicked expression he'd ever seen. "No, n-no, please, I need it, please, don't touch my clothes ... Please give back my collar, please ... "

"Hey, hey, calm down – "

"I need it, it's all I have, *please*, give it back!" Sil tried to push itself up, immediately failing with the weight of all those blankets on top of it. Rayan gently pushed it back down onto the couch, hushing it.

"I'll give it back. I'll give it back right now, okay? I'll put it right next to you, but please, don't put it back on. It's all wet and dirty."

"Just give it back," it repeated brokenly, and Rayan quickly snatched the collar up from the floor and laid it right next to its face. Sil seemed to calm down considerably at that, scooting over so it could press its cheek against the leather. It closed its eyes again, breathing a sigh of relief.

"I'm sorry I took it without asking," Rayan said softly as he sat back down on the floor. "I was just trying to get all the wet stuff off of you, so you wouldn't get sick."

"Please don't take my clothes ... " It looked at Rayan pleadingly, and he just didn't have the heart to say no. He could've – he easily could've. Sil was defenceless and weak; it couldn't even get up from the couch without assistance. He could've taken those clothes and ripped them apart right in front of it if he wanted to. He pushed all the horrible, intrusive thoughts away, almost tearing up at the fact that its previous owner might've done quite similar things to it.

"I won't. I promise I won't."

Sil nodded in response, wincing as it tried to turn over and find a more comfortable position. Seeing that, a theory began to form in Rayan's head as to why a runaway pet would just stay in one spot for weeks, aside from the free food. The constant walking and running it must've had to do was likely taking a toll on its battered body. That was probably why it had decided to put all its eggs in one Rayan-shaped basket ... it didn't have a choice anymore. Not with winter approaching.

He stayed right there until Sil drifted off, wondering how any pet could be so extremely loyal to an abusive owner. It was clearly so attached, Rayan couldn't even imagine what must've finally led to it running off, and the subsequent emotional turmoil it must've caused. It must've been a life or death situation to push it over the edge. And for someone to take advantage of that devotion and love, that *trust* ... He shook his head and got up, grabbing Sil's clothes and bringing them to the closest possible radiator. Maybe they'd even fully dry by the time the pet woke up, and he could just place them back on the floor where they had been without it noticing a single thing.

He tried to shake out the individual pieces as gently as he could so the sound wouldn't wake Sil, but when he got to the pants, something fell out. Thankfully it landed on the carpet, so even though it seemed like a piece of metal, the noise was barely audible. He put the worn pair of slacks on the radiator and picked up the thing, realising with glee that it was a *name tag*. That was perfect! He could track who the owner was, he just had to read the –

Rayan deflated when he turned it around and saw that the engraving was too scratched up and faded to make out anything. He could see some digits of the facility number, and then a capital B ... maybe that was supposed to be Sil's name, then? It seemed too short to be its owner's name. Plus, there was another name right under it, something that resembled his own much more closely. And lastly, maybe a phone number? He couldn't even see the area code.

He sighed and put the trinket on top of the pants, so Sil could find it later; then he thought better of it and slipped it back into the pocket. He had the feeling Sil wouldn't appreciate the fact that he'd tried to read it.

But didn't it say that its owner refused to give it a name? So what was up with that pet name-looking row? Rayan walked back to the couch and sat down on the floor, pulling out his phone and looking up some of the biggest national news outlets, as well as some regional ones. Maybe someone had lost a pet recently. And maybe it was someone whose name fit perfectly into the blanks on that name tag.

GUEST

"Rayan?"

The quiet little voice made Rayan look up from his phone immediately. There wasn't anything interesting on it anyway. No matter where he looked, it seemed there wasn't a single runaway pet within the borders; every pet was happy and right where it was supposed to be, no owner was crying on any social media platforms, and there was no ongoing police investigation. Nothing. To the media, Sil didn't exist.

To Rayan, though, it was the only thing in existence right now.

"What's up?" he asked softly.

"Hurts ... "

He had to admit, Sil did look absolutely miserable. It had barely moved since Rayan brought it inside – granted, it had also spent a lot of that time asleep. When it was awake, it just kept groaning and whining, and now it was looking at him with the most pain-filled, teary eyes that he had ever seen. Its expression was open and vulnerable, a stark contrast to the apparently not-so-permanent scowl he had gotten accustomed to. It was just ... jarring. Heartbreaking.

"Can you tell me what hurts? And how? Maybe I can get you medication for it."

"No – no, no, no ... no pills ... no, please ... " It squeezed its eyes shut, shaking its head weakly. "No pills ... no ... "

"You don't like meds, huh ... Bad memories?"

"*No* memories."

Rayan was confused only for a moment before he realised what Sil was so afraid of. Dirucodone. Of course. It must've had a bad experience with the amnesia drug once, and now it didn't want anything to do with medications. "Hey, painkillers aren't gonna make you forget anything. I don't even have access to the amnesia pill, I couldn't give you that if you asked."

A tear trickled down its cheek, onto the fabric of the couch. "No pills," it repeated stubbornly. "I won't – I won't forget … I can't … "

"You love your owner a lot, don't you?" Rayan asked compassionately, further saddened when Sil nodded. "I'm sorry, love. I wish I could reunite you two. And – and I'll try my best to help, but first you have to get better yourself, okay? And for that, please tell me where it hurts. It could be something serious."

"Everywhere … it hurts – it hurts everywhere … it hurts to talk … "

"Does your throat hurt?" Sil nodded. Of course it had caught a cold outside like that. "Okay, I'll ask you some yes or no questions, then. Do you also have a headache?" Nod. "Nausea?" Nod. "Uh … everywhere … limb pain? Like, arms and legs? Feeling a little achy?" Nod. "Chest tight?" Nod. "That really is everywhere … That's bad. But not horrible." He gently put a hand against Sil's forehead, feeling for a fever, and of course, with his luck, it was burning up. "Okay, we're getting into horrible territory. Sil … I'm gonna need you to take some meds."

"No, no, please!" It tried to scoot farther down on the couch to hide under the blankets, probably jostling some sensitive areas in the process, judging from the whimpers. "Please, please, sir, please, I'm sorry … "

Rayan didn't even know whether he wanted that title to be a little slip-up indicative of it not being fully there and fully lucid, or just a defence mechanism for when it got too scared to be snarky. Neither of the options were particularly promising. "It's not gonna make you forget, Sil, I promise … It's just gonna make you feel better. Why don't we start with a little candy that'll make your throat hurt less? Would that be less scary?"

Sil shook its head frantically. "D-doesn't hurt, it doesn't hurt, I'm fine, it doesn't hurt … "

Okay, they weren't getting anywhere with this. Rayan sighed and backed off a little, trying to think of what would be the best course of action. Was he supposed to let it be? Or was he supposed to force some medication into it in the name of the greater good? At that moment, he really wished he had taken that class on decision-making under pressure.

He had already done quite a lot of things by now to make sure Sil came out on the other side feeling relatively okay, right? Putting his foot down and being a little stern over the medication was just an extension of that same effort ...

Except Sil wasn't fighting anymore, and that was the worst part about all of this. Rayan wasn't going up against that feral alley stray he'd met that first day, he was pestering and tormenting a weak, vulnerable pet. God, he felt so unbelievably awful about this whole thing. He bit his lower lip and stood up, deciding he was going to get those meds in Sil's system by whatever means necessary.

"I'm sorry, I'm sorry, I'm sorry ... " Rayan muttered while getting all the medication together: one for the fever, one for the cold, a painkiller, and a throat-numbing, strawberry-flavoured candy. He could think of nothing else but those times when he'd watched the vet shove medication down cats' throats, and he tried to tell himself that this was similar. Sil needed the medication despite its attempts to dodge it, just like how some animals tried to dodge necessary shots at the vet. "Please, please forgive me ... " He took a deep breath, putting on his most authoritative face.

He walked back to the living room, sitting on the couch and prompting Sil to sit up. It wanted to hide more than anything, but Rayan willed himself to gently but firmly guide it into a sitting position.

"No medication," it sobbed, shaking its head, still trying to get away. "Please, sir, Rayan, please, *please*, you said you care, you said you *care*!"

Oh, Rayan's heart was shattering into a million pieces at the sight. He was doing it to save Sil. He was. He didn't want to hurt it, he *wasn't* hurting it, he wasn't giving it any pills that caused amnesia, he just had to get its fever down. "Sil, I'm sorry, I need you to take these. Please. They'll make you feel better."

That seemed to make the hysteria worse. The phrase set off something absolutely primal in the poor pet, and it put every ounce of its remaining strength and voice into protesting. It was getting way too loud for a little apartment with neighbours on all sides, and Rayan was getting anxious about being busted. In a panic, he decided that if physically forcing it was a no-go ... then he'd just bluff.

"If you don't take the medication here, I'll call the Agency and you can take it there."

Sil went rigidly still within a split second. Its eyes were impossibly wide, full of that animalistic fear Rayan had only ever seen once or twice in particularly bad cases of stray cats and dogs. That, and unbearable betrayal.

It took the pills without resistance, one after the other. Rayan eased it back down onto the sofa afterwards, trying not to think about the long-term effects this stupid trick would have on their relationship.

"I'm so sorry," he whispered miserably. His facade of having it all figured out and under control was long gone, and he slid down onto his knees next to the couch so as not to take up space that Sil might've needed. "Sil, I'm sorry, I had to say something – I had to get you to take those, I'm *so* sorry. I won't call them, okay? I was serious when I said I care, I swear. I – I just – " His desperate excuses came to a sudden stop when Sil closed its eyes, clearly indicating that it just wanted to rest and be left alone. Rayan swallowed and nodded to himself, a silent acknowledgment that he had fucked up. Of course, he had known that the moment he'd decided to force the medication.

He nervously ran his fingers through his hair. He needed help. He needed so much help. But from whom? He didn't want to get his family involved and get them into trouble, plus his parents would've skinned him alive for breaking the law like this. He couldn't ask a doctor – or could he?

He'd heard of ... underground vets before. He'd always thought the entire concept was repulsive. Pets and strays alike were supposed to go to actual vets, ones that were safe and monitored. Rich people also shouldn't have been encouraged to go outside of the system that had been set up to be as protective of registered pets as possible. But now that he had a stray on his hands, one he didn't want discovered ... maybe he could try to find something. Maybe ... god, he hated himself for thinking this way, but maybe he would even be able to bring Sil while it was sick and compliant enough. The fragile, barely-there trust they'd built had already been broken at this point; there was little to lose, and everything to gain.

"I ... I'm gonna be ... right here. In the, um ... in the kitchen. If you need anything ... " he trailed off when he got no response, getting up with a dejected sigh. He was just trying to keep it alive. Why was that so hard to do? Why did every decision that benefitted Sil physically seem like the worst possible option when it came to building some sort of emotional connection?

Rayan dragged himself back over to the kitchen, sitting down at the table and laying his head on his arms. He was an absolute monster for using the PPA as a threat, a thought only further confirmed when he heard the quiet sobbing from the living room. But what else was he supposed to do? He groaned, rubbing his face against his skin. Gross. He was so gross.

He had no idea how long he'd spent wallowing in self-pity before he heard a knock at the door. He jumped at the noise, his head snapping in the direction of his new pet. *Fuck*. He had to get Sil into the bedroom *immediately*.

"One moment!" he yelled, having to disregard the poor guy's consent *once again* as he hastily scooped it up along with its collar and brought it into the bedroom, setting it down on the bed. Thankfully, it seemed he'd woken it from a deep sleep, which meant it didn't even make a peep before the bedroom door was closed. He shoved the half-dried clothes into one of the cupboards, hoping he wouldn't forget to take them out afterwards. "Who is it?" he asked as he walked over, hand already on the doorknob.

"Pet Protection Agency," came the casual reply, and Rayan's blood froze in his veins.

Oh *god*.

Out of the Ordinary

Rayan stared at the door for a moment longer than he should've, only opening it when he was sure he wouldn't immediately throw up from the nerves. The sight of a young female agent greeted him, one that seemed incredibly exhausted and in general very much over the concept of having to talk to him.

"Rayan Kamali? I'm very sorry to bother you, sir," she began with a sigh, clicking her pen against her clipboard. "We've gotten a report about a stray from someone in the area, and we're obligated to ask around a bit. It will really only take a few minutes."

"Yeah – yeah, of course. Should we – would you like to come in?" he offered instinctively, almost flinching when he thought about the possibility of her discovering Sil. Lady Luck smiled upon him that day, because she declined, telling him again that it'd be quick.

The questions were simple enough: Have you seen a stray around? Have you seen anything out of the ordinary? Have you seen anyone stumbling about, looking lost or confused? They were textbook questions, taken straight from the PPA's official website, from the tab about recognising potential strays. It was difficult, given the striking resemblance they bore to people, so it was no wonder that any employee would be a little sceptical or frustrated about having to investigate a tenth false report.

Except this one was not fake.

Rayan answered everything to the best of his ability. He wasn't a very good liar, not even an average one. His palms were all sweaty, his voice broke, the lump in his throat refused to move either up or down. He kept chuckling nervously, repeating that he hadn't seen or heard anything multiple times. Most likely the only thing that saved him from incriminating himself completely was that she didn't let him ramble on, nor did she have the energy to be too suspicious.

"All done," she said after what had felt like an eternity to Rayan's battered heart. "Are you okay, sir?"

"Yeah!" he replied way too quickly. "Yeah, sorry. I get nervous about any questioning. It's like when I exit a store and I know I haven't stolen anything, but I'm like, *'oh god, what if it'll beep?'* That – that kinda thing. Sorry."

She gave him a sympathetic smile, the wariness disappearing from her face. "I'm really sorry if I've made you anxious. It's just a routine check. But please, if you see anything, don't hesitate to give us a call. It's likely nothing, though."

"Of course. I wouldn't want some poor guy to be stuck out there in the cold."

She nodded and went to knock on his neighbour's door, and Rayan forced himself to be slow about closing the door instead of slamming it shut. He took a few steps back, still holding his breath, only exhaling when he was far enough away that he thought she wouldn't hear.

Fucking hell. *Fucking hell.*

He wiped his hands off on his pants, but he couldn't stop the shaking. He'd just lied to a pet protection agent. If this got out, he would be fined *at the very least*. Could he go to jail for this? Misleading authorities? Probably yes. God, he didn't want to go to jail. His life was on track for once, his apartment was fairly clean, it looked like he was about to get promoted at work, he was steadily saving up money for that stupid dessert shop he wanted to open ... He couldn't go to jail.

Tears of pure, overwhelming stress were gathering in his eyes and quickly spilling over. He sat down on the floor, pulling his knees up to his chest, trying to calm himself. He needed to check on Sil and tell it that the coast was clear, the employee had left, and it wasn't going to be brought in. That was the obvious course of action in this situation, not weeping on the floor like a toddler. If he wanted to be a baby about it, he shouldn't have decided to do something so utterly illegal.

Wiping his eyes and taking one last, deep breath, Rayan stood up to go to the bedroom. He could hear the sound of footsteps going from the door to the bed as he approached, and he gave Sil a few moments to properly get into bed and pretend it hadn't been eavesdropping before knocking. "Sil?" No response. "Can I come in?"

It was a little silly. The bedroom was his own; Sil had barely been occupying it for more than ten minutes. Still, he had been so horribly evil, disregarding its consent and opinion at every turn, he felt obligated to at least give it this. Thus, he waited patiently, wondering whether Sil was pretending to be asleep.

Just when he was about to knock again, he heard a faint voice from inside. "No."

Admittedly, he was a little surprised. That wasn't the usual answer most people expected to a simple question like that. It wasn't even a question, really, not in any other scenario; it was more common courtesy, something nice but ultimately useless to say before entering a room. After having violated its consent multiple times, however, Rayan found it impossible to even touch the handle of the door.

"Okay," he said gently. "I just wanted to tell you that it's safe now."

Again, he waited for a good while for a response that truly didn't come this time. He didn't really know how to proceed. Sil had to come out eventually. Would he get his bedroom back then? No, Sil was better off inside, in a room that was hidden from people standing in the front doorway. But he still needed to get his bedsheets, even if he was going to sleep on the couch.

Well, the evening was still a long way away. "I'll come back later with some lunch, okay? Try to get some rest until then. I'm sorry everything is so stressful."

You made it stressful, a nasty voice in the back of his mind whispered. He tried to silence it, to no avail. He eventually decided to busy himself by opening up his laptop and doing some absolutely-not-suspicious research on underground vets. Opening a new tab in incognito mode seemed ridiculous, since he would be up against the government if he got caught, but he did it anyway, hoping to ease his anxiety a little.

There wasn't a lot of available information, of course. Not on sites that could be easily accessed by the masses. Most sources seemed to agree that to get into a clinic like that, one had to have two things: money and connections. As it stood, Rayan had neither.

He tilted his head back, letting it rest against the back of the couch. Connections ... Didn't he have anyone who could hook him up with a vet like that? Who would even have connections like that? People who wanted bad things to happen to pets, or people who wanted the opposite? Definitely people who had a reason to want to go around the system. People who didn't like the system.

Maybe ... people who thought the system was a scam and pets shouldn't have been treated like animals.

He typed in the name of the organisation as fast as he could, scrolling down to the bottom of their website to see their address. They weren't very far from where he lived, ironically, even though their beliefs couldn't have been further apart. He could barely believe he was about to throw himself at their feet.

The Pet Liberation organisation wasn't a very good one. Rayan saw the news about them, all those ludicrous things they kept spewing, trying to confuse people and turn them against the PPA. But even though they were a borderline cult, and Rayan agreed with virtually none of their sentiments, he had to admit that they definitely had a reason to visit or even operate underground pet clinics. But then again, could those clinics be trusted? Or would they employ actual doctors, ones specialised in caring for people?

It was a gamble either way, he supposed. It was a *huge* gamble, a leap of faith that had the potential to kill him. So many things could go wrong, he couldn't even count. What if they turned him away? What if they assumed he was some secret government official, trying to gather information? What if they reported him? What if the doctor they suggested was a complete whacko?

He put down the laptop and got up to pace around the living room. He had to get Sil to a vet one way or another, and this was the only thing he could think of. The only other option was to go to the PPA and let them handle it, but that one was basically out of the picture from the get-go. He just had to do some more research into the organisation's philosophy and pretend he was on board with them, right? Surely, they'd take pity on him if they knew how desperate the situation was. And it had to appeal to them as well, given that he was evading authorities to keep a pet safe. Sil already said he treated it too much like a person.

Or should he go immediately? He glanced at the bedroom door. He had no idea whether time was precious. Would the cold worsen? Was it more than a cold? Was it something serious? Would Sil even be okay in his apartment completely alone? Pets weren't made for independence, they needed someone to help them. But maybe if he just made it a quick errand –

A quiet little sneeze made him stop in his tracks. He could just imagine the poor thing shivering under the blanket. Maybe he should bring it one more layer, just to be safe, just to ensure it really wouldn't be cold anymore.

He grabbed his thickest quilt and made his way over to the bedroom before realising Sil had told him not to enter. He knocked again, deciding that if he wanted to talk to Sil about leaving it alone for a bit, he might as well ask whether he could bring the extra protection inside. "Hey, love? Would you like another blanket?"

"No," it rasped. "Just wanna be left alone."

Well, that's lucky. "Um, that's actually something I wanted to ask you – would it be okay if I left for a little bit? Will you be okay?"

No immediate answer. Rayan never knew what that meant. Was it just annoyed with him? Was it thinking about it? If so, what was the reason for the internal debate? Was it not sure it would be okay, or was it just trying to figure out where Rayan would go?

He could hear the creak of the bed and the shuffling of feet before the door was slowly opened. Sil stood there with the blanket around its shoulders, shaking with either the effort or cold. It had always seemed so small, but now that they were face to face with each other, Rayan could see that the pet was almost as tall as him. It looked ... scared, despite it trying to hide it. "Are you going to the shelter?" it asked quietly. "You can come inside. It's your room. I just ... I wanted to test it, I'm sorry. I won't be a bother." It shifted its weight from one foot to the other, losing its balance and almost fainting. Rayan caught its frail body at the last second, dropping the quilt to the floor. "Please don't call them," it muttered.

"Oh my god," he breathed, astounded by just how ... light and delicate it felt in his arms. It felt like a porcelain doll, about to shatter with the slightest pressure. He quickly brought it back to bed, laying it on the soft mattress and covering its body with the blanket. "I won't call the shelter, Sil. I'm sorry. I – I never meant to make you feel like you couldn't say no to me. I'm *so* sorry about the whole meds situation, I swear I just want to help you. I want you to get better, so you'll have the energy to tell me off like before, yeah?" He couldn't help getting a little choked up at the end, and he had to blink away some tears before he could go on. "I ... I need to get you help. I'm trying to get you help. But I'm not going to any shelter."

"Master ... Master would help ... "

Rayan had some doubts about that. "Can you tell me your master's name?"

Sil shook its head, burying its face in its hands after. It was sobbing again, and Rayan was starting to get very conscious about the possibility of dehydration.

"Hey, it's okay. Um ... if you really want to go back to your owner, then why ... why don't you want me to go to the shelter? They could read your chip there."

"No! No, no owner, no ... "

Rayan furrowed his brows in confusion. Okay, Sil was just talking nonsense. Was it delirious? This whole illness was most likely way worse than he'd thought. He needed to go and get a vet's appointment right now. "Okay, no owner. I'm gonna go and try to get you help, then, yeah? All according to the original plan. No shelter, no owner, just a doctor who can help cure you without blowing your cover. Sound good?"

"Doctor?" Its head lolled to the side, eyes fluttering closed. "Doctors would fix me ... But mutts don't deserve doctors ... "

"Mutts ... what?" It was so difficult to even listen to the things it said sometimes, Rayan couldn't even imagine actually living it. "Sil ... " He sighed heavily, wiping the fresh tears from his eyes. "You'll get better. I promise. I'll take you to a doctor, and they'll fix you up, and it'll all be alright."

Sil hummed approvingly. It took a lot of strength for Rayan to actually stand up and leave it lying there alone, but he wanted to get the contact info he needed as soon as possible. Who knew how long they'd have to wait to get an appointment? Were underground vets busy? They had to be.

He put the quilt over Sil, then brought it fresh water from the kitchen. He couldn't resist petting its hair a little when he checked whether its fever was going down, which, thankfully, felt like it was. "I'll lock the door so no one can bother you," he whispered. "I'll be back before you know it."

Pet Liberation

There was little that Rayan hated more than the Pet Liberation movement. Cult, even, if the media was anything to go by. He didn't necessarily like to jump on any hate trains, but the one against this specific movement seemed to be more than justified. Everything they did, everything they believed in ... It was all nonsense, and they were very angry and violent about it.

Science had long proven that pets were different. Not in a bad way, but in a way that cats were different from dogs. They needed different care, different accommodations ... Their entire brain chemistry was different, their habits, their behaviours, it was all so different from the way people were. Pets were just different. And yet, Pet Lib continued to spew the nonsense that pets and people were one and the same, and the only thing separating them from each other were drugs and conditioning. Hell, they said that any one person could be taken from the street and turned into a pet within a matter of months. They said that was the exact scenario some strays found themselves in.

Rayan tried not to think about all this. He was going to their central office to talk to some very important people; he couldn't rile himself up with the lies right before that. But still, he couldn't *not* think about it. What was wrong with these people? Yes, some strays had lived a substantial portion of their lives thinking they were people. But they could feel that something was wrong! That was why there was an entire process for strays turning themselves over! It caused severe distress in them to be living as people! To call that kidnapping and human trafficking – god, he couldn't imagine what was going through the minds of some people.

He looked down at his hands, fidgeting anxiously. He was going to entrust some seriously sensitive information to these people. If they said something outrageous, like, "Well, let Sil go, let it live as a person!" he didn't know what he was going to say. Should he play along? It'd likely frighten the poor pet if later the vet told it some similar things.

Well, he would think about crossing that bridge when it was at the very least in sight. He got off the bus at the next stop, walking over to the small office building on the other side of the street. This was it, then. He was about to talk to some very strange people.

"Good morning, sir, how may I help you?" a kind woman behind the desk asked, and Rayan suddenly realised he had no idea how to reach the people he wanted to reach.

"I ... um ... I was wondering if I could talk to ... someone. Like, someone who knows a lot about this whole conspiracy." Yes, that was good. He'd seen the word conspiracy used on their website several times in relation to the pet system. "I'm very sorry, I haven't been a follower of the movement for a very long time, but ... it abruptly became ... quite personal to me. To, um, learn about this."

"I'm very sorry to hear that, sir," she said gently. "Understanding the system that causes our grief and working to change it can give our life purpose, I think. I'll try to see if I can reach one of our educators, or you could take a pamphlet in the meantime. We hold weekly meetings and demonstrations, completely free of charge, if you're interested."

"Thank you so much. I'll wait here, then." He took a pamphlet from the desk and sat down, skimming the text.

The faux-science of the Pet Protection Agency. Facts or well-marketed propaganda?

'Strays' are not being saved – the realities of the 'pet test'.

The culture that raised us to let our loved ones be kidnapped and thank the kidnappers.

Corruption, custom pets, and the abuse behind closed doors.

The purposely shocking titles brought back all his memories of the research he'd done, and he felt like he was going to be sick. He quickly stuffed the paper in his pocket, taking a couple deep breaths to calm himself. These people were *evil.* How could they actually spread things like this? How could they go out there and yell all these things at the top of their lungs, as if – as if they were *true*?

They were preying on vulnerable people: ones who had lost a loved one due to them being discovered to have been a pet, ones who had relatives go to jail for pet abuse, strays ... They really were a cult. They had recruited all these ignorant and desperate people who weren't in the right state of mind to join any movement and told them to recruit more. But all that senseless spouting of nonsense could only ever lead to two outcomes, one of which was the complete loss of that friendship, and the other was a successful recruitment. Which meant that these people had ended up with no one but their own cult around them, trapped in the echo chamber of a harmful ideology.

"Sir?"

Rayan's head snapped towards the receptionist woman, then he quickly stood up to go back to the desk.

"One of our educators is available. If it's alright for you, she could be here within ten minutes to answer all your questions." She covered the microphone of the phone, lowering her voice. "I told her that it seemed urgent. I hope that's okay."

"Yes, thank you. Thank you *so* much. I can wait here – or if it's better for her someplace else, I can go there – I can pay her for her time too, I know this was really sudden, and I've never donated to the movement – "

The woman smiled and put a finger up, silencing him. She quickly ended the phone call, then turned back to Rayan with such genuine compassion in her eyes that it pained him to even return her gaze. He was lying to these people. These poor, misguided people who just wanted to do good in the world in their own way. "Denice won't accept a single coin from you, most likely. It's deeply personal for a lot of us, but she's someone who has lost *a lot* to this cruelty. She'll be able to answer any questions you might have."

Rayan nodded wordlessly. He let the woman rant about the injustices in this world, about the fact that she would've moved to Batum long ago if she didn't think they had a chance to change things here. Those people knew what they were doing. They had outlawed the keeping of pets ages ago. They treated everyone as equals.

He wished these people would understand that *people* were treated equally in Lezune. But pets weren't people, that was the whole point, the whole reason behind treating them differently. Treating different beings similarly was just as much of an injustice as treating similar beings differently. He had learned about the effects of the Batumian pet-ban in high school, same as everyone else. Same as the woman sitting across from him, probably. He knew damn well that it had caused serious issues within the country, ones they were still trying desperately to recover from. The pets they tried to integrate into their society of people weren't doing any better than if they had tried to integrate sheep into a wolf enclosure. It just didn't work like that.

When Denice arrived, she suggested they go into one of the more secluded rooms, so Rayan could talk openly. He readily agreed, stiffly settling into one of the comfortable armchairs in the little office she had led him to. He didn't know where to begin.

"I don't mean to assume anything," she started instead, with a knowing look that made Rayan feel like she could see right through him. "But I think you don't really care about the movement. In fact, I think you think we're out of our minds."

"That's – no, of course not – "

She smiled. "I'm not a mindreader or anything, please don't look so worried. I frequent the restaurant you work at, and I've heard you talk about your big dream to adopt a pet so many times I can't even count."

Oh. Rayan's face flushed with embarrassment, and he resolved to share less with his coworkers, or at least do so in a lower volume. He rubbed the back of his neck awkwardly, trying to think of a lie big enough that it would justify him changing his whole worldview. He couldn't.

"I didn't want to lie," he said quietly. "I'm sorry. I didn't know how else to get a hold of ... someone. Anyone who could help."

"Well, I still want to. I didn't come to the office just to scold you and send you on your way. We're not out for people's blood, Rayan. I just didn't want to build this entire conversation on a lie."

He took a deep breath and nodded, meeting Denice's eyes again. "I found a stray. It's very sick right now, and it's also badly injured. I didn't report it to anyone, because I think its previous owner was the one who caused most of its injuries, and from what I gather, it has never been taken to a vet before."

"And you can't take it to a government-approved clinic, so you came here to ask if we had any clinics outside of the system," she concluded. He nodded again. Denice leaned back in her chair, humming in thought.

"You know I'm not a secret PPA officer or anything," Rayan tried weakly. "I mean, if you've seen me at work – you know they don't need to work as waiters and waitresses. Please. If you can direct me to anyone who could possibly help ... I don't want it to go back to a place where it's being hurt. I don't want it to suffer. Even – even if I don't agree with a lot of what you guys are saying, isn't that the whole point? To reduce suffering?"

"You're asking me to break the law, Rayan. You're asking me to give up information I may or may not have on an underground clinic that you could direct absolutely anyone to. You're not part of the movement, in fact you're *against* the movement, and yet you're asking me for sensitive information that could put several of us in jail."

He swallowed thickly, unable to argue. "Yeah. Yeah, that's ... I guess that's what I'm asking. But I'm also already breaking the law. If I contacted the authorities now, I would be in trouble too."

"I don't even know if you have actually found anyone."

"Should I take pictures? Voice recordings? What do you need me to do?" he asked desperately. "What do I need to do so you'll trust me? Please, it almost fainted when it tried to stand. It's alone in my apartment right now and I just want to go home and tend to it, but I *need* to get in contact with a vet. I don't think I can help it alone. I'm already trusting you with all the sensitive information you need to land me in jail, *please*, give me a chance. I'll join the movement if that's what you need."

"We're not that strapped for members." Denice stood up from her desk, motioning for Rayan to do the same. "I'll send someone to check out the situation. If they think you're fine, you'll get to go meet our doctor. Does that sound fair?"

"Why won't you come?" he blurted out, and she laughed.

"I can't visit randos anymore. If I go to anyone's house, the PPA will start harassing them too, thinking they're new recruits. If you're really hiding a 'stray' in there, it'll be discovered within days."

Rayan stood up and nodded. "Right. Sorry. Thank you so much for helping me. I really can't even explain how much it means. I'm so – I'm just so worried."

She put a gentle hand on his shoulder. "Don't take this as an insult, but I think we'll see each other a lot more in the future. You seem like a pretty good guy, and if you're going about this the illegal way, you'll very quickly realise that we might not be the cultists here."

He didn't have much time to react before she passed him on the way to the door, and he quickly followed after her. Before he knew it, he was already on the bus back home, hoping that the Pet Liberation secret agent they were going to send would find everything in order. At least enough to give him the doctor's contact info.

Assessment

On the way back, Rayan's head was full of doubts and concerns. Did he make a mistake? Would Denice report him? No, that'd mean implicating herself. Not to mention what she'd said about the PPA 'harassing' everyone she came into contact with.

On that same note, though, would Rayan be harassed? Would they mistakenly assume he aligned with Pet Lib?

Would they never give him a licence because of that?

He got off the bus a stop too late, but he decided to take it as a blessing in disguise. A little walk would do him good, it'd allow him to clear his head.

No, he couldn't dilly-dally. He picked up his pace, pushing past the people lazily strolling along. He had someone waiting now. Someone very sick.

He made a quick stop at the pharmacy to pick up some more cold medicine, hoping that next time he wouldn't have to resort to cheap bluffs that made Sil's heart skip several beats. He hoped Sil would be better by the time he got home, but he didn't want to get his hopes up. He didn't even worry about it escaping as of now, which was really just a testament to what condition he'd left it in.

"I'm home," he said softly as he finally entered his apartment. Nothing looked amiss, everything was exactly as he'd left it. There was no response from the bedroom, but that could've been for a number of reasons. Maybe Sil was just asleep – still, he would've been lying if he'd said his heart was beating normally.

He tiptoed over to the bedroom door and turned his head to the side, pressing his ear against the wood. There were no sounds coming from inside. He put a hand on the handle and tried to push it down as slowly as possible, just until he heard the telltale click of it popping open. He paused, listening for any sounds – nothing.

The door slid open soundlessly, and Rayan was met with one of the most terrifying sights he could've imagined: an empty bed, devoid of the stray he'd painstakingly carried home with him.

"Fuck!" He pushed the door all the way open, rushing over to the bed in a frenzy. The mattress was still warm in the middle, just where he'd laid Sil, so it must've left not too long ago. Maybe if he ran –

Achoo.

Rayan froze in place. Did someone just ... sneeze? It came from the direction of the bed. From ... under the bed.

He slowly lowered himself to the ground, getting on his hands and knees and bending down until he could see under the bed. There it was, staring back at him with puffy, red eyes. "Sil ... "

Achoo.

No wonder it was sneezing so much, he hadn't cleaned under the bed in ages.

"I wasn't sure it was you," it mumbled, eyes already half-closing. It must've taken so much effort to squeeze under the bed like that, especially in its state. "I didn't want ... others to see ... " Was it dozing off mid-sentence?

Rayan sighed. "It's okay. It's just me. Come on, out we go."

He pulled out his pet without much resistance from it, gently laying it on the bed again. He meticulously removed every last dust bunny that had gotten stuck to its pyjamas before covering it with several blankets again, unable to resist some encouraging words as he worked. Sil didn't seem to mind. In fact, the murmurs seemed to help it relax.

"I went and talked to a kind lady by the name of Denice," he said quietly. "She said she'll send a friend to assess your situation. They're not connected to the PPA in any way; in fact, the PPA kind of hates them. Those are the only type of people I can really talk to right now, I suppose."

"Assess ... ?"

"They'll take a look at you. See how sick you are. Then, if they can help, they'll connect us with a nice doctor. Someone who won't hurt you or turn you in."

"A doctor ... " Sil rubbed its face against the pillow. "I'd like a doctor ... "

"Yeah, I'd like one too. I'm not very good at medical stuff." Rayan slowly reached out, letting the back of his hand brush against Sil's forehead. The fever seemed to be going down at least. He experimentally petted it a little, gently ruffling its hair; Sil leaned into it. "Did you climb under the bed when you heard me enter?"

"Mhm."

"I'll clean out the closet for you, how about that? You can have your little hiding place in there. I'll also clean out the entire room so you don't have to crawl around in filth. I'm so sorry for not having done it sooner, I just had no idea you'd do this ... I don't know why, I should've known you'd get scared ... "

"Rayan?"

"Yes?"

"Can you bring me ... the clothes? My clothes?"

"They're drying on the radiator in the living room." Shit, that was a lie. He totally forgot he'd thrown them into the cupboard. Thank god Sil mentioned it. "I mean, um ... I can bring them inside, put them on the radiator here. If that's okay. I don't want you cuddling wet clothes, they'll just make you sicker."

"Radiator's fine," it mumbled. Its eyes were already closing again, and Rayan wagered it would be asleep by the time he got back from the other room.

"You can go back to sleep, love," he said gently. "I'll place them on the radiator and close the bedroom door again. I won't wake you for the visit if I don't have to."

"I wanna be awake ... Wanna see ... I wanna see the doctor ... "

"This won't be the doctor yet. Just a friend who might tell us about the doctor. Just sleep, sweetheart. Don't even worry about it."

"Mhm ... "

***

The next time someone knocked on the door, Rayan was quick to open it without so much as a question. "I'm so glad you were able to make it," he said to the strange man standing on his doorstep. He didn't ... look like a secret agent.

"Of course, Rayan, anything for my dear friend!" he said cheerily. Great, he already knew his name, while Rayan knew absolutely nothing. "Let's see what we're working with – "

"Can you keep it down a little?" he asked once the door was closed. "It's sleeping."

"Oh, yes, yes, of course." He made a zipping motion from one corner of his mouth to the other. "Not a sound from me. Are they in the bedroom?"

"Yeah, I had to bring it in there because – "

"Ah! None of that dehumanising language until I hear it from their own mouth that they want that. No referring to people as 'it' without their express permission. Or as 'pets', while we're at it."

"Its – their throat hurts. Don't make it – them speak, if you can help it. Please. They're really sick."

The man nodded. "Lead the way, then."

Rayan walked past him and pushed the bedroom door open, revealing a very much asleep Sil. The man peeked inside, then gave Rayan an apologetic look. "I'll have to wake them."

"Well ... I mean, if it can't be helped ... " Rayan sighed. "I'll go wake it instead. Just – just give me a moment." He walked over and sat on the bed, and Sil's eyes already fluttered open. "Hey, sweet. Our friend has arrived, yeah? He'll take a quick look at you now. Are you alright with that?"

The man gave a slightly awkward wave. "Hi. I'm the friend."

Sil glanced at him before its gaze returned to Rayan. "Who's that?"

"Well, um ... I'm sorry, I didn't even ask your name – "

"Not important," the man said quickly. "Let's just get this over with, and I'll be out of here in a second."

The stranger produced an odd-looking device from his coat pocket, the likes of which Rayan had never seen before. He held it up to Sil's neck until it beeped, then stepped back. "Chipped. Poor thing."

Right. All pets were chipped. If this man got it to a doctor, they could simply read its chip, and then the mystery of who its owner was would immediately be solved –

"Can you tell me your name?"

Rayan was pulled back to the present moment as the man started his questioning. He looked at Sil, who looked like it took it a considerable effort to answer. "Dunno."

"You don't know what your name is?"

"Don't have one."

Rayan almost wanted to chime in, but felt like it'd be rude. If Sil didn't want to give its name to this person, he could understand it.

"Alright. Do you have a number?"

Sil frowned. "No. Owner said I didn't deserve one."

Oh, how that pained Rayan to hear. Was Sil's owner someone wealthy? Someone wealthy enough to keep multiple pets and only numbered them instead of naming them? He'd heard of such cases, but didn't realise someone in the area would be like that.

"Did you have a number before your owner?"

"Dunno."

"Alright. Are you a pet?"

"Yes."

"Would you like to be referred to as 'it'?"

"Yes."

Rayan resisted the urge to say 'I told you so'.

"Rayan, I'm going to have to ask you to step outside for a moment."

"What?" Rayan looked at Sil, then back at the man. "Why? What did I do?"

"I want him to stay," Sil said suddenly, and Rayan had never felt more proud in his life.

"It wants me to stay," he echoed.

"It'll just be a moment," he assured them.

"I want him to stay," Sil repeated, more firmly this time. It seemed to be getting really agitated over the idea of having to stay alone with a stranger.

"Okay, fine. I'll just ask in front of him. Is there anything you want me to know about? Did Rayan hurt you at all? Is he the reason you're so sick?"

Rayan's heart dropped. Technically ... yes. Yes, he was the reason why Sil was so sick now. But he hadn't hurt it. Would Sil say otherwise? Would it bring up the way he'd tricked it into taking medication? The way he'd failed to invite it into his warm home until it was halfway frozen?

The man seemed to take notice of his nerves, and Rayan averted his gaze. If Sil said something, he'd deserve it. It might even get Sil taken from him, but maybe then it'd be in the hands of more qualified people.

But then again, it had asked for him to stay. Surely, if Sil harboured any resentment towards him, it would be happy to be rid of him. Or maybe it was just a 'devil you know' scenario for it. Rayan had no way of telling.

"No," Sil said simply, and Rayan couldn't hold back a relieved sigh. "He helped me."

"Understood," the man said with a nod. "Rayan, if you'd be so kind ... "

"Yes, of course. I'm coming." He jumped up from the bed to escort him out, anxiously awaiting the verdict.

"It's most definitely a 'pet'," he started once they were out of the bedroom, doing air-quotes with his hands, "and a very worn-down one at that. It's been a while since I've seen something so severe. I'll write down the contact of the doctor; call her between six and eight in the evening. Don't forget about the chip in its neck, that could get very dangerous for both of you. Get it treated."

Before he knew it, Rayan was standing in his almost empty apartment with a little note in his hand.

He did it. He passed. He now had the contact information of an underground vet.

Doctor's Appointment

Time seemed to slow down as Rayan waited for the clock to strike six. He was sitting on the couch, staring at the one he'd gotten as a housewarming gift from his sister, Dana, bouncing his leg in anxiety as he tried to go through what he was going to say in his head.

"Hi, my name is Rayan. A Pet Lib guy gave me your number and I'd like to schedule an appointment for as soon as possible."

The less details, the better. Right? He could explain everything in greater detail once he and Sil were there. Or she'd see for herself, really. Honestly, Rayan didn't quite know the extent of Sil's injuries, nor how it'd sustained them. The only thing he knew about was it catching this nasty cold, for which he was going to assume full responsibility.

He jumped when his phone's reminder went off. Six o'clock. It was time.

He quickly dialled the number he'd been given, waiting nervously as the phone rang. "Hello?"

"Um, hi." He gripped the phone a little tighter, trying to swallow the lump in his throat. The woman on the other side sounded kind – honestly, everyone associated with Pet Lib had been kind so far – but he still couldn't shake the feeling that this was *wrong*. "My name is Rayan, and I've been given your number by a Pet Lib guy. I don't know his name, I'm sorry. Um, I was just wondering, uh ... if you could give me an appointment? As soon as possible, please."

"I'll give you the address, and you can tell me how soon you can get there. Does that sound alright?"

"Wait, like, today? Right now?"

"You said as soon as possible. I take my job seriously, Rayan."

"Right, right, sorry."

"My office is about five minutes from the address I'm about to tell you. I can't tell you the exact address for safety reasons, but I'll be there to help."

Rayan listened intently as she recited the address, immediately looking it up on his laptop to see where it was. "I can get there in half an hour. Is that alright?"

"That's fine. I'll be there to pick you up in exactly half an hour. What car do you drive?"

None, as of now. But he couldn't say that. He wouldn't be able to carry Sil through the city in the state it was in, so he'd need to ask his sisters for their car. "I don't really know the model, um, it's red. I'll give you the licence plate number, if that's okay."

Once arrangements were made, Rayan hung up and let out a relieved sigh. Everything was going to be fine, he told himself. He hoped his sisters didn't need the car for the rest of the evening.

***

"How much longer?" Sil asked miserably from the backseat. It was lying down with a blanket to cover it, but its shivering was still more than noticeable. "'m really cold ... "

"Two minutes, love. Just hold on a little longer, and the doctor will help you. I promise."

Suddenly, there was a knock on the window. Both Rayan and Sil jumped, and the pet immediately ducked under the covers. Whoever was trying to get Rayan's attention didn't look like the kind elderly lady he'd imagined while talking on the phone – in fact, he didn't look like any lady at all.

He quickly rolled down the window. "Can I help you?"

"You can't park here," he said gruffly.

"I – w hat? Why? I didn't see a sign – "

"I'm telling you that you can't."

Rayan blinked a couple times, confused. If he was made to park somewhere else, there was no telling whether the doctor would find him. "But I have to. I have – I'm meeting someone."

The man raised an eyebrow. "And who might you be meeting *here*?"

"I'm sorry, I don't think that's – "

"Milo, stop bothering the customer."

That sounded more like the voice from the phone call. Rayan craned his neck to look past the buff man by his window, and he spotted a short lady briskly walking towards his car.

The man – Milo – huffed. "I've never seen him around before. He doesn't look the type."

"Well, I'm telling you that he is. Stand down, boy."

Was Milo a pet? In his words, he didn't ... look the type. In fact, he looked like the scariest person Rayan had ever had the displeasure of meeting.

But he did stand down, allowing the doctor to walk up to his car window. "Rayan, am I correct?"

"Yes, ma'am. Can we go to the office now?" Maybe he was glancing at Milo way too noticeably, but the doctor let out a little laugh.

"Yes. Don't worry about Milo; he can be a little overbearing, but his heart is in the right place. And he'd never hurt a fly. My name is Anne, by the way." She stepped back so Rayan could open the door. "Do we need a stretcher for the little guy?"

"No, I can bring it in. Just give me a moment."

Rayan had never been to this part of the city. He couldn't help looking around every two seconds, anxious that someone other than Milo could be following them. The buildings looked old and quite unstable, most of the street lamps didn't work, and rubbish was thrown on the sidewalk in piles. He was honestly a little hesitant when it came to bringing Sil into an office, afraid that it might be in similar conditions.

He couldn't have been more wrong.

The office was as sterile as any other doctor's office he'd seen, if only a little small and not that well-equipped. He laid Sil on the examination table and stepped back, surprised to see it reach out for him.

"Don't leave," it croaked out, and Rayan stepped closer to hold its hand.

"I'm not leaving, love. I'm just trying to give the doctor space to work. I promise, I'm not leaving."

"Quite attached, are we?" Dr. Anne asked as she put on some gloves. "That's good. I would've been really angry if it turned out you were a *bad* illegal owner."

"I love pets," Rayan said defensively. "And I love Sil. I want it to be okay, that's the whole reason I'm here."

"Oh, don't get all mad at me. When you've been an illegal doctor for long enough, you learn not to get your hopes up every time. Many of my clients are the rich fucks who want to avoid scrutiny after beating their pet senseless."

Rayan felt his guts churn, and even Sil whimpered. "And you help them?" it asked in a small voice.

"I do what I do for the pets. What sense is there in turning those people away? The pet would suffer the consequences." She stepped up to the table. "And if I didn't help them, their owners might bring them to worse doctors. I've seen some truly gnarly injuries in my time – I don't trust the other underground clinics. Now, let's see what the problem is with you."

Rayan was trying very hard to sit still as Dr. Anne examined Sil, but it was proving to be quite difficult. She seemed to be causing quite a lot of discomfort, especially when she began moving the badly healed limbs around.

"We'll have to rebreak these if we want them to heal well," she said after a while. "I don't know exactly what happened, but I assume you didn't get medical attention for it."

"Rebreak?" Sil asked, eyes widening in horror. "No! No, please! Don't touch me! Don't hurt me!"

Rayan jumped up from his chair immediately. "Hey, Sil, calm down. Calm down, it's okay. It wouldn't be like the first time at all. It'd be nothing like that." Dr. Anne stepped back so he could take her place and take Sil by the hand, rubbing soothing circles into its skin. "You'd be asleep for it. Right, doctor?"

"Of course," she said without missing a beat. "We're not barbarians here."

"I don't want my limbs broken!" it cried anyway. "We need to go! I want to go home! Leave me alone! Master will be so mad that you broke my limbs again, Master will be furious! Master will save me!"

"Oh, sweetheart ... " Rayan moved on to petting its hair instead, trying to stay calm in the face of it lashing out. "It's okay. We just want to help. If you agree to the procedure, Dr. Anne will be able to make the pain go away. You're in a lot of pain, aren't you? You can barely walk."

"And if I don't agree? Then you'll report me?"

"No, no, of course not. Sil, I'm sorry about that." Dr. Anne shot him a suspicious glance, and Rayan felt his cheeks heat up. "I ... I tried to get it to take the cold medicine, but it didn't want to, so ... so I said ... I said I'd send it to the PPA so they could take care of it ... I realise that was horrible of me. I just wanted its fever to break, I swear. I was so scared."

She let out a heavy sigh. "Right. Well, there will be no more threats like that after this point. Unless Sil consents to the procedure, I'm not touching it."

"But you have to! It can barely walk – "

Dr. Anne glared at him. "Rayan, let me tell you something. The day I start doing non-consensual surgeries on people is the day I'll just apply to work at the PPA instead."

Rayan shut his mouth and slowly nodded. Right. He was being quite a horrible person, wasn't he? Dr. Anne was absolutely right. "I'm sorry," he said quietly.

"I don't want my bones broken," Sil muttered.

"Then they won't be. But let me give you a rundown on how that procedure would go – if you decide against it afterwards, I'll just send you on your way with some medicine for that nasty cold you got."

Rayan sat back in his chair, zoning out a little while the explanation was happening. He was much too preoccupied with his internal dilemma to pay much attention.

Was the PPA right to deny him a licence for pet ownership? Was there something wrong with him? But pets had to be treated without their consent sometimes, right? Like dogs, cats, or even children. Some just can't consent to surgeries that would objectively be good for them. There were no consent forms for pets. Was he wrong to bring Sil to an underground vet? Or doctor. Or whatever Dr. Anne was, he wasn't even sure.

What if Sil wasn't going to consent? Would there be serious consequences? Rayan wouldn't have minded if it was a cosmetic procedure, or something entirely optional, but he'd seen how much pain Sil was in every time it had to move around. This didn't feel optional.

"Rayan?"

He looked up to see both Sil and the doctor staring at him. "I – I'm sorry, I wasn't listening. Yes?"

Sil bit its lower lip, suddenly hesitating. "Would ... would you be here the whole time? During surgery?"

Rayan glanced at Dr. Anne, who gave him a small nod of approval. "Yes. Yes, of course. Anything you want."

It squirmed a little, eyes darting between him and the doctor. "And it wouldn't hurt?"

"Not at all. You'd be asleep for the whole thing, I promise," the doctor said soothingly.

Sil swallowed. "O-okay. I think ... Okay. If it really won't hurt ... But Rayan must stay. Please. Please, don't leave while I'm asleep. Not again."

Rayan furrowed his brows in confusion. "Again?"

"Master disappeared," it mumbled. "I fell asleep, and … and then they were gone."

"I won't leave," he promised again, filing that information away in his mind for later. He wasn't going to pry in front of the doctor. "I'll be right here when you wake up. I promise."

Sil nodded. Dr. Anne moved on to sterilise her equipment.

This would be a long night.

MASTER

Taking Sil home after surgery was easier than taking it there. It was still mostly out of it from the anaesthetics, napping peacefully in the backseat of the car. Rayan tried not to jostle it as he took it inside, then rushed back to take the car to his sisters' apartment. Once everything was settled – and he'd told Dana and Nima some lie about where he'd been – he assumed his guardian position next to Sil's bed.

"Rayan ... " it moaned quietly, reaching for him as soon as he entered the room. "Hurts ... "

"That's okay. It's alright. The doctor has prescribed you a lot of pain medication, I'll just – "

"No ... No pills ... Not again ... "

Fuck. "Sil ... "

"I am not consenting ... " it slurred. "No consent ... No ... "

"Sil, they'll make the pain go away. I have to give you medication for it, otherwise you'll be in pain for *weeks* on end. The doctor gave you medicine too, and you were fine afterwards. You didn't forget anything, did you? And I was right there when you woke up, just like I promised."

Sil's head lolled to the side, and it closed its eyes again. "No medicine ... "

Rayan sighed and grabbed his chair, pulling it right up next to the bed. "Alright. No consent, no medicine. Dr. Anne chewed me out for that bluff enough, I'm not doing it again."

"You said the doctor would fix me ... Why do I need more medicine ... ?"

"Well ... it gets worse before it gets better, a lot of the time. It will get worse for a bit – "

"Worse?" Sil looked up at him, its eyes full of horror. "Worse than how it was? But you said she'd fix me! You said ... I wanna be better, I wanna be without pain ... "

"You will be. If you don't trust me, trust Dr. Anne. She promised your limbs would go back to how they were. You'll just need a few weeks – "

"Weeks?" Sil let out a heavy sigh. "I don't wanna wait weeks ... "

"You don't have to wait out those weeks in pain. That's what the medication is for. It won't make you forget anything, it'll just make your weeks bearable. Don't you want to give it a try?"

Sil shook its head frantically. "No medicine. No pills."

It was Rayan's turn to sigh. "Alright. No pills for now. But the offer is on the table for whenever you change your mind."

A horrible little thought weaseled its way into Rayan's mind as he watched his pet all out of it. Would it be easier to get information out of it now? If he were to ask about its master, would it clear up some of the confusion? If he asked about the collar or the tag, would it answer?

These were all horrible thoughts, but they were almost impossible to ignore. He needed answers if he were to help this poor pet. He needed to know where to return it, whether its master was really a horrible person ...

"Sil?"

"Mhm ... "

Rayan was fidgeting with the hem of his shirt, not even really looking at the pet as he spoke. "Was your master a good person?"

Silence. "Yes. I love my master."

"Did they ever hurt you?"

"No."

Rayan's heartbeat picked up. Did he make all the wrong assumptions? "How did you get all these injuries, then?"

Sil shivered, even under the blanket. It must've been the anxiety. "Owner hurt me."

Rayan frowned. "But you said – "

"Not Master. Master would never hurt me."

Slowly, painstakingly slowly, it was starting to dawn on Rayan; Sil was talking about two different people. Owner and Master were not just synonyms to it, they marked two very different personalities.

"Oh," he breathed. But that was strange. Pets with several owners over the years should've been wiped between rehomings. How did Sil remember its previous master? "What was Master like?"

"Kind ... Always so kind to me ... I can't remember very well ... I remember little things, like – like Master holding me, singing me to sleep ... I remember a lake, and – and sitting on the shore in the grass ... The sun reflected off the water so prettily, I loved sitting there ... "

A lake? There was no lake near Laka. The only water near Laka was maybe the river Vezi, but that most definitely wasn't a lake. "Don't you mean the river?" he tried.

"Lake ... It was a lake ... Master loved the lake, and I loved it too, and we'd sit on the shore, and they'd brush my hair, and it was all so calm ... "

A lake. Lake Havey, maybe? But that was hours away from Laka. Maybe this was the wrong line of questioning. "What was your owner like?"

Sil shivered again. "*Bad*. Bad, horrible, mean ... Everyone was mean ... Owner was mean, his sister was mean, the other pets were mean ... It always hurt, something always, *always* hurt, and they'd yell at me, and beat me ... "

Rayan's heart twisted in pain. "Sil, I'm so sorry."

"He broke my bones too. But he never let me be asleep. He'd break them while I was awake, and he'd never take me to the doctor, and he'd yell at me for being in pain ... "

The topic was clearly upsetting the poor pet, and Rayan decided to try to shift the conversation. "Do you remember his name, maybe? Even just a first name?"

Sil shook its head. "Never told me. I don't know. I just called him master, or sir."

"Were you still by the lake when this new owner took over?"

"I don't know. I was never allowed outside."

Rayan winced. That was absolutely horrible. "How did you escape, then?"

"Owner left my door open one day on accident. Or maybe on purpose ... I was in a lot of pain, so maybe he thought I wouldn't get up anyway ... But I did. I ran. I ran until I collapsed and couldn't anymore. I got on random buses that looked like they'd take me far away. But then my leg started to hurt a lot ... "

"How did you get on buses? I thought – "

"I stole money. I stole food. I stole whatever I could. I just wanted to get back to the lake. I wanted to find Master."

Rayan nodded solemnly. "I get that. I'm sorry about ... everything that happened to you. It's awful."

"Master will fix it. Owner said Master sold me, that Master didn't want me anymore, but I know it's not true. Master loved me, and I loved Master so much. I know they'll fix it, once I find them ... They'll fix it all ... I'll never be in pain anymore, once I'm back with Master ... "

"The collar you love so much, is it from your master?" Sil nodded. Rayan didn't bring up the tag he'd found in Sil's pocket. It seemed inappropriate, even during an already inappropriate questioning. "I see. Well ... you should probably go back to sleep now. I don't wanna bother you. I'll make my bed on the couch, and if you need anything, just call for me. Okay?"

Sil looked up at him with the saddest eyes he'd ever seen. "You won't stay?"

"I, well ... I assumed you wouldn't want me to," he admitted. "Should I just stay here? Sleep on a mattress on the floor? I'll be waking up early tomorrow to go to work. Won't I bother you?"

Sil shook its head. "I don't wanna be alone ... I'm scared ... "

Rayan couldn't say no to that. "Alright. I'll take out the spare mattress and sleep here with you. And again, if you need anything, don't hesitate to wake me up."

Bubbles

The next day, Sil didn't remember having a conversation about its master. Rayan tried to allude to it, tried to gently prod and see just how much he could reveal ... but apparently none of it. Sil was oblivious.

This was bad.

"You don't remember talking about the collar either?"

Sil looked at him with big, innocent – albeit a bit suspicious – eyes. "My collar?"

"We ... we talked a bit about it."

Sil narrowed its eyes. "What did we talk about?"

Rayan squirmed on his mattress. "Well, um ... "

"I was barely there yesterday. I don't even remember anything. Just *what* did you ask me about in that state?"

"Sil ... "

"No, I want to know. I have a right to know. I don't have many rights – I barely have any at all. But I do know I have a right to know what you asked me about when I was half-asleep and barely conscious. Right out of surgery."

Rayan sighed. "I asked you about your owner. And your master. I ... I know they're two different people. And – " Was this the time to share the fact that he'd seen the tag?

"And ... ?" it prompted, leaning closer. "What else?"

"You ... um ... I mean, *I* ... " Rayan averted his gaze, shifting awkwardly. "When I first brought you inside, your clothes were sopping wet. I had to put them on the radiator. As I was doing that, something fell out of your pocket ... "

Sil's eyes went wide as two saucepans. Its good arm shot out to touch its pocket, the tag nestled safely inside from when Rayan had put it back. "You're disgusting!" it hissed. "You went through my things!"

"I didn't! It was an accident!" Rayan tried not to raise his voice, both to avoid scaring Sil and to avoid alerting the neighbours to its presence. "It was an accident, I swear! I – at that point, I couldn't just leave it ... I just wanted to see what it was, so I – "

"So you looked at it! You read it!"

"I'm sorry!"

Sil wanted to say more, but it turned into a coughing fit. Rayan had to resist the urge to rush over to rub its back – he assumed that wouldn't have been taken kindly. Instead, he just sat there, looking dumb and useless.

"Sil ... " he started gently once the coughing stopped. "I'm sorry. It was just right there – I just wanted to help. I wanted to know who your owner was so I could help you. I didn't even know back then – I didn't know you've gone through multiple of them."

"What did it say?" Sil asked.

"Huh?"

"What did my tag say?" it asked again, more urgent.

"I ... You don't know?"

Sil shook its head. "I ... I can't read. I can sometimes read – if something's written out in large, clear lettering, I can spell it out. But the tag ... I can't read what's on it. It's all I have of Master. What did it say? Did it lead you back to Master?"

"It's too faded," Rayan admitted, and he saw the same emotions cross Sil's face as the ones he'd felt on that day.

"Oh," it breathed.

"But I can try again. If you'll allow me."

Sil glared at him. "Don't try to be all polite now. You've already read it."

"I'm just trying to make it right. Sil, I'm sorry."

Its glare softened as it let out a quiet sigh. Its hand dipped into its pocket and it fished out the tag, holding it close to its chest for just a brief moment before it handed it over to Rayan. "Anything you can make out is more than I have. If there's even just a letter, anything ... Maybe it'll jostle my memory. I don't know how much the medication took from me, I just know that it was a lot."

"I'll try my best," he promised as he gingerly took the tag again. "I can make out a capital B in the row that I think is meant to be your name."

"A B?" Sil's brows knitted together in concentration. "B ... My name, starting with a B ... Is there nothing more? How many letters, can you make that out?"

Rayan tried, but to no avail. "Maybe six? Or seven. There's an L in there, I think. Or is that an I? It's hard to say."

"B ... L ... What pet names are there with those letters? Don't you have – don't you have one of those books? Those pet name books? I remember seeing them at the facility."

Rayan perked up. "I have one! Wait here."

He rushed outside to retrieve it and noticed he'd left the TV on from earlier. There was a pet medication ad playing – or was it a pet medication ad? Rayan frowned in confusion, grabbing the remote and increasing the volume a bit.

"Mr. Barlowe, is there anything the public can do to help?"

It was Tarquin Barlowe, the man behind the famous pet med company. They sold vitamins or something; Rayan had looked into it more than once during the times he was daydreaming about owning a pet and giving it a good, proper life. Nutrition was a very important facet of keeping one.

"Just keep your eyes open, please. I have no idea what my precious Bubbles might look like after so much time without an owner, but I'm sure it's not good. Its characteristics are pale skin, brown eyes, brown hair ... It's also very tall, although the poor thing might try to hide in small places. It is very traumatised. It might've

also sustained some injuries while trying to find its way back. It's important that we find it as soon as possible so it can be properly cared for."

Bubbles? Tarquin Barlowe had lost a pet?

Wait a minute –

"Rayan?" Sil called from the bedroom.

Wait a minute ...

"You heard it here, everyone. Mr. Barlowe is looking for a tall female pet with brown hair, brown eyes, and possible injuries it might've sustained while on the streets. Its name is Bubbles, but it might not respond to it right away, instead deciding to hide away from curious eyes and strangers. The best thing to do would be to call the PPA right away if you spot it."

B ... L ...

Bubbles.

Tarquin Barlowe had to be Sil's master. The kind master, the master from near the lake –

"Rayan?" Sil limped out into the living room with its crutches, its gaze finding the man on the TV screen. The remaining colour drained from its already pale cheeks. "Why is he there?" it stammered, tripping over itself in an attempt to get away. "Why – why is he – what is he doing there, why is he there?"

"Sil, love ... Isn't that your master?" Rayan asked softly.

"No!" it screamed. "No! No! I won't go back! I won't be hurt again!"

"Sil, calm down, quiet – "

"I won't ever go back!"

"Sil!" Rayan rushed over, clamping a hand over its mouth. "Quiet! The neighbours will hear!"

Suddenly, Rayan's phone went off. He let it ring, focusing instead on stabilising his flailing little pet – when Sil *bit* him.

"Ouch!" he cried, pulling his hand back. "Sil!"

"I'm not going back!" It limped back to the bedroom, slamming the door shut with a loud *bang* that echoed through the small apartment. Rayan had no time to really digest what had just happened, he had to take the call from ... Dana?

He swiped his finger across the screen and muted the television. "Hello?"

"Hi."

Silence.

"Everything okay?"

Dana sighed on the other end. She sounded like she was on the verge of crying. "Can I come over?"

Rayan glanced towards the very much occupied bedroom. "Um ... Why? What's up?" He tried to sound as casual as possible, but he had a feeling that if Dana didn't suss out that something was wrong, it wasn't because of his acting skills. "Is everything okay?"

"Yes, um ... No, not really. Um ... " Rayan swore he heard a quiet half-sob. "I shouldn't be telling you this, but I can't really keep it a secret until the last moment, I guess ... Nima and Bo are expecting again."

Rayan almost dropped the phone. "What? You mean – Nima's pregnant?" Little Destin, Rayan's baby nephew, wasn't exactly a baby anymore; still, this was a stark reminder of the flow of time. "Right now? There's a baby on the way?"

"Yeah ... "

"But ... Wait, does that mean ... ?"

"The flat is small, even for the four of us. Nima and Bo ... they deserve a nice place to raise their kids. Without ... without me breathing down their necks. They're very nice about it, or they had been until now, um ... "

Oh no.

"Dana ... "

Another half-sob. "I didn't wanna trouble you with this, but ... "

Rayan swallowed. "Dana, I – "

"I know it's a lot to ask. I know."

She had no idea how much it was to ask. Why now? Why now, of all times, when he had a post-surgery illegal pet in his bedroom? But there was no way he could send her back to their parents' house. Not when ... not when they were the way they were. There was a reason they had all moved out as soon as possible.

"Please," Dana asked, voice small. "Can I move in with you?"

FIGURING IT OUT

"Dana, can we – can we talk later?"

"Please, Rayan, I know I'm asking a lot, but can I just come over? Just to talk it out? You don't have to decide right now, I'm just ... I'm in a very sticky situation. Please, I just want to talk."

Rayan thought about Sil trembling under the covers. "I'm not at home right now," he lied, voice shaky.

"No? I thought – I thought your shift was already over?"

"I'm still at the supermarket."

"Oh ... It's very quiet. I didn't realise. I'm sorry."

"We're definitely gonna talk, okay? You can come over on, um ... " *Think fast. Think fast. Think fast.* "Tomorrow," he blurted out.

Stupid.

What was he going to do with Sil in a single day?

"Okay," Dana said, sniffling a little. "Thanks. I won't bother you. Just tell me a time and I'll come over. And please don't tell Nima that I told you. She said she wanted to keep it a secret for a bit longer."

"I won't tell her. I promise."

"Thanks. See you tomorrow, then."

Rayan hung up the phone and let out a sigh.

This was *not* good. Dana and Nima living together worked out just fine when the two of them were single; once Bo entered the picture, they'd had to make some compromises. But even with one kid, at least Dana could babysit ... but with another on the way, it was clear that Dana couldn't stay for much longer. Everyone had to know that.

But Nima wasn't going to just kick Dana out, right? With how nice she was, she would probably try to downplay it ... God, and Rayan was living all alone. Even though his apartment was a one-bedroom, it was very clear that the responsibility of letting his sister move in was now on him.

Later. He would think about this later. He had to check on Sil and figure out what this Tarquin Barlowe business was.

He tiptoed over to the bedroom door and gently knocked. "Love? Are you okay?"

"I'm not going back!" it yelled.

"Shh, please, keep your voice down!" He opened the door and quickly slipped inside, closing it behind himself and leaning up against it, as though that way he could prevent the PPA from busting through and taking him to prison and Sil to a shelter. "Please."

"You don't understand!" it said, flailing with its good arm. "You don't know what he did! He's the entire reason – he's the reason I'm like *this*!" It pointed to its leg, now in a cast. "He's the reason Master left me! No, I'm sure they didn't even leave me, I must've been stolen! He must've stolen me! He gave me the pills too! He did everything bad to me! Him and his sister and his other stupid pets!"

"Woah, woah, woah, slow down, calm down, quiet down ... "

Sil pulled the blanket over itself protectively. "I'm never going back."

"Tarquin – the man on TV, he ... he isn't your master? The master you love?"

"No!"

That didn't make sense. Barlowe owned a whole company dedicated to making pets' lives better ... How ... Why would he have so many pets if he was just going to treat them so badly? There was no way he could've done all that to Sil, right? But it seemed so sincere ... and it had no reason to lie.

"Tarquin has a lot of pets," he tried cautiously. "All of them in pristine condition. His whole business is focused on the wellbeing of pets, he's under a microscope."

"Then that's why he never let me out," Sil growled. "Those other pets – they were paraded around. Happy. Content. They got regular meals and pretty clothes. I got scraps and the basement."

"You said he didn't even give you a name, but he said he was looking for a Bubbles."

Sil froze for a moment. "Bubbles," it said slowly, turning the name over in its mouth. "Bubbles ... Is that ... is that me?" It looked down at the tag in its hand. "Is that what Master named me?"

"Can I see that again?"

Sil hesitantly held it out for Rayan to take, and he inspected it once again, this time even more closely. "Yeah, I think that's Bubbles on here. I think that must've been your name."

"So why?" it asked, choked up. "Why did he never call me that? Why did he call me a mutt? A stupid thing? If I had a name, why was I only ever called bad names?"

Rayan's heart shattered at the sight. "Sil ... "

"Don't!" it snapped. "That's not my name! That's not my *real* name! That's a stupid, made-up name that I myself had to come up with! That wasn't what Master had named me!" It snatched the tag back and held it close to its chest, sobbing quietly. "Bubbles ... My name is Bubbles ... "

"I'm sorry," Rayan said clumsily. "I truly am. I ... I would've never guessed that Tarquin – god, it's horrible. He's ... he's so influential and – and such a big name in the industry, I looked up to him ... " Sil – Bubbles – looked at him like he was completely insane. "I thought he was a good owner. I thought he was a good *person*."

"Well, he's *not*."

Rayan's heart suddenly dropped. "And now he's after us," he breathed. "He has all the resources and connections in the world ... If he realises I have you and didn't report – holy shit, I'm in *huge* trouble."

Bubbles looked terrified at the prospect too. "What does that mean? *What does that mean*?" it demanded, more and more urgent. "That doesn't mean you'll report me and send me back, right? That can't be!"

"No, no, that's not – wait, *fuck*. Fuck, I didn't ask about the chip at the doctor's!" Rayan slapped himself on the forehead. There were too many things to keep in mind, too much happening all at once. "We need to get that chip out! We need to get it out before something happens! That's basically the only way they can reliably send you back to Tarquin, I think. We need another doctor's appointment."

"I have a chip?" Bubbles looked alarmed. "Where?"

"In the back of your neck. Every pet has one – it's to aid in identification."

"We have to get it out!" It put its good hand on the back of its neck, and for a moment, Rayan thought it might try to claw it out itself. "How do we get it out?"

"It's ... gonna be another surgery. But not right now. I mean, as soon as possible, but not right now. We're gonna have to deal with Dana as well ... God!" He buried his face in his hands, overwhelmed by this whole ordeal. "One thing at a time ... Just one thing at a time ... "

Bubbles grabbed him by the shirt. "Call the doctor!"

"I can't right now!"

"Why?"

"The last time I got a very specific window of time for when I could call her! She likely won't pick up! And we have a more urgent – or at least just as urgent matter to talk about." He put his hand on Bubbles', gently prying its fingers off. "My sister's visiting tomorrow. You're gonna have to hide for the duration of the visit; under the bed, or in the closet ... We'll figure something out. She's ... in need of a new place to stay, and the most realistic outcome is that I'm gonna be providing that place. I don't know how, yet, but um ... That's ... t hat's what's happening."

If possible, Bubbles looked even more alarmed. "You can't bring her here! You pushed me to have these surgeries, now I can't even run away, and now you want to bring someone here? A stranger?"

"It's gonna be fine," he hurried to assure it, though truth be told, he didn't know whether it would be fine. "I promise. It's gonna be fine. I'm gonna protect you. She's not moving in right away – we can probably try to find out more about your situation before then! You can be out of here and back with your nice, loving owner before push comes to shove."

If that loving owner was really a loving owner. If Bubbles was really right in assuming Tarquin somehow stole it ... however difficult that was to imagine.

"I'll try to secure a doctor's appointment for you as well. We'll figure this out. It's all going to be fine."

***

"Thanks for letting me come over," Dana said as she settled down on the sofa. Rayan had carefully hidden away all of Bubbles' clothes and cleared out a space for it in the closet – now it was just a matter of it not sneezing or coughing during her visit. The cramped space must not have been good for its post-op limbs either ... They just had to make it quick. "I don't even know what I want to talk about, really ... I mean ... It's clear, isn't it? I've become a nuisance there. Nima would never say it, but that's how it is."

"Don't say that," Rayan said gently. "You're not a nuisance."

"I'm a nuisance here as well, aren't I?"

"No! No, not at all."

"It's just that ... I don't think I can go back home. To Mom and Dad, I mean."

Rayan swallowed, trying not to say the wrong thing. He didn't know *what* to say. Their parents were ... good people, really. It was just that they were a bit ... strict. "I understand," he assured her. "I do."

"But you don't want me to move in."

"No! Dana, listen to me." He scooted closer, grabbing her hands and holding them between his own. "I love you, okay? We'll figure this out. I'm happy to have you stay here. It's just ... very sudden, yeah? We have a whole nine months to figure this out."

Achoo.

Rayan froze.

"What was that?" Dana asked, confused.

"The ... the neighbour," he stammered. "It – it really sounds like it was just like in the other room, huh? The curse of these apartments. Paper-thin walls. Um, back to Mom and Dad – "

"I can't go back to being slapped around," she blurted out. Rayan deflated at the mention of that. He hated thinking back to those times, before they had moved out. He hated to think that Dana might have to go back to that.

Maybe he should just come clean and introduce Bubbles and Dana. Maybe she would be understanding?

No, that was too risky. Too many variables.

"You won't have to," he tried to say as confidently as possible. "We'll make it work."

"I can pay you rent. I can ... maybe bring my bed over? Put it ... somewhere."

"We'll figure it out," he repeated for the thousandth time.

"You look ... a bit frazzled," she said with a chuckle. "Everything okay on your end?"

Oh, if she knew.

"Yeah. I'm just a bit shaken by all the new info. The new baby and all."

The conversation took a more pleasant turn, but Rayan couldn't push Bubbles out of the back of his mind. With every passing second he thought of it, all alone in that dark, cramped closet. By the time Dana was ready to leave, he couldn't be fast enough to let it out.

"She's gone," he said as he opened the door, and Bubbles slowly crawled out. "C'mere ... " He lifted it up in his arms, and the poor pet was too worn out to really protest. "It was a long time, wasn't it? I'm sorry. I didn't want to be rude."

"I'm tired ... " it muttered. "But the chip – can you call now?"

"Right. The chip." Rayan gently set it down on the bed and pulled out his phone. Just after six o'clock; maybe Dr. Anne would pick up.

"Do you think ... do you think there's a chance the chip belongs to Master? Not ... not my owner, but Master? Do you think there's a chance they didn't switch it out?" it asked. "Because, um ... I don't remember being chipped. Maybe ... maybe if my owner knew he wouldn't ever be letting me out of the basement, then he didn't feel the need ... "

For the first time in a little while, Rayan's heart leapt with hope. "It could be. Dr. Anne will surely help us figure it out."

Un-Chipped

This time, as Rayan was led into the doctor's office by Milo, he didn't even flinch at the way he glared at him. He was a lot less nervous and a lot more full of tentative hope – this chip might just prove to be the way to Bubbles' owner.

"Dr. Anne?" he called hesitantly once they reached the little office. "It's Rayan. I've come for the appointment."

"Yes, yes." She stepped out of an even smaller room with a gentle smile on her face, gesturing for the two of them to come closer. Even with the crutches, Bubbles needed some help to move comfortably. "Chip surgery, was it?"

"Um, first – "

"I want to know who I belong to," Bubbles cut in. "You can read this chip, right? Before you take it out? Or after. I don't care."

"You don't know?" she asked, a little surprised.

"I'm ... not sure. Maybe it's still in Master's name. I need to know."

Dr. Anne hummed. "That might be tricky. I don't really have access to the database, but we'll see what I can do. First things first, though, we'll get it out of you."

Bubbles swallowed audibly. "It's ... it's gonna be like last time, right? I'll be asleep?"

"No, no. We'll just inject you with a local anaesthetic."

It noticeably bristled at that. "No, I want to be asleep."

"We can't just put you to sleep for every procedure."

"It's gonna be fine," Rayan tried gently. "I'll be right here. You can hold my hand while she injects you."

Bubbles' eyes were darting between the two of them, glare deepening. "No. I don't like needles."

"Then you're not getting that chip out," Dr. Anne said, staring it down even stronger than it was staring her down. She spoke with authority, and Rayan was just about to cut in and try to ease the tension when Bubbles backed down.

"Fine," it muttered. It was gripping its crutches so hard its knuckles were white. "Do the stupid injection."

"I'll be right here the entire time," Rayan assured it again as he led it to the operating table. Bubbles lay on its stomach, its good hand in one of Rayan's. It was already squeezing. "You're gonna be okay, love."

"I just need to know whose chip is in me. I just – if there's any chance that it's Master's ... if I'm legally still Master's, with this chip, could I maybe go back to them?"

"I don't know your specific circumstances," Dr. Anne said as she was preparing the syringe. "That could be the case. But why wouldn't your new owner change the name on the chip?"

"Because he wanted to keep me a secret," it hissed. "That's why. I never saw a doctor, not after ... not after he gave me the pills. I never saw a doctor at all, as far as I can remember."

"*He* gave you pills?" Dr. Anne raised an eyebrow. "That's sketchy. That's usually administered by the guys at the shelter or facility."

Rayan opened his mouth to say something, then closed it again. Right. Dr. Anne was right. How did he not catch that detail earlier? That must've been why Bubbles even remembered its previous owner. Master, as it called them. Tarquin must've somehow messed up the dosage or something – his business might've been a pet vitamin business, but he was a businessman, not a vet. "Is that even allowed?" he asked her.

"In some cases, yeah. If the client's a big shot."

Rayan bit the inside of his cheek. "It's Tarquin Barlowe," he blurted out. Dr. Anne stopped in her tracks.

"Come again?"

"It's Tarquin Barlowe. Bubbles confirmed it."

"Bubbles?" Recognition sparked in her eyes. "Right. He was on TV, looking for his lost pet. He never mentioned a chip. I knew there was something off about that announcement."

"Can we just get this over with before we start chatting?" Bubbles interrupted.

Dr. Anne chuckled. "Sure. I'm gonna inject you now, hold still."

Rayan had to look away as the needle was pushed inside, but he knew exactly when it hit skin; Bubbles' grip became ten times tighter, then it relaxed. "Is it still inside?" it asked hesitantly.

"Not anymore. Can you feel me poking you?"

"No."

"Good."

Bubbles didn't let go of his hand. "My neck feels weird."

"That's the anaesthetic working. Now, keep quiet. I need to focus so I don't cause you to be paralysed."

As Dr. Anne leaned over, Rayan caught a glimpse of ... a scar? There was a scar just above the collar of her shirt, right around the place where ... where she was marking Bubbles' neck to be cut into.

Rayan's eyes widened, but he didn't make a peep. He wouldn't until she was done with the surgery.

But that could only mean one thing, right?

No, there were many ways to obtain scars. There was no way the doctor was a pet. An ex-pet. Were ex-pets a thing outside of Pet Lib propaganda? His mind was reeling.

But all thoughts were pushed aside when he saw her take out the scalpel and put it at the base of Bubbles' neck. He immediately looked away.

"Squeamish, are we?" she asked teasingly and Rayan could only nod.

The seconds ticked by and Rayan waited, studying every pattern on the wall while he held Bubbles' hand. He didn't know how long it took to fish a chip out of someone's neck, and he didn't need to. That was where the professionals came in.

"Done," Dr. Anne said abruptly and Rayan looked back. The wound was all bandaged and – Rayan assumed – stitched up underneath. "I'll try to take a look and see who this chip belongs to and I'll give you guys a ring. How's that?"

"It's already out?" Bubbles blinked like a confused child. "I can get up?"

"Yeah, go on, go on. You're a free little critter now."

Bubbles pushed itself up and gently moved its neck, stretching it a little. "I'm ... free? What does that even mean? I don't want to be free. I want you to find who that chip belongs to and I want to go back to Master."

"All in due time."

"Dr. Anne – " Rayan interrupted quietly. "Can we have a word? Please? Just the two of us."

Bubbles narrowed its eyes at him. "About me?"

"No! No, I ... I mean, I guess it doesn't have to be just the two of us. If Dr. Anne's fine with a bit of a, um ... personal question about, um ... "

"I used to be a pet, yeah," she said easily. Rayan's eyes almost popped out.

"H-h uh?"

Bubbles was similarly baffled. "What?"

"You saw my scar, didn't you?" She smiled and tapped the back of her neck. "That's where my chip came from. I ran and hid and studied medicine. Now I'm an illegal doctor – part-time, at least."

Rayan opened his mouth. Then closed it. Then opened it. Then closed it again. "How?" he managed to force out.

"You talked to the Pet Lib guys, arranged for a whole illegal doctor meeting, and you still believe in this pet bullshit? Hats off, you're blinder than I thought."

Rayan flushed deep red. "I don't understand," he said softly. "I'm sorry. I don't ... I don't get it. How ... how can a pet be a doctor? What do you mean you *used to* be a pet? If you're a doctor, shouldn't you ... shouldn't you especially believe in the system?"

"Get it together, boy. It's all smoke and mirrors." She snapped her fingers in front of his face a couple times, making him flinch. "Pets aren't a thing. We're all people."

Rayan frowned. "No, that's ... "

"That's not true," Bubbles said, and Rayan couldn't have been more grateful.

"But it is. Look around. Milo's an ex-pet too, I am an ex-pet, and tell you what – if I did the pet test on you right now, you'd probably be a pet."

That hurt. "That's not true!" he said desperately. "I'm a person! There's not a single pet in my family tree, that's stupid!"

"Wanna try it?" she asked with an insufferably smug grin, and Rayan couldn't turn it down.

"Yes. Let's try the test."

Bubbles didn't interrupt or ask to go home. As far as Rayan could see, it was just as curious to see the infamous test as he was. And the results.

Dr. Anne brought out a folder full of papers and sat down in the chair across from Rayan. "I'm going to say statements, you say whether they're true or false for you. First one: I am a person," she said in full seriousness. Rayan almost laughed.

"True."

"There are no pets in my family."

"True."

This was easy.

"I like being around pets more than people."

Rayan stopped for a moment and thought about his time spent volunteering at the local shelter. "Um ... " Okay, one wrong answer couldn't be too bad. Was it even the wrong answer? He didn't know. He didn't know much about this test, for all the faith he'd placed in it all his life. "True."

The statements went on. "*I get along with both of my parents.*" "*I have plenty of friends.*" "*Solving life's hardships comes naturally to me.*" "*People often scolded me as a child."* Rayan soon found he felt he was answering incorrectly to most of them. He was squirming more and more in his seat.

"Congratulations," Dr. Anne said when they were finished. "You'd be cast as a pet. Don't ever let the PPA get their hands on you, you'll be memory wiped as soon as you set foot in that building."

"B-but – but there's a medical exam too – " he stammered. "They – they'd know – "

"The medical exam is complete bullshit," she said simply. "They check this, they check that, they write whatever's convenient based on this sample test. You were nervous the whole time too – that would get put down on paper as a sign that you're a pet as well. They'd spot you from a mile away. The only thing protecting your cushy little life right now is the fact that no one has reported you yet, and that you haven't been caught committing petty crimes."

"We're done here," Rayan snapped, standing abruptly. "Thank you for your help, Dr. Anne. I trust that Bubbles will heal well and we won't have to see each other again."

Dr. Anne smiled, softer than before. "Rayan ... listen to the people around you, yeah? They've had plenty of experience you'd do well to learn from."

"Thank you," he said curtly. "Goodbye."

Tragic Backstory

Thoughts were swirling inside Rayan's head at a rapid speed. What did that stupid sample test mean? He knew he wasn't a pet. Dr. Anne must've lied about the results to prove her point. But she didn't seem the type to do that ... As Rayan was helping Bubbles out of his sisters' car and into the building, he was too far away to even notice it talking to him.

"Rayan!" it snapped after a while, and Rayan was brought back to the present.

"Huh? Sorry, I – sorry. What were you saying?"

"What will you do now?"

"What do you mean?"

"You're so devoted to the system. Will you report to the PPA now? Let them take you? You can't leave me here alone. I won't let you. Not before the doctor tells me whose chip that was."

"Of course I won't report to the PPA," he said indignantly. "Whatever test that was, I'm sure it was just some made-up stuff. Dr. Anne wanted to convince me that pets didn't exist, so she made me out to be a 'pet' – but that doesn't mean anything. I don't have to report anything to anyone."

Bubbles nodded. "Okay. After I'm back with my real master, you can do whatever you want. But until then, no messing around with the PPA."

Rayan smiled at the way Bubbles tried to order him around, like ... like it was the owner and he was the pet. His guts churned at the notion.

If he had met Bubbles in any other circumstance, would he have mistaken it for a person? If Bubbles had met him in any other circumstance, would it have mistaken him for a pet? Was the line really so blurry?

Was the science behind it not as sound as he thought?

"Rayan!" Bubbles snapped its fingers in front of his face to get his attention. "What are you thinking about? That doctor didn't get into your head, did she? Pets exist – I'm living proof. Don't start believing all that crap, not now. Not before I'm out of here."

"Sorry. You're right." A pet ordering a person around ... They were an odd couple for sure, but that didn't mean Dr. Anne was right. "Let's get you back to bed so you can heal. I'll do some internet research about Tarquin, maybe something about your previous owner will pop up."

***

Rayan went down a rabbit hole of information about Tarquin Barlowe. He had a sister, Pandora Barlowe, with whom he'd started his company decades ago. The two of them had a lot of pets, which was to be expected – Bubbles was in none of the photos, though. As he researched more and more, he found several interviews Tarquin had given on the subject now that his pet was missing.

"I didn't want to expose it to the public given its shy demeanour and traumatising backstory," one article read. *"I realise now that if only I had taken at least a couple photos of it, this whole thing would be easier. It was just so reclusive and skittish, it didn't even occur to me ... To think that it's now out in the big wide world all alone, it breaks my heart."*

Traumatising backstory? "Bubbles?"

"Yes?" came the muffled reply from the bedroom. Rayan stood up, laptop in hand, and walked over there.

"I've been reading some articles, and Tarquin seems to always highlight some tragic backstory you had. Do you have any idea what he might be talking about?"

Bubbles made a face. "He stole me away from Master. That's tragic enough."

"I don't think he means that. He wouldn't be very public about that."

"I don't know ... I don't know. He gave me all those pills, they made me forget a lot of stuff. They made me forget the face of my master, their voice, their name ... I'm lucky I didn't forget about them entirely."

Rayan hummed. "Tragic backstory ... He never explicitly says what it is and I can't really find articles on it. I'll go back to looking."

Just as he was about to exit the bedroom, there was a knock on the door. He quickly pulled the bedroom door shut and put down the laptop on the coffee table, then went to open it.

"Who is it?"

"Pet Protection Agency."

Rayan froze. Again? They'd just been here a few days ago. "Uh ... Um ... " He opened the door, but he was unable to find the right words to express just how unwelcome this visit was. "Is this about the reports again?"

"I'm afraid so," the agent said. It was a woman, not much older than Rayan himself, who wore a uniform and a serious expression that made him wary. "I know my colleagues have been here not too long ago, but ever since then, we've gotten more reports about suspicious activity in the area. Can I come in?"

Rayan swallowed but stood aside, motioning for her to enter. She did so while observing everything in the flat, probably looking for clues. She seemed much more ruthless than the agent who had come before her. She seemed ... convinced this wasn't just a random report.

He could only hope Bubbles had already made it into the closet, into the little space that had been cleared out to serve as a hiding place.

"So, um ... what sort of report was it?" Rayan tried to ask nonchalantly.

"You live alone here, yes?"

"Yeah, just me."

"The neighbours keep hearing strange noises and even arguments."

Rayan kicked himself that he couldn't keep Bubbles more quiet. "Uh ... Yeah, that's ... Sometimes I have people over. Like my sister, Dana. She just visited. And sometimes I argue with my parents on the phone ... doesn't everyone? We don't have the best relationship – I won't go into details, if that's okay."

The woman regarded him with a suspicious look. "The neighbours said they never see anyone come or go."

Rayan furrowed his brows. "Well ... I don't assume they stand by their door all day, watching my flat. Right?"

The woman hummed. "I suppose not." She turned towards the bedroom door, and Rayan already knew he was going to be made to show her around. "Can I take a peek inside that room?"

"There's a bit of a mess there, but um ... sure. I mean, why not."

"I assure you, I'm not going to judge. The only thing I'm looking for is a stray pet. You must've seen the announcements about Mr. Barlowe's pet that's gone missing; we need to take reports much more seriously around this time."

Oh. So it was a money thing. Everyone wanted the reward that came with finding a millionaire's pet. "Of course. Bubbles, was it? It's deeply troubling." He led her to the bedroom door and tried to open it without much hesitation, hoping that Bubbles was already under the bed or in the closet.

Sure enough, the bed was empty.

"You use crutches?" the woman asked, immediately spotting the two that were laid against the bed.

"Y-y eah. Yeah, I ... My legs are a bit ... weak, recently. The doctors don't know what's wrong with them – you see, I'm a waiter in the small Italian restaurant in town. I walk a lot, I have to be on my feet all the time. Anyway, I've been experiencing some muscle weakness, so they prescribed some mobility aids for m e."

She narrowed her eyes at him but didn't pry. "I see. It must be hard."

Rayan could only nod with the lump in his throat. He thought if he said another word, he would immediately faint. He wasn't a good liar, or a good actor, or a good anything.

"Can I see the bathroom as well?"

"Yeah, of course. Right this way."

By some miracle, the woman found nothing amiss. By the time Rayan escorted her out and closed the door behind her, the nausea got so bad that he immediately had to rush back to the bathroom to retch.

"Fuck," he breathed. "Fuck. Fuck. They're onto us. They're so onto us. I can't do this."

He managed to get himself together enough to stumble back into the bedroom, quietly opening the closet door to find Bubbles huddled inside. It was looking up at him with big, tear-filled eyes – the poor thing must've been scared out of its mind too.

"She's gone," he whispered. "We have to be much more quiet from now on. The neighbours ... I don't know exactly what they're saying, but everyone's on high alert because Tarquin's lost a pet. They're taking reports much more seriously."

Bubbles nodded mutely. "I can't go back," it mumbled. "I can't – not when I'm so close. The doctor will find Master, I'm sure. I'm so close. Please, please, don't let them take me now. Don't let them take me back."

Rayan crouched down in front of it so they were at eye level. "I won't let them, love. I promise."

***

It was at least a week until Rayan got a call from an unknown number, and he took it with shaking hands. If it was the PPA again, he might not survive without a heart attack.

"Hello?" he almost squeaked.

"It's Dr. Anne," came the swift reply, and Rayan let out an audible sigh of relief. "What, were you expecting someone else?"

"It doesn't matter."

"It doesn't. Listen, I'm gonna be quick. I have good news and bad news: good news, the chip in Bubbles' neck really did have its previous owner's name attached. Wynn Havard."

"That's amazing – "

"Bad news is, Wynn seems to be dead."

On the Run

It was like the rug had been pulled out from under Rayan. He had been carefully building a Jenga tower of questionable pieces, of surgeries and PPA visits and family conflicts, all to try and get Bubbles back to its owner ... and its owner was dead. Wynn Havard was dead.

"Wh – what?"

"I can't talk much right now. I'm sorry, Rayan. I don't even know what Bubbles will say; try to be very patient with it. I have to go."

And she hung up.

Rayan collapsed onto his sofa, tears springing to his eyes. How was he meant to explain this to Bubbles? They'd been so close ... He'd promised it'd be back with its owner before Dana moved in.

"Who was it?" came the question from the bedroom. Bubbles limped out with its crutches, looking at Rayan inquisitively. "Was it Dr. Anne? Did she find my owner?"

"It was in Tarquin's name," he said without thinking.

Bubbles stopped in its tracks, its face immediately falling. "Oh."

No, this wasn't right. It wasn't right to keep this information from it. Rayan took a deep breath and tried again. "Love ... Come, sit down."

"No, I ... I think I'm gonna go back to my room."

"Bubbles. Please."

Bubbles gave him a puzzled look but tentatively agreed, plopping down onto the sofa. "You said it was in my owner's name, what else is there to talk about? I get it. I'm not gonna freak out and start yelling. I'm gonna lay low until my limbs heal, then I can go out and find Master."

"I lied," he blurted out.

Bubbles looked even more perplexed. "What?"

"It wasn't in Tarquin's name. Bubbles, I – listen, please don't get mad at me. And please keep your voice down."

"What is it? What's going on?"

"Dr. Anne has found your master's name."

Bubbles' face lit up. "She has?"

"They're dead."

It was as though he'd punched it in the gut. Its face became distorted with pain beyond Rayan's understanding, and it slowly reached out to grab him by the shirt, pleading without words.

Please, tell me you're lying.

"I'm sorry," Rayan whispered.

"They can't be dead," it muttered. "They can't be. What are you even saying? This is stupid. Dr. Anne is stupid. What was their name? Let me look for them, I'll find them – "

"Their name was Wynn Havard."

"*Is* Wynn Havard."

"Bubbles – "

"Don't. Don't call me that." It let go and leaned back, tears now freely pouring down its face. "Don't. Don't say anything. I don't want to hear it. This is wrong. You're all wrong."

"You said you didn't think your master gave you up, and yet you somehow ended up with Tarquin. That, coupled with the fact he's saying you're highly traumatised – "

"He's saying that because he abused me!" it snapped.

"Keep your voice down," Rayan said, pleading. "The PPA – "

"I don't care about the PPA!"

"Please, Sil – "

"Don't call me anything! I'm leaving! I'm gonna go find Master! Wynn, I'm gonna find them, I'm gonna – "

Rayan grabbed it by the good arm and pulled it into a hug, holding it tight. He could feel it sobbing against his shoulder as it eventually gave up struggling, wrapping its thin little arms around him. "I'm sorry."

"I can never go back to being Bubbles?" it choked out, and Rayan tried to keep his own tears to a minimum. "I can never go back to having a loving home? I can never go back to ... before?"

"I'm sorry," he repeated. "I'm so, *so* sorry."

"Where do I even go from here?"

"I don't know ... "

"I can't stay here. The PPA will hunt me down. You'll go to prison, I'll go back to my stupid owner – "

"We'll figure something out."

"What?" it snapped again. "Your sister wants to move in too – it's all a mess! I can't stay here, but I have nowhere to go!"

"Shh ... " Rayan rubbed its back in circles, trying to soothe it. "It's okay. I mean, it's not ... But we're gonna figure it out."

In truth, Rayan had no idea what to do. He was already eating through his savings trying to keep the two of them afloat, especially with the illegal doctor's visits. The PPA was clearly increasing their security checks. Nima's baby was on the way.

Sil pushed him away, crossing its arms and looking absolutely defeated. "I ... Maybe I should just give myself up."

"No, no, Sil ... "

"What's the point? My owner was right – there's no one coming for me. He'll make up some story about how I injured myself while on the run and he'll get off scot-free. I'll go back to being a punching bag."

"That can't be the only solution! That's no solution at all! What if I went with you to the PPA and explained – "

"They won't believe you."

Rayan frowned. "But ... but they're called the Pet Protection Agency ... They're supposed to protect pets like you ... "

Sil scoffed. "Grow up. They've never protected anybody."

"Don't take this as an insult, but I think we'll see each other a lot more in the future. You seem like a pretty good guy, and if you're going about this the illegal way, you'll very quickly realise that we might not be the cultists here."

"Listen to the people around you, yeah? They've had plenty of experience you'd do well to learn from."

Denice and Dr. Anne's words echoed in his mind, making him dizzy. If the PPA was corrupt, if Tarquin was lying on live television, if his neighbours were constantly reporting suspicious activity, if he didn't even trust his own family to have his back in this sketchy situation, then ...

"I'm gonna go back to Pet Lib," he exclaimed. "They'll know what to do."

***

"Leave the country."

Rayan recoiled. Denice was sitting across from him at a small table, looking deathly serious. "What?"

"If you really want to protect that poor guy, you'll help it leave the country. You'll go somewhere where pets are outlawed."

"I can't do that! I have all my family here, my savings, I – "

"Rayan." Denice leaned over the table. "Your window of opportunity is very quickly closing. They're cracking down on us all around the country because Tarquin has lost his pet – I'm not even gonna ask whether that's the same pet you keep in your flat. If you truly want to help, and you want us to be able to help you in return, you'll leave *right now.*"

Rayan left the room more disoriented than he'd gone in. He couldn't just leave. Leaving his parents behind – that was long overdue. But his sisters? Bo? Little Destin? There was no way.

As he neared his apartment, he noticed a van parked in front of the building.

Pet Protection Agency.

His heart skipped a beat.

Sil.

"Rayan!" someone hissed from behind and he spun around, finding a very dishevelled Sil motioning for him to follow into an alleyway. He quickly dove behind the wall, just as a few agents exited the building. "They almost got me," it explained in a hushed voice. "We can't go back inside. Or at least I can't – but I heard them mention some arrest warrant."

"Oh god," he breathed.

"We need to leave. I brought some food along, maybe we could go to your family – "

"We can't. What if we get them into trouble too?"

Sil frowned. "So then what? Do you wanna live behind dumpsters with me?"

"I ... I don't know, can't I just go talk to them?"

"Rayan, they're out to *get you.*"

Rayan shivered. He never wanted this. He just wanted to help. "Okay. We'll take a shortcut and go to my sisters' place. Can you keep up with those crutches?"

"If my life depends on it, yeah. I told you: I'm *not* going back."

***

Rayan almost collapsed into Dana's arms when she opened the door. "Please, help," he whined. "Please ... please, I'm in so much trouble."

"Who is it?" Nima called from the living room.

"What's going on?" Dana asked.

Sil was standing behind him, holding on to his shirt like it was scared that at any moment Rayan's sisters might turn on it. "We'll explain when we're inside," it said hurriedly. "Just let us in."

"Who is that?"

"Let us in," Rayan pleaded and Dana stepped aside. Sil hurriedly waddled inside.

"Rayan?" Nima came out with Destin following in tow, quickly wrapping a towel around her hair to keep it out of view of strangers, her eyes widening as she took in the sight in front of her. "Who is that?"

"Sil – Bubbles – Tarquin Barlowe's lost pet, but he kept it a secret and abused it, it can't go back, we need a place to stay, the PPA wants to arrest me – "

"Woah, hey, okay, what lost pet?"

"Don't tell them!" Sil snapped.

"I have to!" Rayan sobbed. He couldn't keep it in anymore. He was in shambles. "Dana, you can have the flat, I need to leave the country! The Pet Lib people said I need to – and – and I don't wanna go to jail, I ... I have to somehow leave – and I can't stay here, they'll arrest you too – "

Through effortful half-sentences told between sobs, Rayan finally managed to get the story together. His sisters were both horrified at the state of affairs and Sil was furious that he'd just told everyone, but there was no going back now.

"This will likely be the first place they'll look for me," Rayan finished in tears.

"We'll just go on the run while they get us fake papers," Sil said. "You said they can get us fake papers, right?"

"Don't be silly," Nima tried gently. "This is all so silly. All you have to do is give Sil to the PPA, and they'll handle everything."

"No!" Sil snapped.

"I can't," Rayan said as well. "I – I'm not sure about this pet thing anymore – "

"I'm sure about the pet thing, but the PPA is useless!"

Dana motioned for them to keep it down. "Okay, okay, what about this? I'll go look after your flat until you can send Sil on its way, and then you can just come back. How's that?"

"You need to tell me whether they really want to arrest me," Rayan begged. "Please. Please, you can stay there for as long as you want, just please, tell me. I'd love to come back – I'm just not sure I can."

"We talked enough," Sil said gruffly. "Let's go before the PPA comes."

"But the PPA is the authority in this case," Nima said, still apprehensive. "This is madness. Rayan, you can't possibly be going *on the run*. What would our parents think? What about your job?"

"It was a mistake to tell them," Sil cut in.

"No, Sil, they'll help – "

"We'll help," Dana assured him. "Nima, please take Destin back to the bedroom. I'll go with Rayan to his apartment. We'll figure it out. If the police come here, don't say *anything*."

"This is madness! Dana, you can't seriously be telling me that!"

"We have to go. *Now*." Sil grabbed Rayan by the hand and shoved him towards the door. "Bye. If the PPA comes after us, we'll know who told them where we are. So don't. Say. *A word*."

With that, the three of them left.

Smoke and Mirrors

Things were not looking good.

Through Dana, Rayan quickly figured out that there really was an arrest warrant out for him. His parents were apparently more than happy to work with the police and the PPA, eager to seem like good, upstanding citizens of a country still so foreign to them after decades.

"It's not good," Dana whispered into the phone one night. Rayan was huddled close to a very protective Sil, using the last of his phone's battery power on a call with his sister. "Dad said – I don't even want to repeat what Dad said. But the flat is okay, I put everything back in place for you. Um ... are the two of you okay?"

"I'm cold all the time," Rayan said quietly. "And scared. There are agents around every Pet Lib place, we'll ... have to find another way to contact them. Dana, I'm so sorry."

"You have nothing to apologise for. You were dragged into this – maybe it wasn't the best decision to keep an illegal pet, but we understand. Mom and Dad, not really, but ... me, Nima, and the others. We understand."

"I don't think there's a way around it," he muttered. "I think I really have to leave. The country, I mean. I think there's no other choice."

"Rayan ... "

"I ... I'm never gonna open that dessert shop, huh?" He let out a small, miserable, humourless chuckle. "To think my life was normal up until a few weeks ago, and now it's come to this ... "

"It will go back to normal, love," Dana insisted. "I – "

"Hang up," Sil hissed. "There's someone coming."

"Dana, I have to go," Rayan said quickly.

"Wait – "

"I'll call you back!"

He hung up before she could've said anything, and both of them pressed themselves up against the wall of the alley. Rayan could hear the quiet buzz off the phone in his pocket as it powered off. He wasn't going to call her back.

"It's not the PPA," Sil whispered. "Just some guys."

"You lived like this for a whole year?" Rayan asked, bewildered. "I – this is horrible ... "

Sil shot him a look. "Well, get used to it. If you don't, I'll just leave you behind."

That wasn't an option. Sil still needed crutches to move around – the two of them could only survive on the streets together.

"What if we went to Dr. Anne? She would be able to connect us with the Pet Lib guys."

"Fine. Just follow my lead. We have one big advantage, and that's that pets look just like people. *Don't* look suspicious or nervous. If you walk confidently, they'll never be able to tell."

Confidence. That wasn't something Rayan had ever possessed, especially not since the day his girlfriend had broken up with him publicly. This was a matter of life and death, though, so he straightened his back and followed Sil across the street.

No one batted an eye.

The only thing protecting your cushy little life right now is the fact that no one has reported you yet, and that you haven't been caught committing petty crimes.

Was this whole thing really one big sham? Smoke and mirrors? Was he no different to Sil? Were the two of them no different to the guys on the other side of the street, having fun?

They didn't seem to be. No one called the PPA on them as they walked into another alleyway that would lead them to Dr. Anne's office.

"You're doing better than expected," Sil said, and Rayan felt like that was the most he was going to get as far as compliments went. "We'll sleep behind that dumpster. Maybe *in* the dumpster, depends on the temperature."

Rayan wrinkled his nose. "I'm not – "

"That, the police, or freezing to death. Pick your poison."

He sighed. "Let's just try our luck outside first."

As they settled down, Rayan realised just how hungry he was. He hadn't eaten in at least a day, when he and Sil had shared a pack of biscuits. Even though it'd only been a good twenty-four hours, Rayan could see why Sil became so protective of even the mush he'd unknowingly fed it.

"Seriously," he said quietly. "How did you do this?"

"It's not even that bad," Sil groaned. "Quit whining so much."

"And your ankle was busted too – "

"*Quit whining.*"

Rayan's mouth snapped shut. It would've been funny how quickly the roles were reversed, had it not been absolutely tragic.

After a few minutes of silence, Rayan could hear quiet sobbing. When he looked up, it was too dark to make out Sil's face, but he could see the outline of its shoulders rising and falling with each choked breath.

"Sil ... "

"Don't."

Another few minutes passed, and Sil abruptly scooted closer.

"For warmth," it mumbled, and Rayan had a feeling he would've been reprimanded for pushing it.

They stayed like that for hours, dozing off every now and then. Rayan could only praise and give thanks to whatever higher power was out there that he didn't need to go through this alone.

***

It took three days for Dr. Anne to show up to the illegal clinic. In those three days, the two of them had lied, cheated, and stole, trying to evade both PPA and police in their quest to stay alive and safe. Sil caught a glimpse of her and immediately alerted Rayan, then instructed him to walk over there and go inside with her. It'd follow in a few minutes, it had said.

"It'd look too suspicious if we approached her all at once," it explained. "Go. I survived out here for a year, you couldn't handle five minutes on your own."

Rayan got to her just before she closed the door. "Dr. Anne?"

"Rayan? I thought – oh lord, where's Bubbles?"

"Can I come in? Please? I'll explain – "

"You're asking me to hide a criminal."

"You're a criminal yourself!" he said desperately. "Please? Please, I won't make a peep."

Dr. Anne sighed and opened the door wider, letting Rayan slip inside. "Where's Bubbles?"

"It goes by Sil again. Ever since ... the news."

"Oh."

"It's hiding out in the alley next to the clinic. It said it would follow in a few minutes, but that it didn't want to cause a commotion."

Dr. Anne pushed up the glasses on her nose. "Well, you two have caused *quite* the commotion. Out of every runaway, did you have to find Tarquin Barlowe's? He's offering an insane reward for whoever brings you two to justice, you know. I could get rich and never look back."

Rayan's blood turned to ice in his veins. "You – you wouldn't – "

Dr. Anne waved him off. "Of course I wouldn't. I'm just saying, you're very lucky."

"So we can stay here a while? Just – we'll be gone in a minute. We just need to ask something of you. Please."

There was a knock on the door and Milo went to go get it, ushering a rough-looking Sil to the centre of the room. "We need your help," it said curtly.

"I can see that. All this running around isn't very good for those bones, is it?"

Sil scoffed. "Whatever. We need you to bring us to the Pet Lib people without them seeing. Or bring the Pet Lib people to us."

"Quite demanding, aren't you?" She sat down in one of the chairs and motioned for Rayan and Sil to take the other two. Milo stood guard at the door. "You two are *very* lucky that I decided to put my life on the line every day to help people just like you."

"So you'll help?" Rayan asked, leaning forwards. "You'll help us?"

"I'll do what I can."

"Um ... " Rayan averted his gaze, fidgeting with the hem of his shirt. "Do you think ... Would there be a way for me to ... to stay here? Maybe put Sil on a boat – "

"You can't stay in a country where Barlowe has such a reach," Dr. Anne said without hesitation. Rayan deflated.

"I see."

"It's only fair," Sil muttered. Dr. Anne said nothing, eyeing Rayan cautiously, probably waiting for him to blow up.

He didn't. Sil was right – it had lost everything, it was only fair that Rayan would now lose it all too. Or, well ... maybe not fair, but ... something close to it. Rayan wished there was another way, but he also couldn't fault Sil for any of it.

"Just ... please connect us with the Pet Lib guys. That's the last thing we'll hopefully ever ask of you," Rayan said quietly. "And I'm sorry I ran away like that last time. I was ... I was running from a lot of things. I'm really grateful for all you've done for us."

Dr. Anne rewarded his heartfelt apology with a gentle smile. "You're doing the right thing, you know. You just have to persevere. You both do. I'll see what I can do on my end."

Comrade

"We need to stay alert," Sil said, sitting on Dr. Anne's operating table and glaring at a very sleepy Rayan who was about to doze off in a chair. "You can't just let yourself go like that."

"We're safe for now," he tried. Sil made a face.

"We don't know that. We barely know her intentions."

"She's an ex-pet who's probably also on a couple hit lists. She won't sell us out."

"*We don't know that.*"

"Sil, please ... "

It slapped Rayan in the upper arm with its good hand. "Stay awake," it hissed. "If we have to run, we run together. Isn't that what you promised me? Isn't that what you said we would do? I can't keep looking after you all the time, I need you to pull your weight."

"I looked after you for – "

"I know!" it snapped. "I know, and now I'm looking after you! Why won't you just make it a bit easier for me?"

"As if you ever made it easy!" he yelled back. "As if you ever considered my stance! My situation!"

"Oh, don't try to play the victim."

Rayan let out a frustrated sigh. "I *am* a victim. I left everything behind to help you!"

"You left everything behind to run from the police," Sil shot back. "Don't try to make yourself out to be a martyr. You're just as selfish as I am, but you could at least be grateful that I stole some food for you. Without me, you'd be rotting in a cell and eating whatever they gave you."

"Maybe that'd be better than sitting here with *you*."

Sil recoiled at the sharp words, its mouth snapping shut. It blinked a few times, giving Rayan enough time to massage his temples and try to collect himself.

"I'm sorry, I didn't mean – "

"Okay." Sil leaned back against the wall, crossing its arms. "Fine. I don't care. Do you think I care? Go and give yourself up for all I care."

"Sil ... "

"Shut up. I guess I should be grateful that you finally showed your true colours."

Rayan wanted to respond, but all that came out was a choked little sob. He didn't mean to say that. He was just angry. "Sil," he whimpered, tears trickling down his cheeks. He couldn't say any more before the floodgates fully opened and he dissolved into a wailing mess.

"Fuck," Sil breathed. "Stop that. *Stop*."

He couldn't. All he could do was bury his face in his hands, tears falling onto the ground below and collecting into a little puddle. He was a mess. He was hungry, he was scared, he was cut off from his family, and he snapped at Sil and said some things he hadn't fucking meant to. Sil was all he had. If he lost it, what would he even do?

Suddenly, two thin little arms were wrapped around him, enveloping him in a warm hug. He threw his arms around the other, pulling it close and sobbing into the crook of its neck. "I'm sorry," he cried. "I'm sorry, Sil, please, I'm sorry, I just wanna go home ... I just want this all to be over ... "

"It'll be over," it said gently. "It will be. At some point, one way or another, it will be over. I'm ... " It took a deep breath, rubbing his back a little. "I'm sorry too. I've said some things ... Whatever. You know what I mean."

He did. And he was grateful.

When Dr. Anne came back, she found them still hugging it out, clinging to each other like two people who really had no one else in the world on their side. Thankfully, that didn't seem to be the case.

"They're ready for you," she said with a smile. "So stop the pity party."

"Sorry," Rayan said, wiping his face. Sil also returned to scowling as soon as the two of them separated, and Rayan found he much preferred that to its teary little face from before. "Who are 'they', exactly?"

"Denice and the guys. I let them know you two need a temporary place to stay – I didn't need to explain much. They watch the news too; they know your exact situation, like everyone else in Laka. Maybe the whole of Lezune."

Rayan glanced at Sil. Sil glanced back at him. "But we'll be safe there, right?" it asked, looking back at Dr. Anne. "They can keep us safe?"

"You won't even have to go outside," she said with a grin. "Hop off the operating table."

Sil did so and Milo immediately stepped up to push the table to the side. Dr. Anne grabbed a handle Rayan hadn't noticed until then, pulling part of the floor aside to reveal an underground tunnel.

"Woah," he said softly. "Was that there the whole time?"

"No, we just dug it yesterday," Dr. Anne said sarcastically. "How do you think I go in and out of this building? I can't be seen entering any place too many times or they'll come investigate it. Come on, jump down."

Rayan was the first to enter the tunnel so he could then help Sil land softly enough on its ruined ankle with the crutches. They said their goodbyes to Dr. Anne, who only sent Milo with them to show the way.

"I can't believe I never noticed that," Rayan marvelled.

"You never notice anything," Sil retorted. "I'm not too surprised."

"Quiet," Milo hissed. "We're below a pretty quiet street, we don't need them finding out there's a tunnel underneath."

Rayan clamped a hand over his mouth. "Sorry."

The journey was pretty much smooth sailing until they reached another trap door. Milo knocked on it in a specific pattern and it was soon opened, and Rayan found himself staring straight at a smugly grinning Denice.

"What's up, comrade?"

Rayan thought back to the way he'd criticised Pet Lib and Denice's vocation and blushed deep red. How the world had changed in just a few weeks.

He climbed out with Milo, then the two of them helped Sil get up. They were in some sort of cellar with a bunch of people around, or ...

"Is everyone here an ex-pet?" Rayan asked quietly. Denice's grin widened.

"Why don't you try and guess?"

"We don't have time for stupid games," Sil growled.

"No, no, I think this is quite an important game. Go on. Guess who's an ex-pet."

Rayan looked around and realised the task was impossible. Everyone looked like an ex-pet to him, mostly because everyone looked like an enemy of the state. Who else would rebel against a system if not ex-pets? "Um ... I ... Uh ... "

Fuck.

Denice clapped him on the shoulder. "Yeah, exactly."

"B-but pets look like people – "

"Because they *are* people, silly."

Rayan looked around again, trying to make sense of a reality that was rapidly shifting from second to second.

"You look like an ex-pet right now too," a woman said from the corner. "Are you?"

"No! No, I'm ... I look like an ex-pet ... ?"

She shrugged. "You look rough enough to have been abused by a bad owner. I looked much the same when I escaped."

"We don't have *time* for this," Sil said again. "You." It pointed at Denice. "Help us get out of here. Out of my owner's reach. Out of this stupid country."

"We're working on your fake papers now," Denice assured it. "You're gonna have to stay put for just a bit longer. Don't worry – this place is safe."

***

Through talking, Rayan learned that at most half the people in that cellar were actually ex-pets. *People*. They were all people, the lot of them. There was no way for him to differentiate between people from facilities and normal homes, and while Sil seemed especially opposed to the idea that the system was built on lies, Rayan was believing it more and more.

"You failed a pet test?" he asked one of the men – Axel – absolutely horrified. "So they took you away from your parents? I mean, I knew that was a thing, I just ... "

"Yup. They didn't do a damn thing to protect me." He pulled his shirt collar aside to reveal a similar scar to Sil's. "They put a chip in me first thing to prevent me from escaping. Apparently the one I had functioned as a tracker – someone paid good money to have me be processed. Have you heard of 'custom pets'? The sick fucks at the top can have people be abducted and processed into the system."

"There's no way ... "

"Oh, but there is. They pay the PPA to have people be turned into slaves, they pay the PPA to leave them alone as they abuse them, they pay the PPA to turn a blind eye when those pets suddenly disappear one day ... I'm not saying everyone at every level knows what's going on, but I'm sure as hell saying the top fuckers know."

"Rayan, Sil," Denice called as she descended the stairs. "We've got your papers. Get your things together and let's go."

"R-right now? Like, immediately?"

Sil didn't seem to have such hang-ups. It grabbed its backpack and stood up, pulling the crutches under its arms. "Let's go. Don't tell me you were still holding on to the notion that we might be able to stay."

Sil's vehement objections to befriending any of the people here suddenly seemed to make a lot more sense. Rayan let out a defeated sigh and followed it up the stairs.

"It's the dead of night, but you never know," Denice said as she fitted Rayan with a beanie and an eye-patch. "Your face is all over the news. Change into these clothes."

Sil was given different clothes as well — a dark blue jacket instead of its regular red one that had become iconic in the past days, dark pants to match, and even a wheelchair.

"You can lift it, right?" Denice asked. "You'll need to lift it into the boat when you get to the shore. There'll be new crutches for you on the ship, but you can't use them until then. Everyone is on the lookout for a pet with crutches."

Sil swallowed. "So I'll just have to rely on Rayan pushing me around?"

"For a little while." Denice shot it an apologetic smile. "He's trying his best. Give him a chance."

"One chance is *all* I have."

"All *we* have," Rayan amended quietly. "I promise, I'm in it as much as you are. I won't mess up."

Sil hesitantly gave up its crutches and sat in the chair. Rayan exchanged good-byes with all his new friends and, lastly, Denice.

"I knew you'd come around," she said with a warm smile. "And hey, if you get caught, rest assured that we have a small, radical team on our side, specialising in busting out people from prison."

Rayan let out a small chuckle, shocked at the surreal idea. "Thanks, Denice. Well ... this is goodbye, then."

"It's just see you later. We'll get pets outlawed here sooner or later, and you guys will be welcomed back with open arms. Just you wait."

He didn't want to say it, but Rayan knew there was a very small chance of that happening. Not with most of the revolutionary action taking place across the ocean, where they were now headed. "Yeah. I'll be waiting."

"Let's go," Sil said gruffly, and Rayan immediately put his hands on the handles of its wheelchair.

"Right. See you later."

— • —

The Ship That Sailed

The streets were dark and quiet as the two of them followed the path set out by Denice and the others. They were going through narrow alleyways and streets barely illuminated by the streetlights, getting closer and closer to the ocean. Rayan could already smell it. It wasn't too far now.

"Hey," someone yelled from across the street and Rayan froze.

"Don't stop," Sil whispered. "Go. Go, go, *go*."

"Hey, you!"

Rayan couldn't will his legs to move. He swallowed thickly as he turned to meet the gaze of the man shouting at him, hoping he didn't look as suspicious as he felt. "Yes?"

"There's a curfew order in place, didn't you hear?"

Curfew?

Denice hadn't said anything about a curfew.

"N-no, I'm sorry." As the man got even closer, Rayan got to take a good, close look at the PPA badge on the front of his uniform. "I was just taking my sister out for some fresh air," he tried as nonchalantly as possible. "It – " *Fuck.* "She gets very sick sometimes if she has to lie down for a long period of time. She gets these asthma attacks – we were just going to the shore for – "

Sil suddenly stood up, balancing on its one good leg. Rayan's eyes widened as he watched it gain momentum and –

Bang.

It smacked the guy across the head with the cast on its bad arm, wincing as the healing bones took the impact. The PPA agent was out cold.

"You can't just do that!" Rayan whisper-screamed as Sil sat back down.

"Go," it hissed. "Come on. Go!"

Rayan couldn't stay calm anymore. He raced down the streets with all the stamina he had, grabbing Sil and holding it in a bridal carry once they reached the sandy shore, where the wheelchair became quite useless. There was a little boat waiting for them, according to Denice.

But where?

"There it is!" Sil suddenly said, pointing to a shadow on the water.

"Hey! You there! Stop!" someone yelled. Rayan ran even faster. "*Stop*!"

Sil buried its face in his chest as the two of them rushed to the boat, almost not wanting to let go when Rayan basically threw it on one of the benches. "Row!" it screamed in a panicked frenzy.

"I'm on it!" Rayan shouted back, trying to push the boat onto the water. He could hear the man running across the sand to catch up to them, and he pushed with all his might, trying his best to get out of reach.

"Stop immediately! You're under arrest!"

Rayan jumped into the boat and grabbed the paddles, rowing as fast as he could. The two of them started gaining momentum as he did so, leaving the PPA agent behind.

Sil let out a relieved sigh, carding through its sweat-damp hair with its good hand. "Fuck," it breathed.

"Fuck indeed," Rayan agreed quietly, still rowing like his life depended on it.

Because it kind of did.

When the two of them caught a glimpse of the promised ship in the distance, even Rayan started to feel the knots in his stomach loosen. It was floating in place with the anchor down, and they went up to it as close as safely possible.

"They're here!" someone on board yelled, and the lifeboat was soon lowered. Rayan helped Sil into it before climbing over himself, and then the two of them were pulled up, both utterly exhausted from the cat and mouse chase they'd just endured.

"We did it," Rayan panted on the floor. For the first time in all their days together, he saw Sil *smile* as he looked over.

"We did it!" it said, more enthusiastic. "We did it! We're out! We're out!"

Rayan sat up and looked over the railing into the ocean, thinking about the family he was leaving behind. "We did it ... "

Sil crashed into him for a big hug, holding on tighter than ever. "We did it," it whispered. "I never have to be hurt again. I – I'll miss Master more than anything, but we ... we did it. I'm sorry about your family. But we did it. We're out."

Rayan hugged back, more aware than ever that they were all each of them had. "We did it."

***

"Rayan!" Silja yelled as it barged in through the front door. "Rayan!"

"What?" he yelled back from the kitchen, putting a freshly baked batch of muffins on the counter and pulling off his oven mitts.

Instead of answering, Silja rushed into the kitchen with a wide grin on its face, holding a piece of paper in front of its now-less-scrawny body. Rayan immediately knew what it was – the only thing that had mattered in these last few days.

"You graduated?" he asked with a grin now matching Silja's, taking the paper from its hands. "You scored ninety-eight out of one hundred! Sil, that's outstanding!"

Silja threw its hair back and twirled around, then bowed with great flourish. "That's Silja for you."

"We're celebrating today, then! I knew you'd do it, love. I've prepared some muffins for you!"

The two of them sat down at the kitchen table, and after they'd let the muffins cool for a while – and Rayan had taken a sufficient amount of pictures of Silja's graduation papers – they began to eat.

"I told you I could do it," Silja said with its mouth full of delicious, chocolatey goodness.

"I never doubted you," Rayan responded with a warm smile.

"You would've doubted me way back when! When you thought I was just a dumb pet!"

Rayan reached over and ruffled its hair, making Silja laugh and swat his hand away. "You'll never stop bringing that up, will you?"

"Never ever."

Rayan looked back at the piece of paper proving that Silja was now a high school graduate and found that one particular detail warmed his heart more than even the incredible score written on the front. Tears sprung to his eyes as he took it in, and he tried his best to wipe them away as discreetly as possible.

Silja Kamali.

As much as he missed his family abroad, there was always a little sister here for him to be proud of.

About the Author

Zi Trone is but a humble fear enthusiast with a passion for writing. An undying love for scared and crying characters has been the driving force behind hundreds of thousands of words already written, and hopefully many more to come.

Bonnie and Guy

Nox Spacey

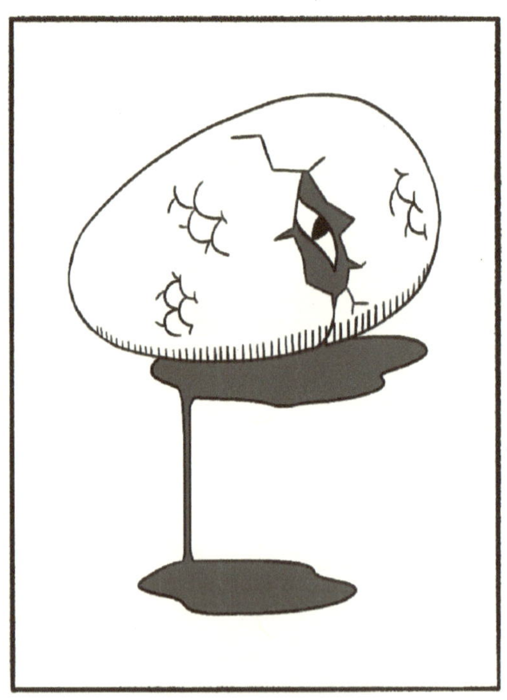

Cover Design by Nicole Alessi

Cover Illustration by Hen Towers

Also by Nox Spacey

Magnanimous Moonrise & Savage Sunset

Contents

CONTENT WARNINGS

This story contains the following content:

- Animal attacks
- Broken bones
- Referenced character death

If this book isn't for you, no worries! But if it is, we hope you enjoy this story about a dragonrider and his unexpected ally...

1

The rest of Guy's unit was definitely very, very dead. But that was okay because he hadn't let himself get attached. Not attached at all! So really, it was fine that everyone was dead.

The mad howling of creatures up in the sky was less intense way down here amidst the wreckage on the pavement, but Guy knew better than to think he was safe. He was a sitting duck.

He probably would have been the only one in the unit who knew what a duck was since they'd been extinct for decades.

They'd all been kids. Well, not kids. Late teens, early twenties. Kids to *him*. He'd been the only one of the lot that had even been alive before the Tribulation, and honestly, he'd known as soon as he'd met them that they weren't going to last. So he hadn't gotten attached. Hadn't let himself get attached. Easy as that.

And then a building had fallen on their whole unit mid-flight, proving him right. He would rather be alive than right, which was part of the reason why he'd survived and the rest had died instantly when the massive, decrepit, vine-covered skyscraper had collapsed on top of them.

The only one he let himself get attached to these days was Bonnie, and even that seemed to be backfiring.

Explosions continued to sound in the distance on top of the echoing calls of roaring creatures, and Guy tried to extract himself from under Bonnie's flank where they'd fallen, anxiety mounting. Oh, his leg was definitely broken. Definitely definitely definitely. Bonnie had landed on her side and probably smashed his bones into a million pieces, pinning his leg to the cracked pavement. She wouldn't respond to his calls to get up.

"You have to get up, Bonnie." He choked back a sob, and tears blurred his vision. He needed her to get up. Not only because they would die if she didn't, but because he needed her. His sweet Bonnie. He'd raised her from almost the moment she'd hatched from her egg. His heart twisted seeing her pinned under the rubble of a Pre-Tribulation building.

The looming stone monuments of Pre-Tribulation cities were only good for serving as battlefields these days, and Guy hated them even more now that one had been pushed over on top of them all. The humans in the unit would definitely have died instantly; the dragons would still be alive, invulnerable to being killed by something as mundane as crushing concrete, but there would be no way to dig them out before the flock of Wellspring creatures could get to them for their next meal, so they were as good as dead.

Guy and Bonnie might be too. Bonnie was severely hurt from the fight, and they hadn't managed to clear the falling building in time, so they were now half-stuck under it. They were an easy meal for the starving, ravenous creatures swarming the city, and he could hear the leader of the attack calling for everyone to retreat. Even if they didn't die right here, right now, they were going to be left behind among the dead.

Bonnie was still alive, at least; he could tell by the laborious rising and falling of her sides. He slid his hand over her flank, feeling the softness of her powder blue feathers. The tears did spill over, then. "Bonnie. Bonnie-onnie, my sweet girl. Please. You have to get up, BonBon." He very gently tugged at the reins, which jingled with the motion. "Please."

He heard an infernal clicking behind him, and he craned his neck to see a pack of raptors picking their way over the rubble towards him, their huge talons scraping over the debris.

Those things weren't usually a problem. But then again, *usually* Guy was a hundred feet up in the air with the ability to just torch them in a cone of fire.

"Bonnie," he said, his voice pitching up with renewed urgency. "Bonnie, you have to get up, sweetheart. Please get up." He pressed his palm to her side again and pushed, trying to pry his leg out from under her.

Bonnie gave a labored, animalistic moan and started to writhe, claws grabbing at the air and tail thrashing, trying in vain to push the debris off herself.

"There you go," Guy encouraged. "There you go, girl."

The raptors had spotted him, though, and were now locked onto him, the pack making guttural clicks to call to each other.

"Faster," Guy squeaked. "Faster, Bonnie, faster, faster."

The raptors reached him before Bonnie could free herself. Their heads bobbed and cocked to the side to observe him.

"You can't eat me," Guy said, as though he had any chance of negotiating with them. "You don't want to kill me! I'm just some guy! Wait – wait!"

One of them lunged forwards and seized him by the arm he'd extended to shield himself, shaking its head savagely and pulling.

"Ow! Fuck! Fuck, fuck, stop! Ow!"

The rest of the pack pounced, then. So this was how he was going to die. It'd be a lie to say he wasn't disappointed. After all this, he'd die like carrion being eaten by a pack of scavengers. He and Bonnie had survived a quetzalcoatl, a storm flier, a whole herd of unicorns, a whole pack of feral hawk wyverns, a flock of cherubim, a cluster of rock drakes. Hell, Guy had survived the damn Tribulation. And he was going to die here because a stupid building collapsed and nearly crushed them, leaving him vulnerable to the stupid little critters running around on the ground he never thought he'd have to worry about.

Guy screamed as the pack pulled him out from under Bonnie, finally wrenching his broken leg free. He flailed as much as he could, but there were at least five of them taking turns nipping at him.

The armor of his riding suit and his helmet had protected him from the worst of the hurt from the fall. It was all made with Wellspring material and therefore could only be damaged by other things made from Wellspring material, which unfortunately included the teeth and claws of the predators now savaging him. The fabric that had been indestructible under concrete and rebar tore under their talons, drawing blood and more screams from him. Realistically his only chance at survival would have been his WS rifle, but he'd used up his bullet ration trying to keep Bonnie alive in the fight, so the weapon hung empty on Bonnie's saddle.

He reached down to his belt and pulled out the Bowie knife sheathed there. It was also made of Wellspring material and therefore could hurt the raptors if he managed to land a hit before one of them clamped onto his arm, which he didn't. He dropped the knife and screamed as the beast's teeth pierced his armor, pulling his arm like it meant to pull it off.

He thought his comm wasn't working anymore based on the static it was transmitting instead of voices, but on the off chance his mic was still hot, whoever was listening must be getting an earful.

Bonnie let out a whine and flopped her wings, trying to muster up the strength to push off the debris pinning her. The raptors finally managed to snap the lines keeping him attached to Bonnie's saddle, which whipped back with a *twang*. Now that he was completely untethered, the largest raptor clamped his torso in its jaws and ran off, his legs dragging across the dusty ground. The others followed, growling and jostling to try and take Guy from the pack leader.

"Bonnie!" he screamed, because for some reason the thought of dying away from her was *so* much less bearable.

Bonnie lay her head down limply, braying and moaning.

One of the raptors managed to get its jaws around his helmet and pull hard enough to rip it off. His hair came free. One of them seemed to find that interesting, nibbling at it and then getting a mouthful and tugging, taking out the cord he'd used to tie it back.

He hit the dirt with a *thud*, under the claws of one of the raptors, the others still squabbling over him. Multiple jaws and claws tugged him in different directions.

The rest of their force could be seen retreating overhead, the sky darkening intermittently with shadows of fleeing dragons. It felt odd, quiet, to not be able to hear the constant radio chatter that always accompanied being in an attack.

He tried to crane his neck to catch sight of Bonnie, but he'd been dragged too far away. He was alone. He hoped Bonnie could make it back on her own.

The pain was so intense he could hardly feel it anymore. His body was shutting down. He was so tired. Maybe this wasn't so bad. Maybe he shouldn't fight anymore. He let his limbs fall limp.

He closed his eyes and waited for it to happen.

Suddenly there was a huge stomping sound and the ground shook. The raptors gave alarm calls to each other and turned their attention towards something out of view, hissing and posturing. Then they fled entirely, leaving him completely exposed and limp on the pavement. Alone.

At first he thought Bonnie had managed to get up and come to save him. He weakly dragged his head across the ground to face the direction the raptors had fled from.

Oh, there was a new beast there. Big. Bigger than Bonnie herself. It stood on its hind legs and balanced with a heavy tail, and rows of curving spikes branched from its head down its back. It had a solid jaw like a saw, in which one of the raptors was currently hanging limply.

It dropped onto all fours and let the dead raptor fall to the pavement, then sniffed it, licked its lips, and started eating it. It used the massive claws on its forelegs to tear it apart.

Ah. He'd just be prey for a different predator, then. He let his head fall back down, trying to regulate his breathing. His mind swam in the pain, making it hard to think.

He watched the beast eat its meal, bones and all, cracking it apart into pieces and swallowing it without chewing, just tilting its head back and letting it slide down its throat. Like an alligator. Those were extinct now too.

The raptors came back in a nervous wave, picking their way towards Guy slowly in the hopes of not drawing the ire of the larger predator. Its eyes burned on them, and it trundled over towards Guy and shooed them away, dragging the bloody corpse of its half-eaten meal behind it. The raptors darted towards him in turns, rebuffed by the occasional claw or snarl from the beast claiming him as its meal.

He closed his eyes and just listened to the sounds. The squeaks, barks, thumping growls he could feel in his chest. A clawed foot pressed down on him from above, just barely not crushing him any more than he already was.

He bit his lip to keep from crying out. He was so tired. He lay there limply.

He felt hot breath on the back of his neck, a stinky exhale that disturbed his hair. He started to tremble, then, despite himself. This was it.

He cracked an eye open and saw the bloody muzzle of the big beast inches away from him, nostrils flaring to sniff him. Bits of the dead raptor were scattered about, a few stray bones and sinews still hanging from its teeth. The raptors were all gone, so the beast must have completed the first course of its meal and was now ready to eat him. This was it.

He squeezed his eyes shut again and turned away.

Its thick, coarse lips brushed against his skin, painting him with warm blood. He shuddered on the ground, still pinned under its broad claw. It nosed at him with something akin to curiosity, and it started to nibble on him. He let out a pathetic cry as its teeth scraped his skin, drawing even more blood. His head spun.

It drew back. He opened his eyes and looked up at it, chest heaving with terrified breaths. Its eyes were dark and inscrutable, but it was *looking* at him. Making eye contact.

"H ... hello?" he said. "Hi. I'm just some guy. Eyyyyyy."

Its jaw hinged all the way open, then, and clamped around him, adding even more punctures to his already impressive collection. He screamed and squirmed as it hefted him up in the air. It was so big he fit in its mouth sideways from shoulders to knees, only one arm left dangling outside of its mouth.

"Not a fan of jokes, then?" he managed to choke out before the shifting of its jaws drew out another terrified squeak.

The crushing force that he'd expected to come down and kill him didn't come, though. Instead the beast started walking. He swayed in its jaws, its teeth prickling him with the shambling motion. Carrying him away.

2

Guy expected the beast was taking him back to its nest to feed its young. There was no other explanation for why it would kidnap him, rather than just eating him on the spot. It was what Wellspring creatures did. They killed and ate and raised young and did basically nothing else.

It took him into one of the skyscrapers, one of the ones leaning precipitously into its neighbor. A huge hole had been blown in the side, and the creature picked its way across the wreckage carefully.

It crossed what would have once been a lobby, blue marble cracked and plants growing up through it and smothering the reception desk. It walked past what would have once been an elevator and mounted what remained of the stairs.

It barely fit in the stairwell, having to go partially up onto the wall to navigate the corners. A few times, it leapt over spaces where the stairs had collapsed entirely. It was a smart place to build a nest. Larger predators wouldn't be able to fit in the space, and smaller ones wouldn't be able to get over the obstacles or wouldn't be smart enough to climb the stairs at all.

The beast pushed past a broken door to exit the stairwell and come out onto a floor that looked like it had once been an office. The cubicles had all been pushed into one corner and piled up to form a sort of little shelter, facing away from the broken windows that would let in rain. Leaves and unidentifiable fabric and bones and dried blood lined the nest. Guy would almost call it cozy, even if it smelled terrible.

There were no young in the nest. No egg. Nothing at all. Guy's mind swam through the upstream of terror to try and make sense of it.

The creature gently set him onto the ground in the nest, then curled around him and put its head on its paws.

Guy swallowed, sweating. This ... wasn't what he'd expected. He palmed the floor to try and push himself to his feet, but the creature let out a savage growl and narrowed its eyes at him, nostrils flaring. He fell still immediately.

The beast's breathing gradually began to slow down, and when he looked over and saw its eyes sliding closed, he realized it was falling asleep. He waited a few minutes before once again trying to stand up, but it immediately snapped awake and growled at him again, even angrier than before. He froze, quaking.

He lost track of how long he lay there. The light outside started to dim as the sun set. Despite the whole situation, he was tired too. He was bone-deep exhausted. Despite the pain, he eventually fell asleep too.

***

It was still dark when he jolted awake, scrambling to remember where he was and what had happened.

The beast was gone. His heart pounded at the realization. It was gone, and everything was quiet, and *goddamn* did his everything still hurt, but he had to do something.

He had to get back down to the street, navigate the terrain through the dark, dodge hungry Wellspring creatures, find Bonnie, and get back to Wasp Nest.

... There was no way he could do that, not really. But he had to try, right?

Gritting his teeth to keep from crying out, he pushed himself to his feet, using a nearby desk to steady himself. *Okay. So far so good.*

He hobbled across the room. This was harder than he'd thought. He needed something to use as a crutch. Anything that could prop himself up.

There was a bent stop sign on the ground nearby. Sure. Why not. He bent down painfully to pick it up, then used it to brace himself and keep the pressure off his leg.

He made it to the stairwell okay. It was an agonizing pace, but he took the steps one at a time, wheezing.

It'd been a while since he'd been in a building this tall. It was giving him flashbacks to the before times. His father taking him to work in a building like this. Lots of paper and electronic devices and men in suits looking important.

He came to a section of the stairwell where the stairs had crumbled away. Ah. He'd forgotten. It was too far to jump, but there was still a bit of a lip attached to the wall. Maybe he could shimmy across it?

He put his good leg onto the ledge, and it crumbled instantly and tumbled down into the darkness below, sending him scrambling back.

Okay, so that wouldn't work. Maybe he could find something to lay across it, or a rope to swing across?

As he was in the process of assessing the surrounding rubble for anything useful, he heard the shuffling motions of the beast coming back upstairs.

Shit, oh shit shit shit shit. He froze with panic, having no idea what to do.

The beast's head appeared around the corner, and its eyes landed on him. It flicked an ear.

"Um," he said. "Hi."

It snorted and crouched down like it was going to jump. Guy scrambled backwards to get out of the landing zone, and when it leapt up, its claws slammed down a few inches in front of him.

It took a step forward, over him. He scrunched himself down, trying to become one with the concrete. "Hi," he said, voice getting even more mousey. "Um. Sorry."

He let out a scared *eep* as its mouth closed around him again, teeth prickling at him. He went limp in its jaws.

It carted him back up to the office nest and dropped him back where he'd been. He curled up in the corner, wrapping his arms around his legs. "Can't blame a guy for trying."

It made eye contact with him.

"A guy? Because I'm ... "

The beast turned away and walked back down the stairs.

Guy craned his neck to try and follow its motion, but its tail disappeared down into the dark. "Okay. Um, bye."

It came back up a moment later, this time with another dead raptor in its jaws. The corpse swung limply as the beast trotted over.

To his dismay, the beast leaned over and dropped the carcass directly onto Guy's lap.

He winced and squirmed, blood dripping down over his lap. "Um."

The beast lowered its head and sniffed at the corpse.

"Um." He held his hands up and leaned away, awash in discomfort and terror.

The beast bumped the corpse with its nose, pushing it towards him.

It suddenly clicked. "Are you ... are you trying to feed me?"

The beast sat back on its haunches, tail swishing.

Guy looked from the carcass to the beast and back again, utterly amazed. "Thank you, but. Um ... I can't eat this. I'm not sure what you want me to do."

It gave a bovine low and shook its head, ears flicking.

"Um, I'm sorry. Don't, uh, don't be mad at me."

It tugged the corpse off his lap and dragged it away, tearing it open and starting to eat it. Guy let himself relax a little, trying to wipe the blood from himself. Between the blood and the smell in here and the sweat and tears and everything from earlier, Guy felt *disgusting* in a way that would be intolerable if the fear of his imminent demise wasn't so looming.

Although ... given the way the thing was behaving, maybe it wasn't so imminent after all.

3

Guy watched the beast for a bit, studying it. It was behaving ... strangely for a Wellspring creature. He'd never encountered one that didn't just try to eat him as soon as it clapped eyes on him. It seemed smarter. More on the level of the hawk wyverns the guild members rode, which could be cooperative and trained, the only Wellspring creatures capable of that kind of behavior. Except for this one, apparently. The beast seemed relatively normal other than that, cracking the bones of its prey and swallowing it down in an animalistic way.

Guy stretched his legs out, the injury in his left leg twinging with pain now that the adrenaline had worn off. The beast was currently facing away from him, and it seemed inappropriate to do so, but he examined the space between its hind legs. There was no evidence of maleness there, so it was probably female, although Wellspring creatures could get pretty freaky about that sometimes. Guy had spent his fair share of time in the library at Paramount reading up on the cataloged information on Wellsprings and the phenomenon associated with them. Everyone was required to do so as part of their training to become a dragonrider, but he'd been among the few to take it seriously. The younger trainees just kind of blew it off, in his experience.

So the beast was a girl beast. "Beast?" he said.

She raised her head and looked at him, blood dribbling from her maw.

"Can I name you Bea?"

She flicked an ear and lowered her head, going back to her meal.

Guy felt silly. A Wellspring creature could not possibly care less what you called it, but for some reason it felt like he needed to name it. If she was a *she* and *Bea* and a familiar beast, that was less scary. As though he could will it into existence that this creature could be won over, just like he'd won Bonnie over.

Guy shakily got to his feet, steadying himself on the nearby furniture. "Hey, Bea?"

Bea ignored him this time, unwavering attention on finishing her meal.

Guy limped closer. "Were you really trying to feed me?"

The last of the raptor finally disappeared down her throat, and she licked her chops, sniffing the ground to make sure it was really all gone.

"Why are you keeping me here?"

Her eyes swung towards him. He really could not tell what was going on behind them – if there was any intelligence there. It felt like there was, but maybe he was imagining it.

"I appreciate it," he said. "I do. I can't eat Wellspring creatures, though. It's just –"

She abruptly got up and disappeared down the stairwell, snorting and flicking her tail dismissively.

" ... Okay," he said quietly.

***

Guy spent the alone time imagining what would happen if he did eat the meat of a Wellspring creature. His stomach acid couldn't break down the meat any more than his punch could hurt its body while it was still alive. Very best-case scenario, he'd throw it back up. Though it'd probably just sit in his gut like he'd eaten a piece of metal.

He thought better about trying to go down the stairs this time. He doubted he could make it all the way down to the ground floor, and even if he did, his reward would be facing whatever creatures were down there. Not as puzzlingly inclined to nonviolence towards him as Bea, but surely just as hungry.

He limped over to one of the broken windows, leaning on it and looking outside. He watched the sunrise with a strange sense of inner peace. Everything felt like it mattered less, here, his world shrunk down to whether or not Bea was going to eat him in this nest.

A pack of fox wyverns flew by outside in the distance, the *pop* of their teleportation powers echoing off the buildings. Guy gasped and dropped down, below the window. He'd managed to forget for a moment where he was. The kind of danger he was perpetually in.

He sighed and looked around the room. In his haste to make an escape, he hadn't picked over the debris of this floor very much. It had been an open office concept of some sort, he guessed, because it seemed like most of the floor was one giant room.

His stomach growled. He really was starting to get hungry. He hadn't eaten since breakfast yesterday, before leaving Wasp Nest to join the battle against the horde of creatures that had been menacing the farming settlement across the river.

He found a rusty metal pipe this time to use as a crutch, balancing on it as he hobbled around broken desks and chairs and moldy cubicles and bits of rubble from the collapsed upper floor. He poked around for anything useful.

A dirt-filled pot, some houseplant long dead and gone. Trinkets and doodads people had used to decorate their desks, brightly-colored plastic figures lying faded and broken on the floor. Paper, ever-present paper, yellowed and tattered and molding. Electronic devices that hadn't worked in decades – broken touchscreens, ripped power cords, hardware snapped in half. Conference rooms with the glass barriers smashed out. A water cooler, the interior long bone-dry. A bathroom, the toilet in an unspeakable state. He tried the faucet just to check – a rusty sludge came out. It would probably be more dangerous to drink than puddle water from outside. He left it on just in case it eventually started running clear water.

At last, something useful: a vending machine. It was still upright and fully stocked. He tried pressing the buttons first – they didn't work, of course, without power. But worth a shot. Next he tried jamming his arm up in through the dispensing port to grab whatever was on the lowest shelf. No chance. He resigned himself to having to pick glass out of whatever he grabbed and smashed the front with the metal pipe.

The dirty glass cascaded down, giving him a clear view of the contents inside. Some of the snacks had clearly rotted and started growing mold even through their sealed packaging, but some of them looked like they might be okay. He reached in and took one, shaking it to get all the glass off, and tore it open. It was some sort of chocolate pastry, desiccated and discolored. It smelled off, so he tossed it to the ground and reached for the thing beside it. The label printed on the side indicated it had expired in 2067. He shrugged and tore it open. He took a nibble despite his better judgment, then immediately spat it out.

He sighed and reached for one of the cans of soda. This one had no expiration date, and when he cracked it open, it still fizzled. Of course. These kinds of manmade liquid abominations lasted forever.

He took a sip. It was ... *incredibly* sweet. He didn't entirely like it. Had he really eaten and drunk things like this every day before the Tribulation?

It wasn't filling in the slightest, but it did give him some much needed energy. He continued rifling around to find anything useful until Bea came back.

He heard her before he saw her, big stomps up the stairs. He came over to meet her. "Hey, girl! Did you have a good day at work?"

She flicked her tail and narrowed her eyes at him. She approached and lowered her head.

Guy took a nervous step back.

She opened her mouth, and a handful of dented cans tumbled out, rolling across the floor.

Guy stared at them in amazement. Canned pineapples, potatoes, and pumpkin puree. That's what they were.

"Oh my God. You *are* trying to feed me." He got down on his knees and collected the cans, trying to calculate how best to take advantage of this strange blessing. "Thank you. Um. Thanks."

She sat down, curling her tail around her front feet. Guy kept the cans in his arms and walked with some difficulty over towards a pile of debris he'd seen earlier, where a twisted metal bar had a jagged edge he'd noted he'd need to avoid.

He held the can up to it and twisted, using it as a can opener. Pineapple juice spilled out.

"Thank you, Bea," he said. "Thank you. Holy shit." He sipped at the juice – it tasted funny after drinking the soda. He reached a dirty finger in and scooped up a pineapple ring. A *pineapple ring*. He hadn't eaten pineapple since before the Tribulation.

It was sweet and acidic in his mouth. He couldn't stifle the little moan of satisfaction. "Bea, you're beautiful. You're a gem."

She stalked over to where he was, watching him. He made eye contact with her, trying to make it obvious that he was making use of what she'd brought back, eating it with exaggerated glee.

"We used to make a really good kind of cake with these, you know," he said wistfully. "With brown sugar. You'd bake a cake using pineapple juice instead of water, then turn it upside down at the end. The glaze would all dribble down." He sat down, hunched over. He was imagining the pineapple upside-down cake so vividly he could almost taste it.

He sighed and took another bite of pineapple ring. "The rest of my unit wouldn't have even known about that kind of cake. I wonder if any of them ever even ate pineapple. They were all so young."

Bea sat down, ear twitching.

"They were just kids, Bea. My God, they were just kids. They didn't even understand the difference between the magic of the Wellsprings and the technology of, like, the mics in our helmets and stuff. They thought Awsk was a person and not an AI. They didn't even know what an AI *was*."

But he hadn't gotten attached to them, so it was fine. He hadn't gotten attached to anyone since his first unit. He'd learned. "I knew they weren't going to last, Bea. They were stupid and reckless. Too eager to fight. Too excited about the thought of dying in battle." When had he started crying? He reached a sticky hand up and wiped the tears on the back of his palm. "They never last. Even the kids. Especially the kids."

He startled as Bea shoved her snout under his hand. After a moment, he slowly lowered his hand down onto her, touching gently. "Thank you," he said around the lump in his throat. "God, I'm going to have to drink something other than Pepsi to stay hydrated if I'm going to be crying, huh? Haha."

***

Bea ended up bringing back an entire refrigerator the next time she left, the old, dirty appliance dragging on the ground in her jaws as she excitedly brought it back like a retriever. It was completely empty, but she seemed to know it was associated with food somehow, because she dropped it at his feet the same way she'd done with the cans earlier.

"Thank you," he said very seriously. He opened it and put the remaining canned food and soda in it, despite the fact that it was sitting on its side and unpowered. It did give him some weird feeling of normalcy. *Food goes in the fridge.*

He managed to collect some water when it rained that afternoon. He left some of the drums from the empty water cooler by the broken windows and torn-away walls, and they managed to catch some of the rainwater.

With imminent death staved off – relative safety, and starvation and dehydration kept at bay – he was now free to be incredibly in pain. His leg was very, very broken, and he still had multiple open wounds from the raptor attack – not actively bleeding, but threatening to reopen if they didn't get some proper treatment soon. He couldn't afford to pass out from blood loss.

Fuck it. If he was going to be stuck here with this beast of unknown intentions, he might as well try. "Hey, Bea?" he said tentatively.

She raised her head off her paws.

"I need some medicine." She seemed capable of understanding more than expected. Could she understand that? Would this unexpected blessing stretch that far? "I'm hurt. I'm sick."

She got up, stretched, and came over to him, shoving her snout in his face. He scrambled backwards. "Medicine?" he said hopefully.

She nosed at him. A pit formed in his stomach. Had he made a mistake?

Her jaws opened and clamped around him, lifting him bodily up. *Oh fuck.* Yep, yep, yep, definitely a mistake. Somehow.

"Wait, Bea!" he cried, squirming in her jaws. Her iron-hard teeth prickled at him. "Wait, I'm sorry. I'm sorry."

She ignored his thrashing around and carried him down the stairs, effortlessly leaping over the gulfs that had given him trouble. They came out onto the ground floor, and Bea galloped over the uneven pavement, still keeping him clamped in her jaws.

A large shadow passed overhead, the outline of a predator far larger than Bea herself. She huddled under an overturned bus until it passed, then continued on with her mission.

"Where are we going?" Guy asked, trying not to sound too pitiful.

She grunted, and Guy felt the vibrations in his core. All she'd need to do would be to clamp down and break him in half, and that would be it for him.

She didn't, though. She toted him through the ruined streets and passed through a few tunnels, coming out into –

The world tumbled over as Bea dropped Guy onto the linoleum. He rolled over, groaning, and froze when his foot touched something.

A box. Bandages. *A box of bandages.*

"Holy shit," he said, nearly weeping with relief. He looked around and saw the destroyed remains of a pharmacy. "Holy shit. You're a lifesaver. Thank you, thank you."

He crawled along the floor, collecting bandages and ointments and bottles of pills. "Holy shit. Bea, I don't know what the hell you are or why you're doing this, but thank you. You're a lifesaver."

He managed to find a case of bottled water, then turned a chair over so he could sit on it. He stripped his shirt off and started pouring the water over his open wounds. He brushed the dirt off a bar of soap he'd found and used it to clean out the many, many bite marks littering his skin as best as he could. He found a rubber band to tie his hair back and keep it out of his face.

He applied the antibiotic ointment and wrapped his bites up in the bandages. He then wiggled out of his pants to repeat the procedure for the wounds on his legs.

Bea snorted, lying down on her haunches and tail wiggling.

Guy froze, self-consciousness suddenly creeping over him. "Don't look at me like that."

Bea had an amused glint in her eye, and she snorted.

"Don't objectify me!"

She crawled forwards and hooked his pants with one claw, dragging them away.

"Hey! You little pervert!"

He finished washing out the cuts on his legs and wrapping them up, feeling woozy from all the blood he'd lost in the past twenty-four hours. There was probably more Pepsi and pineapple juice than blood in his veins at this point.

He pulled his top back on, bandages now showing through the holes, and reached towards his pants. Bea had them in her mouth.

"Please?" he said, trying not to sound too desperate.

She snorted and tossed her head. The pants landed on Guy's face.

"Thank you." He stepped back into them, trying mightily not to jostle his broken leg. The very expired acetaminophen he'd swallowed earlier could only do so much.

He hunted around and found a boot and a splint, which he used to immobilize the leg, as well as a very high tech first aid kit. There was a syringe inside that the leaflet instructed him to use in the event of broken bones. He never knew what was in those things, but he'd been told they worked.

He tried to confirm the needle wasn't too dirty before stabbing it into his leg. As soon as he injected it, pain ripped like wildfire through the area, and he fell down squirming.

"Jesus Christ," he moaned, rolling over. "Fuuuuck me. This is it. This is how I die."

The pain passed after a minute, and his hazy vision cleared to see Bea standing over him and nosing him with concern.

"I'm all right." He heaved in big breaths and used her head to help stand up, using the horns as handholds. "Shit. Fuck." His leg *did* feel a bit better now, but that might just be compared to how it'd felt when the injection hit.

He found an honest-to-goodness crutch nearby, and with that, it was really all he could ask for for a broken leg right now. He hunted around and found a backpack lying open on the ground – it'd belonged to some ill-fated scavengers, no doubt. He hung it on his front and loaded the remaining bottled water into it. He'd need it to stay hydrated if he had diarrhea later, which he suspected was coming from all the very expired food he was eating.

He collected the rest of the bandages, pain meds, first aid kit, and whatever else he could find that seemed useful and stowed it in the backpack, limping along with his crutch.

All things considered, this was good. Very good. Maybe he *wasn't* going to die. Maybe he could survive, somehow. Maybe he could ...

Maybe he could find Bonnie.

Bea clearly had some level of irregular intelligence and some inclination to use it to help him. He didn't want to push his luck, especially since he couldn't guarantee how Bonnie would react to Bea, but *damn* did he want to go find her. The longer he waited, the less chance there was of finding her alive.

"Hey, Bea," he said slowly. He walked towards the thumping of her big feet. "So, I was wondering. Can you – "

He stopped as he rounded the bend and saw that the thing that had been stomping around was *not* Bea. It had a tail, which was a writhing snake, pointing at him. As soon as its slitted eyes clamped onto him, the second head at the front, which was a lion, looked over its shoulder at him.

Chimera. "Fuck," Guy said, scrambling backwards and stumbling into an overturned store shelf.

The chimera backed up to get him within range of its tail, and the snake lashed out and bit him.

"Fuck," he said again, and he smacked the snake head with his crutch. It did nothing, of course. He had nothing that could hurt it, not his knife or his gun or his dragon.

He did have Bea, though. She barreled around the corner and pounced on the chimera's head, cracking its skull with her enormous weight. The lion claws came out and sunk into her feet, and the wings flapped and the tail writhed.

Bea closed her mouth around its head and crushed it. It fell still, the tail still wiggling directionlessly.

"Thanks, Bee," he said. He started to sweat. "I really thought – I didn't know if – you were – were ... gonna ... "

The strength bled out of his limbs. *Oh no,* he thought, skin crawling. *No, no, I'm fucked. I'm so fucked.*

The chimera's paralyzing venom kicked in fully, sapping his ability to speak and stand. His knees collapsed from under him and he went down.

All he could move were his eyes, which bounced around at floor-level. He felt the floor vibrate with shaking footsteps. Bea, for real this time, he hoped.

Tears streamed down his face and onto the floor. *Fuck.* No way Bea would be able to keep him alive like this, right? He had no idea how long it was going to take the venom to wear off, and that was assuming he hadn't been given a fatal dose. He tried to move, something, *anything*, even to twitch his fingers, but all he could do was gulp in panicked breaths and look around.

Bea's snout came into his field of view, snuffling over him.

"Bea," he managed to get out.

She nosed at him, pushing him over onto his back. His head lolled.

"Bea," he faintly said again.

Her teeth closed around him, and as she carted him off this time, he wasn't even worried about where they were going.

4

To add insult to injury, the venom had forcibly relaxed *all* his muscles, including his bowels, and his earlier predictions about his bodily functions came true. So now he had to sit in that.

He was limp like a doll in Bea's jaws, swinging like the corpse she'd brought in earlier. He wondered if Bea would mistake him for dead and finally eat him, although maybe she would be too grossed out by him shitting his pants to do that.

She dropped him in her nest like she always had, and this time he just lay there where he'd been dropped, overwhelmed tears prickling at his eyes again.

She nosed at him, rolling him over.

"Bea," he gasped weakly. "Please."

She snorted and nosed at him again, as though urging him to get up.

"I can't. I can't move."

She circled around behind him and hooked her teeth in his shirt, dragging him back and leaning him against the wall of the nest. That was better than lying on the floor, at least, even if his head lay limply on the furniture next to him.

***

Bea circled him relentlessly, occasionally nosing at him to get up. When she eventually got bored of that, she lay down and curled up around him again.

When all was quiet outside, he fell asleep despite being terrified he might not wake back up.

He did, though. Bea had laid out on her back, belly up in the air.

His mouth was so, so dry. "Bea? I'm so thirsty. Can you get me water?"

She rolled over, ears flopping, and looked at him.

"Water?" He would have pantomimed drinking something to give her the idea, but he still couldn't move.

She rose to her feet and stuck her snout into the backpack that was still dangling from his chest. She came back out with a bottle of water delicately clenched between her teeth.

"Yes," he said, relief flooding through him. "Yes, yes, water. Thank you."

She let it fall onto his lap. He groaned, trying not to cry and become even more dehydrated. "I can't move, Bea. Please. I need help. Please help."

She nosed at the bottle of water.

"I need help."

She delicately clenched the bottle again, raising it up to his face.

"You need to open it."

Her teeth punctured it, and the water all drained and fell onto his lap. He tried not to let out a hopeless whimper, but it happened anyway.

Growling with frustration, Bea went into the backpack again and came out with another bottle of water. This one she gripped in her claws, but it was obvious she didn't have the manual dexterity needed to open it that way. She pawed at it like a dog, and eventually this one crumpled and burst under her claws too.

Guy tried to stifle his sounds of despair. Bea growled and shook her head, crinkling the water bottle and ripping it up.

"Bee," he said desperately. "Please. I'm going to die here. I'm going to die if you can't help me."

Bea paced back and forth, swinging her head and chuffing to herself. Then she stopped and turned around, nosing open the fridge and clamping one of the cans in her mouth.

She held it in her mouth and turned it over and over until her top fang pierced the lid of the can. The juice inside welled up.

Guy was so thirsty it almost hurt to look at. "Please."

With as much dexterity as she could muster, Bea positioned herself above Guy and tilted the can so the juice dribbled down. Wonder of wonders, she managed to get a decent amount in his mouth.

***

Bea repeated this strategy with the cans of potatoes, and Guy never thought stinky potato water would taste so good. The pumpkin puree was a bit of a mess – it sloshed down all over him, adding to the mess, but it kept him alive through the day, then the night, then the next day, until –

He managed to twitch a finger. He sobbed with relief, then. By that afternoon he was able to reach down and grab a water bottle for himself, twist it open, and take sips.

"Thank you, Bea," he said. She drew near, lowering her snout so he could pat it weakly. "You've saved my life yet again."

She let out a rumble.

Guy took a few hours to get back on his feet and although it was wobbly, he could walk around now. He collapsed back into the nest at nightfall, exhausted once again and ready for a good night's sleep.

5

He was feeling almost normal the next morning. Even his leg was hurting less – apparently the emergency bone juice he'd shot into himself was helping, or maybe it was just the boot. Bea hadn't taken the crutch he'd found at the pharmacy, but he couldn't really blame her for that and resorted to once again finding a metal pipe and propping himself up.

He ate the last of the canned food – dry, raw potatoes weren't his idea of the breakfast of champions, but it was what they had. "Hey, Bee. I'm filthy. Do you think we could find running water somewhere for me to wash off and change my bandages? We're going to need more food soon too, maybe we can look for that while we're out?"

She grunted her assent and then seized him once again in her mouth. He was going to have to figure out a way to ask her not to do that.

She carefully picked her way through the ruins again, sticking to cover to avoid the notice of predators that could fly or were bigger than her. She eventually prowled into what had clearly been a public park at one point, the trails long overgrown and the benches and playgrounds sitting in disrepair.

Trees crowded in on the path and blocked it from overhead view, and the shade felt nice. Bea approached a drop-off and slid down it through the dried leaves and underbrush, sliding to a stop at a creek bed.

She dropped him on the edge, and he dipped a finger in. "Oh, this is lovely. This is such a nice spot." He raised his head and closed his eyes, feeling the dappled sunlight on his skin and remembering what birdsong had sounded like in a place like this. Forests were quiet these days. He hadn't seen a wild bird in years, and even insects were typically in short supply as the smaller Wellspring creatures had devastated their populations.

The plants were abundant, though. Wellspring creatures were all carnivores.

Guy waded into the creek and found it a pleasant temperature, cool but not too cold, having been warmed by the sun. It went up to about his waist. Relieved to finally have some reasonable way to wash himself, he stripped his shirt, then his pants. He washed them off as best as he could, then lay them out flat on a nearby rock to dry.

He unwrapped his bandages and let them flow away in the stream. He dipped his wounds in the water carefully – he wasn't sure the water was clean, but surely anything would be better than not cleaning out the filth he'd been sitting in for the past few days. Luckily the antibiotic ointment seemed to be pulling its weight and all his injuries were scabbed over with little inflammation.

He bent down and dipped his upper half in the water, scrubbing his hair out and dislodging the last of the nasty layer that had accumulated all over him. He waded back to shore and knelt to dig in his backpack to retrieve the bar of soap he had.

Bea was looking directly at his exposed genitals.

Guy froze, cheeks heating up. Should he be embarrassed by this? Should Bea be embarrassed? Was she capable of feeling embarrassed?

"Like what you see?" It was all he could think to say.

She flicked an ear and looked away. Guy scrutinized her very hard, trying to figure out what exactly was going on in her head.

He shrugged and retrieved the soap, wading back into the water. Bea continued to watch him as he scrubbed himself clean, looking extremely interested.

"Do you want to get clean too?" he asked carefully. Maybe if she washed off, everything in the nest would smell less horrible.

She tilted her head.

He made a motion like rubbing soap in the air. "I can clean you off."

Bea hauled herself to her feet and cautiously waded into the river after him. It barely came up past her knees.

"Go ahead and get nice and wet," Guy prompted.

She lowered herself down and rolled around in the creek, water splashing, sending a small tidal wave rolling over Guy.

"Hey!" he giggled. "Watch it!"

She rolled over, water dripping from her horns, watching him.

He playfully splashed her back. "How do *you* like it, huh?"

She let out a bray that sounded suspiciously like laughter, and a mighty swipe of her paw sent another huge swell of water crashing over him. He laughed and let himself float with it.

The water sloshed around her legs as she waded towards him. She peered over, toothy delight on her warped face.

He splashed her again.

She reached her paw out and pinned him under the water.

All playfulness immediately fled Guy's body, visceral panic overtaking him as he flailed his limbs and tried to yell for her to let him up. In his panic, he simply swallowed a mouthful of water.

Oh God, oh my God, oh my fucking God, she's going to drown me. She has the strength to drown me with one hand and I can't do anything about it and maybe she doesn't even realize she's drowning me but –

In reality it must have only been a few seconds, but it felt like minutes. She let him up, and he immediately coughed up the water he'd inhaled, flailing and backing away from her.

Her face shifted downwards into a frown. Guy scooted backwards and braced himself against the pebbles on shore, water dripping down from his hair.

"Don't hurt me," he tried. "S-sorry, I'm sorry."

Bea looked *heartbroken.* He'd never seen any Wellspring creature emote, let alone with such clarity. It was even clearer than the body language of the hawk wyverns he was used to.

Guy coughed again. "Um. It's – "

Fear surged through him again as Bea's snout drew closer, but she merely rested it in his lap. A mournful rumble vibrated her throat.

Guy's hand slowly lowered down to stroke her head.

"It was just an accident. You just scared me a little. I'm not hurt."

Her eyes flickered up to him.

"We just gotta be a bit more careful when we're goofing around, I guess."

She closed her eyes.

"Now come on, let me up so I can put fresh bandages on."

Still looking downtrodden, she removed herself from him and stayed low to the ground. He rifled in his backpack to find the bandages and ointment, wrapping himself up liberally. His clothes were still pretty damp, but he didn't want to wait here too long for them to dry, so he stretched the wet fabric of his suit over his shoulders and put it back on. He then replaced the boot on his leg.

"Hey, Bee, I need your help with something. Will you help me a little more?"

She raised her head.

"My best friend is named Bonnie. She's a lot like you. She's still out there, hurt and scared. Will you help me find her?"

She got to her feet and made a motion to clamp him in her jaws. "Ah-hah," he said, sweating. "Could we maybe, um, do that some other way? Your teeth hurt m e."

Bea lowered her head and moaned mournfully.

"It's okay! I promise it's okay. You just didn't realize. What about if I sit up on your back?"

Bea looked over her shoulder, then slowly lowered down.

Guy used her spiked horns as handholds, navigating carefully to sit down on her shoulders. Okay, this wasn't so different from a dragon. He would have to use more upper body strength than core this way, but he felt much safer up here in the familiar territory of riding a huge beast.

Except Bea didn't have a saddle and reins, and also hadn't been trained to understand the cues with his boots. He went to dig his heels into her flank out of muscle memory before remembering she'd have no idea what that meant.

"Um, okay," he said instead. "Do you remember where you found me? Can you take me back there?"

Bea moved off. Okay, this wasn't too different. Hawk wyverns usually took verbal commands pretty well – they were wicked smart, relatively speaking, and understood what you were telling them sometimes. They couldn't hear you well during flight, though, hence the need for nonverbal cues.

Hawk wyverns were the only Wellspring creature who could understand spoken speech, as far as he knew. Just another reason why Bea was unusual.

Bea meandered around a while as though she couldn't quite remember the way, but eventually she corrected herself and made a beeline for the site where he and Bonnie had fallen.

His heart sank. Bonnie wasn't where he'd last seen her. The debris lay scattered over empty concrete. That was good, he told himself. As long as he hadn't seen her body, there was a chance she was still alive.

He asked Bea to let him off and he rummaged around until he found his Bowie knife. He sheathed it, pleased to no longer be *completely* helpless. His helmet was nearby, scraped and banged up but still perfectly functional. Good, he'd need it for when he found Bonnie. "Can we look around a little for her?"

He got back up on Bea's back, and they walked around, still sticking to cover to avoid notice. Guy wanted to call out for Bonnie like a lost cat; she'd come running if she heard his voice, but probably so would the other million monsters infesting the ruins.

Just as they were crossing from a bridge to a tunnel, Guy heard the distinct and in this case *terrifying* sound of a fox wyvern teleporting, *terrifyingly* close.

Talons closed around his shoulders, yanking him off Bea's back, too fast for him to react. His suit protected him from the worst of the claws, but it wouldn't save him from –

There was another *pop* of teleportation, and suddenly he was a million miles off the ground. And in free fall a second later when his assailant released him.

"Oh God!" he screamed, tumbling head over heels. "Bonnie! Bonnie! BONNIE BONNIE BONNIE!"

And wonder of wonders, Bonnie answered. Guy had been right about her coming running if he shouted for her.

She gave an alarm call and launched into flight from some unseen crevice where she'd been hiding, pumping her wings to get up into the air. He'd never seen her move so fast, not even to get treats. She looked incredibly disheveled but otherwise okay.

The fox wyvern snarled and maneuvered itself to intercept Bonnie. Clearly it intended to just follow him down and have its meal after the fall did the hard work of killing him – not a sophisticated strategy, but an effective one without another creature meddling.

He willed Bonnie to meddle faster.

Bonnie was quite a bit larger than the fox wyvern, and so she simply barreled straight through it, knocking it away in the air, completely ignoring its bites and claws raking over her in favor of getting to Guy as fast as possible. *That* was not a reaction a young rider would have gotten from their dragon, not until after years of bonding.

Her talons clamped around him, knocking the wind out of him as he was jerked sideways. Above him, Bonnie and the fox wyvern spiraled around clamped onto each other, snarling viciously.

But the fox wyvern was fighting for a meal and Bonnie was fighting for her human's life. Bonnie opened her mouth and exhaled a column of fire at the fox wyvern, and that was all it took for it to decide it wasn't worth the effort and fly off.

Bonnie alighted on a nearby rooftop, dropping Guy and chirping at him anxiously. He groaned and rolled over, pushing himself up. Her snout prodded at him, almost pushing him over. "I'm here, I'm here, girl."

He took her snout in his encircling arms and gave her a little kiss between her eyes. "Thank you so much. I missed you. I was so worried about you."

Bonnie let out deep, happy rumbles, tail thumping against the ground.

Okay, Bonnie's saddle was still here and usable even though the anchors had been snapped. He had his helmet and his riding suit. They were both banged up but in good enough shape to travel.

The logical next step was to just leave the city and head back to Wasp Nest. That was it. There really was no reason to hesitate and do anything else.

It would be stupid to not just immediately leave.

... It would be stupid.

Guy was realizing he was a little bit stupid.

"Hey, girl, I met somebody here who took care of me while we were separated. Do you want to go meet her?"

Bonnie looked at him and trilled nervously, hesitation written all over her features.

"She's like you. She's a big, um, a big, pointy gal. But she's nice. I was in a real bad spot and she made sure I didn't die. She's probably worried about me." Why the hell should he care if a Wellspring creature was "worried about him"? What on earth could that even mean?

... And yet the thought of Bea wandering around, anxiously looking for him in the rubble, was too much.

And Guy had never met any creature like Bea before. Maybe nobody had. It was extremely unusual. It could be important.

Bonnie did not seem convinced. Her tail twitched, feathers fanning out.

"She can't fly," Guy offered. "If she decides to attack, we can just fly away."

Bonnie hesitantly lowered her wing down so Guy could access her saddle and climb on.

It felt good to be back in the saddle, even if it was hard to settle in with his foot in a boot. The leg straps were still functional, so that should give him some security to not fall out of the saddle. Her reins were gone, but he could manage well enough without them for a while. Bonnie usually knew what to do.

Bonnie trotted over and climbed a building to get up high enough to throw herself into the air so they could start circling the city.

6

It was hard to find Bea. She knew to avoid being out in the open where aerial predators could take a swipe at her – the fact that a fox wyvern had managed to snatch him off her back had honestly been incredibly unlucky.

He spotted her tail disappearing underneath a ruined overpass. "There," he said, and knowing Bonnie probably couldn't hear him, gave Bonnie's left shoulder a series of rapid taps. Bonnie took this as instructions to dive left and descend.

Her feet thumped in the dirt for a few paces before she stopped and folded in her wings. Guy could just barely make out the glow of Bea's eyes in the shadows under the overpass.

"Bea," he said, waving to her. "Bea, I'm here! I'm okay! Are you okay?"

Bea warily crept out. Bonnie hopped backwards, fanning her wings out and hissing defensively. Bea responded by crouching low to the ground, all her spikes facing outwards, and baring her teeth.

"It's okay!" Guy shouted. "Sh! Sh! Girls, girls, it's all right!" He slid off Bonnie's saddle, hobbling forwards a few steps, trying not to imagine himself being ripped in half as the two massive creatures did a tug-of-war. Ironic – being fought over by two large women had once been a fantasy of his.

"This is Bea," Guy said. "She saved my life. See?" He very cautiously reached a hand out to Bea, who slunk forwards and pushed her snout into his palm. "Bea, this is Bonnie. She's my best friend."

Bonnie gradually smoothed out her feathers and folded in her wings, cocking her head in a birdlike motion and lashing her tail. She let out a curious chirp and stepped forward, head bobbing.

Bea gradually untensed, keeping low and sniffing. Bonnie leaned in to do the same, and the two both jerked backwards as they accidentally bumped each other.

"It's all right," Guy said with a laugh. "We're all friends here. See?" He put his other hand on Bonnie's snout. "There we go. See?"

Bea flattened herself against the ground, as though trying to hide behind Guy.

"What is this?" he laughed. "Suddenly you're shy now?"

Bonnie's head snaked around and she very cautiously touched her lips onto the furthest tip of one of Bea's spikes, taking an exploratory nibble. Bea didn't seem bothered by it, instead very curiously sniffing Bonnie's talons.

"Bee, here's the deal," Guy said. God, this was going to be ... something. "Bonnie and I have friends at the outpost south of here. We have to go back there. But I don't want to just leave you behind. Do you want to come with us?"

Bea slowly raised her head, ears flicking, eyebrows raising. She grunted.

"Yeah?"

She turned her head unsurely, bobbing and lowing.

"It'll be okay. I'll tell them what you did for me. They'll be able to see you're ... different. Not a threat. They'll take care of you, I know they will. They'll be so interested to learn everything about you." He pulled on Bonnie's saddle to reseat himself. "We should get going now so we can get there before sunset. What do you say?"

Bea shuffled along to follow as Guy gave Bonnie the command to move out.

***

He'd have to have Bea wait out of sight until he could get back to Wasp Nest and talk to General Hobby about it. Bea would be killed on sight unless everyone had been informed and told to hold off, even if they saw Bea approaching alongside Guy.

Bea seemed extremely unhappy now that the shoe was on the other foot and *she* had to trust *Guy.*

"I promise I'll come back. I *promise.* I just need you to stay here until I can tell everyone about you so they don't attack you. Okay?"

She gave an anxious moan and hunkered down.

Guy made sure she was hidden from the air before jetting off with Bonnie towards Wasp Nest. The sandy, limestone cliffs came into view, and there was the station itself perched atop. A massive building, half of which was the structure that gave Southern Station its nickname: the stables where the dragons nested was a lumpy structure twisting out from the building, with honeycomb-shaped nesting caverns.

Bonnie didn't need directions to climb to the top of the roost and swoop down in. Dragons, startled by the sudden appearance of an active dragon while the rest were trying to settle into their nests for the evening, flapped and barked at her.

"Is that Guy?" said the errant voice of a rider elsewhere in the room.

Bonnie found her preferred nest and landed, barely giving Guy enough time to dismount before flopping on her side and covering herself up with her wings.

"You did good," he said, patting her side. "Thank you. Make sure you get some dinner before you go to sleep."

"Lieutenant!" someone called. "We thought you were dead!"

Guy peered over the edge to see a loose group of other riders clustered on the ground, looking up at him.

"I told you you don't have to call me Lieutenant," Guy shouted back. "I'm really just some guy."

A chorus of groans came from below. "That's him, all right."

Guy swung around and started climbing down the ladder. "In the flesh."

"Where's the rest of Unit 24?"

"They didn't make it back, unless they showed up here while I was gone."

"Another unit wipe? Isn't this the third time? I'm starting to get suspicious."

"You got me. I'm a double agent. The Wellspring creatures are paying me to off my teammates." His boots hit the ground. "Where is the general? I need to talk to him right away."

***

The glowing lights from Sonny's giant computer screen shifted as he scrolled down. The screen had the words *ARCHIVE OF WELLSPRING KNOWLEDGE* at the top, and pictures of different Wellspring creatures flashed past.

"I'd say she's in the medium size category. She's bigger than Bonnie, but definitely smaller than Patches and Lucifer."

"Got it," said Awsk, and the images shifted once again, winnowing out all the ones that were too big or too small.

General Hobby thoughtfully stroked his beard. "Did she display any abilities we could use to narrow it down? What's the species' cheat?"

"I have no idea. I didn't see her breathe fire or teleport when either of those would be useful, so probably not that. Maybe her cheat is just being really smart?"

"Mmmm," Sonny said doubtfully.

"I haven't recorded anything like that yet," Awsk said, its disembodied voice just coming directly from the screen. "This sounds really unusual. You're sure this is correct?"

"Yes," Guy answered instantly. "I wouldn't be alive if it wasn't."

"This could potentially be something very important for the guild scientists to know," General Hobby said. "If we can confirm it."

"More spikes," Guy said. "None of these have enough spikes."

The images filtered further, until Guy saw a familiar one flash past. "There! There, that's what she looks like."

Awsk maximized the image.

"Damn, it looks a lot ... meaner than she does." It was bigger, had even more spikes, and perhaps most importantly not a hint or gleam of intelligence in its eyes. It looked like Bea's stupid older brother.

"It's called a porcupine, apparently," Awsk said. Guy could see that, maybe, if he'd never laid eyes on a porcupine before. "We see them rarely enough down south that we can tell there aren't any breeding populations here. They're not unheard of, but definitely more common in the north."

"What information do you have about them?" Guy pressed. "Are they an unusual species in any way?"

"Doesn't look like it," Sonny said.

"Yeah," Awsk confirmed. "Their cheat seems to be regeneration, since multiple units have seen them get back up from fatal injuries looking fresh."

Guy's brow furrowed as Awsk showed them more photos and videos of the porcupines in action. They were just as aggressive as every hostile Wellspring creature Guy had seen, and they all looked bigger and meaner than Bea. One particularly graphic video showed one batting a rider off their dragon and then stomping them to death.

"This isn't what she's like at all," Guy said. "I mean, it's definitely the same species, but ... "

"Just seems like your run-of-the-mill stupid, violent monster," Sonny said. "Don't see any reason why it would be special."

"She *is*, though," Guy insisted. "I can't emphasize this enough, she kept me alive even though there was no real reason to do so, as far as I could tell. She brought me food. She can understand spoken words to an extent like the dragons can."

General Hobby was thinking very hard.

"Well, what should we do about it?" Sonny said.

"We should leave soon," General Hobby said slowly, "if we want to go meet her before it gets too dark."

***

Patches was the oldest dragon at Wasp Nest and therefore the largest, having cleared out the space of several honeycombs and destroyed the barriers between them, so he had enough room to curl up. Lucifer, the second-in-command's dragon, often spent his nights curled up and nuzzled into Patches's side. They both dwarfed Bonnie, and he really hoped their overwhelming size didn't make Bea too nervous. Bonnie could probably fit on one of Patches's outstretched wings.

"Up and at 'em, old boy," General Hobby said.

Patches cracked an eye open and glared at him.

"Sorry, I know it's bedtime, but there's something important we have to do. It won't take long, promise."

Patches whined and moaned, dramatically stretching. Lucifer raised his head with bleary eyes, disgruntled at having his drowsing disturbed.

"Saddle on."

Patches continued to grumble, but he crawled over to the area where General Hobby had the stepladder he used to saddle him. The general tightened the straps and then hauled himself up. "Is your saddle too damaged to fly?"

"No, me and Bonnie are okay on that front. My mic is kaput, though, so you'll have to shout loud."

General Hobby lowered his visor. "Got it."

All the dragons began chirping and barking as Patches scaled the wall, too big to even spread his wings to take off inside. He came out on the lip of the roost, spreading his massive wingspan and lifting off, buffeting the topmost dragons quite rudely. Bonnie flitted up behind him, drafting on his tailwind.

Guy really, really hoped that Patches didn't scare Bea. General Hobby was generally pretty easy to talk to, and Guy knew he would be interested in Bea, but his attitude might be different if he couldn't be convinced Bea was safe to be around.

Bonnie led the way to the rocky alcove where Bea had hidden. She touched down amidst Patches's shadow, the huge wyvern coming down after her and leaning over to examine the ground where Bonnie was scuttling around.

"Bea!" Guy called. "It's me! I promise it's safe! We won't hurt you! This is my – my friend! I know he's really big, but – but he's nice like Bonnie is! Promise!"

Bea's face appeared amidst the sandstone, looking at Patches warily. Patches, unlike Bonnie, was large enough that Bea barely registered as a threat. He merely thrashed his tail and grunted in her direction.

"I see her, boy," General Hobby said. He patted the dragon's flank and pulled the reins back slightly, indicating *stand down*. "It's all right. No need to get agitated. Don't attack."

Patches seemed happy to not have to do something, so he laid down with his belly flat against the ground.

Bonnie trotted over and raised the feathers on her head, trilling at Bea. Bea slowly crept out, not taking her eyes off Patches.

"This is General Hobby and Patches. They're in charge of keeping everyone safe here. They want to meet you."

Bea kept low to the ground and slunk to Bonnie's side. Guy dismounted, coming over and putting a hand on Bea's snout. "See? No fighting. Nothing to worry about."

Bea's eyes flickered around Patches.

"Fascinating," General Hobby said. He slid out of his saddle and down to the ground, approaching slowly. "My name is Jairus," he announced cautiously. "Lieutenant Reed told me you saved his life."

Bea snorted and nervously flicked her head.

"I owe you for bringing him back. He's a fine rider. It would have been a shame to lose him."

Bea crept closer, out from Bonnie.

"General, can she stay here at the station? I don't want anything to happen to her. We usually have leftover food, anyway."

It couldn't be that easy, could it? Just walking up and asking?

But apparently it was. "Yes. I think the folks at Paramount will be interested in her, so we should make sure she's around."

***

Bea herself took some convincing once they got close enough to the station.

She seemed to accept Patches same as she'd accepted Bonnie, and she walked under their wings as they flew without issue.

When all the other humans came into view, along with the errant dragon circling, she started to get more nervous.

As they approached the stables, Bea started to fidget and low at the dragons gathered feeding on the corpses outside the ground floor. The dragons, in turn, raised their heads and barked with interest, nervously jostling and posturing, showing their teeth.

"All right, all right," Guy said. "Come on, now. We're all friends."

The other dragons didn't seem convinced. Bea didn't either, not moving any closer.

Patches, by contrast, spontaneously decided that he was very annoyed with everyone else and moved towards the kill pile, grunting and lashing his tail. The smaller dragons hissed at him, but backed up as he approached. Patches unfurled a wing and decked the boldest member of the group, scattering them amongst outraged honks.

Patches lay down and nibbled at the kill pile, getting a mouthful of meat and swallowing it down. Bonnie trilled and followed him, staying low to the ground as a sign of submission and tiptoeing forwards to also take a few bites. Patches allowed her.

"Are you hungry, Bea?" Guy said. "Go ahead if you want."

Still keeping a nervous eye on Patches, Bea slunk over, keeping her spikes oriented between her and Patches. She stretched her neck out to take the foot of one of the dead creatures, sliding it further away from Patches and towards herself. Patches ignored her, completely disinterested.

"Can we move her into the stables?" Guy asked.

"Yes," the general said. "That's probably the best place for her. If Patches is calm, the rest of the flock should accept her."

Bea ate considerably more than either of the dragons, more even than her bulky frame would suggest. Maybe she was nervous about the next time she would be able to eat, or maybe she was more underfed than he'd guessed.

"There you go, girl," Guy said, patting Bea on the flank. "You took care of me, so I'm gonna take care of you."

When all three beasts had eaten their fill, General Hobby led Patches into the stables. Guy encouraged Bonnie to follow, then kept his hand on Bea's snout. "Do you wanna go inside?"

Bea kept her head low and let out a moo.

"Stay close to Bonnie if you get nervous."

Guy kept his hand on her as he walked inside the shelter. In the dim light of the sunset shining in from the top, the rest of the dragons could be seen peering out from their nests. A few of them growled at her. Bea hunkered down under their glares.

"Go stand by Patches," Guy said. "So everyone sees you're with us."

Bea crept forwards and crouched in Patches's shadow. Patches snorted and sniffed her, then sat down, tucking his limbs under his chest. Bonnie came up on his other side and started to groom his feathery head crest, which he allowed her to do with eyes sliding shut.

"Everyone, this creature is Bea," General Hobby shouted up. "She will be staying here for a little while. Let's keep everything nonviolent."

The rest of the dragons slowly went back to snoozing.

"Bonnie, I'll bring the vet out to check you over tomorrow morning, all right?" Guy was really looking forwards to getting his own medical care, a real shower, and a rest in a real bed.

Bonnie leaned down and licked him.

"Bea, I'll be back out in the morning, okay?"

She grunted.

Guy turned and walked towards the exit. He heard the sound of a heavy creature moving behind him, and felt something gently pulling him backwards.

Bea had very gingerly taken the back of his shirt in her teeth. When he gave her a questioning look, she dropped it and looked at the ground.

Guy smiled and turned back to her, scratching behind her jaw. "You okay?"

She let out an anxious whine.

He patted her snout. "Okay. How about I come back in and sleep in the stables with you and BonBon tonight?"

She pressed her forehead into him.

7

She'd started to think of herself as Bea, just because Guy called her that.

She'd had a name, she thought. She already had a name, from before. She couldn't remember what it was. She couldn't remember a lot of things from before.

She liked the name, though. Bea. It was small and nice and pretty, everything she wasn't anymore.

Guy wanted her to stay in this weird building full of dragons, and she didn't like that idea at all. She wouldn't be able to fight them off if they got mad at her. When aerial predators attacked, all she could ever do was hunker down with her spikes out to keep them from hitting her. That didn't work for ones who could do things like breathe fire, though.

Bonnie could protect Guy better than she could. Bea secretly hated Bonnie, but it was only because of jealousy. Bonnie had been able to save Guy from falling to his death, and Bea couldn't do anything against aerial predators except save herself.

At first she thought he'd lied about coming back out with how long he was gone. Bea waited by the door, hating the fact that she was too big to fit through and go after him. Who knew what was going on beyond that door? Were the others mistreating him while he was helpless, without even Bonnie to protect him? Were they killing him to eat?

But no. He came back eventually. His hurt foot was in a brand-new boot, and he was walking more easily. He also smelled a lot cleaner, and she could smell he'd eaten – good food, not the raw, inedible meat she'd so stupidly tried to give him.

It was a miracle he even wanted her around anymore. She was stupid and ugly and dangerous and unlike Bonnie, she couldn't even fly. He didn't need her anymore.

Despite that, he came over and patted her snout. "Miss me?"

Yes.

Bonnie's head snaked around and nudged him from the other side. She nearly pushed him over with her nudging, and he laughed and pushed her back.

Bea wanted to hold Guy so badly, but her claws were too big. Every way she had to pick him up would hurt him. She flexed her claws, imagining for a moment that she could use them to cradle him without tearing his skin.

"You good, Bee?"

She grunted.

"The vet's going to come out, okay? He's the one who takes care of our dragons, so he's going to take care of you too."

She sat down with her limbs tucked under herself. Her defensive position. She was nervous. What if the vet didn't like what it saw? What if it saw that Bea was weird and dangerous, and it told Guy to send her away or kill her?

What *was* a vet, anyway? She couldn't remember what the word meant. Guy was talking about it like it was a doctor, though.

If the vet was a threat, she could probably kill it, unless it was bigger than the dragons.

It turned out to be a second man. She didn't like this one as much. It was uglier. It was bald, instead of having a nice strip of hair she could think about tugging on like Guy. Nevertheless, its words were kind as it directed Bea to stand up, move her limbs, open her mouth. The vet seemed pleased and surprised by her cooperation and told Guy that Bea seemed perfectly healthy and didn't need any medical care.

Maybe that could be her advantage over Bonnie. She didn't need medical care, but Bonnie obviously did if they needed a whole vet to take care of the dragons. Bea couldn't remember any time when she'd needed medical care.

"How ya feeling, girl? All good?"

Bea grunted and leaned into Guy's proffered hand.

"Good. We're gonna just hang out here for a little while then, okay?"

Bea sat as close to Bonnie as she could without hurting anyone with her spikes.

***

Guy slept nestled in Bonnie's wing, and Bea watched them both with burning jealousy.

The next morning was easy and slow and calm. Guy lavished attention on Bonnie. He took her down to the base of the nesting structure and sprayed Bonnie with a hose. Bonnie tried to bite the spray of water, and after they were done, she sat preening her wet feathers.

"Do you want to be hosed off too, Bea?"

Bea grunted and shuffled forwards. She couldn't really keep herself clean, and things accumulated between her spikes. The only time she'd ever get clean was going to the river like she'd done with Guy, but it was too far out of the way to travel there just for that. Just so she could feel clean.

She felt clean now, though, as Guy power washed all the accumulated dirt and muck and grime off her back, her thick skin keeping her from even feeling the pressure very much. Guy had her lift up her paws and washed her claws too, which felt like a nice massage.

"There we go. You smell a lot better now."

Had she smelled bad? Had she been disgusting? Was that something she should worry about, smelling bad?

Guy didn't seem overly worried about it. "We have some time to kill while Jairus talks to the commander general. Do you want to walk around outside?"

She shuffled excitedly. Being out from under all these dragons would be a relief. She hadn't slept well with their eyes on her.

She followed as he walked outside the building. The landscape was rocky, barren, and open – perfectly defensible for aerial predators. Perfect for the dragons. Very bad for her. Guy didn't seem worried about that either.

He walked around the outside of the nest, pointed out things to her, telling anecdotes. "Bonnie smacked into that tree when she was younger. Got a bit too excited and overshot her landing. That was our first major crash. Luckily I was okay, and well, she was okay, of course. Sometimes when it rains, that basin over there accumulates a small lake and everyone is down there all day like it's a beach party. We get flash floods sometimes, but we're up on the hill so usually it doesn't cause too many problems. This spot is a great place to sit to watch the dragons eating. They have the cattiest drama sometimes. It's hilarious. Bonnie is too shy for that, though, she always gives up right away when anyone is mean to her. Some of the meaner dragons have a soft spot for her because of how sweet she is, though, so she doesn't get bullied or anything. I'd show you the inside of the base if I coul d."

The man Guy had been treating as very important came and found him outside. "Lieutenant, the commander general is on his way down. He wants to talk with you this afternoon."

"What?" Guy suddenly seemed very nervous. Did he need Bea to take him away from here? Would she have to fight the commander general if it tried to eat him? "He's coming down here to talk to *me*?"

"Yeah, he wants to see Bea for himself."

Guy shifted from foot to foot. Bea bumped him with her nose, and he smiled at her and rubbed her head. "Okay, thanks, General."

Guy walked away, very deep in thought. Bea followed, giving a concerned rumble.

“The commander general,” Guy said to her. “He’s a living legend. He’s the leader of the whole guild. He’s the one who figured out how to tame dragons. He’s – he’s – he’s coming here to talk to *me*?” He tugged on his collar.

Bea eased forwards and nudged her head under Guy’s arm. His nervous expression broke into a smile, and he patted her head. “Thanks, Bee. I know you and Bonnie are gonna be there to support me.”

She would. She’d wanted nothing more than to take care of him ever since she’d seen him lying broken and endangered on the pavement. It stirred something in her, something she hadn’t felt in a long, long time.

8

Guy was sitting in a honeycomb brushing Bonnie when the commander general showed up.

There was a huge *boom* as something heavy landed on the outside of the stables, and some of the more skittish dragons started calling and took to the skies, funneling out with a flurry of wings.

A very, very large head with cobalt blue feathers peered down into the stables, neck snaking through.

God, Yough was *huge.* Commander General Eckron's dragon was the oldest dragon in existence, the first one hatched during the Tribulation, and dragons never stopped growing for as long as they lived. Guy had seen the enormous beast occasionally during his training at Paramount, mostly in the form of his colossal shadow falling over them as he passed overhead.

Yough's enormous black eyes looked directly at Guy as he turned his head, peering down. God, one of his eyes was probably as big as Guy's entire head.

"Commander, Commander General," Guy squeaked, then realized he hadn't talked loudly enough to be heard over the din of the stables. "Commander General!"

Commander General Eckron's voice boomed out with mechanical amplification. "Lieutenant. Come meet me outside, why don't you?"

Okay, thank God. Guy wasn't sure Yough would even fit in the stables. "Yes, sir!"

Guy scrambled to put down the brush he'd been using on Bonnie, patting his pockets, trying to think if he needed anything. He picked the brush back up and put it in his pocket, then put it back down again. "Bonnie, can we go down there?"

He didn't stop to put her saddle and bridle on, just jumping on and directing Bonnie down to Bea. "Bee, we're gonna go outside, okay?"

Bea was bristling in the corner, spikes turned outwards, clearly on edge by Yough's recent appearance.

"The commander general wants to meet you. We're just gonna talk, okay? His dragon is really, really big, but he's not gonna hurt you. He's friendly." He didn't know that for sure. Yough's eyes looked mean.

Bea crept forward.

"There you go. Come on."

Bea followed obediently as Bonnie took Guy outside. Yough was roosted on the ground outside, and Eckron was casually leaning against his flank.

"Commander General!" Guy said. He pulled up and slid off Bonnie's back. God, Bonnie was like a kitten next to Yough. The smaller dragon crouched fearfully, not moving any closer.

Eckron flipped his visor up, revealing his salt-and-pepper bearded face. "Riding bareback, are we?"

"Yes, sir! Sorry, sir! I won't do it again, sir!"

Eckron smirked. "Relax. I just think it takes a lot of skill to direct a dragon in flight without a bridle. You have quite a bond."

Stupid, stupid, Guy was being stupid. Stupid, dumb, idiot. "Thank you, sir!"

"Not to mention it means you have no fear of falling off."

"Thank you, sir!"

"It's handling skills like that that make me – "

"Thank you, sir! Oh, sorry, sir! Please, go on, sir!"

"That's quite all right. Just relax now. I was saying you seem trustworthy."

"I'm a trustworthy guy, sir!" Oh no, had he really just made one of his stupid jokes to *the commander general?*

Luckily Eckron seemed to find it funny. "Yes, I suppose you are. That's why I trust you know what you're talking about when you say you found an unusual Wellspring creature."

Guy swallowed nervously. "Yes, sir. We've been calling her Bea."

"Jairus told me she saved your life and brought you and Bonnie back when you were left for dead out by the ruins of Memphis."

"Yes, sir."

Eckron looked past him to Bea, who was hunkered down behind Guy. "It's a pleasure to meet you."

Bea shuffled her feet nervously.

"She certainly does behave more like the dragons than like the other Wellspring creatures."

"She really does. Nobody has any idea why."

"Right ... It's certainly unusual." Eckron stroked his beard. "She responds to verbal commands and gestures the way the dragons do?"

"Mostly, yeah." Guy stepped to the side and gently coaxed Bea forward. "Come on, it's all right."

Bea nervously stepped forward, tail flicking.

"She's nervous around all the dragons, I think."

"Logical. They're quite scary." Eckron held his hand out. "Friendly, are you?"

Bea crept up to his hand at an agonizing pace, sniffing it suspiciously, tail lashing.

Eckron put his hand on her nose. She snorted and bobbed her head, but didn't pull away.

"Interesting. Very interesting." Eckron withdrew his hand. "This is certainly an anomaly worth attention. It could lead to some ... interesting discoveries. Dr. Zhao has been bugging me about some theories she wants to test – she's been pleading with me to let her take a Wellspring creature to the hawk wyvern Wellspring. Bea could help with that. Lieutenant Reed, I'd like for you and Bonnie to help me escort this creature up to Paramount."

"Yes, sir!" Guy choked out. "Yes, absolutely! Sir!"

Eckron waved a hand, clearly starting to get a little annoyed. "All right, at ease, soldier. I'll talk to Jairus about making the preparations and we can set off first thing tomorrow morning."

***

Eckron decided that Major Sinervo would escort them back to Paramount.

That was ... something. Major Sinervo was ... something.

As the only major at Wasp Nest, he was theoretically in charge just behind General Hobby and Colonel Quinn, but usually the more junior riders around him took on the role of babysitters more than subordinates. No one had ever gotten killed following his orders, but missions inevitably took a lot longer when Sinervo was there.

It was an unspoken consensus that Sinervo had only been promoted up as far as he had because of his dragon, Raki. Raki was a freakish anomaly among dragons, huge as a general's dragon without being nearly as old, albino with white feathers and pale red eyes, and wicked smart. Probably smarter than the man strapped to his back. Raki could do most of Sinervo's missions by himself; Sinervo could be swapped out for a training dummy and it probably wouldn't affect their performance at all. It was remarkable Raki managed to get as far as he did with such an idiot pinned to him.

Eckron and Guy waited on the runway, Yough and Bonnie saddled up and ready to go. Bea waited down below, peering up at them and waiting for her cue to follow.

"You're sure he knows he's coming?" Guy said.

"Yes," Eckron said, exasperated.

Guy had asked Sonny to fix the comm in his helmet, so thankfully he was now able to take action to ask about what was going on. He sighed and touched the mic in his helmet. "Hey, Sonny?"

"Tech support?" said Sonny's voice.

"Do you know where Major Sinervo is?"

"Uh ... he's scheduled to be on the runway with you and the commander general five minutes ago."

" ... Right. Thanks."

Raki slithered up out of the stables, grunting and chuffing. He wasn't even wearing his saddle yet.

"Good morning, Raki," Guy said.

Raki growled and tapped his claws on the stone of the runway.

Bonnie trilled and raised her head crest at him.

Raki threw back his head, opened his mouth to show his rows of icicle-like teeth, and let out a bone-jarring roar.

A few seconds later, the door to the castle flew open and Major Sinervo came out, dragging a saddle behind him. "Sorry, sorry, here I am."

He threw the saddle onto Raki, whose tail was swishing irritably, and started doing up the straps. "Well, then, I'm here now, so we can be off on our special mission! Let's get going!"

The second Sinervo's feet touched the stirrups, Raki stood and bounded away, seemingly without consideration for his rider's readiness or lack thereof. Sinervo was still trying to do up the leg straps as Raki tossed himself off the cliff and into the open air.

Bonnie followed, swooping down low enough that Guy could signal to Bea to follow. Bea gave a moo and broke into a gallop.

"We'll probably want to roost for a short rest after about an hour," Guy said into his comm. "Bea can't run for much longer than that without needing to stop, as far as I can tell."

"I don't suppose we can just pick her up?" Sinervo said. "Ol' Raki is certainly big enough to carry her."

Guy looked down at Bea, a hunk of spikes kicking up a dust cloud to follow. " ... I don't think she'd like that very much."

"Aw, come on, Lieutenant, you never know until you try!"

" ... I think I know on this one, Major. Respectfully."

Storm clouds were gathering on the horizon, but Guy wasn't worried. With someone as experienced as Commander General Eckron, he had no doubt whatsoever they would make it to Paramount safely. Raki being here was nice extra insurance in case they ran into any Wellspring creatures.

"What's the agenda when we get to Paramount?" Sinervo said.

"We'll have Dr. Zhao examine Bea and give us her assessment. Since Bea is so unusual, we'll want to catalog her as a case report in the archives. After that, we'll take her to the Wellspring by Paramount."

"What for, Commander General?" Sinervo broke in.

There was silence for a moment, Yough's wings flapping. Guy could feel disapproval radiating from Eckron. "Major Sinervo. Wellsprings are the source of magic that Wellspring creatures draw from, so an unusual creature like Bea might have a reaction to a Wellspring."

"Uh-huh," said Sinervo.

Tense silence filled the communications line. Guy wanted to pipe up and ask if everything was okay, but he was too scared. He'd never seen anyone interact with Eckron this way before.

The conversation was light after that, and eventually Guy noticed Bea starting to lag behind and called for them to take a break. The dragons found an open space to land on, and Bea followed, panting.

"You're doing great," he told her, patting her side.

Bea's tongue was lolling out of her mouth when she reached them, and Guy held his hand on her nose. "Can we find some water nearby?" Despite the clouds, sweat rolled down his back. He could only imagine Bea and the dragons would appreciate some water.

"I'll go scout for some," Sinervo said.

"Be careful," Eckron told him. "We've had recent reports of poxies in the area."

Raki took off.

"How ya holding up, girl?" Guy said, rubbing Bea's head.

Bea gave a nervous moan and shuffled closer to him.

"You're doing great. We're going to a bigger station, and there will be more food and more people to meet there."

She shifted from foot to foot, jittery.

"Me and Bonnie will be with you. Nothing bad is gonna happen to you there."

She crouched down on the ground, flicking her ears and bobbing her head.

Sinervo came back and reported a shallow watering hole nearby, so they moved over there. Bonnie lay down and stuck her snout into the water.

"We should be safe enough from poxies," Guy offered. "They usually need more shadow than this to manifest in any decent numbers." The overcast sky meant shadows were ill-defined and weak.

Eckron scanned the horizon. "Safe enough."

Raki had been circling in the air but now came back at top speed, touching down and sliding to a stop and kicking up a huge cloud of dirt, panting. "Commander, there's something over there! Under the storm clouds."

Guy looked in the indicated direction, squinting. "Awsk?"

"Let me get a closer look at it." Awsk took control of the zoom function on Guy's visor and focused on the area beneath the roiling clouds. A huge creature jumped into focus, one with long, knobby limbs and an impressive set of antlers. The entire creature glowed soft blue, and sparks danced around its antlers, the occasional jolt of electricity arcing between the points. Despite its resemblance to a very large, twisted deer, its mouth hung open in a predatory snarl.

"Lightning elk," Awsk said.

"Shit." Guy swung back into Bonnie's saddle. "That could be a problem." This was one of the strictly terrestrial Wellspring creatures that it was nevertheless not safe to fight from the air. Being closer to the sky put you in better range of its primary weapon.

Unlike natural lightning, the elk's lightning would go wherever the creature directed it rather than anything to do with heights or magnetism, so they couldn't even try to make a lightning rod to keep themselves safe. It had to aim, though, so if they kept moving, it would have a harder time hitting them. If they kept low to the ground –

Thunder clapped as a bolt of lightning streaked down and absorbed into the elk's antlers. The flash of bright light threw shadows all around and –

Ah, symbiotic hunters. Smart.

The poxies erupted out of the shadows a moment later, all snarling teeth and claws. Guy unsheathed his knife and stabbed it into the one that had leapt at him, its blood spraying out and adding more red to its already crimson fur coat. "Commander?!"

Yough picked Eckron up and tossed him into the saddle. "Sinervo, go deal with the elk! Guy and I will protect Bea."

"Right!" Sinervo said. "Up, then, Raki, m'boy, into the sky."

Sinervo tugged the reins up to signal gaining altitude, but Raki snaked his head down and raced forward, staying low to the ground.

"That works too, whatever you're feeling, Raki."

Guy watched nervously as Raki ignored more commands from his rider and approached the elk, but Raki's ideas seemed to be safer than Sinervo's, so maybe that was for the best. He was sure anyone else displaying this level of incompetence in front of Eckron would have been dismissed instantly, but Raki was bonded to Sinervo and likely couldn't be ridden by anyone else, and that dragon was way too valuable to lose. He demonstrated why as he expertly dodged multiple lightning strikes, weaving deftly to attack his prey.

Meanwhile, Bea didn't seem to need much defending; the poxies attacking her couldn't figure out a way past her spikes, and she took them out easily with broad sweeps of her tail. They were small enough to die underfoot.

They were more of a threat to Guy. He kept stabbing until he could get up onto Bonnie's back. Bonnie instinctively lifted off to get them out of danger.

A lightning bolt cracked down a few feet from her, sending her flapping backwards with a startled roar. More poxies appeared in the fresh shadows, and a few of them hopped up onto Bonnie's back and latched onto Guy.

Bonnie swiveled her sinuous neck to try and bite the ones off Guy, but that exposed her neck to the ones in front of her. She roared and reared back as their teeth sunk in.

"Steady, Bon!" Guy shouted. He was having flashbacks to the raptors as the teeth and claws worked at his armor, trying to find his weak spots.

Bea's hulking figure cast a shadow over Guy, and her huge claws swiped at the ones attacking him. She overshot and her swing hit Guy straight in the stomach – it was the flat of her claws and not the point, thank God, or he would have been toast. It knocked the wind out of him and sent him spinning, the saddle sliding slightly as the restraints tried to find a middle ground between keeping him in the saddle and keeping the saddle on Bonnie's back.

"Bee," he gasped, unable to say much more.

Bea let out a worried moan, hugging close to him with her spikes facing the poxies.

Bonnie tried to pull away, clawing at the poxies with her back feet

"Bee, let Bonnie – "

Bea panicked as Bonnie left her and took Guy. She spun around stomping on the poxies and knocking them back, roaring, and then turned tail and ran.

Another bolt of lightning aimed at Eckron thankfully missed, but it did summon even more teeth and claws from the shadows.

"Major!" Eckron yelled into the comms as Yough knocked back his assailants.

"On it! Sorry!"

"Awsk," Guy said, pulling Bonnie's reins to go after Bea. "Any useful info on lightning elk?"

"Hmmm," Awsk said. "So, its antlers are immune to electricity, but the rest of its body isn't. But it knows not to strike itself with lightning anywhere else."

"Major, kite the elk over to the lake," Guy called, keenly aware of how inappropriate it was for him to be giving orders to the major ... but Sinervo didn't seem to have his own plan.

Raki swooped down and dive-bombed the elk, prompting a rapid series of lightning strikes that the dragon expertly dodged.

"Lieutenant, you and I move over the lake," Eckron added.

"Yes," Guy said.

He pulled Bonnie away from where Bea had disappeared to fly low over the water. The poxies followed, splashing in the shallows.

Raki swooped over the elk again, and this time it gave chase. Raki expertly weaved to dodge its bolts, then flew over the water.

The elk's hooves splashed through the shallows around its poxy allies, braying angrily. Guy pulled up further away from the water as a final lightning strike came down and touched the water.

With a crackling sound, all the poxies and the elk convulsed with electricity, then fell dead with the smell of smoking meat.

" ... Whew," Sinervo said.

Yough splashed back down into the shallows, sniffing at the electrified corpses.

"Good work, Lieutenant Reed," Eckron said, pointedly not saying anything to Sinervo.

"Good job, Raki," Sinervo said, patting the dragon's side. Raki moaned and rolled his eyes, coming over to join Yough and mouth at the corpses.

"Well, at least that's the dragon's feed for the day sorted out!" Guy said, trying desperately to handle the strange tension building between Eckron and Sinervo. It was way above his rank.

9

Guy managed to find Bea cowering behind a rock nearby. Her snout had some shallow scratches where apparently the poxies had managed to get past her spikes. She seemed embarrassed, ashamed to come out.

"Oh, sh, sh, it's okay," Guy soothed. He took out a cloth and wiped the blood off her snout. "It's all right. You're okay."

She rumbled and stuck her nose to his chest, quivering.

"I'm okay too. We're all okay. Come get something to eat. There's plenty of bodies around."

Fortunately, their meal and the subsequent rest of the trip to Paramount went without issue. The looming stone castle came into view over the horizon.

"It's been a while for you, hasn't it, Lieutenant?" Eckron said.

"Yes, sir." He hadn't been to the guild headquarters since training.

"Feel free to reminisce. Dr. Zhao isn't going to be available until later today, so we have some time to kill until then."

They touched down on the runway. Guy had Bonnie swoop down to where Bea was still laboriously climbing up the pathway to the summit.

"You good?"

She grunted, seemingly embarrassed that she couldn't fly.

Bonnie landed and folded her wings in. "We'll go together, how about that?"

Bea perked up a little bit, stepping with renewed vigor.

When Bonnie slithered up onto the runway, a chorus of voices greeted him, riders he'd been beside in training that had stayed at Paramount instead of being shipped off to a point station.

"Guy! Hey, it's Guy!"

"That's *Lieutenant Guy* to you! I'm an important guy, you know!"

"Haven't changed a bit, I see."

I really have, and not for the better.

"Word on the street is you have a new pet monster."

"It's true, so you better be nice to me before I sic her on you."

"Ooooh, *her*, is it? You finally lucky in love?"

"Come on, I already made tender love to your mother and we all know she has the face of a monster."

This prompted a smattering of laughter. Guy secretly thought these people were extremely stupid, but the only way to get them to leave you alone was to play along, make them laugh, and then disappear as fast as possible. A joke about one's mother was just enough to get the job done, and he was able to get them to leave him alone long enough to make sure Bea was settled in and not too scared of the dragons in the stables.

The Paramount stables were much nicer, big enough for the oldest dragons to nest in. He found Bea a nice cavern tucked into the wall down on the ground. Bea seemed most comfortable when she could hunker down out of sight.

"This okay for now?"

Bea bobbed her head and flicked her ears.

"Bonnie will stay here with you. I'm going to go get some lunch, okay?"

She grunted. Bonnie came over and started licking her head, which seemed to annoy her.

"Lieutenant Reed!" someone shouted above him from dragonback. "Rainer heard you were going to be at Paramount today and begged me to get you to come help him train the new recruits!"

Guy sighed and tried to hide his expression, fixing his face into an enthusiastic grin before turning back. "Oh, that sounds great! Sure, when?"

"Today's hatching and matching for the new squads, so whenever you can get to the stables!"

***

He had fond memories of Rainer and the people who'd hatched Bonnie. They were kind, patient, and helpful to a fault. The only thing they cared about was making sure the dragons were taken care of – their babies. Guy hoped that one day he'd be able to do that – not until Bonnie had passed, though. None of the hatchery workers had dragons of their own.

"Trainer Rainer!" Guy shouted with glee, coming into the training center. Rainer was the one who'd given him instructions on how to bond with Bonnie. They barely knew each other, but Rainer was like an old friend to Guy.

"Sorry, who's that?" Rainer said with feigned ignorance. "I don't remember who you are. You look like just some guy!"

The students all groaned as Rainer and Guy clasped hands, grinning.

"So, Rainer, I've been told these new recruits are meeting their dragons today?" Guy started.

"You bet! I was hoping you'd have some words for them."

Guy suddenly felt very serious, his stomach dropping. *Did* he have words for them?

What would *he* say?

To a bunch of *kids*?

He looked out over their eager faces. They looked the same as the ones that'd been crushed under that building that nearly took him out. Identical. Even though he couldn't remember the faces of the ones that had died.

He hadn't gotten attached, not at all –

The kids never last –

"Don't die," he said, and was horrified to find his voice thick with emotion. He cleared his throat and swallowed the tears. "Don't die," he said again, voice steadier. "It's tempting to get caught up in all the glory and excitement, but I promise you it's more impressive to survive than it is to die in a blaze of glory. Your dragon is going to be your best friend, and they're depending on you to survive."

"Well put," Rainer said. "Now, Lieutenant Reed is going to join us in the hatchery. It's always a reason for celebration when we have a successful clutch of newborns."

The hatchery was deep in the protected belly of Paramount, well away from the stables, since they couldn't risk the adults attacking the newborns. It was a dungeon-like room with stone walls, shrouded in quiet darkness, and everyone whispered as though in the presence of something holy.

He wished Bonnie were here.

The air lit up with the cheeping of dragon chicks. The newborns were fresh and wet, gangly creatures with limp feathers sitting among their eggshells looking confused. They looked oddly humanoid here, this small and this undeveloped. A barely bipedal creature with wings like arms sprouting feathers, an animalistic snout in place of a face, a tail to balance out the heavy back legs, balancing on feet sprouting claws they did not know how to use. A few of them were screaming at the horror of being brought to life.

Relatable.

***

Dr. Zhao was finally available. She was one of the few people at Paramount Guy had never met. She was important, gravely so, since she was the foremost expert on Wellspring science. She'd been the one to identify the mechanism of Wellspring creatures' near-immortality. She'd been there to help Eckron raise the first brood of dragons.

She rarely appeared in public. She would only show up when Eckron asked her to, and sometimes not even then.

There was no mistaking her, though. A petite, graying woman moving far faster than would be expected of someone her age. Her leg bounced as she stood in place. "Where is the creature, then?"

"Down here," Guy said. He leaned over the ledge and beckoned Bea up. "Come on. Want to meet the nice doctor?"

Bea shyly crawled up, staying low to the ground.

"Ah," Zhao said. She took a screen out of her pocket and pulled it open, the glassy surface flashing with images as she used her thumbs to navigate it. "A porcupine, certainly. Underdeveloped."

"She's smart, though," Guy said. "Smarter than even – " He stopped as he realized Zhao wasn't even listening to him. She'd pulled up an entry about porcupines and projected a holographic image of their typical appearance, comparing them with her eyes bouncing back and forth. Just as Guy had seen before, the image was bigger, meaner, more savage, more spikes.

"Ah," Zhao said. "This is a first-generation. That explains it."

"First-generation ... ?" Guy said.

Zhao manipulated the images floating above her screen with a series of rapid-fire finger movements, leg still bouncing. "Creatures born directly from Wellsprings are smaller and more docile. Once they establish breeding populations, their phenotype changes. It's a phenomenon called form progression."

"Form progression ... " Guy echoed. "Um, okay."

Zhao didn't elaborate, rapidly typing on her electronic device.

"You've faced feral hawk wyverns before, right?" Eckron offered. "They looked different from our domestic ones, didn't they?"

"Oh, yeah," Guy said, realization dawning. They'd been bigger, faster, and far more aggressive. "I'd wondered why they were like that, but everyone told me that's just what feral wyverns were like."

"Our dragons are all first generation. Their eggs are pulled directly out of the Wellspring. Second generation wyverns are too temperamental to train for riding."

"We've tried," Zhao cut in.

Guy had never seen eggs come from Wellsprings before. He knew theoretically that was where Wellspring creatures came from, but he'd only heard about it from the riders who came back laden with new eggs for the hatchery. "Okay," Guy said. "So Bea is rare because she came directly out of a Wellspring, then?"

Bea pressed her forehead into Guy, and he put his hand on her ear and rubbed. "What does that mean, then?"

Zhao snapped her screen shut and put it in her pocket. "Dunno. I'll meet you at the Wellspring tomorrow morning, though. Bye."

She walked out.

"Um," Guy said. "Okay. Thanks."

***

When Guy didn't know something, he went to the library. And there was a lot he didn't know.

He checked out one of the screens, going to one of the docks and contemplatively browsing the archives. Hand on chin and deep in thought, he flipped through pages about Wellsprings. Wellspring creatures, Wellspring phenomena. The eggs that came out of Wellsprings, and hatched into monsters that bore children that became even more monstrous.

What was the difference between a creature from a Wellspring and one born to Wellspring creatures?

He couldn't find an answer. If anyone would know, it would be Zhao, right? She hadn't seemed at all interested in it, though.

He looked up Zhao's biography. She had studied molecular genetics before the Tribulation, apparently. Her name was on dozens of academic papers about cytokines and aquaporins and interleukins. Guy lost interest before he could fall too far down that rabbit hole. It was way too complicated to understand.

Her biography said how she'd met Eckron. She'd heard of his project to try and tame Wellspring creatures and joined up with his group to establish what eventually became the guild.

There was a picture, from the early days of the Tribulation. Eckron, looking much younger and with more hair, kneeling with General Hobby and General Lively, along with Zhao, also looking much younger. There were three people he didn't recognize. The caption read:

Lawrence Eckron, Jairus Hobby, Amotz Lively, Wei Zhao, Alastair Yough, Raki Kaya, Ansel Müller, 2072.

Yough had been a close associate of Eckron's during the Tribulation; everyone knew about him even though he'd died during the Tribulation because Eckron's dragon was named after him. And Sinervo's dragon was named after Raki, although Guy didn't know anything about him. Ansel Müller was a name he'd never heard before, either human or dragon.

Yough was an imposing man with a very serious face. Ansel was a young woman with long, brown hair. Raki was ... tall. The tallest in the group. And he looked like he had albinism. His eyes were pale pink. Guy stared at him, thinking very hard.

"Lieutenant Reed."

Guy jumped, clutching his chest and looking over at who'd spoken. It was Sinervo. "Hello, Major."

"Doing some reading, are we?"

He put his head in his hand and flipped the screen closed. "Just realizing there's a lot I don't know."

"That's true for all of us. At least you realize it." Sinvero looked around nervously and then leaned in. "You can't go to the Wellspring tomorrow with Eckron."

Guy furrowed his brow. "Why not?"

Sinervo shifted from foot to foot. "If I told you – "

"You'd have to kill me? Come on." Guy plugged the glass tablet back into its socket and started walking.

Sinervo hesitated, then followed and whispered. "Take Bea and leave. Run from the guild. Go south."

"No offense, Major, but I'd listen to the commander general over you."

Guy left Sinervo standing there directionless in the library.

10

Guy's eyes bounced from Eckron in front of him, mounted on Yough's huge shoulders as they flew, down to Bea running in front of a dust cloud underneath them.

"General?" Guy said hesitantly.

"Yes, Lieutenant?"

"Permission to speak freely?"

"Granted."

"What are we going to the Wellspring for?"

"To meet Zhao for some research."

"But what exactly will we be doing there? It won't hurt Bea, will it?"

Yough's wings flapped. "No," Eckron said slowly. "It won't hurt Bea."

A pit of anxiety formed in Guy's stomach. "How is Zhao getting there? Is she meeting us?"

"She's being escorted by General Lively."

Guy looked back at the sky behind them – empty. No other dragons following. "When?"

"They'll be behind us shortly. No need to worry about the logistics, Lieutenant, I have it all sorted out."

If Guy had been given less time, he wouldn't have paid Major Sinervo's words much mind. But as it stood, with a trip to the Wellspring in silence, Guy had nothing to do but second-guess himself.

It was too late for that, though. If for some reason he'd wanted to take Sinervo's insane advice for no reason at all, peeling off now would raise a lot of questions from Eckron, and he couldn't outrun Yough.

The Wellspring came into view: the guild had built an iron structure around it to keep it safe, since it was critical to the guild's function. It was empty now, though Eckron informed him it was quite lively around egg-production season.

"Roaming Wellspring creatures would have no reason to mess with this Wellspring, as far as we know, but we keep it secured anyway just in case."

"So this is where all the Wellspring creatures came from?"

"Good heavens, no. Each species has their own individual Wellspring. They're scattered across the globe. I'm not surprised you didn't know that, though. It's not common knowledge anymore ... This one is just for the hawk wyverns."

Eckron landed and dismounted, approaching the door. Guy had Bonnie touch down, then turned to watch Bea catch up. Bea was panting when she arrived.

"Good job, girl," Guy told her. "You're doing great."

Bea gave a lopsided smile and rumbled happily, laying flat out on the ground.

"Lieutenant, let's make sure there aren't any eggs inside before we let Bea in. Sometimes the wyverns will smash the eggs or attack juveniles."

Right, wyvern eggs were a precious commodity they couldn't risk. "Okay, sir. I'll wait here with Bea."

"I'll need you to help me carry the egg if there is one inside."

Guy still sat in Bonnie's saddle, glad his visor was hiding his expression. Eckron stood there waiting for him to come over. Guy was doing calculations about whether or not he could take Eckron in a fight, whether or not Bonnie and Bea could take Yough in a fight, and he didn't like the results he kept getting.

"Yes, sir." Guy slowly untethered himself from Bonnie's saddle and slid down. Bonnie, sensing his anxiety, nudged him. "It's all right, girl, just wait here and watch Bea, yeah?"

Bea flicked her ears and bobbed her head.

"Just wait there and watch Bonnie, okay?"

Eckron used his fingerprint to open the lock on the door, and Guy followed him inside.

It was dark inside, with only reinforced glass from the high vaulted ceiling letting in some sunlight. Guy could hear running water, and as his eyes adjusted to the darkness, he saw the Wellspring itself: a pond with a gentle current, a small spring bubbling up from the center. Not what he'd expected. All told, it was pretty underwhelming.

"So this is where all the wyvern eggs come from?" Guy said.

"Yes. Some unknown force we are still researching deep underground is connected to Wellsprings across the planet, fueling the Wellspring creatures through this water."

"Well, there aren't any eggs, so we can have – "

The door shut and locked mechanically. Sweating, Guy walked over and tried his fingerprint to open it. As he'd feared, it didn't work.

"No need to be nervous, Lieutenant," Eckron said, taking his jacket off.

"Why are we really here, Commander?" Guy said. His eyes darted around the room – the only thing he could think of was that Eckron was going to drown him, or bash him over the head with a rock, and neither of those made very much sense.

Bonnie gave a nervous little yowl from outside.

"I'm here to tell you something that very, very few people in the guild know, Lieutenant. There's a reason the wyverns all have to be first-generation."

Don't tell me. Don't tell me, because then you'll have to kill me.

"The Wellsprings produce eggs for us, but to do that the Wellsprings ... have to be fed."

"Commander General, why are you telling me this?"

"Because I want to give you the chance to do this willingly. People that go into this process kicking and screaming make for particularly uncooperative dragons during training."

Guy's fear instantly ratcheted up to maximum, suddenly piecing together a *lot* of pieces he suddenly wished he hadn't seen.

"No," he said. "No, no, it can't be true. You're – you're a *hero*, you tamed the dragons. You haven't been *throwing people into the Wellspring* to do that, have you?"

Eckron held out his hand. "Come on, Lieutenant. The guild would fall apart if everyone knew, so we have to keep it secret. You know too much to continue serving the guild as a rider, but I know you'll make a fine dragon."

"No," Guy said, stumbling backwards, numb. "No, no, no."

"The hard way, then."

"General, wait!" Guy shouted as Eckron seized him. "No, no, wait! Wait! You don't have to do this! Fuck!"

Bonnie and Bea roared from outside, and Yough could be heard stomping around.

Guy unsheathed his knife and tried to stab Eckron, but the blade glanced off the thick armor of the arm dragging him towards the Wellspring.

"I won't tell anyone! I'll be your accomplice!"

"Come on, Lieutenant, don't fight it."

Guy bent over to try and twist out of his grip, and the two men dissolved into wrestling, breathing heavily and cursing at each other.

Bonnie and Yough were clearly getting into it outside, snarling and hissing. Yough suddenly gave a pained sound as though he'd stepped on something sharp, and the wall to Guy's left dented inwards as though hit by a great force.

"Bea!" Guy screamed. "Bea, Bonnie, help!"

The dent came in further under another blow. Bonnie and Yough didn't have the strength to pierce through the metal, but maybe Bea did. She was heavier, spikier, stronger.

A miracle: a third blow split the metal open, and Bea's claw came in, groping blindly. She stuck her face in, but it wasn't wide enough to get into. She disappeared as she backed up for another blow. Bonnie and Yough continued to give outraged howls as they fought each other. Guy prayed for Bea to do this quickly; he knew Bonnie wouldn't last long if that fight kept up.

"Call her off," Eckron demanded, putting Guy in a headlock. "If I die or if word of this gets out, the guild will fall apart and everyone under our protection will die."

"Let go of me! Get off!"

"*Call her off.* You're going to doom humanity a second time."

Metal screeched as the wall split open further as Bea hurled herself at it, and this time it was enough for her to wiggle through, spikes scraping against the metal. She pounced on the two men on the ground, slapping Eckron away and accidentally standing on Guy and knocking the wind out of him.

Bonnie appeared a moment later, also forcing her body through the hole. Yough, far too large to follow, jammed his head in and gave an outraged scream.

"Bee – " Guy wheezed. "Bee, let me up."

Bea removed her crushing foot, and Guy staggered to his feet, leaning on Bea as Bonnie swiftly put herself between him and Eckron.

Guy locked eyes with Eckron. "This whole time," he said, trying not to cry. "You're the one who figured out you had to throw people into a Wellspring to make a dragon you could ride, and you hid that from us."

"I had to!" Eckron said. "Nobody would throw themselves into a Wellspring willingly! If I wanted to harness this to save humanity, it had to stay secret! Even if it meant getting my hands dirty!"

"People would!" Guy argued. "You don't know that! You didn't have to do – *this*!"

Yough's claws scraped against the metal as he tried to peel it back to follow, but he didn't have the same force as Bea.

"It doesn't matter now!" Eckron said. "What's done is done, and we can't have the guild falling apart when we're the only thing standing between us and a second Tribulation!"

"Bea was a person," Guy said, tears now sliding down his cheeks. "And she just got unlucky enough to fall into a Wellspring somewhere out there, didn't she? And she just had to figure out how to deal with that? She just had to figure out how to survive out there among monsters?"

"Lieutenant ... "

"*Bonnie* was a person – a human woman, and you – you did this to her!" Bonnie's head swung around to block him from advancing on Eckron, moaning worriedly. "She was an innocent person and you made her life into a nightmare!"

"A nightmare?" Eckron said. "Come on. She seems happy, don't you think?"

"She doesn't understand what you did to her!" Guy screamed, and now Bea pulled him back, sandwiching him between Bea and Bonnie.

The metal grinded as Yough's claws tore it back a little, then shoved his head in to try and fit again.

"Come on," Eckron said. "It's not too late for you. You can either take this secret to your grave, or you can live on in some way. We'll just say this beast you brought went wild for no reason and had to be put down, and you can still be with Bonnie – closer to her, even. I'll make sure you're assigned together."

"Fuck you!" Guy said. "Fuck you, sir!"

Yough finally managed to get his head in, but when he tried to snap at Bea, he got a faceful of her spikes and pulled back out.

It was then that Bonnie did something that she almost never did: she made an executive decision.

Guy was still a mess, swimming in his revelations and anger at Eckron. Bonnie turned her head sideways, seized him in her jaws, and darted through the opening Yough had just made.

Yough's head snaked around to follow them as Bonnie flitted past, and he spread his wings to take off and give chase. Bea came out next, though, and clamped her jaws around Yough's leg. The wyvern reared back with an outraged bellow.

That was the last Guy saw before they disappeared, swallowed by the rock hurtling past them as Bonnie fled the scene.

***

Guy hadn't been able to stop crying. Bonnie eventually made the effort to find a small stream of water, and she plopped him down into it pointedly with a splash.

"Thank you," he choked out. He turned over and crawled on his hands and knees, splashing his face, still sobbing. The water was cool and clear and felt nice.

He looked up at Bonnie with puffy eyes. She cocked her head, turning one brilliant blue eye towards him.

"This is so messed up," he said. He wobbled to his feet. "Bonnie."

She trilled, raising her head crest.

"I'm sorry, Bonnie. I'm sorry. I didn't know."

Bonnie's eyes followed him as he staggered over and undid her bridle. "I'm sorry," he sobbed. "I'm sorry. I didn't know. I would never have guessed. I'm sorry."

He dropped the bridle into the stream, then undid the saddle, letting it slide off. "You can leave," Guy said. "You didn't choose to be here. You didn't choose to be with me. You didn't choose any of this."

Bonnie trilled in a concerned way and nosed at his hand.

"You don't even understand what's wrong," he wailed. "You can't understand!"

She turned her head sideways, nose in his hand. Her eyes were watery.

Maybe she *did* understand.

"Can you understand what I'm saying right now? Blink twice if you can understand what I'm saying."

She rumbled magnanimously and pulled her head back, nuzzling Guy's shoulders, closing her eyes. She brought her wing around and nestled him in it.

Maybe she didn't. He had no way of knowing.

He did know one thing, though: she had nowhere to go without him. She would be consigned to roaming around the wild like an animal, like Bea had been, if Guy abandoned her. And despite his moral grandstanding, she didn't seem to *want* to leave.

Guy sniffled and took her head in his hands. "If you want to stay, I'm with you for life," he said, voice shaky. "It's you and me, Bonnie. I want it to be your choice, though."

Bonnie leaned down and delicately picked the bridle up with her teeth, setting the dripping implement in Guy's hands.

Guy wiped his face on his arm. "Thank you, Bonnie. Thank you for being here with me. I don't know how to help you understand what's going on, but I'll always take care of you. I'll always do whatever I can to help you."

Bonnie perked up, head turning towards where a heavy thumping sound revealed Bea, claws scraping over the rock to join them in the stream. She was covered in burns and bite marks, blood and embers running down through her spikes.

"Bea," Guy called, rushing over.

She collapsed to the ground, lowing sorrowfully. "Bee," Guy said, cupping her jaws. "Bee, you did so good. Thank you. Thank you for coming to find me."

Her eyes slid closed, and she exhaled slowly.

"Let me help you. I'll get you bandaged up and everything, and – and just like you did for me."

Bonnie came over and covered her with her wings.

Guy put his one hand on her, keeping the other hand on Bea. "We're gonna be okay."

He looked up to the sky, the clouds pink and puffy from the sun. "South, huh?" He never in a million years would have taken Sinervo's advice to flee the guild unless something this drastic had happened to him firsthand.

But now he knew he had no choice. Everyone would believe whatever version of the story Eckron told them, probably that Bea had gone berserk and attacked like he'd said earlier. At best, Guy would have to leave Bea behind for dead and go back to being a rider. With the knowledge of what the dragons really were forever burned in his brain. He could keep killing Wellspring creatures that had never been human at all, but how could he ever look any dragon in the eye again knowing they'd been drowned, transformed, mindwiped, and made to submit without anyone even knowing what they really were?

How could he possibly just go back to normal after this?

Guy tangled his fingers in the soft feathers of Bonnie's abdomen, using the other hand to reassuringly rub Bea's head. "I'm gonna take care of the two of you. I don't know how, but I'm going to find a way to help you. I promise."

About the Author

Nox is a lover of all creatures and people in sci-fi and fantasy and loves stories about persevering through horrors to come out better on the other side.

The Dark Side of the Sun

Harper M. Tremblay

Cover Design by Nicole Alessi

Cover Illustration by Hen Towers

To the best friend I've ever had and the strongest mother anyone could ask for —
I love you.

Contents

Content Warnings

This story contains the following content:

- Torture, including unethical scientific experimentation
- Slavery
- Captivity
- Suicidal ideation
- Terminal illness

If this book isn't for you, no worries! But if it is, we hope you enjoy this story about an unexpected reunion...

— • —

"Do you know why you're here before me, Cassius?"

The creature looking down at Cassius was an ugly thing. Few of King Myndill's kind truly remained pure, but King Myndill was a fearsome creature indeed. His lupine amber eyes marked by the blackness of Taint never ceased to glow. His long, sabertooth-like teeth stood out, even when he took that regal human form.

Cassius dared not face King Myndill's true form. Even just the silhouette of a large wolf could send villages fleeing in fear – for good reason too. That creature brought destruction wherever his dirtied paws found purchase.

"You're a fucking revenge-driven bastard, Myndill. I know you hate me and my kind. What, am I just your latest revenge piece? I know how you are."

Anger flashed in those charred eyes of his. "Watch your fucking mouth, Cassius."

The guards that held his arms down quickly pushed Cassius to the floor, agonizingly so. It took everything in Cassius not to give Myndill the satisfaction of a cry.

"I have much worse in mind for you than 'revenge,' dear Cassius." King Myndill used the edge of his boot to tilt Cassius' chin up in his direction. "You hate *my* kind. I know that well."

"Who wouldn't hate your kind? You were punished by the Judge for what you did. You're all rotten."

Myndill grinned wildly. "Most of us are here for very similar reasons to the suffering that you've imparted on others, Cassius. You're just lucky." Myndill used his boot to twist Cassius' head to the side. Then his boot came crashing down on Cassius' jaw. If his jaw hadn't immediately fallen out of place, Cassius might've screamed. "Don't forget who owns *your* life now."

Cassius let out a stifled groan. He couldn't move his jaw. It was an injury easily fixed with alchemy, but that didn't take away the humiliation of the moment.

"I don't plan on ever letting you go, Cassius. After a certain time, everyone's going to assume that I've killed you. I don't have such a merciful fate in mind for the likes of you."

Cassius let out a small growl as he narrowed his eyes at the King of the Tainted. He tired already of the creature's games. It was all overdone hysterics, anyway. Though Myndill was a fearsome creature, many of the other Tainted could overthrow him easily.

At least, that's what Cassius thought from his research. The Tainted each held a fearsome might. Every specimen he got his hands on seemed to be increasingly powerful. He wondered how this king even stayed in power. Most had to be afraid, he thought. Yet the king hadn't attacked any villages in the past hundred years on his own. That, to Cassius, was just a show of weakness and insecurity.

"Oh, it'll be so much fun to make you beg at my feet for scraps of that precious food you humans find yourself needing oh-so-very often."

Cassius doubted that Myndill would ever make him beg for anything.

"You'll regret ever crossing one of us, dear Cassius. You'll regret ever insulting me. You'll be one of the toys I'll enjoy shattering the most. I might even keep you longer. You'll last longer than most of the other toys I've had, after all."

That much was true, at least. Cassius knew his body could last many more days than most. He never planned on spending those days with a sick bastard like Myndill. No, he wouldn't waste his precious life with that false idol.

***

Screams soon filled the halls of the palace. Hakon was far used to it after fifty years as a Tainted. He was lucky enough to have come under the protection and kindness of the king. Somehow, those fifty years he'd spent in that Tainted body of his, under the rule of a king he once found to be a beast of his night terrors, were the best of his life.

Today, though, something *felt* different. He was more acute to emotions now as a Tainted. How could he ever get used to hearing and feeling everything around him? It gave him headaches and overloaded him often when he was in crowds. The king had assured him that it was because he was only recently taken over by Taint.

Hakon begged to differ.

Memories of his time as a human came back to him easily when he heard those screams.

"Hakon?"

The Tainted next to him – a gentle fellow that Hakon was close to calling a friend – looked him in the eyes. "Are you okay?"

Hakon shook his head. "I thought I recognized the voice of His Majesty's new toy."

His friend was eerily quiet. Hakon's stomach dropped.

"You probably do, Hakon."

Hakon looked at his friend in confusion. Fear swarmed in his head, stinging his mind like hornets. "N-none of the humans I knew are alive anymore. If they are, they're too old for His Majesty's tastes in toys."

His friend shook his head. "I'll let His Majesty tell you himself. He requested to see you before you go about your regular duties for today."

"What? You know!? Tell me! Tell me before I see him!" He couldn't hide the panic from his voice.

"I can't disobey His Majesty's orders, Hakon. You should see him as soon as you can, if you're so anxious."

Hakon nodded. He forced himself to take a deep breath, to focus on his heart beating in his chest as he held it. Once he'd brought his entire mind to his heart, letting his breath go through his mouth in a long, gracious stroke, his lungs seemed to fill more. His heart began to slow.

"Thank you. I'll see you soon." Hakon gave his friend a small smile, then went to his rooms to put on the necklace that his king had given him all those years ago.

***

King Myndill's blood sang with wine and lust as he awaited Hakon's arrival on his throne. He wasn't quite deep in his cups yet, but he was certainly going to be. Whether because of celebration of Cassius' capture or because he genuinely enjoyed the bottle he found himself drinking, Myndill didn't know. He wasn't sure he cared either.

Hakon came quickly once that friend of his had passed along the message. He came dressed in ceremonial robes, a scarf tied over his eyes. On his neck, Hakon bore the necklace he was always polite enough to wear when around Myndill.

Indeed, Hakon was a treasure as the Chaplain of the palace and the Seer of his kingdom. Few Tainted had the magic he did. He needed not sight nor smell to know where he was. His mind's eye was acute enough to guide him.

Not too many paces forwards or too many back, Hakon fell to his knees in a bow to his king. Myndill smiled. *A valuable asset, indeed.*

"You may rise, Hakon."

Hakon stood and bowed at the waist. "Yes, Your Majesty."

Myndill didn't need Hakon's magic to know that the young Tainted had a grave question on his mind. "What is it, Hakon? You may speak freely."

A look of surprise washed over Hakon's face. "Your Grace, I've had the feeling that I might know your new toy. Something tells me who he is and – I recognize his screams. His voice."

Myndill smiled. He hadn't told Hakon about Cassius' presence purposefully. Though it felt a little cruel to give the boy such a test, Myndill needed to know the strength of Hakon's magic – and the strength of his resolve. Myndill always had a sense that Hakon had an acuity that other Western-bound souls didn't have.

The resolve remained despite the tremor in the boy's voice.

"Who did you think it might be?"

Hakon looked hesitant, afraid almost. It wasn't unusual with the Tainted, for them to have been hurt by others before. Few were the Tainted whose sin was entirely random. Myndill was used to it by now.

"All is well, Hakon. You may speak to me. You're a valuable part of the palace. You don't have to fear others like you did when you were human."

Something flashed on that gentle skin of Hakon's. "I thought it might be Cassius. The one who – "

Hakon's voice caught and struggled on the words, so Myndill held his hand up.

"I understand, Hakon," Myndill soothed. "Indeed, I've taken Cassius as my new toy. He'll be fun to break. Imagine – the one who's hurt us for the past hundred years groveling at our feet for scraps of food. It'll be a long time before I get there with him. The day it comes, though, will be glorious."

A small smile parted Hakon's lips. The idea pleased him too.

"He's a bastard. He deserves everything he has coming at him, Your Majesty."

Myndill laughed a hearty laugh as he looked at Hakon. Despite his covered eyes, Hakon was able to meet his gaze. "He deserves every last part of it. I had the guards start him off easy today – we branded him to ensure that if he escapes our territory, he's returned immediately."

Hakon's smile faded a bit, turning into that shy smile of his early days at the palace.

"I know it's a sensitive subject, my dear Hakon. It's for his own good. He'd be killed instead of returned if he didn't bear our mark."

Hakon grimaced. "All the better. The world is better off without him, Your Highness."

Myndill smiled a bit, lapping up that little bit of defiance he'd cultivated in Hakon like a thirsty dog would water.

"I understand your wish, Hakon. I think that seeing him break first will be the perfect punishment for what he's done to us. Death would be a mercy for someone like him. He has two hundred years ahead of him, at least. Plenty of time to make sure he suffers before he dies."

Hakon nodded. "I am forever your loyal servant, My Lord."

Myndill smiled and stood from his throne. He ruffled Hakon's hair a bit. Admittedly, the boy was something of a son to him, even though such a relationship didn't exist in Tainted society or the one he came from. Where that paternal energy came from fascinated Myndill, even if the origin of the idea planted so deeply in his mind baffled him.

"I know you are, my dear. I couldn't be more thankful to have you around here. You're an invaluable asset to this kingdom and very dear to me." Myndill took a breath. "I imagine you'll want to see him."

Again, Hakon nodded. "Yes, Your Majesty."

Myndill hummed. "I want you to walk there with someone you trust." He held a finger up to shush the comment he was sure Hakon had. "I'm worried about how it'll affect you to see the one who made you the way that you are. They don't need to go into the room with you. They just need to wait outside for you and get you back to your rooms."

It was one of those genuine, unselfish concerns that Myndill had. They were rare, but not as much with Hakon.

"I'll survive. I've survived worse, Your Highness."

"I know you have." Myndill looked at the stained glass of his throne room. "I know you have, Hakon. You're strong. Stronger than you know. My goal as your liege is to have you save that strength, not to have you expend it on fools. If you need anything, you know that you can call on me, right?"

Hakon gave a small nod. "As you wish, Your Majesty."

Myndill smiled softly at him. "We're keeping him in the dungeons. You're welcome to come and go as you please. The guards all know who you are already."

A smile crossed Hakon's face. "Thank you, Your Majesty."

"Of course. Take good care of yourself. You are to make sure you have someone the first time. I don't mind if you touch him or anything this time. He's yours as much as he is mine."

"Thank you for your kindness, Your Majesty. I would like to go see him now."

"Of course. Make sure you eat something tonight too. You're looking thin."

Hakon chuckled and smiled. "I always look thin, Your Majesty. I had consumption as a human."

"Then it'll be easier to eat!"

The two laughed before Myndill gave Hakon a pat on the shoulder. "Take good care, my dear."

***

The dungeons were a musty place. Cassius immediately hated it there, though he had more pressing issues than his running nose.

Rage flared in his mind every time the brand on his side ached from the rough handling of the guards. He wanted to punch them. He wanted to fight back.

It was a stupid idea to do either, though. Cassius knew better. Neither guard found a punch to the side. The brand would limit his movement for days and his jaw was somewhat broken.

Once I'm alone, I need to see if I can fix my jaw.

Broken bones were surprisingly easy to fix with alchemy. They were all minerals, something that alchemy excelled at changing. Skin made of human flesh, on the other hand, was not easy to fix. It was too complex compared to the simplicity of bone cells.

Once the guards had dumped him on the mossy, slightly damp floor of the cell, Cassius wasted no time meditating. His focus had to be unshakeable. The most pressing matter was fixing his jaw. *Then I need to destroy those stupid motherfuckers.*

Just as Cassius had gotten a feeling for the weather patterns in the area – a good pattern too, with lots of wind – he heard a familiar voice.

"Triple Onyx Cassius. I never expected to see you again, much less here of all places."

Cassius immediately lost all his focus as he looked out into those familiar honey-gold eyes, now lined with the black Taint of his kind.

"Elijah?"

The face of the Tainted before him changed. "I'm not Elijah anymore." His eyes narrowed. "I'm Hakon now. After what *you* did."

Cassius smiled a bit. "Hakon now, eh? Well, then, I see you've become one of my greatest successes if you've actually become one of the Tainted."

His words only seem to twist that once-innocent face more. It hurt him more than he cared to admit to speak with a half-fixed jaw, but the anger rolling off the Tainted like waves and filling the room was worth every second of pain.

"Shut the fuck up. I'm here because of my own decisions, not your stupid fucking experiments."

That only seemed to make Cassius smile more.

— • —

Seeing Cassius smiling and laughing at him brought Hakon right back to those days in Cassius' lab with a needle in his arm. He forced himself to swallow the lump in his throat as he looked at his former captor, shirtless and sitting in cheap breeches.

The brand, King Myndill's mark, burned red and hot on his side. Of course, he was an alchemist and would be able to fight off infection much more easily. Hakon was still surprised to see that the brand wasn't covered.

Somehow, as he was watching Cassius smile from the ground, he found himself regarding the sight as rather pathetic. *This* was the man who'd tortured him? *This* was the man who'd kept him captive and made him accept punishment by the Judge?

The notion filled Hakon with rage he thought himself hardly capable of.

In fact, it made him want to punch that smirk right off of Cassius' stupid, smug face.

"Somehow, I doubt that quiet little Elijah managed to grow up into a big bad monster all on his own."

"Shut up. Shut up right now, you bastard!"

Cassius gave him that smirk he knew all too well. It only served to make Hakon angrier.

"What? Was it really all bad? Come on, if you want to hit me, go ahead. Hit that stupid fucking brand Myndill put on me. If it really was *that* bad with me, show me how angry it made you."

From his position above, Hakon soon realized that he was giving Cassius control over the situation. He hated how easily he'd let Cassius put him right back into that position he was all those years ago – fifty-five, now, wasn't it?

He wanted to beat the shit out of Cassius. Hakon wasn't the weak child that Cassius had tortured anymore. In fact, he was stronger than Cassius. Hakon didn't rely on hurting others for his self-esteem. Hakon knew he was powerful – probably stronger than Cassius, in fact.

It left him with a sense of pity for his captor. Part of him was angry that he was so weak back then as to let such a pathetic man torture him. Part of him knew it wasn't his fault – just like King Myndill had taught him.

Yet, because Hakon was stronger than Cassius in spirit and in magic, it was easy for him to figure out what he wanted to do.

"You're pathetic," Hakon spat. "Here you are, on the floor. You think you still have power over me. You still somehow think that taunting will get you anywhere. You see, Cassius, I'm not that person you knew all those years ago. I've become the Seer for His Highness, King Myndill. In my presence, you will address him with respect."

Cassius scoffed.

"I pity you."

Cassius' face changed. That simple phrase had wiped the smirk off of his face with more grace and ease than any punch to the face would've.

"You pity me?" Cassius asked incredulously.

"You're a sad, pathetic worm of a man, Cassius."

Hakon pulled a small knife out of his boot. Cassius looked at Hakon with a glint of fear, entirely unsatisfying fear, in his eyes. Hakon didn't want Cassius to fear him, not anymore. Cassius' fear would not heal the hurt in his heart. It was best to leave that fear as a bitter taste in his mouth.

With the knife, Hakon cut a strip of fabric from his plain, white robes. He didn't really mind, in all honesty. What he was about to do was worth more than any old robes he'd thrown on to go see Cassius.

"Stay still, Cassius. I'll be able to see what you're going to do before you do it."

As Hakon reached to open the door of the cell, Cassius snapped like a rabid dog. "What the hell do you think you're doing? Are you trying to dress my fucking wound? Just who do you think you are?"

"I'm not sure who I am. I never was. Probably never will be. I might have you to thank for that. I don't know." Hakon took a deep breath. "I know one thing, though. You're weak and you're injured. You need my help."

"If I'm so weak and pathetic, what does that make you?" Cassius hissed. "I broke you so beautifully back then. A weak little orphan, suddenly an adult and alone in the real world."

Cassius' question gave Hakon pause. Still, Hakon continued in silence. Bafflingly, Cassius let him dress his brand wound. Hakon had never expected him to stay still.

"I'm not sure what it makes me." Hakon wrapped the bandages around Cassius' torso, pulling them snug, but not too tight. Cassius flinched in pain and groaned each time a new layer was added. "But *this*." He motioned to the bandages. "This makes me stronger than you."

To that, Cassius had no answer. Instead, Cassius let Hakon finish dressing his wound, then allowed Hakon to help him relocate his jaw.

"I know you can fix the rest with alchemy."

Cassius nodded.

As Hakon turned to leave, Cassius muttered something from behind him. "Seer suits you well, Hakon. You were always so observant."

Hakon said nothing as he walked back up the stairs. The comment made him feel a little sick. Why, he wasn't sure.

***

Cassius spent longer than he would care to admit thinking about his conversation with Hakon.

The boy was so different from the orphan he'd taken in. Back then, he was a rather scared boy who was just barely an adult and had to face the horrors of the world on his own. People of that stripe made amazing prey for research subjects. Nobody would miss them. Nobody would ever even look for them. Nobody would lash out at the alchemists for keeping someone like that.

Back then, he was Elijah, with not even a family name to call his own.

The day they met, it was raining in sheets. Elijah had been sitting under the roof of the back entrance of a church – the entrance to the soup kitchen. He was thin and had the biggest bags under his honey eyes.

Cassius had been looking for someone to test an idea on. He'd managed to purify the bone marrow of a Tainted he'd killed with an affinity for curses. All that was left was to try injecting it in the corresponding organ area of someone else. Cassius had a theory back then that because mages stored their magic in organs, Taint originated in the same area.

Taint spread like a blight from person to person. One day, after an ill deed, people would turn into depraved, evil fae creatures with black sclera. They always reported a strange dream before Taint took over – at least, the ones that would or could talk to Cassius about their experiences.

Sometimes, Taint would infect an entire household. Cases were rare of a Tainted spreading their corruption, but it was typically in mage families with similar magic that it happened.

Thus, Cassius thought that if he could identify the direction of the soul of his subject and inject the purified version of the Tainted's bone marrow, he could corrupt their soul and create "artificial" Tainted.

His theory would prove deadly for many, so someone like Elijah was the perfect target. No alchemist accomplished much of anything without a few sacrifices along the way.

"You look hungry."

Elijah had perked up immediately. Cassius was holding an umbrella over his own head. It made him look particularly well-off.

"Sir, if you have any change to spare, I'd like to buy a warm meal. The soup kitchen only serves food once a day."

A small smile crawled onto Cassius' lips. He knew it made him look friendly to the scared child at his feet.

"Come, I'll feed you. You look so awfully thin."

Elijah shook his head. "S-sir, I can't. I have consumption. You'll catch it from me if you take me in."

"Consumption doesn't scare me." Cassius prepared himself to tell his little lie. "My brother had it and I grew up with him. I never caught it. I doubt you could give it to me if my own brother didn't."

That convinced Elijah.

"Tell me your name, child?"

"I-I'm not a child. I just turned eighteen three months ago." He ducked his head as he trailed behind Cassius when he started walking. "I'm Elijah."

Cassius nodded. "Eighteen is still very much a child. I'm Cassius. I'm an alchemist. I can help you, though. We aren't bad people. Lots of nasty rumors out there."

It was the honest truth. *Alchemists* weren't bad people. He wasn't a bad person, either, though he knew some would disagree. Some simply envied a man in the pursuit of knowledge. Not everyone had the stomach to handle when the pursuit of knowledge wasn't as noble as most thought it to be. It was a fact of life.

Little did Elijah know at the time that he would never step foot near that church again. Elijah would become something much greater than a street urchin.

Cassius thought he wasn't capable of regret. Yet seeing Elijah, now Hakon, a Tainted just like he'd intended all those years ago, filled him with an indescribable emotion that *hurt*.

Was that what regret felt like?

Cassius wasn't sure.

***

King Myndill waited with a giddy sort of pleasure for his new toy to arrive. Cassius was a fighter, though that was more of a perk than the point. Cassius was a nuisance. Better a toy than a nuisance, King Myndill presumed.

Of course, his new toy came kicking and biting the guards like a feral beast. King Myndill smiled. *Perfect.*

"Leave him unrestrained and exit."

The guards bowed and shut the door to Myndill's personal torture chambers. The walls were lined with cabinets that held all sorts of materials he needed for his pets – materials to feed them, hurt them, and heal their wounds, eventually.

How would Cassius react today?

"That little shit Hakon came to visit me last night."

Of course, King Myndill knew already. He'd prepared time for him and Hakon to speak about how it had gone. "Hmm? What happened to make you so angry?"

A look of annoyance flooded Cassius' face. King Myndill had to stifle his chuckle. For such an arrogant man, Cassius certainly had never won a game of poker.

"You wouldn't believe it, but the little bastard still cares about me. He came and wrapped up my side, without your permission, I'm assuming."

King Myndill had noticed the bandages. He'd given Hakon permission to do what he pleased, so it didn't bother him. Hakon had a beautiful empathy within him. It was a gift – a helpful one at that. Seers needed empathy to be good at their jobs.

"I'm surprised he didn't just punch you in the face."

Cassius laughed. "Something we can agree on." Cassius got a wicked smile on his face. "He's oh-so-loyal to you, Your Royal *Highness*. He demanded that I call you by a proper title," Cassius scoffed.

"I was thinking about working on that with you, actually." A smile materialized on King Myndill's face. "Mocking me is a piss-poor idea, Cassius."

"If you want to see a piss-poor idea, just look at your kingdom."

King Myndill wasn't smiling anymore. That just egged Cassius on.

"Why take in a pathetic kid like that? When I had him, he could hardly wipe his ass without my permission."

"Keep speaking, Cassius, and I'll make you regret the day you were born."

Cassius took that as a challenge. "Really? Like I made *Elijah* regret ever being born?"

That was the end of King Myndill's rope. He threw a hard punch at Cassius' face, hitting him squarely in his already-injured jaw. A sharp kick to his abdomen, right on top of his brand, came next.

Cassius fell to the ground in a heap, coughing, biting back a scream of pain.

"Get up now. Face me."

Cassius didn't comply. King Myndill knew he couldn't.

King Myndill kneeled down and picked up Cassius' chin, tilting Cassius' head to watch the contorted look of pain wash over his face.

"Do not insult any Tainted, much less one as talented as Hakon, in my presence. They're like children, brothers, and sisters to me." He squeezed Cassius' jaw with his hand until Cassius was whimpering. "I'll make everything extremely clear to you, understand?"

King Myndill took a deep breath. "You will be *my* plaything from now until the day you die. If you're respectful and good, I'll treat you well. If you can't keep your damn mouth shut, you'll find yourself hurt. It's only natural. Humans don't understand anything other than pain."

Cassius scoffed, but King Myndill only squeezed his injured jaw more until the only noise he made was whimpering.

"From now on, dear Cassius, you have no god other than me. You will obey my every command. It'll take you a while to get there, I know, but you will. I promise you that I will learn every secret in your head, every horrible memory you'd rather forget, and every weakness you have."

Cassius, for the first time, had a horrible look of fear in his eyes. King Myndill smirked. "You know that I always make good on my promises, right?"

Cassius said nothing, but his silence confirmed that he was already beginning to break down a bit. He was starting to understand.

That just made King Myndill giddy as he prepared himself for what he would do with Cassius that day.

"You'll call me 'liege' before this day ends. However long that takes is your choice, Cassius, but it will happen."

The look of doubt on Cassius' face only served to make King Myndill more excited for what laid ahead.

— • —

Cassius lay there, freezing, on the ground of the torture room.

"Come on, dear, it's so easy. You can do well."

He hated that mocking tone of his captor – King Myndill. His body was littered with bruises and he was sure one of his ribs had cracked. Worst of all, the torture room of his captor was freezing cold and he was drenched with cold water.

Apparently, he'd needed a bath after the torture session, so King Myndill had taken to washing him by dumping a bucket of cold water on him.

Now –

"Come on, dear Cassius. All it takes is one word."

He was cold and naked and in desperate need of a towel. He was shaking, trying to warm up in any way possible. His wet breeches stuck to him, zapping away any heat his body could produce.

"Just call me 'liege' and I'll come to towel you off."

Myndill's smile was wicked. Cassius wanted to punch him in the face and wipe that smile right off of it. His one shoulder was almost certainly dislocated, and it ached, reminding him that he didn't want to tempt Myndill to break the other one.

"Look at you! You're sweating so much. Poor dear." Myndill clicked his tongue mockingly. "Do you need another bath?"

"No! I do not need more of that cold fucking water." Cassius' teeth were chattering, making it difficult to make out what he was trying to say.

"You don't need to be like this, Cassius. You're doing this to yourself. It's so easy. It's just one word to behave properly."

Cassius couldn't take the cold anymore. "My Liege."

Myndill hesitated. "Good boy."

His smile grew only more wicked and gleeful. Cassius hated it, but he was pathetically helpless. He was lucky that Myndill had decided against restraints, otherwise it would've been a lot worse.

Myndill tossed the towel to Cassius with a clean pair of breeches. "Get yourself dressed. I'll have someone bring you your food and water later."

***

Some types were more prone to Taint than others. The hedonists, like King Myndill himself, and the revenge-prone were always more likely to develop it than others.

Taint always fed off of those selfish, dark emotions. It was a double-edged sword – becoming a Tainted meant a life of never-ending persecution. Be that as it may, it also meant that those selfish, dark creatures no longer had to hide their darker self. In fact, that darker self was the source of a Tainted's power.

For King Myndill, becoming a Tainted had been a gift beyond measure. As a fae creature, he was always weak. As a Tainted, he was powerful. He stood above all others in pure strength.

With that power, he built a kingdom. His kingdom grew to such might that it could take land easily. His people were never without food. His people never suffered death at the hands of those who hated them. They could all sleep easily at night. King Myndill couldn't be more proud.

Despite King Myndill's best efforts, the Kingdom of the Tainted was missing many things. For one, they had little healing magic. Healing types almost never fell victim to Taint. It was only one of the numerous concerns of having a high concentration of individuals whose magic was largely destructive in nature.

King Myndill didn't know why he went out to collect the new Tainted that day. Had he thought to scare the creatures outside his kingdom? No, that didn't make sense.

That day was fifty years ago now – a short time to a five hundred year old creature, yes, but still long enough to lose memories.

It was a miserable day too. One of the worst blizzards King Myndill could remember had moved in. His patrols couldn't encounter any issues or else risk leaving new Tainted out to die. He preferred being out in the field, anyway, helping them. It was thrilling compared to royal life. He could let his wolf out too, and run like he didn't have a care in the world other than the mission.

They'd almost missed Hakon that day.

"Your Majesty, I think someone's in the snow!"

King Myndill stopped immediately. Patrol members hurried to begin digging in the snow. They could hardly see a few stone tosses in front of them, but the Tainted who'd found the young man was very talented in sensing the soul of another.

As it turned out, she was absolutely right.

A young man with black sclera and honey-gold eyes laid under the snow. His skin was flushed with frostbite.

"Get me some blankets!"

King Myndill allowed one of the patrol members to wrap the young man in blankets and lean him up against Myndill's warm, furry body.

"He won't be the only one. You can leave me with him here," Myndill ordered the patrol members. "I'll see if he can be saved."

The patrol members nodded. They wouldn't disobey the orders of their king.

They left Myndill with extra blankets. He didn't want them to linger.

From the look of the young man, Myndill figured he was probably once human, which meant that he would need a fae name.

"You look like a Hakon."

It was a fond name for King Myndill. He, admittedly, wasn't the best at sensing the nature of a person, but even he could tell that something was very different about the young man. King Myndill would later learn that he had one of the rarest magics of all for a Tainted – Western magic.

A small smile parted King Myndill's lips as he warmed the young man with his hot breath. He couldn't wait to meet this honey-eyed gift to his kingdom.

***

"How did your meeting with Cassius go yesterday?"

King Myndill sat at a table this time. Sometimes he and his consumptive Seer would eat together. Though neither of them really *needed* to eat, it was definitely more pleasant *to* eat than to use worldly energy to sustain themselves.

Hakon was hardly a consumptive anymore. He couldn't spread his disease nor would it progress beyond what it did while Hakon was human. He still sometimes suffered coughing fits and was always thin and pale, so Myndill did what he could to encourage him to eat regular meals, even if they weren't necessary for Hakon to survive.

After all, surviving wasn't living.

"It went well, Your Majesty."

Myndill knew that wasn't the whole truth.

Hakon, just as he was about to take a bite of his food, broke down in a coughing fit. Once Myndill was sure that he wasn't choking, he allowed Hakon to finish coughing.

"Sorry, Your Majesty."

Myndill shook his head. "No reason to apologize." He moved his food around before he decided on where to take a bite. "He said a lot of things."

Hakon froze, but Myndill gave a reassuring gesture. "It's okay. I won't go into details, but I see why you hate the bastard. You should've beaten him up. I would've understood."

Myndill loved the thoughtful look Hakon got when he was deeply considering what to say next. Quietly, Hakon ate a bit in between thoughts. That was one of his Seer's quirks. Eating and thinking didn't come as naturally to Hakon as it did to most.

"It felt wrong." Hakon put down his fork. "Wouldn't I be just as bad as him if I did that? I – I just can't imagine hurting him. I don't think that it's the way for me to reclaim power over my life. Not at all."

Myndill hummed a little. *You're an interesting Tainted, Hakon. What did you do to get to this place?*

"Hmm ... I'm not sure. That's a very personal question, Hakon." Myndill smiled at him, glowing a bit with pride. Hakon was young for a Tainted but held none of the youthful vengeance of a young Tainted. "I wouldn't have given him a lick of mercy. But I'm also Southern-bound. You're unique. You're Western-bound. Your soul wants different things from mine."

Hakon nodded. "Thank you, Your Majesty."

Again, that look.

Myndill stayed silent.

"If it's well with you, Your Majesty, I would like to keep visiting him. I don't think I can put my soul to rest until I find what it wants with him. It wants something, Your Majesty, and it will not allow me to lay in peace until it gets what it wants."

Myndill nodded, intrigued. "Of course, Hakon. You may visit as often as you want. You know his tricks better than I do. I know you'll be safe." Myndill took the last bite off of his plate. "I saw you tended to his wound. Would you like to try to bring him his meals? His water? He is still a human. I need him in good shape for what I want to do."

Hakon considered it for a long time. "Yes, Your Majesty. It would please me to give it a try."

Myndill smiled at Hakon. Glancing at Hakon's plate, he frowned. "You need to eat more."

Hakon couldn't help a chuckle. "Of course, Your Majesty."

***

Hakon picked up the food for Cassius in the kitchen. The cooks definitely looked at him differently, but Hakon didn't care. He was the Seer, after all. The Seer never got a normal look from the Tainted around him. Uneasy, weary, suspicious looks. Sometimes ones of admiration or envy, maybe, but not the look of any passerby.

Why did I agree to this? Why did I say that I wanted to see that bastard again?

Hakon couldn't answer any of those questions.

He wanted more with Cassius, but what exactly he was hoping to accomplish was unclear.

I wish I could cast a spell on myself.

Sometimes, Hakon used his magic to help others make decisions. Perhaps cruelly, though, he could never use his magic on himself. At least, not spells like that. He could enhance his senses and the like, sure, but never help himself with anything practical.

A dangerous pang of self-doubt flared in his chest.

I'm doing the right thing. Hakon shook his head. *I'm doing the right thing. I just don't know what that is right now. I always figure it out.*

That was true. Whether with Cassius or with King Myndill, Hakon always figured something out.

Hakon took a deep breath.

I'll be okay.

After all, Cassius had no power other than the power that Hakon gave him now. Hakon wouldn't let Cassius have any power over his life. He wouldn't allow Cassius to take away what he had, not like in those days.

The guards moved aside quickly for Hakon. Even the guards in front of Cassius' cell were quick to leave in his presence.

A chuckle came from the cell.

"Aren't you quite the celebrity?"

Hakon knew that Cassius was grinning, even if he was hiding in the shadows. He could also see ...

Wounds? His shoulder looks dislocated. Are his ribs okay?

Hakon didn't know what he was expecting. Of course Cassius would go get himself beaten up by King Myndill. King Myndill didn't tolerate disrespect for authority. Hakon wasn't sure that Cassius even knew what authority *was*. Other than his own, maybe.

"They respect me." Hakon set the tray of food on the ledge of the cell made for such things. "Unlike someone I know."

Cassius raised his one hand as he limped out of the shadows. He looked worse than Hakon had expected. He had a black eye and a large bruise on his already-injured jaw. His left arm hung incorrectly from his shoulder.

Hakon felt a cough coming on. He quickly took out the cloth he kept in his pocket and coughed into it.

"Still a consumptive?" Cassius took the food from the ledge.

"Becoming a Tainted doesn't heal disease. It just prevents it from spreading and progressing."

Cassius looked genuinely surprised. Hakon smiled a bit. *He must not have known.*

It felt amazing to have known something that Cassius hadn't.

Cassius didn't admit it.

He never would have.

Hakon sat in silence against the wall for a while.

"Do you really need to stay here while I eat every bite of my food?"

Cassius' mood was quickly turning foul. Hakon might've scoffed if the sound of that irritation didn't send chills down his spine.

"I need to collect the tray."

"You seem a little high-ranking to be collecting dishes from me."

Hakon shrugged at the comment meant to agitate him. "I am. You're a special case."

Cassius grinned. Hakon hated the look of it.

"Do you want me to help you set that shoulder? It'll heal faster if I set it now."

Cassius' grin faded. A small smile of triumph split Hakon's mouth.

"No. I'll deal with it on my own."

Clearly, the question had soured his appetite. He returned the tray.

"The food's shit. Get me something better tomorrow."

—•—

Were the times with Cassius all bad?

The question haunted Hakon more often than he cared to admit. As he laid in bed, resting that morning, he found himself thinking back to that time when he was "Elijah."

Cassius kept him in a single bedroom with a small, doorless bathroom. The door to his tiny, cramped bedroom was always locked in the beginning. Cassius didn't trust him not to run.

Even with the benefit of hindsight, Hakon wasn't exactly sure why. He had nowhere to go. He was a consumptive orphan. Nobody would've taken him in, especially since he didn't have any job skills. His only hope would be to be sent to a sanatorium. Even then, nobody would believe that an alchemist kidnapped him and tortured him. They were too secretive.

That assumed he could even outrun the alchemist. His lungs simply might not hold.

Cassius, at some point, realized that Hakon wasn't going to run. One day, he'd actually asked why. Hakon had been naive enough back then to believe that the alchemist might've asked out of care.

His answer had changed everything.

Cassius had burst out laughing. "I can't believe I didn't think of that before!" He needed a moment to calm down from his laughter. "You're right. You couldn't run from me, even if you tried. At least I know where to drop you off if this experiment fails. I heard the sanatorium near here isn't bad. Maybe you should've gone there. I would've never come to get you."

Hakon didn't know why he was so hurt by Cassius' response. Cassius was an ass, of course. He always was, no matter the day. He should've expected the cruel response. He felt stupid for expecting anything else.

Of course, Cassius was also right. The alchemist was more acute than he gave himself credit for. Maybe Cassius hadn't realized it that day when Hakon had sat at the steps of the soup kitchen, fighting off a fever, but Hakon well and truly had nowhere to go. He'd slept on the streets before Cassius. At least he had a warm meal once in a while and a place to sleep with Cassius.

From then on, Cassius would *sometimes* allow Hakon out of his room between tests, so long as he didn't enter the kitchen or any of the other bathrooms. One night, he'd forgotten to lock Hakon back up. Hakon was smart, even back then, and knew not to anger Cassius. Thus, he'd decided to wake Cassius up.

He immediately took Hakon by the throat and squeezed until Hakon was coughing and spitting, struggling helplessly for air. Cassius' hands were going to leave bruises, Hakon was sure.

He squeezed a little tighter. "Don't you fucking dare watch me sleep."

With that, he dropped Hakon to the ground. Hakon was simply left in a coughing pile, using the cuff of his sleeve to cover his mouth. If Hakon didn't know that Cassius was largely immune to disease like consumption, he would've thought Cassius stupid for strangling a consumptive.

"Let's get you to your room before you cause any more problems for me."

"P-please let me finish coughing."

Cassius had thrown a sharp punch to Hakon's face in response. "I said get to your room. You have the audacity to not use a proper title for me too. I'll punish you for that." Cassius narrowed his eyes. "Since you're so worried about that disease of yours, how about I wash that mouth?"

The taste of the caustic combination of vinegar, lye, and alcohol lingered in Hakon's mouth as he fell asleep that night, afraid of seeing Cassius the next morning.

***

Hakon happened upon a sleeping Cassius. Hakon never knew Cassius to be a particularly deep sleeper, but Cassius' body was injured and his mind was surely weary. Stubbornly refusing medicine would have only casted an even deeper sleep spell.

Cassius was sweating and his face was flushed. *Did his wound get infected?*

Cassius' weakness then made Hakon deeply uncomfortable. Fifty years ago – the years Hakon lived as a Tainted passed so quickly. In those years of unrivaled health, Hakon had forgotten that even powerful alchemists like Cassius suffered infection in deep wounds.

That familiar fear – the taste of the lye mix too – lingered in his chest. Waking Cassius felt like waking a rabid bear.

Even after working himself up over the task, Hakon didn't have to wake Cassius that day. As he opened the door to the tray-deposit ledge, Cassius stirred.

Hakon expected to see rage. Hakon expected Cassius to yell and admonish him for watching him sleep.

Instead, all Hakon got out of Cassius was a simple, "Wow, I was really asleep."

Wincing, he stood and came to get the food. Cassius, for perhaps just a moment, seemed human in his fatigue and pain.

"I hope you made sure that the food isn't shit today. If it still is, I'm going to tell that fucking king of yours that you're making me starve."

Hakon was quiet.

"He wouldn't touch me. He doesn't punish his subjects – not like you."

Cassius scoffed. "I beg to differ. I'm surprised you're so loyal to *His Majesty* when you were a total brat for me."

"You aren't one of his subjects. You're free game," Hakon retorted, though his heart wasn't in the insult.

Cassius gave Hakon a little look of surprise. "The food's still shit, by the way."

Hakon scoffed. "Glad to hear it."

Cassius gave a laugh that ended abruptly.

Neither of them said anything else until Cassius finished half his tray. "Going to let him know that you're intent on starving me."

"Go ahead. Who do you think he'll believe?"

Cassius scowled, but he said nothing.

A long moment of silence passed between them.

"The weather here is really turbulent."

It was Hakon's turn to be confused. *What does that have to do with anything?*

Cassius' eyes narrowed. "I need you to help me relocate my shoulder, dumbass. I think that brand he gave me is infected too."

Hakon was indignant. "That's some way to ask for help."

For once, Cassius had to swallow his pride. "I can't do it myself. My Source is atmospheric convection. The convection here is too unpredictable. I'm not used to controlling it. I hate this just as much as you do, Hakon. You're a pathetic, weak kid. I shouldn't have to stoop down to asking someone like you. But you offered last night, and at least you know what it is to fear me. I'm stubborn, but I'm not stupid. I know when I need help."

Hakon wanted to growl and hurl harsher words than he could think of at Cassius. He wanted to punch him and wipe that horrible smirk off of his face.

Yet something in him told him to help Cassius. Hakon didn't want to add to Cassius' misery, not the same way that Cassius had to Hakon's. He was so much better, so much stronger than Cassius now.

His heart didn't believe that.

"The thought of helping you makes me sick." Hakon sighed. "I'm going to help you either way. I don't enjoy watching others in pain."

"Whatever helps you sleep at night, *Tainted.*"

Hakon knew the venom in those words well. "At least I'm not a bastard alchemist who kidnaps people to torture them."

Cassius frowned. "The progress of science won't be stopped by some Tainted with too many opinions."

A frustrated groan escaped Hakon as he entered the cell. Cassius stubbornly refused to stand to meet him, so Hakon had to kneel reluctantly. He knew Cassius could stand; what Cassius wanted was always more important. "Maybe don't say that to the person relocating your shoulder."

"Good idea."

The words caught Hakon off guard. Cassius wasn't being sarcastic. He tried to shake off the surprise, but it lingered as he took hold of Cassius' shoulder and gave it a strong push. Cassius let out a small cry of pain as his shoulder *snapped* loudly into place.

"Anything else?"

Cassius shook his head. "Unless that king of yours can change the weather, I don't need anything else." He motioned to the tray. "Take the food with you, busboy. I don't feel like getting up."

Hakon got up and picked up the tray, the potentially infected brand long forgotten. He hated obeying Cassius. He hated how easily it came to him. Most of all, he hated Cassius and his *attitude*.

It took all the self-control he had to hold back a punch as he left the cell.

***

Hakon spent most of his time alone. The reason wasn't exactly that he enjoyed his own company, but that he found difficulty in the company of others. There was only one other person he trusted – a Tainted much older than him, Alfie.

Alfie worked in the stacks of the library most of the time. However, they and Hakon had found a certain kinship that pushed them to be Hakon's personal assistant during his Seer duties. That meant that Alfie fetched Hakon when it was actually time to perform his duties.

Sometimes, Alfie came to his quarters regardless. Always good company, Hakon welcomed the opportunity to have them around. Though they had about one hundred years on Hakon, they had the understanding to converse with someone much younger – and someone who had been human once; Alfie had been some genderless fae creature all those years ago. They looked up to Hakon and his role as Seer. They were exceptionally untalented with Western-bound magic, despite being Southwestern-bound themself.

The role of Seer actually afforded Hakon quite a lot of time off. Aside from his regular readings that took him at most three hours, he sometimes had to perform other readings or help with an interrogation. Those were somewhat rare occasions, so he spent a lot of time journaling and writing about what he read. Anything that could keep the outside world on the outside and his internal world inside of him.

"Hakon!"

Alfie always greeted him with a smile that reached their black-green eyes.

"His Majesty wishes for you to complete a special reading today. He wants it completed as quickly as possible. It sounds important."

Hakon nodded and stood up from his desk, placing his pen down gently. "Let me prepare."

"Of course."

Alfie waited patiently in the hardly-touched entertaining room of Hakon's quarters while Hakon prepared himself. He first drew the Seer's symbols on the palms of his feet and hands and over his heart. Then, careful not to smudge the wet ink, he closed his eyes and placed ink over them. Finally, he tied a blindfold over his eyes.

Slowly but surely, those golden threads appeared in his vision to guide him. They guided his feet through the marks on his palms and brought him to Alfie. In those golden threads, Alfie looked like a crocheted doll with hollow eyes. It was like that for all the Tainted – he could never see the eyes.

"I'm ready."

Alfie nodded.

Together, the two of them made their way down to the Seer's Library. Hidden deep underground, only the librarian and those who saw the threads could enter.

Some things in the world held on to the threads very well and were almost spools. At first glance, the daily task of unwinding the spools and detangling what they recorded from every corner of the world might seem like difficult but enthralling work. Yet to call it "work" would be deceiving. Hakon read the spools so quickly that he hardly noticed time passing.

"Which spool does he want me to work on?"

Alfie, with their gloves on, brought over a particular spool. It was made of bones from a Southeastern-bound soul, though perhaps a little aged. For some reason, their ability to linger persisted long after death and made their bones an excellent conduit for threads.

Quietly, Hakon put his fingers to the thread as Alfie left the room. Each string through the conduit was a link between him and the threads in a completely different area.

This one – Hakon recognized. He recognized it a little too well.

An alchemist's college! What does he want me to read?

Hakon ran his fingers up and down the thread, trying to see where in time King Myndill wanted him to read. Though it was possible to read the past with threads, the length of time he could go back depended on the strength of the conduit. Because of the state of the bone, Hakon could read back about a day, which only served to make his work harder.

That was until he happened upon what King Myndill probably wanted him to see.

"Cassius has been taken by King Myndill of the Tainted."

A group of alchemists shrouded by their robes and cloaks gathered in the center of a meeting room. Vaguely, Hakon recognized them. It took everything in him not to lose his focus as he continued his reading.

"If you ask me, he was asking for it. You would've gotten away with it two hundred years ago. Not today! King Myndill is simply too powerful, too defensive over his kin."

Someone else in the room scoffed.

"He was too reckless." *That was the leader, right?* "I don't know if we'll be able to rescue him. He's too far into Tainted territory. They would easily overwhelm us unless we received aid from the Hall or one of the Strongholds. I doubt we'd receive it because it isn't an act of aggression against alchemists, just against one person."

The other alchemists in the meeting room nodded.

"I think it's still worth a try, though. Cassius is reckless, but he's intelligent and has some of the best leads on Magnum Opus that we've had in centuries."

Again, the alchemists all nodded their agreement. A miasma of disdain, perhaps even hatred, hung in the room.

They're agreeing because they have to.

Hakon swallowed.

"I'll contact Valentina's Stronghold. She has experience fighting the fae."

"She's rather far to contact. Plus, she's still recovering from that assassination attempt. Couldn't we find someone on our continent?"

"There's nobody better than her."

They all nodded their agreement. The sense of closure among the alchemists told Hakon he could let go of the string. He felt nauseous and exhausted in a way that was simply different.

Alfie's concerned gaze hardly registered.

"Are you okay?"

Hakon shuddered, more disturbed by the image than he wanted to credit it for. "Sorry. It was just – the reading was of one of the colleges I went to while Cassius held me captive."

Alfie nodded. "I'm the one who should be apologizing. Are you still able to read? Maybe it'll help you take your mind off of what you just saw."

Hakon thought over their question for a while. "I'll try."

After all, they both understood that the only way that Hakon coped with his flashbacks and disturbing memories was work.

***

"So they're too weak to attack us directly?"

The smile on King Myndill's face told Hakon everything he needed to know. King Myndill was talented in many realms of trickery – a poker face was not one of them. Perhaps it was because he'd spent a good portion of his life as a wolf. Regardless, he wasn't among that small pack of the last of his kind anymore. He was King of the Tainted.

"Yes, Your Majesty."

He chuckled gleefully. "Who's this Valentina character?"

Hakon took a deep breath. "From what I gather, she's a combative alchemist from another continent. I don't know which one, but to ask for her means that she has to be rather powerful."

King Myndill looked puzzled for a moment. "I'll need you to gather information on her. If they plan to have her help in attacking us, I want to know everything there is to know about her."

Hakon gave a dutiful nod. Even if watching alchemist society would be difficult for him, Hakon was the only Seer that the Tainted had. It was his responsibility to serve his kingdom in the way only he could.

King Myndill ruffled his hair as he sat there, waiting for more orders.

"You're a good man, Hakon. I'm proud of you. You've done very well for us. You've also grown more than I could've imagined. We're very lucky to have a strong, driven, and *kind* Tainted among us."

Hakon grinned, glowing at the praise. He could tell it was genuine. After all, King Myndill was more of a father than Hakon ever had. Cassius certainly had never filled that role, nor did any of the attendants at the orphanages.

"Thank you, Your Majesty."

"You're like a son to me, Hakon. Of course."

Sometimes, Hakon wondered if he would be in line for the throne. The relationship he had with Myndill was special. King Myndill had a will that included the name of his successor, but nobody had ever seen it.

The thought of going from an orphan to potentially a king always struck Hakon as terrifying. Would he want that position? Could he even handle it?

He found himself entirely unworthy, even if King Myndill had worked Hakon's whole life as a Tainted to change his warped view of himself. At his core, though, he was a weak kid that had been tortured and used for an experiment by an alchemist.

In King Myndill's eyes, that was a strength. In Hakon's eyes, it couldn't be more of a weakness. What would happen, come the day that the alchemists wanted more from the Tainted? Would Hakon even be able to stand up to them without being filled with terror?

What if they chose Cassius to lead them, knowing that Cassius was his one true weakness?

As King Myndill pulled Hakon into a warm embrace, Hakon forced himself to think about something else. Self-doubt was a dangerous emotion for someone like him. He needed to be confident to perform his duties.

Anyway, that's a long time from now.

King Myndill was too kind, too powerful, to fall so easily.

— • —

"Useless! Fucking useless!"

Cassius remembered well throwing down all his instruments under the fearful gaze of his experimental subject. He'd managed to get ahold of a mage's compass. He knew it was possible that Elijah didn't have any affinity for magecraft, but he didn't plan for *what* kind of magecraft Elijah would be talented in.

"You're fucking Western-bound."

His voice was a low hiss as he stared daggers into Elijah. Elijah whimpered pathetically on the table. He was completely immobilized, strapped down with leather onto Cassius' workbench. Cassius somehow doubted that he'd be moving, even if he wasn't strapped at practically every major joint.

"S-sir?"

"Didn't you hear me?" Cassius shouted. "I can't follow the fucking protocol. You're Western-bound. Do you have even the slightest clue what I'm talking about?"

Elijah shook his head fearfully. "No, I-I-I don't, sir." He sounded on the verge of tears.

Cassius growled his annoyance.

Everything about his experiment had fallen apart in an instant. It took everything inside himself to not pull Elijah off of the table and beat him to a pulp. The only two directions that would be difficult to inject with the serum he'd made were Northwest and West. Even then, he was sure he could manage Northwest. The heart was the only organ that was completely impenetrable.

Elijah watched him as he stormed over to his books, trying to figure out anything he could do. Cassius stared at those blood vessel charts for a long time. It would be incredibly risky to use a vein near the heart to access it, especially when he was unable to see anything.

He looked back at Elijah.

The kid could die if he attempted what he was thinking. Granted, there was a good chance that the Taint didn't take and he died regardless. Elijah *was* going to die in the next few years, anyway. He was consumptive. What did it matter if he died?

The idea didn't sit well with Cassius. Almost nothing stopped him. But this, cutting a conscious, terrified person – a twenty-something-year-old who might've become a mage – open for his own purposes pushed the limits of what he would do.

He stormed to the door of his lab and quickly shut it behind him.

"Somebody get me some fucking saline! And some piping."

The supplies arrived quickly afterwards. The ability to give fluids through a vein was a well-kept secret of the alchemists. It might've easily cured cholera and dysentery, if not for the fact that the alchemists didn't want people knowing what they really used it for – surgeries and experimentation.

Cassius didn't re-enter the lab until he had everything ready. He grabbed one of his bottles of whiskey just in case.

"Alright, kid, we're doing this."

He doused his hands in the whiskey, caring little for the bit of residue it left behind.

He offered the bottle to Elijah. "Do you want whiskey?"

Elijah froze. Cassius' patience eventually wore thin while Elijah laid there, anxious and unable to put words together to answer him. Cassius said nothing as he took a swig of whiskey and headed over to the supplies.

In theory, the Taint would target Elijah's heart. Therefore, if Cassius injected the serum directly into a vein with saline, he might be able to test his theory. He wouldn't have to use a catheter to enter his heart that way. It would be a lot less dangerous of a procedure.

As he prepared Elijah for the infusion, Elijah gave him a panicked look.

He had his chance for pain relief.

Cassius attached extra straps to Elijah's right arm. He couldn't have Elijah moving.

"Stay. Still."

The warning was enough. Elijah froze again as Cassius quickly placed the needle and hurried to hook him up to the saline.

The drip started soon enough. Through the access port, Cassius injected Elijah with the Taint serum slowly.

The screams that came from Elijah over the next few hours still haunted Cassius. He wasn't one to be haunted by such a thing, but the nerves of potentially succeeding combined with the heartbreakingly shrill tone of Elijah's screams were what made the sound *stick*.

Did he regret it?

He didn't regret the pain he put Elijah through, even if it was all for nothing in the end. No, he only regretted that the experiment had failed. Elijah had remained human.

***

The question still bothered Cassius – if his experiments hadn't turned Hakon into a Tainted, then what had?

Cassius knew it was poor taste to ask a Tainted what had caused them to succumb to Taint, but he felt his relationship with Hakon was just ... different. It still wouldn't be polite, but after what he'd done, he felt he had a right to know.

Dinner was when Hakon stayed the longest. He always looked a little tired when bringing Cassius his dinner. If Cassius remembered correctly, when Hakon was tired, he tended to answer questions more easily.

Fifty years didn't seem so long before.

When Cassius thought about it, those fifty years were about a quarter to a sixth of his life. The thought didn't bother him, exactly. His memory of that time with Hakon was so clear that it just didn't feel like a quarter of a lifetime ago.

"I've been meaning to ask you," Cassius started. Hakon looked up at him with that delightful distaste. "What exactly made you a Tainted?"

Hakon scoffed. "What makes you think I would tell you? Don't you know it's awfully rude to ask a Tainted what made them succumb?"

"Well, I just wanted to know." Cassius shrugged a bit. "I wanted to know who your maker is if it isn't me. If you don't tell me, I guess I can just assume that I really did succeed. You'll have been my biggest success. When I get out of here, I can get another subject and just repeat what I did with you."

Cassius knew that Hakon fell for taunts easily.

"You aren't my fucking maker."

Cassius could tell by the rage in Hakon's eyes that he was about to tell him exactly what he wanted to hear.

Hakon took a deep breath. "I'll make a deal with you. I know you alchemists can at least hold a promise." He gave an expectant look, to which Cassius nodded. "I'll tell you how it happened, because for years I've wanted to tell you how you ruined any chance I ever had at being happy as a human, then you'll tell me why the fuck you did what you did."

It wasn't as weighty of a promise as Hakon clearly believed it to be. "I promise to give you the honest answer, if you're honest with me."

Reasons were in no short supply.

"I don't even know why I'm telling you this," Hakon muttered. "The day after you let me go, I ended up in a bad street fight. You see, people knew something was wrong with me. It wasn't the scars or how scared I looked. They felt the remnants of the Taint that you put in me."

Cassius stayed quiet, intrigued. He'd let Hakon – Elijah, then – go a few months after his final experiment with the Taint failed.

"I didn't trust any decision I made. I was scared that the Taint was warping my mind. I was scared that it would turn me into an evil person. I couldn't trust myself. Still, someone tried to be my friend. She was kind and smart and so, so tough. She was also a consumptive, like me."

Hakon took a sharp breath. Cassius did his best to look entertained. The backstory didn't matter. He wanted to know the moment it happened.

"You see, Cassius, succumbing to Taint doesn't happen all at once."

Cassius couldn't keep the look of shock off his face. Hakon only sadly smirked.

"I couldn't make any decisions. I was swallowed entirely by self-doubt. I couldn't tell the truth from the lies anymore. As you know, Western-bound souls need to have a good sense of self. We can't suffer in self-doubt nor lose sight of what's important. I'd done just that.

"One day, we got into a street fight. She died because I froze. I couldn't trust myself to not die in the process of saving her. You see, Cassius, indecision is as much of a decision as any of those decisions you've made. I learned that the hard way."

That struck Cassius into silence. A pang of something that resembled guilt struck him, but he quickly pushed it aside.

"One night, I had a nightmare. An odd woman came to visit me in my dreams and told me that my soul had been swallowed by its weakness. You see, every soul, depending on its direction, has an emotion it loses itself to. Mine was self-doubt. She warned me that I needed to turn myself in to those who bring the Tainted to King Myndill's kingdom. That they would protect me to the border."

"That was the Judge."

Hakon nodded. "She isn't a judge at all. She just ... she warns us. She tells us what happened to us. She guides us."

Cassius couldn't help a small laugh. "The gods don't forsake you after all."

"If anyone was forsaken by the gods, it's you."

Cassius went quiet again. He hated the power that Hakon had over his words. The man could make him speechless like none before. Nothing made him angrier.

"Well, you wanted to know why I took you, right?"

Hakon nodded, hesitant.

"You were so pathetic there on the ground that day. I figured nobody wanted you. I was right too, it seems. I'd had a theory I wanted to test for a while, but I didn't have anyone to test it on. You were just too perfect to pass up. All I had to do was offer you food. I knew that you could disappear and nobody would care if you never showed up again."

Cassius took a small, dramatic breath. "See, I don't let anything as silly as principles stop my research. Some alchemists have more principles than me – most of them do, in fact. But I don't think that's the right way to go about things. You were perfect. I did what I did because you were a means to an end, nothing more, nothing less. Like I told you before, nothing personal."

Hakon was quiet for a very long time. "You've said that all before. You couldn't be more wrong." There were tears in Hakon's eyes. "There are a lot of people who want me here. They value me. I'm the Seer. I can look at the past, present, and future of *any* part of the world. I'm stronger than you ever were. I overcame the weakness of my soul."

Hakon looked up at Cassius, tears rolling down his face. "I'm not the person who you hurt anymore."

Hakon stepped forwards with some pills in his hand. "This is a blend to help your infection. King Myndill asked me to give them to you. He says he wants that fever gone as soon as possible."

He put them on the tray door and looked at Cassius expectantly. Cassius reluctantly took them, downing them with his glass of metallic water.

"Do you need any of your joints set before I leave?"

Cassius shook his head, surprised at the sudden change in attitude from Hakon. There were still tears in his eyes as he took back the tray.

"Make sure my water doesn't taste like piss tomorrow."

Cassius would never let Hakon off the hook at the end of the day.

That seemed to get under Hakon's skin. Cassius smiled as Hakon left without another word, the marks of his tears on the floor drying as he walked away.

— • —

Every alchemist had a maker. Now that Cassius thought about it, his life might not have been that different from Hakon's had he not been found by the right person.

Even if that part of his life was one hundred years ago, some institutions were immortal. Soup kitchens came to mind. Wherever people were, there was poverty. Where there was poverty, there was somewhere to feed the few impoverished lucky enough to make it in the door that day.

Times were different back then, weren't they? Though poverty always existed, the attitude changed over the years.

Back then, weren't they cruel? Cassius was just another orphan of the Tainted, after all. His family had all died by the time he was fifteen. Doomed to be nothing, Cassius hung in the soup kitchen as though it were a tavern. He was smart – if he volunteered to help with the cooking and cleaning and things nobody else wanted to do, they'd feed him first.

Nobody would hire an orphan of the Tainted with no skills. So, Cassius sought a way to have skills – the soup kitchen. If he could learn to cook, maybe he could find a home on a ship. He could be fed. He could do something. He might even *become* something.

That was until he met Janus. Janus came every day, without fail, to the soup kitchen. Cassius was long used to talking to the lonely souls that made up the soup kitchen's clientele, but Janus was different. Janus was as sharp as a razor. He had hopes and dreams. Janus gave Cassius energy in his quest to become *something*.

Best of all, Janus didn't judge Cassius for being from a poor village. Things like that mattered back then, more than they did in the modern times.

One day, time seemed to freeze around them.

"You want to become something, don't you?"

Cassius had nodded frantically. Was it an offer of employment? Or was he about to be recruited into some underground organization?

"My dear, you have the makings of an alchemist."

The word sent fear down Cassius' spine at first. Alchemists weren't always good news. If this man was an alchemist, his very life could be in danger.

"You're brilliant. You've learned the streets as if you wrote the guidebook on survival out here. Yet I imagine you as someone who forges paths that lead to wonders beyond our imaginations, writing guidebook after guidebook. My boy, you could become more than something. You could become *great*."

Those were the words that sold Cassius on the deal. He'd do anything to become better than a something. The promise of a chance at greatness would've taken him anywhere.

Nothing would stop Cassius from becoming great. That youthful ambition never left him. It was ingrained into his very soul like the image of his family murdered by a wild Tainted.

Even in his worst days, it kept him going.

Now, Cassius began to wonder if it might have led him astray. If only Janus was still around to talk to. Maybe then, he'd know if he'd achieved that greatness.

***

Cassius' walls were crumbling more and more every day. Would he have embarked on this life if he knew that it would end with him strapped and tortured by the king of the creatures that had murdered his family?

Almost certainly.

Cassius wasn't dumb enough to believe that something that far ahead would've stopped him.

"You see, dear Cassius, I don't think those feet are doing you much good."

King Myndill was smiling wickedly at him. Cassius was strapped down to the table, per usual. The days of torture took all the health left in his body. Every morning, he was hardly able to move. The guards had needed to carry him to the torture room rather than having him walk. Maybe it was the mix of tonics and poisons that Myndill liked to feed him when he was misbehaving that was causing the fatigue. Regardless, Cassius was growing more and more concerned for the state of his body.

He could only hope that someone would rescue him from the pain before Myndill killed him.

"You experimented a lot on poor Hakon, right?" His tone was mocking as he circled Cassius, grinning. "Well, I've always wanted to do an experiment of my own. See, Cassius, I have quite an ability with the cold. I've always wondered what would happen if I used my magic to freeze the blood inside a person. What would happen to their cells? What type of pain would they experience?"

King Myndill got another one of his mock-caring faces on as he continued. "You see, I have quite a number of prisoners who come through here. You're different, of course. You're a toy of mine. I'll keep you until I get bored. Yet, because you're my toy, you make for the perfect test subject."

Myndill laid a hand on Cassius' strapped leg. "What do you say?"

Rage bubbled inside Cassius to cover the fear he was feeling. He knew better than Myndill did what that would do to him. Myndill must've known that too.

"Silent? That's new."

"You're mad. You're absolutely mad. I could lose my legs."

Myndill broke out laughing. "Good. Then you won't run."

Cassius growled, but it was quickly cut off as overwhelming pain filled his toes.

"We'll start small and move up."

The ice through his veins tore his flesh apart. His nerves snapped like thin threads as a million knives were being shoved through his skin, inside out.

He couldn't help it.

He screamed bloody murder.

"That much for just the beginning?"

Myndill clearly didn't understand that though his body could endure such things, Cassius was still human and had the limitations of a human body.

"Stop! Fucking stop!"

The pain as Myndill escalated, crawling up his foot, was so bad that he began to feel faint. He didn't want to give the bastard any pleasure from his fainting, but he wasn't sure he had much of a choice.

Stars began to form in his vision. How long would it last? It already felt like hours had passed, even if Cassius knew that to be impossible.

He didn't have much time to think as he let out another scream. The pain was moving up his leg. He could've sworn that his leg had torn open and was gushing blood. Nothing made sense anymore. He was slipping. His vision was darkening on the sides. Eventually, he felt that familiar pang of panicked dizziness before he slipped into unconsciousness.

***

Cassius awoke to the feeling of drowning. Something was over his face. He couldn't breathe.

Maybe the bastard had finally left him to die. It wasn't a thought that particularly bothered Cassius. Meeting his tragic end infuriated him, yes, but the idea of breaking under Myndill's grasp was more infuriating.

The cloth was yanked off of his face.

Myndill's black-edged eyes glared down at him.

"Hello there, sleeping beauty."

Cassius finally understood what was happening. It wasn't as though he'd never waterboarded anyone. He just didn't recognize the suffocating sensation until he was lifted out of that void.

"You're a monster! A fucking monster! I hate you. I hate your kind. You're all evil."

King Myndill's smile dropped as he looked at Cassius. "You have the audacity to call me a monster? *You*, of all people, Cassius?"

Cassius growled. "I didn't give in to Taint like you did."

A lupine growl escaped King Myndill's lips. His teeth were sharp, as were his horns. For a moment, Cassius could've sworn he saw the ghost of a wolf in Myndill, black ears, amber eyes, and tall form instead of that human that stood before him.

"And you think this world is fair, Cassius?" King Myndill snarled. "Do you think it's just that kind children like Hakon get outcasted for being so distraught and lost that they lose themselves to their emotions?"

Cassius narrowed his eyes and glared at King Myndill. "I care not what happens to orphan consumptives once they've served their purpose."

King Myndill backhanded Cassius. "And weren't you a poor orphan once too? Where is your empathy? By the Judge's name, you might've helped the world. Instead, you chose to torture *my* people. You chose to strap us down to tables, torture, and murder us. For what? Your own ambition?"

That flash of a wolf became clearer as Cassius watched Myndill hold back his own rage. "Do you think that would've brought you greatness?"

"Your kind are a blight on this world. *Your* kind murdered my family. Hakon was unwanted from the start. *I* had people who loved me. My research is more important than the lives of a few creatures too weak to hold up under pressure. I want to help heal people. Real people. Strong people. Not ones who'd easily give in to Taint. People like me who've had to endure and find a way in a world that didn't care. I want people to remember me."

Myndill released Cassius from his restraints for a moment, before his hands wrapped around his throat.

"Let me tell you something, Cassius."

His voice was a dangerous hiss.

"I was happy, once, too. I had people who loved me. But, you see, humans saw it fit to take that all away from me. I lived with my mother and father, my sisters, my brothers, and some others in a pack. I didn't always have this human form. I was once only a wolf, a fae creature, but still a wolf."

Cassius was struggling for air as Myndill was speaking. King Myndill was holding back to ensure that Cassius could still breathe, but squeezing the sides of his neck tight enough to leave bruises.

"I was their defender. We weren't wild wolves. One day, when I was away to look for one of my sisters who'd gone missing, humans came and murdered everyone. My sister's body was only the first I found. Every. Single. One. Murdered by humans.

"I felt so helpless. There was nothing I could do. The humans were long gone. Even then, murdering them would never bring my pack back. One day, I got the dream, and awoke in human form as a Tainted. I've kept both forms, though with years it gets harder to move between the two."

Myndill's hands squeezed tightly around Cassius' throat. "We never bothered humans. We never ate their livestock. So, why did they murder us?" Myndill squeezed a bit tighter. Cassius knew he couldn't last much longer. "I never held it against humankind the way you hold it against the Tainted."

Finally, Myndill let go. "This world isn't fair. There isn't divine justice. I only built this kingdom to repent for not being able to save them. People, *creatures* like you, are the ones that I need to defend my people from. I'm not the evil one. Like Hakon, I simply lost myself to my own soul's weakness. I'm happier here than I've ever been since losing my family. You will not ruin that because you naively believe in justice."

Myndill grabbed Cassius' arm and began to twist. The first snap was horrible and loud. Cassius screamed in pain, shouting, perhaps even begging, for King Myndill to stop.

"You will repent. You'll understand that it isn't strength that kept you from becoming Tainted. It was merely luck and privilege. I will break you. By the end of the week, you will be clay in my hands."

Myndill kept pulling on Cassius' arm. A second, then a third snap came as tears welled in Cassius' eyes.

"You will never be great. You'll always be a pathetic kid who never moved on."

The final snap of Cassius' shoulder breaking freed the tears in his eyes. For the first time in more years than he cared to count, Cassius cried true tears of agony.

"There will be many more tears for you, Cassius. I promise you that. You're going to regret the day that you decided to torture my people. You're going to regret every bad decision you've ever made. And you'll apologize. You'll apologize to Hakon personally and beg him for forgiveness."

Somehow, Cassius found a part of himself believing that he really would do all those things, no matter how much he resented the idea. No, Cassius couldn't even manage to smirk at the idea.

— • —

Cassius sneered when Elijah emerged from his room. "You look awful."

Elijah already knew it, but seeing the look of disgust on Cassius' face was still painful, even if he knew he should've been used to it. His eyes were sticky from his untreated allergies and his skin glittered from his consumptive night sweats. Some days, the weakness was worse than others. That day was one of the worst that Hakon could remember from his mortal life.

He dropped a knee to Cassius, bowing his head. He shook, though whether from the fatigue or the fear of him, Elijah didn't know.

"You may rise." Elijah could hear Cassius' smile in his voice.

Elijah immediately complied, keeping his gaze squarely on the ground and ensuring that he didn't look too large.

Cassius grabbed Elijah's chin and made him look up. "I like this version of you much better. So compliant. Quiet." Cassius tilted his head further up. Elijah didn't move except to allow Cassius to look at his neck. "You're losing a lot of weight."

The truth was that his weight loss wasn't entirely due to his consumption. Elijah seldom found the energy to eat. He'd resigned himself to dying, whether by his own hand, Cassius', or his disease's. There was no hope for him. Even if he somehow left, he would never have a life. He would never do anything. He was pathetic. He was weak. He allowed himself to be someone else's experimental toy. All the decisions he made were stupid. Yes, it would be better if he died.

"You probably don't have much longer."

Elijah's stomach sank. Even if he wished for death, it still scared him. He didn't want to die in that painful way that consumptives did.

Cassius put a hand to Elijah's forehead. "Bad fever. Yeah, kid, you don't have much longer."

The insouciant way that Cassius talked about his death scared him. *Maybe I can ask him to kill me. Maybe he would.*

"S-sir?"

"You may speak."

Cassius was annoyed. Elijah shrank, but not enough to make Cassius upset because he moved away from his touch.

"If – if you would be so kind, please kill me. I – you have to have the methods. I don't want to die of consumption."

Cassius seemed to seriously consider it for a moment. Elijah swallowed as Cassius moved his hand away from his forehead. He knew the slap was coming before it happened, but still cried after the sharp backhand.

"How *dare* you think of me as a murderer! I don't kill humans like that."

Elijah whimpered.

"Your use is coming to an end anyway."

Cassius threw him to the ground and kicked him hard in the side. "First you fail to fall to Taint, then you have the audacity to ask me to kill you. Since when have I cared about what you want?"

"Never, sir. I'm sorry, sir. Please. Please forgive me, sir. I can't go out there, sir."

Cassius glared down at him. "That's right. You won't survive out there. It *would* be like killing you to send you out there alone."

Elijah's whimpers turned into keening. He was fighting back tears.

"That's what you want, though, anyway."

Elijah froze. "Please, sir. Please, no, sir. I can't, sir."

"Silence!" Cassius shouted. He kicked Elijah even harder, throwing Elijah into a bloody, violent coughing fit.

"You asked for death. I'll fucking give it to you. On my terms."

***

Cassius felt like he was going to die. Sure, he'd felt that yesterday when King Myndill had waterboarded, then choked him, but this, this was different.

Another wave of electricity crashed through his body. He let out a bloody scream.

Every muscle in his body ached. He wanted it all to stop.

Memories of that horrible day when lightning came from the sky at the will of that wretched Tainted came flooding back.

Suddenly, he found himself panicking.

He couldn't breathe.

He could smell the burning flesh.

Just as he continued to panic, a wave of electricity crashed through his body again. There were tears in his eyes as he heard the screams of his family. Suddenly, his screams seemed to be mixed with a phantasm of every scream they'd cried that day.

"This won't stop until you beg."

Myndill had paused with the shocks and instead gently wiped a tear from Cassius' eye.

"Come on. I know you can do it."

No. No. He's going to –

The next wave came with enough force to make his eyes roll to the back of his head. He thrashed in his restraints, bloody gashes cutting into his wrists and ankles. He was in so much pain. He couldn't take it anymore. He was going to die if he didn't do something. He couldn't even breathe.

A whip cracked down on him while the electricity raced through his body, leaving bloody, excruciating marks on his chest.

That was it.

It was all suddenly too much.

Cassius needed it to stop no matter what.

Funny.

This is exactly how I broke Elijah.

Just as Myndill threatened another wave worse than the last, Cassius finally gave up. Tears flowed freely from his eyes.

"Please, make it stop."

"I didn't hear that. What did you say?" Myndill touched the glowing orb he'd been using to generate the electricity.

Cassius knew exactly what he was looking for.

"Please, Liege, make it stop. I can't take it anymore. I'm too weak. Please, please, please, I'll do anything. Just make it stop. Just make it stop, please."

He was hysterical as Myndill threatened to electrocute him again.

"I can't take the screams. I can't take the memories. I need it all to stop."

A smile parted Myndill's lips. "You'll be obedient from now on?"

"Yes," Cassius replied with enthusiasm. "Yes. I'll be perfect and obedient, just please make it stop."

Myndill chuckled. "Well, then, I think we've made enough progress for today."

With relief beyond measure, Cassius watched Myndill release his restraints.

"Not so fast."

Cassius' heart sank as he sat up. Myndill grabbed his broken wrist with crushing force and pushed deep down on the broken bones, grinding them to a pulp and setting them further out of place. He'd managed to fix some of it with alchemy the previous night, but with each second that passed, Cassius doubted he'd be able to fix his wrist at all.

"I want you to remember this day. You're *mine*."

Myndill pushed him off the table using his broken arm, which made Cassius scream in pain.

"Guards! Get him back to his cell. Make sure Hakon gets him something to eat. He hasn't eaten in a day."

Cassius couldn't even be happy at the notion of food between his sobs.

***

Hakon didn't know what he would be greeted with when he heard that Cassius had finally broken. He thought back to when Cassius had broken him, what he had done. Hakon was sure he'd hidden in a closet and refused to eat for days.

Seeing Cassius hiding in the farthest corner of his cell, curled up in a ball with a clearly broken and disfigured arm hanging to the side and blood running down his wrists and ankles, was somehow not at all what he expected.

Something in him immediately was horrified.

Why do I feel bad for him?

The answer was easy – Hakon had morals. Cassius didn't. He was stronger than Cassius. He was *kinder* than Cassius.

Hakon pushed the tray of food through the door, but Cassius didn't respond. His head was turned to the side, his gaze not even looking at him for a second.

"Cassius?"

"Come to see me now that I'm broken?"

Hakon's heart fell when he heard the tears in Cassius' voice.

The truth was that Hakon had long forgiven the man. Sure, Cassius was a madman. Just another someone driven by something that Hakon would never understand. Nothing that had happened was Hakon's fault. Cassius singularly held that blame.

Hakon refused to hold on to the pain and allow Cassius to control his life. The only way that he knew to make that happen was to forgive what Cassius did, even if it was unforgivable, make peace with his own emotions, and move on.

Without resentment and an urge to take revenge, Hakon had been free to become Seer and make a life for himself. Did that mean that what Cassius did never bothered him? No. Did that mean that Hakon thought it was all justified? Definitely not. However, it meant freedom. A freedom he didn't have without it.

"Can someone get me bandages, cheap spirits, some leather, and some stiff wood?"

The guards quickly followed his orders. They brought what he had asked for with no question.

"Cassius, I'm going to take care of your wounds."

Cassius looked at Hakon with genuine shock in his eyes. Hakon knew that look well. Cassius had only expected cruelty, even from someone who'd never shown him any.

The look sent chills down his spine. He knew that he'd looked at everyone like that at the beginning. Seeing Cassius, the one who'd broken him, looking at him like that brought him no pleasure or joy. It simply made him ache. He'd have never wished that pain on anyone, even Cassius.

Hakon opened the cell door and entered quietly. He didn't really know where to start with tending to Cassius' wounds. He figured he'd start with his ankle gashes.

"I'm sorry for the pain, Cassius."

Cassius looked at him like he had no clue why Hakon was apologizing. Nonetheless, his hoarse whimpers started as Hakon gently poured alcohol onto the cuts and dabbed at them with gauze.

Once the dirt and old blood was cleared and he was sure the wound was disinfected, Hakon moved on to his bloodied and bruised wrists.

He lightly dabbed at the gash on his deformed wrist. The swelling caused the gash to open wider.

Gently, Hakon wrapped the wound in bandages.

"Will you be able to fix your shoulder and elbow with alchemy?"

To his absolute shock, Cassius shook his head. "The winds here are too hard to control. I can't do a good job."

Hakon just nodded in response. Quietly, despite the yelps and small screams from Cassius, he tied each joint straight with wood and leather. He gave small apologies the entire time he worked on Cassius.

Eventually, with tears in his eyes, Cassius looked at him. It took them a while to get through all the cuts that needed to be disinfected and covered. Then Hakon fed him carefully. He needed all the strength he could get. He had a difficult road of healing ahead of him.

Cassius didn't speak until Hakon was picking up the bloodied scrap bandages and the dirty dishes.

"Hey, Hakon?"

His voice was hoarse from the crying and screaming. Hakon found it deeply unsettling to hear the person who'd tortured him talk like that.

"Yeah?"

Cassius was silent for a really long time, before he finally got the courage to speak.

"I'm sorry for what I did to you."

Hakon didn't really know what to say. He didn't need Cassius' apology. He didn't even know if it was genuine or born out of self-pity. It was probably the latter, all things considered. Cassius never regretted anything. He only cared about himself. He probably thought that apologizing was better than saying "thank you" like a normal person.

"No apology will make up for what you did to me."

"I know."

Hakon left shortly after. He didn't know what to make of the conversation, so he didn't think about it. He needed to go complete his readings. He didn't have room in his mind to ponder *why* Cassius had apologized and what exactly King Myndill had done to break him so completely.

When he finally found himself ready to sit down to do his readings, he was simply too unsettled. Alfie brought him tea and the two of them talked about nothing.

For once, the smile came easily to Hakon's face as they talked about the snowfall that evening. Anything to get his mind off of what had happened with Cassius.

— • —

Sometimes, what Hakon saw in his readings was incomprehensible in the moment. Most of the time, Hakon found himself missing some important context that he didn't understand until he thought through similar jobs. Rarely, though, what he saw shook him so deeply that it took him time to be able to comprehend i t.

It seemed that with Valentina, he was having more and more trouble comprehending her actions. He understood all the context. He'd kept surveillance on her for long enough to understand her modus operandi. However, the *why* of what she did was completely impossible to understand.

Dare he say that he might've found someone more heartless, more ruthless, than Cassius himself?

The image of having the woman invade his home and tear it all apart terrorized Hakon. He saw what she did to the areas she targeted. There was nothing left in her wake. She brutalized the dead bodies and hung heads from spears at the village gates.

Hakon would die. King Myndill would die. Alfie would die. Worst of all, he knew King Myndill to be too prideful to give up the fight now that he knew about it.

"Alfie?"

They came from the other room. "Hakon? What can I help you with?"

He put down the bones he was reading off of and pulled his blindfold off. "Can you get me some cloths and a glass of tea?"

Alfie raised an eyebrow. "Are you sure?"

Hakon nodded, looking at them with his sharp golden eyes.

They shrugged. They knew better than to question when the Seer wanted to stop with his readings.

They were quick to return with damp cloths. Hakon quietly wiped the ink off of his body, closing the link to the golden threads. It was something of a relief – sometimes, they were a rather overwhelming phenomenon. Too much information, too much going on to comprehend fully. It was perhaps best compared to trying to keep track of a thousand conversations – impossible, even for the sharpest minds.

Once Hakon was finished removing the ritual marks, Alfie put a hand on his shoulder.

"What's wrong?"

Hakon startled. "What do you mean?"

They looked at Hakon gently, kindly. "I can see on your face that something's wrong."

That much was true. To Alfie, Hakon was an open book. He just wasn't used to showing his emotions so obviously. Maybe his readings lowered his inhibitions. Or maybe it was just a comfort around them that he found so foreign he couldn't recognize that he was actually comfortable around someone.

"We can't fight Valentina," he blurted.

Alfie looked at him curiously. "What makes you say that?"

With a panicked edge to his voice, Hakon continued at their prompting. "She's awful. She kills everything in sight. Even if we beat her successfully, we'll lose too many people. His Majesty won't back down, though. I know he won't."

Alfie was quiet for a long time. "So, this alchemist is so powerful that we don't even really stand a chance?"

Hakon shook his head. "Our kingdom is too new. Our forces are not trained enough. Cohesive enough. Our territory is easy to defend, yes, but how many are we willing to lose over one prisoner?"

They watched him cautiously, motioning for him to continue.

"I think His Majesty would forgive me if I did what was best for his kingdom, even if it isn't the action he would take."

The images of bloodied battlefields flew through him. He couldn't allow the people he loved to be hurt in such a way. He'd have failed at his job as Seer – to make important decisions with knowledge of the past, present, and future, knowledge that only he had.

"I – " Hakon forced himself to take a deep breath and try to stay in the moment. "I hate what I have to do. I couldn't even describe what I saw to you. Just bodies covered in blood, decapitated, with limbs torn off."

"You know I'm always here by your side. My role is to support your decisions and to help you do what is right by this kingdom, not His Majesty. What is it that you want to do with your knowledge, Hakon?"

Alfie quietly pulled Hakon into a hug, just before grabbing one of their signature glasses of chamomile tea and handing it to him.

"I have to let Cassius go. I need him to go to the alchemists and tell them not to attack. They'll listen to him. I've seen how they respect him."

Alfie paused. "Are you sure?" Their voice was a whisper.

"Completely. I hate the idea too, but it's the only way to save this place. My home."

Alfie swallowed, then nodded. "I understand. Just let me know what I should do."

Hakon nodded, taking a deep sip of the tea. Tears were forming in his eyes as he looked down at it. "Why me?"

"Asking why is always futile in confronting helplessness. I don't like it either."

***

Hakon quickly dismissed the guards from where Cassius was held. He needed total privacy for what he was about to do.

Cassius looked at him blankly when he arrived without food and made no comment. The absence of any of his snarky remarks unsettled Hakon beyond measure. Cassius' jaw hung open a little limply and he could see the remnants of tears on his face.

Suddenly, the idea that Cassius might not be able to run with him struck him. He was in horrible condition. *What am I getting myself into?*

"Cassius?"

"Yes?"

It was the most polite response he'd ever gotten from Cassius.

"I – we need to talk."

Cassius gave him a familiar, curious look. "About what?"

Hakon had a sad smile on his lips. "They're sending Valentina after you."

Hakon didn't know why he decided to be honest with Cassius. He had no reason to. All the cards were in his hand and to tell Cassius was to give him leverage in the negotiation. However, that human part of him that saw Cassius hurt wanted to speak to him as an equal about matters of life and death.

"She's going to rip this fucking place apart."

"I know. I saw it all." Hakon rubbed his hands together.

"What? You've come to ask me if I can call her off from here?"

"No." Hakon swallowed. "I have two choices right now: either have you work with His Majesty and arrange a counter defense against her, knowing that there's going to be a lot of casualties, or let you go and have you call off the offensive."

A small look of curiosity flashed across Cassius' face before it quickly disappeared under the immensity of his despair.

"Why should I help the Tainted creatures that tortured me?"

That was exactly the question that Hakon had anticipated and the one there was no easy answer for.

"I'll be honest. My reasons for releasing you are purely selfish. I want to preserve what's mine, not help you." Hakon took a deep breath. "However, I also know you want to make it out of here alive. So, we both win. You make the alchemists call off the offensive and take all of the blame. If you do that, I'll make sure you're left alone for the rest of your days."

Cassius seemed to seriously consider it. "Lie – King Myndill would let you do that?"

"He doesn't have to know, does he? Anyway, if you tell him, he'd never believe you over me."

Cassius nodded without argument. Again, Hakon was shocked.

"I don't want to owe Valentina anything." Cassius began to cough, but the bruising on his ribs was obvious. Hakon hoped that his broken ribs weren't too bad.

"Then be ready." Hakon swallowed. He didn't want to thank Cassius. Instead, he left quickly, calling the guards back and heading to speak to Alfie.

***

Cassius couldn't believe that he was escaping. He wouldn't have to live through the torture soon. It seemed almost too good to be true. Nevertheless, if he knew one thing about Hakon, it was that Hakon wasn't a liar.

What a surprise it had been to see him here, healed and doing well for himself. The feeling it left Cassius with was almost indescribable. It was an odd mix between nostalgia, sadness, and victory. He'd succeeded. Seeing Hakon reminded him of a time when others didn't look down on him so much. However, his life had mostly stagnated, while Hakon's had exploded.

Cassius broke out in another coughing spell. Even if there were no clocks and no windows, he knew it was time for a meal soon.

Just as the thought crossed his mind, Hakon came down the stairs. *Hakon, right. Not Elijah.*

The two were becoming separate entities in his mind. Hakon was strong. Hakon might've been his equal in a different life. Elijah was pathetic. Elijah would always be inferior.

Hakon slid him his meal.

He picked at it a bit. There were questions on his mind that he couldn't leave the Tainted's kingdom without having an answer to, not after everything he'd been through with Hakon.

"Hakon, can I ask you something?"

For some reason, as he set his tray down, Cassius found himself somewhat afraid of the answers to what he was going to ask.

"Yes."

Hakon was curt.

"When I broke you, how was it?"

Hakon looked offended. Cassius hated the way he shrunk away from the angered face of the Tainted in front of him.

"Why the fuck do you want to know that?"

Cassius, with as genuine a voice as he could manage, answered simply. "For me, it happened within a moment. I just couldn't take it anymore. Suddenly, the price of holding on was too much. I had to give in."

Hakon, with thinly veiled hostility, was quiet for a long time. "It was the same for me. Suddenly, I couldn't resist *you* anymore. I couldn't stand up to *you*. Everything was too awful because of *you*."

The emphasis of his role in Hakon's torture wasn't lost on Cassius. "I'm sorry that my experiment failed."

"What? You're only sorry that your experiment failed? Not for the hell I went through?"

Cassius didn't doubt that answer for a moment. He went quiet while trying to think of a way to change the subject before he was forced to answer with something Hakon wouldn't like.

Hakon said, "We all fight at the beginning. We all want out. Eventually, we all realize it's never going to fucking happen. We realize that the pain is forever. We realize that we're going to die there, huh? You're lucky I've spared you. You're so lucky that I was kind to you. I have more strength than you ever will, Cassius. I have thousands of years ahead of me. You'll be a speck in my history, a bad one at that."

Cassius flinched a bit at the final bit of Hakon's rant. However, he didn't want to respond to that.

He stayed quiet as Hakon continued on his rant, allowing Hakon to dig into him for the first time. He did not have the mental strength to stop him. In some sick way, it made him feel better to know that Hakon was no saint. He was flawed, just like Cassius. His forgiveness was imperfect. He still harbored his anger and his flame.

I always failed to extinguish it, huh?

Yes, Cassius had failed in every way with Hakon.

Somehow, that comforted his broken soul. He'd been right in what he did, but at least when he failed, it wasn't the end for someone. At least Hakon had been able to make a life for himself.

— • —

Facing King Myndill the next day felt oddly final. Cassius imagined that it was more similar to being carried off to the gallows than the moment before freedom.

No, his mind would never be free. Never again. Not after knowing what he knew now about himself. Breaking for King Myndill, that first time where he begged King Myndill to stop, would haunt him forever. King Myndill would be there for what remained of his life – a phantasm of a time where he was, for a moment, breakable.

After all, he was only made of onyx. Hakon, well, he was made of diamond. Though difficult, one could shatter onyx. Diamond, on the other hand, was unbreakable.

Hakon had never truly broken, Cassius suspected. He'd failed from the outset. Nothing would break Hakon if he couldn't break him. Cassius was strong, but Hakon was stronger. Accepting the fact that he had been bested by someone he'd looked down on for so long was difficult.

Being strapped to the same board every day made the torture feel routine, even if it carried that finality of being bested.

"You're awfully tame today, Cassius."

King Myndill wore a wicked smile that made Cassius' stomach knot. How was he to respond to such a question? King Myndill had left him alone for a few days. It seemed like mercy back then, but Cassius was left to wonder if he'd been devising some sort of horrible plan for his next tortures.

He had so many things he wanted to say. *You broke me, remember? That's what happens after weeks of torture. What did you expect?*

However, he knew that saying something like that would only earn him more pain. He wasn't stupid. He wouldn't put himself in danger for an insult, not anymore.

"Quiet. I think I like that." King Myndill hung over him, his black-edged eyes burning into him. "In fact, I've had something of a headache today. I think I need you to *stay* quiet."

King Myndill went over to one of his drawers and pulled out a thick cloth and muzzle.

"I've always had a hatred for these things." King Myndill walked over with the muzzle and thick cloth. "Humans used them against my kind for so long that when I see one, I'm filled with anger."

King Myndill grabbed Cassius' jaw and pushed until Cassius was tearing up with pain. The force slacked his jaw and King Myndill stuffed the cloth in his mouth.

"However." King Myndill began to tie the muzzle on Cassius' face, locking his jaw around the cloth. "Seeing it on a human? That makes me happy. Especially one as despicable as you."

Cassius felt himself folding inside as the muzzle's last strap was secured and King Myndill stepped back to admire his work. He hated the proud way that King Myndill gazed upon him, like a project that had finally gone right.

I must've looked at Hakon like that. I wonder if he hated it so much.

He probably did.

Good.

After all, it was the natural order of the world. He was strong, stronger than King Myndill, so he would escape after being the toy of the weaker creature. However, Hakon was stronger and thereby the one to rescue him. To be so powerful, he needed the pressure that Cassius had put him under – back when he was weak.

There was always a fire going in the room. However, today, there were hot rods in the fire. King Myndill, without being burned by them, picked one up from the fire and moved over to Cassius.

"I think we'll use these today. It's been a while since I branded you." He ran a gentle, caressing hand over Cassius' brand.

Of course, Cassius couldn't say a thing in response. He could only accept the pain. That had been the plan, anyway, but somehow, when the poker hit the soles of his feet, the pain of forced silence amplified the pain of flesh blistering.

***

"Dammit!"

Hakon wanted to scream when he saw the burn marks on the soles of Cassius' feet. He'd lined everything up for the escape to happen once King Myndill was satisfied with his toy for the day. He hadn't anticipated that King Myndill might burn Cassius' feet as part of his fun.

Cassius had flinched back when Hakon had shouted. That was definitely new.

"Fucking hell ... "

There was a slight tremor in Cassius' hands. "I-I'm sorry. I should've tried to stop him."

"No, you shouldn't have." Hakon shook his head. "I just didn't expect him to do this so early on ... without provocation."

Hakon remembered how he was around yelling in the beginning. He realized that he should definitely calm down to avoid scaring Cassius and making the whole situation harder on him.

Scaring Cassius. Hakon would have chuckled at the thought had the situation not been so dire.

"Could he have known?"

Hakon shook his head. The genuine, unadulterated fear in Cassius' voice scared him. "There's no way."

Hakon needed to be the confident one for this all to work.

"Did His Majesty use his magic on you at all, Cassius?"

Cassius seemed to go distant for a moment before he answered with a simple nod. That sparked some hope in Hakon. Maybe, just maybe, if the wounds had been made worse by manipulation magic, he could revert Cassius' skin back to its original state.

"You – you're Western-bound, right? You should be able to use restoration magic, right?"

Cassius was desperate. That much was obvious.

"I am, but I have no skill outside eclairer. Let me try something."

Hakon approached Cassius quietly and closed his eyes. He always had a connection to those threads, but they were hazier when he wasn't connected through ritual.

Those shadows of golden threads were tangled around Cassius' feet. Hakon knew immediately what to do.

As he began to manipulate the threads and straighten them out, Cassius began to scream and cry in pain. It was almost like Hakon was giving Cassius stitches without any pain medicine.

"Hold on, Cassius. I need you to stay conscious." Hakon offered Cassius his hand. "Hold on to me. It's okay."

Cassius immediately took hold of Hakon's hand. He gripped until Hakon thought that blood flow was cut off to his hand. However, the healing was done quickly. The relief of the end was tangible for them both.

***

Nothing stopped Cassius. Elijah had learned that the hard way early on, but after a few years with the man, it was a lesson easily forgotten. After all, the suffering he thought was abhorrent in the beginning had become somewhat mundane. Of course Cassius would torture him. It was what Cassius did.

However, after realizing that, though Cassius was intent on not murdering him, he still wanted to be the cause of Elijah's death.

Walking out that day, in the cheapest clothes that Cassius had bought him, was like walking to the gallows.

He would never return to the lab. Somehow, it brought him no relief. See, Elijah had come to understand one simple truth: there was no life for him outside the lab. He would simply be left to die.

"Please, Cassius! I don't want to die."

Elijah had been hysterical when he saw the village that Cassius was going to be dropping him off at.

"Do you think I care?" Cassius towered over Elijah, making Elijah shrink in his skin. "Do you really think that after you ruined my experiment and attempted to end your own life, that I can really believe that you *don't* want to die? That I should care about what you want?"

Elijah looked up at him in horror. "Please."

Cassius threw Elijah to the ground and hooked a sharp punch across his jaw. "Silence. You'll need to walk the rest of the way there yourself."

Elijah looked at Cassius with horrible fear in his eyes. "Please. Please! No."

Another hard punch in the same spot. There were tears in Elijah's eyes.

"Start walking. Don't you dare follow me back," Cassius growled.

Then, just as quickly as he'd come into Elijah's life, Cassius walked away for the last time. Elijah had laid there, alone, on the ground for a while before he finally decided to get up. He only had one option that day – forwards. He either died there or tried to create a life for himself now that he was no longer Cassius' captive.

Though nobody stood by his side, Elijah still had himself. Despite everything, that day, he'd decided to move forwards and see what his life would bring him, even if that was just more misery.

***

The border villages were never rich. As such, they were always riddled with crime and fear the moment a Tainted stepped foot into them. It was the perfect place to drop Cassius off. Everyone would turn a blind eye to his presence. He could recover some strength before he contacted the alchemists again, now that he was out of the Tainted's territory.

Being together with Cassius, staring down the village in the distance, was perhaps an all-too-familiar scene.

Cassius was struggling to stay on his feet, but he was holding together well enough.

"Hakon?"

Hakon looked at Cassius curiously. "Yes?"

Cassius began to cough. Hakon thought he might be choking until he put his head in his sleeve. The fit lasted a rather long time – long enough for Hakon to worry.

"Do you remember, a few days before I abandoned you, that you attempted to take your life? You said that you didn't want to die by my hands?"

Hakon froze a little. "How could I forget?"

Cassius swallowed, his chest uncomfortable. "I told you that day that it would be on my terms that you would die or not at all."

Hakon nodded solemnly. "Then I didn't end up dying at all. I became Tainted. I'm practically immortal now."

"Well, I'm not." Cassius swallowed again. He was sweating a bit. "Life has a bitter sort of irony, Hakon. I genuinely believed back then that you couldn't give me your consumption, that I was immune."

Cassius broke out in another coughing fit. "You'll end up killing me by circumstance, not the other way around." Blood tinged his sleeve.

"What do you mean?" There was a nervous edge to Hakon's voice. *Did he catch it?*

"You gave me your consumption." Cassius looked at him with the most gentle look he'd ever seen from the man. "I don't know how many years I have left. The doctor told me maybe five if I'm lucky."

Hakon had no idea what to say. He simply froze as Cassius took those few steps towards the village ahead of them.

"What I wanted to say to you, Hakon, is have a good life. Don't worry too much about me." Cassius smiled back at him, now a few paces ahead on the path to the village. "I know you will. I don't deserve your worry. I don't need it, either."

Hakon stood there, stunned, watching Cassius walk away into the sunset, towards the village he'd get to call home until the alchemists came for him.

When he got back, King Myndill had already found out. Once Hakon's reasoning came out with Alfie's help, King Myndill was quick to forgive him.

That didn't stop Hakon, over the next few days, from feeling empty, like a failure somehow. He'd let Cassius have the last word, again. He'd let Cassius walk away, again. Still, after all those years, Cassius could make him go silent.

Cassius held to his word. The alchemists never attacked. The threads gave no indication of any such thing.

Still, even weeks after King Myndill had found his next toy, Hakon was left to wonder whether having that last word would've changed the hollowness of knowing how weak that man from his past really was.

Probably not, Hakon concluded.

But it would've felt good.

About the Author

Harper is a long-time writer turned whump enthusiast. She enjoys a variety of different types of whump and likes to not leave any genre unturned. She has a love for fantasy and combines intricate soft worldbuilding with hurt to create stories that explore the human and nonhuman condition. She also has a love for surrealism. Though a private person, Harper incorporates parts of her life in her stories to create pieces that she hopes are both comforting and difficult to read at times.

Also by The Whumpy Printing Press

Anthologies

Hurt and Comfort

Once Upon a Blade

The Whumpboratory

High Stakes and Bloody Business

Zines

ABCs of Whump

Novels

Cry of Fangs

Magnanimous Moonrise & Savage Sunset

Novellas

Bloodbag

Lux in Tenebris: Poena et Salus

Hunting Static

The Windows to a Shapeshifter's Soul

Never, Never

Creatures From the Caldera

Deepest Canyon

Showstopper

The Kill Touch

Chipped

Silence

Bonnie and Guy

The Dark Side of the Sun